Silver Screen Sleuths

Curated By Nicole Petit

SILVER SCREEN SLEUTHS
An 18thWall Productions book published by
arrangement with Nicole Petit
verba mea in minibus
desiderium meum
Cover by Johannes Chazot
Design by Johannes Chazot & SJS Design
Text design by Sophie Iles
Text Copyright
Green Hell, Red Murder © Josh Reynolds
A Scandal in Hollywood © Jon Black
Nice Work If You Can Get It © Nicole Petit & James Bojaciuk
The Unfilmable © C.L. Werner
Screen Time © M.H. Norris
Death Among the Marigolds © John Linwood Grant

Table of Contents

Vincent Price starring in...

GREEN HELL, RED MURDER

Josh Reynolds

It was the worst heat wave the City of Angels had experienced in almost forty years. The forty odd thousand square foot confines of the interior jungle set for James Whale's latest picture were almost as sweltering as the real thing. The stage hands were in a war of attrition with the humidity, and production assistants were waving clipboards like fans, trying to keep the cast from melting. There were rumours that Fairbanks had collapsed from heat stroke, and that George Bancroft was running amok somewhere.

All in all, I was quite happy to be dead, and lounging in the shade.

"About five of the worst pictures ever made are crammed into this one," I said. I was on my third cigarette of the morning. I held out the pack to Ray, who took one.

"The doctors say these will kill me," he said, before lighting up. "And that's being a bit harsh, Vincent. We've both been in worse films." He gave me a flat smile. "And will be for many years to come, if the fates are kind."

"Speak for yourself," I said. "I suspect I've reached the apex of my cinematic journey. Two poisoned arrows to the chest and a bit of melodramatic writhing." I tapped my chest for emphasis. "Hardly a praiseworthy career." It was a bit part, but I got last billing. It's said that last billing is better than no billing, but I was having a hard time seeing the upside, career-wise. Such is the lot of the bit-player.

"Four years ago, I shared top billing with a horse and a dog," Ray said. "Now I'm playing a jungle savage, with fewer good lines than a character who got two poisoned arrows to the chest." He quirked an eyebrow and blew smoke at me.

"Don't forget the writhing. I am quite proud of the

writing."

"Almost Shakespearean."

"Well, I did get my start on the stage."

Ray laughed. There was nothing quite like watching Ray Mala laugh. His face, usually about as expressive as a chunk of teak, broke into canyons and crinkles. He clapped me on the shoulder, coughing slightly.

"That's why I like you, Vincent. You make me laugh."

"My talents are many and varied, Ray." I puffed on my cigarette and studied the interior of the subterranean Incan temple that had led to my most recent death. The studio had spared no expense on it—it rose wild, a blossom of heathen idolatry, crammed into a sound stage. It was the dais that drew the eye—a slab of faux-stone, surmounted by an immense menhir, ringed by a quartet of stylised, vaguely capric statues. Deer or goats or antelope, they didn't quite fit the theme. None of it did, really, despite the profuse amounts of plastic and paper flora clumped and scattered over the set in haphazard fashion.

Even so, it was a masterpiece far out of proportion with its current display. Cyclopean and intimidating, with an air of primitive mastery to it, it hinted at far better stories than the one currently playing out within it. I had no doubt Universal would use the set again, whenever they had need of something suitably exotic. Trade out the vines for sand, and it'd be a perfect Temple of the Seven Jackals or what have you.

"I heard Douglas tried to swing on one of the vines," Ray said. "Came off in his hand and dumped him on his ass."

"Serves him right. This isn't Zenda, and those aren't chandeliers."

"Did he swing on any chandeliers in that one?"

I blew a plume of smoke. "Not during the film."

Ray smiled. "You're just annoyed because he ran off with your wife."

I choked as smoke went down the wrong pipe. As I bent over, wheezing, Ray patted my back sympathetically. I knew he'd meant Joan Bennet, who played my late character's wife. My part was so miniscule that I hadn't had a chance to meet her before I was out, she was in, and the jungle was a-swelter with illicit romance between her character and Fairbanks' dashing adventurer. But for a moment—just an instant—I'd been thinking of Edi. My Edith.

Not unusual, all things considered. We'd been having some difficulties, of late. Broadway wasn't being kind to her, and none of the usual comforting pabulums were doing the trick. My successes, meagre though they were, weren't helping matters. Nor was the distance—she was still on the East Coast, while Hollywood had caught me up in its sun-drenched claws. I'd suggested we split the difference and move to Kansas, but she hadn't appreciated my attempt at humour. Edi was a tougher audience than Ray.

I forgot about Edi when the first scream echoed over the lot. Ray and I looked at one another. Then, a second scream followed the first, rising up like the wail of a fire engine. It was coming from the temple. We started forward, along with everyone else with two legs and a pair of ears. There was a stampede towards the looming eidolon, with its fake greenery and grisly decorations. One of the native girls—really, a former waitress from Long Island—stumbled into the open, eyes wide. She screamed again, showing off a set of lungs that would have made Weissmuller jealous.

Members of the crew were already crawling over the artificial edifice, seeking whatever it was that had set her to sounding the alarm. As we arrived, they found it.

Him, rather.

To the surprise of no one, shooting was cancelled for the rest of the day.

The next morning, I found myself in the scrap of a lot office that James Whale had claimed for his own. It was early enough that the drunks were singing in accompaniment with the birds on Cahuenga Boulevard, but the Universal backlot was silent. No scratch of tools or shouting teamsters. It was unnerving, I admit. You get used to the noise—the constant pressure of a hundred voices, all speaking at cross-purposes. It's only when it goes silent that you realise just how big and empty a sound stage truly is. An infinity of possibilities.

Whale looked like a man who'd been subsisting entirely on coffee and cigarettes for too long. He was still handsome, in that brittle British way, but you could see the cracks in the facade. The rumour was, he was on his way out. A shame, but then, I wasn't even *in*, so who was I to commiserate? Whale had been a name, once. A director on the rise.

But then the Laemmles had lost control in '36, when the studio went bankrupt. *Showboat* had sunk them, for all that it had been a success. And with the Carl and Junior out, Whale's rising star had turned into a falling one. I'd heard about the mess with the Germans and *The Road Back*—everyone in town had. Whale had won the battle, but lost the war. Rogers, the new studio head, was trying to figure out a way to get rid of him without breaking their contract, but Whale wasn't having any of it.

Thus, the great man had found himself directing a string of B-movies, including the currently in-production *Green Hell*. Whale was beaten down, with a hangdog look on his long, English features. Nonetheless, he eyed me keenly. "You made for an engaging Albert, when I saw you on stage a few years ago."

"It wasn't difficult. He was a charming man." I had played Prince Albert in the American production of Houseman's *Victoria Regina*. Not one of my more well-known roles, but one I was proud of, nonetheless.

Whale smiled. "Have you ever given thought to a more hardboiled part?"

"I'm open to opportunity," I said, trying to hide my eagerness. Was I being offered a part, in another film? My last starring role had involved being invisible for the majority of my screen-time. I don't recommend it.

The door closed behind me. I turned, and saw the familiar figure of the studio fixer, Earl Hoskins, looming in front of it. Imagine a chunk of granite, chopped carelessly, and stuffed into an expensive suit in an effort to hide the flaws in its shaping. That was Hoskins. Officially, he was just another studio executive. In reality, his purpose was more colorful than corporate. Hoskins was a new breed of middle man, designed and built by the studio system to make sure scandals stayed quiet, and that all the moving parts performed their function without interruption. "You ask him yet?"

"I was getting to it."

"Hurry up. I can't keep the cops off of the set forever."

"Then don't."

"This film is already over-budget and behind schedule." Hoskins spat the Four Deadly Words like bullets. Whale twitched but didn't otherwise react. I shrank slightly in my seat, trying to inch out of the line of fire.

Whale glanced at me. "You were on set yesterday? When they found it?"

"Yes. Poor Harold." I reached for the pack of cigarettes in my pocket. The body they'd found had been that of Harold Gummer. A security guard, and something of a fixture on the backlot. Elderly, even by the standards of Universal security guards. I hadn't known him well, but he'd seemed pleasant enough the few times we'd chatted. "Heart attack?"

"Arrows."

I stopped, the pack half out of my pocket. "Arrows?"

"Poison arrows. Just like the ones that did you in."

"But those are just props, surely?"

"Not when you break one in half and slide it between a guy's ribs," Hoskins grunted. He leaned against the door, arms crossed. "Better than a jailhouse shiv." The voice of experience, I assumed.

"The props department will be pleased to hear it." Whale looked at me. "It was murder. He was killed sometime the night before. The body was hidden."

I lit my cigarette. Given the heat, I was surprised someone hadn't stumbled over the body sooner, but I kept that little bon mot to myself. "Then why keep the police off the set?"

Hoskins set a heavy hand on my shoulder. "I thought you said he was smart?"

I glanced up at him. "This is about money?"

Hoskins grinned, despite my withering tone. "Look at that. He already found a clue."

9

Whale sighed. "The police will shut down the set. We're behind schedule already. But, if we can wrap things up nicely for them, before they start poking around, they might be inclined to accept our gift horse without first checking its teeth."

I sat back. "I'm starting to see where this is going. But why am I here?" I tensed. "Am I a suspect?"

"No. You'll be playing the detective." Whale tried to smile encouragingly. He didn't quite manage it.

"Why me?"

"You got a reason to be on set, even if you aren't doing anything. We hire a private dick, word gets out, the schedule goes to hell." Hoskins spoke flatly, grudging every word. He cracked his knuckles repeatedly, as if longing to thump someone.

"I know you're at loose ends, Vincent. I also know you're a good deal smarter than you pretend to be. You were an art procurer, for a brief time."

"Still am, in the slow months." When it came to buying art, it always helped to have a second pair of eyes. I was only too happy to provide those eyes, for a modest fee. Enough to cover the cost of a piece or two for my own collection.

"You have to have a good eye for forgeries in that line. The ability to see what a layman might miss. The little details."

I sat back, digesting this. As parts went, it wasn't the kind I'd had in mind. But, at the same time, I wasn't doing anything at the moment, being in something of a professional dry spell. And house rentals in the valley weren't cheap, on a bit player's income. Besides which, I'd liked Harold. No one ought to die on a film set. Not for real, anyway. I looked at Whale.

"I've always wanted to don the deerstalker. How much does it pay?"

"We're over budget," Hoskins growled.

"It will be worse, if the police get involved," Whale said, pointedly. He looked at me. "We'll bump your salary. You'll get what the leads are getting, in cash. Off the books." Behind me, Hoskins made a choking sound. Whale ignored him. "Does that sound fair?"

"More than adequate," I said. "I assume I am to begin by digging for suspects, among the cast and crew."

"I already know who did it," Whale said, bluntly. "I just need you to find them."

I stubbed out my cigarette in the ashtray on the table. "And who are they?"

"The Nazis," Whale said.

"It's not the Krauts," Hoskins said.

"I didn't say it was the Krauts," Whale said. "We've got plenty of goose-stepping pricks here. Can't throw a rock in Illinois without hitting a Nazi." He leaned towards me, the shadows turning his face into a Greek tragedy mask. "Mark my words, Vincent—it's the Nazis. They hate my work. The only thing worse than a fascist is a critic."

"And the only thing worse than that is a critic who's a fascist," I said. Hoskins gave me the side-eye, and I quickly sheathed my rapier-like wit. I recovered quickly. "Why do you think it's the Nazis?"

"They've had it out for me since *The Road Back* premiered. You heard about it?"

"Who hasn't?" Whale's sequel to *All Quiet on the Western Front* had ruffled some feathers, including those of George Gyssling, the Los Angeles consul for the current German government. He'd squawked that the film had been unfair in its representation of the German people. Threats had followed, and the whole thing became one of those messes someone will inevitably write a book about, in a decade or two. "And you think they killed a security guard in order to shut down production?"

"I think there's nothing they wouldn't stoop to."

I leaned back, already in need of another cigarette. Instead, I nodded. Never argue with a director. A glance at Hoskins told me he felt the same. Whale's theory was unlikely, if only because he was no longer important enough to sabotage. At least not by the German government. But it was best to keep that to myself. I pushed myself to my feet.

"Even so, best to be thorough. I'll begin with the young woman who found the body, and go from there."

"You got a day, Price. That's all the budget allows for," Hoskins growled. "And I'll be watching to make sure you earn every penny."

"I feel more productive already. If you gentlemen will excuse me?"

As I left, another argument began. Or perhaps it was the same one. Directors and producers were uneasy allies in the eternal war against rival studios, and Whale was harder to clamp down on than most.

Days like this, I was glad to be a humble thespian.

I found my witness in the studio cafeteria, nursing a cup of joe. She was a mild thing, with a face for cinema and a voice for a bus depot. Too much yelling, not enough speaking. "I recommend tea with a dash of lemon and honey. Does wonders."

"What?" She looked as I sat down across from her. "Say, ain't you the dead guy?"

"That's what it says on my tombstone."

"What?"

"Yes. Vincent." I extended my hand. She shook it.

"Imelda."

"Really?"

"Yeah. Got a problem with it?"

"Not at all. Fine name." I cleared my throat. "*Amarti, e nel martoro...*"

She stared at me. I floundered for a moment, tripped by my own erudition. I fancy that I'm terribly cultured, but sometimes I fear I'm simply cultured terribly. "Donizetti's *Imelda de'Lambertazzi,*" I continued, lamely. "The opera?"

"Oh." She laughed, more to be polite, I suspected, than because she was taken by my wit. "Hey, being dead pay well?"

"Oh, I'm as happy as a clam. Can I finish your coffee?"

"Sorry, this has to get me through the day."

I nodded sympathetically. "I understand you had a rather

tough one, yesterday."

She blanched. "Poor old Harry."

"You knew him then?"

"Didn't you?"

"Not well." I took out my cigarettes and set it down between us. She glanced at it, and I nudged it towards her, in silent invitation. "You?"

"He was a card. A real cut up." She took a cigarette and I fished out a matchbook. She leaned forward, and I struck a match. "Why you asking?"

"Curiosity, mostly." I lit a cigarette for myself. "Did Harry have trouble with anyone on the set?" It seemed the sort of question a detective might ask. Then, what I knew about detectives came mostly from books.

"Besides whoever killed him?"

"Well, ideally they're one and the same."

She sat back. "Why are you asking me?"

"Curiosity, as I said."

She frowned. "Not that I know of. He was a sweet guy, like I said." She puffed on her cigarette. "Yola—one of the other gals—said somebody stabbed him."

"Yes, with a prop arrow, sometime the night before you—ah—stumbled over him."

She shuddered. "Nasty way to go."

"How did you come to stumble over him?"

She looked at me as if I'd accused her of something. "I was having a smoke in the chimney." Seeing my expression, she clarified. "The big stone. You know the one?"

"In the temple?"

"It's hollow, or mostly. Lupita showed me. She was in *Dracula,* you know."

"Really." Lupita was one of the other bit players in the cast, and a familiar face. She'd had some success in Spanish language remakes, like the aforementioned *Dracula*—a fair amount, in fact—and in a few early talkies for Fox.

"Oh yeah. Said Lugosi liked to get fresh, when they were filming *The Veiled Woman.*" Imelda smiled. "She showed it to me, like I said. Good place to duck out of sight, for a few minutes, if you need a smoke or for…you know." She flushed. I did know. Movie sets were highly pressurised environments, and sometimes, you had to release that pressure however you could. Even if it wasn't strictly hygienic.

"Yes. I suppose the killer must have thought the same."

"Say, I thought you were an actor, not a detective."

"A man who limits his interests limits his life," I said, aiming for worldly. From the look on her face, I fear I came off more as pompous. I made my excuses and cleared out, hands in my pockets.

I interviewed a few more people as the morning wore on, and cast and crew arrived. Despite the murder, the show would go on. Hollywood's guiding ethos, and Hoskins' influence. Nonetheless, I knew time was pressing close about me. Every so often, I caught a glimpse of Hoskins lurking in the background, watching me like a hawk. There's nothing so intimidating as a pushy producer.

I spoke to Imelda's fellow natives, including an Italian doing his best to sound like a Cherokee, a few stagehands, and one very surly teamster in short order. Most of them said the same thing—Harold Gummer had been a fine fellow, and a diligent security guard, if a bit deaf and doddering.

Nothing I learned was helpful. In the stories, it always seems so easy. A quick chat with the witness, bob's your uncle. The murderer hadn't even tried to bop me on the head, or drop a sandbag on me. Maybe I was being too inconspicuous in my poking around. Or maybe it was simply that a movie set was no place to conduct a murder investigation.

Nonetheless, I was determined to earn my increased salary.

By late afternoon, I was sitting above the set on the catwalk, puffing on the second to last coffin nail in my pack, pondering the imponderable and fanning myself with a folded up copy of the *L.A. Times*. The pieces were there, I knew it. Harold had been killed at night, after filming had stopped for the day. Which meant he'd have been making his rounds. I studied the soundstage, trying to think like Sherlock Holmes.

I was certain by now that Harold had been a victim of circumstance, rather than intent. If you were looking to murder someone on a movie set, why kill the guy who doesn't even get bottom billing?

Had Harold seen or heard something? But what would someone be doing on the set after hours? Whale's mention of sabotage came back to me. Perhaps one of the theoretical Illinois Nazis he'd mentioned had been lurking around, and Harold had surprised them in the midst of some skulduggery. But why hide the body, if that were the case? Leaving poor Harold strung up somewhere public would have effectively brought filming to a halt, and not even Hoskins could have swept that under the rug.

Too, there was no evidence of sabotage. No mysterious accidents. No accidents at all, save the usual lethality associated with the Universal backlot. No figures seen creeping about the catwalks, nothing stolen or out of place.

Just a dead man, killed with a prop, seemingly for no reason. Too many questions, not enough answers. Like all good actors, I needed a writer to feed me lines. Unfortunately, this was real life, and unless I started coming up with theories, a killer would walk and I'd be out of a job. I thwacked the rail with my newspaper. "It doesn't make sense."

"What doesn't?" Ray asked, from behind me. Startled, I nearly plummeted from my perch, but Ray steadied me. "Whoa there, Vincent. We don't need another accident." He was dressed for work, in a grass skirt and a necklace of prop ivory.

"Not an accident, I fear." I filled him in. Gossip is the currency of the backlot, but Ray knew how to keep his mouth shut. He wasn't quite Nigel Bruce, but I needed a sounding board. One can only monologue for so long.

When I'd finished, he sat back on his heels, looking solemn. "So you're getting more money," he said, finally.

"Focus, Ray. I need help."

"Are you having fun?"

"Oh I'm having a ball," I said.

"Give me a cigarette." He held out his hand, and I complied, sacrificing my last cigarette for the cause. He puffed away for a few moments, crouched on the balls of his feet, arms over his knees. Finally, he said, "My first thought is that it's probably not Fairbanks."

I threw the newspaper at him. He caught it and flipped it open. I shook my head. "You're not helping, Ray."

"Well I'm not being paid to play detective. Not this time around."

I looked at him. "Wait, what?"

Ray ignored me. "Have you seen this?" He folded the paper and displayed it. I took it back and scanned the article. I'd noticed it before, but had been too distracted to read it.

"A robbery," I said. "An auction house in Beverly Hills got knocked over a few days ago. Police are still searching for one of the men involved. He's believed to have gotten away with…diamonds. Hunh." I glanced at Ray, in his native get-up, and suddenly, it struck me. Much like a poisoned arrow, in fact. "Say, Ray, anyone new on set these past few days?"

"A few. You know background talent, Vincent. They tend to go where the wind takes them."

"Could you be a pal and find out if they've hired anyone new recently? In, say, the last week?" I tucked the paper under my arm and peered down at the soundstage, the faint inkling of a theory tickling the underside of my brain. "I have a suspicion that our killer is hiding in plain sight."

It was contrived, I admit. The sort of crime Agatha Christie might assemble out of a collection of random events. But it all seemed to fit. Still, one had to be sure. That meant going spelunking.

I waited until everyone broke for lunch, and then began my quest to conquer the summit of the ancient temple. It wasn't that hard. The dais, like the rest of it, was hollow, and it was a simple enough matter to wriggle my overlong frame beneath the whole setup. From there, I climbed a short web of support timbers, until I found myself standing in a wide space. The stone might have been fake, but it was solid.

I found the spot where Harold had been left easily enough, with the help of light bulb wired up inside the stone. The bulb was there for the stagehands to use when they made repairs or disassembled the scenery. The light it cast was weak, but serviceable. There was a stain, obviously, and I admit I stared at it for far longer than a real detective might have. It was a sad place to die, I thought. A quiet, cramped little tomb.

It was also a terrible hiding place for a body. It was the centre of the scenes being filmed currently, which meant that someone was bound to stumble over the body sooner or later. Not to mention the stifling heat. Anyone working on the set would've known that. But what if hiding a body hadn't been part of the plan? As I tore my eyes from the dark stains, I noticed a scuff mark on one of the timbers. There was a second scuff mark on another timber, some little ways above.

Curiouser and curiouser.

It was the little details, as Whale had said. Paintings were made of little details, hundreds of them, one blending into another, forming a whole. I fancied a mystery was much the same. Little clues, adding up to a big crime.

I was starting to think like a detective now, my little grey cells firing. Bracing myself, I began to climb the skeleton of the stone. As I did so, I felt around. When I found what I was looking for, I resisted the urge to shout 'Eureka!', and satisfied myself with a grunt of triumph. Holding onto my perch, I pulled it down.

The bag was soft and black, like the kind you find in a jeweller's. A quick peek told me that it was full of ice— diamonds. More than enough to make a man homicidal, if he'd already gone to the trouble of stealing them.

Agatha Christie herself couldn't have laid it out better— where better than a backlot to hide something? Lots of people coming and going, every day. So intent was I on my own cleverness, I didn't notice Hoskins until he caught my ankle. I squawked, nearly dropped the bag, and looked down into the producer's hard-edged features.

"Don't do that! You nearly scared the life out of me."

"What are you doing in there?" Hoskins growled.

"What you're paying me to do. Solving the case."

"Get out of there, before someone sees you."

"Did you hear me? I solved the case."

"Great. Maybe we can bring it in under budget. Get out here."

I began to clamber after Hoskins, still holding the jewels. After a moment's hesitation, I stopped, and placed them back where I'd found them. The beginnings of a plan had begun to form. When I clambered out from under the set, Hoskins caught me by my collar and swung me back against the dais.

"Explain."

"Take me to Whale."

Hoskins growled.

"Time is money," I said, quickly. "And you're wasting both."

Hoskins released me, and I straightened my shirt. A bell rang, somewhere, signalling the end of lunch. As cast and crew started flooding back into the soundstage, I caught sight of Ray hurrying towards us. Seeing the look on Hoskins' face, he said, "Vincent? Any trouble?"

"Quite the contrary, Ray. Did you find out what I asked you about?"

Ray fell into step beside me as we walked. "Not really. Background comes and goes. Some only work for a few days. We filmed the native attack scene yesterday, so most of them will be gone today, looking for something else."

I nodded. That meant whoever it was, was likely to come looking for their loot tonight. I caught Ray's shoulder. "Ray, do me a favour—guard the temple."

"What?" Ray stopped, frowning.

"The temple. Guard it. Keep an eye on it." Hoskins was pulling ahead, leaving me behind. I turned to catch up, leaving Ray scratching his head.

Whale kept us waiting long enough for Hoskins' face to shift through several spectrums of colour. When the director finally arrived, I jumped to my feet before the producer could explode. Whale closed the office door behind him and looked at me expectantly. "Well?"

"There's a bag of diamonds hidden in your South American temple."

Whale blinked. "Real ones?"

"Yes."

"That's a first." He sat down heavily. "And how did they come to be there?"

I gave him the bullet points, conscious of Hoskins' glare. "Jewellery heist, auction house, Beverly Hills. It's not really important. They're here and I think they're the reason Harold was killed."

"He was in on it?"

"More mundane than that, I'm afraid." I cleared my throat. "I think whoever our murderer is got a job as background talent so that they'd have a reason to be wandering around the set. Think about it…where better to hide something small and valuable than a movie set? And no one notices background— it's right in the name."

"So you think Harold surprised them while they were hiding it?"

"Or attempting to retrieve it. It's a good hiding place, but Harold knew the supernumeraries used it for…extracurricular activities. So of course he'd check it, when he heard a sound or saw that the light was on. He must have surprised them, they panicked and…well." I shrugged. "The question is, what do we do now?" I paused. "We could question all of the background talent…"

"That'll take too much time," Hoskins growled. "We're over budget as it is, and I've got the cops circling, asking me why we ain't reported a dead body yet. Nothing they like better than poking around a backlot. No, we need this handled now."

"Which is why I left the diamonds where I found them. I think whoever it was will come back tonight, looking to retrieve them before the cops start poking around. We'll have one shot at catching them red-handed."

Whale looked at Hoskins. Hoskins looked at me. "What are you suggesting?"

"Simple. We have the bait. Let's set a trap."

When night came, and the shooting day ended, we were waiting. Me, Hoskins, and Ray. Once he'd realised what was going on, Ray demanded equal billing, so to speak. Even Hoskins wasn't tight enough to turn down an extra pair of hands when it came to catching a murderer. Whale had left it with us, serene in his confidence. Or maybe he was just good at pretending, after all these years.

The trap wasn't clockwork, but it was as good as. Ray was waiting on the catwalk, and Hoskins was out of sight in the wings. And I had the centre stage—right inside the chimney. Mostly because of the three of us, only Ray and I fit, and Ray had declined the honour. It was stifling there, in the dark, and cramped. By the time I heard the sound of someone walking across the set, I was a bundle of aches and pains.

I forgot all of that the moment someone began to mess with the dais, and clamber underneath. I heard muttered cursing—a man's voice, I noted—and a grunt of effort. He was a big one, not quite as large as Hoskins, but large enough to have rammed a prop arrow through poor Harold. I tensed, ready for my big scene.

If this had been Agatha Christie or Conan Doyle, there'd have been a moment of recognition when the bulb flickered to life, revealing the face of our murderer—perhaps he'd have been one of the stars, or someone I'd questioned. Instead, it was just another face in the crowd. I'd seen him a few times, a background player, shooting arrows at befuddled explorers. He stared up at me in confusion, his jaw working. All that came out was, "What?"

"Looking for—oh damn it! Hoskins!"

He hadn't even waited for me to get the line out. He scrambled out of the scenery, cursing a blue streak. I followed, more awkwardly. Blessed—or cursed—with long limbs as I was, it was all but impossible to swiftly slither out of hiding. I kept shouting.

The murderer was running, when I finally got free. I caught sight of Ray shimmying down from the catwalk, and

Hoskins bulling out of his hiding place. I envisioned a tense, ill-lit chase through the prop department, perhaps a shoot-out on one of the other lots. Instead, Hoskins' fist hammered across the intruder's jaw, spinning him around. The producer was quicker than he looked. Then, so was an avalanche.

The man, big as he was, went water-kneed and stumbled back towards me. I put my fists up, but there was thankfully no need for me to show off my pugilistic skills. Ray tackled him a moment later, hitting him low about the legs, as is the fashion in Republic serials. The bruiser went down with a yelp, and kicked at Ray, trying to throw him off.

By the time he wriggled free, Hoskins was waiting to ring his bells again. The producer hit him twice, in quick succession. The murderer folded over and sagged. Hoskins hit him again, just for good measure. I winced, as he collapsed to the floor.

"Well. That was easy."

"Over budget," Hoskins grunted. He crouched beside our captive and rolled him over. "Either of you recognise him?"

I looked at Ray, who shrugged. I shook my head. "No. How disappointing."

The police were, of course, called at that point. They were not so put out as one might expect. My name was left out of it, as was Ray's. Hoskins claimed the credit, in the same way a lion claims an expanse of savannah. It had happened in his territory, and was, ipso facto, his. I was happy enough to leave the producer to it, so long as I got paid.

It wasn't the first time I'd played a bit part.

And last billing was better than no billing, as they say.

Basil Rathbone starring in...

A Scandal in Hollywood

Jon Black

"Honestly, I'm surprised the movies do so well," Basil Rathbone said. "Sherlock Holmes is an anachronism in the age of Raymond Chandler and Dashiell Hammett."

While the reporter from *Motion Picture Magazine* took notes, Basil stirred his coffee as the pair sat in the Universal Studio commissary.

"It sounds as if you don't like Holmes very much?" The journalist, a middle-aged gentleman with a bushy white walrus mustache, had a trace of the Continental in his accent.

That relieved Basil. His English accent often so charmed American reporters that they didn't pay attention to his words. "After shooting on *Dressed to Kill* wraps up next week, I will have played Holmes twelve times. Twice for Fox. The rest for Universal. After playing one character a dozen times, any actor would be ready to move on."

Basil paused, deciding whether to continue. "Counting my stage career, I've played fifty-two roles from twenty-three of Shakespeare's plays. My first professional acting work was with the official company at Stratford-on-Avon. I gravitate toward roles with nuance. Even a bit of darkness. I've played Iago, Cassius, Tybalt, Dickens' Murdstone, Pontius Pilate, even Judas Iscariot. Even my screen villains like Sir Guy of Gisbourne in *The Adventures of Robin Hood* had some depth."

"Don't you have anything good to say about Holmes?" The reporter sounded shocked.

A true fan of Sherlock Holmes, then. Basil met them often. Though their enthusiasm for the character mystified him, he felt a pang of sympathy accentuated, perhaps, by the band of pale skin around the reporter's finger. An absent ring meant a likely widower. "I will say this," Basil began, "Sherlock Holmes is unwavering in fighting for good even in danger's face. In that, he is an example to all of us."

The four o'clock interview had been his last task for the day. Leaving the commissary for his studio dressing room, he looked forward to relaxing before driving home. Jane, Basil's personal assistant, intercepted him. "Mina Reeves is here to see you. She had a key to your dressing room so I told her to let herself in."

Basil often found his assistant's dark eyes difficult to read. This time Jane's expression clearly asked *Did I do right?*

"Very good, Jane." Basil glanced at his pocket watch. "Isn't it time for you to head home? I'll see you tomorrow."

It surprised him that Mina came calling after so many months. True, they'd spent time together last year. But they had drifted. Such things happened. Yet now she warmed his chair. Blonde curls bounced with a will of their own and her curves were precisely as the year 1946 declared they should be. Like many others, she had chased big dreams to Hollywood from the Midwest. But Mina never learned to project her real life beauty onto the screen. So her career languished amidst walk-on parts and bit roles.

Despite efforts at touching up her makeup, she'd clearly been crying. "Oh, Baz." She looked at him with despair.

Perhaps it was that tender diminutive, Baz, which got to him. It hadn't passed her lips since they'd grown apart. Feeling unexpectedly protective, Basil knelt beside her. "Mina, what's wrong?"

Suppressing a sob, she handed Basil a cream-colored paper from her purse.

Miss Reeves, I possess photographs of you and a certain Universal Studios actor in a private moment at Arroyo Burro Beach during August of last year. If you do not wish those photographs made public, be at 3627 Mission Road at 10 P.M. this evening and bring your actor friend.

Basil remembered the day. After picnicking, they slipped further up the beach to a secluded spot. How someone had obtained photos, he didn't understand. But he understood Hollywood's hypocrisy. Photos would barely touch him. They would ruin her. A gentleman did the right thing, and he had been genuinely fond of Mina. Of course, he would help her.

Basil reached for the phone, wanting to tell Ouida he would be home late, before remembering she had was in New York for a screenwriter's conference. That was just as well. Explaining would be complicated. Ouida was the love of his life. And he, hers. But they had an understanding. Neither asked how the other spent private time.

Escorting Mina to the Universal Pictures parking lot, they left the studio in his beloved '39 Packard. At the lot's exit, a portly security guard he knew only as "Chester" gave a friendly wave. But Basil was not unaware of the slight tightening around the corner of the Chester's eyes, as if to say *Oh, are you two together again?* Inwardly, Basil sighed. Studios were like giant small towns. Negotiating through the tight Universal City streets, Basil nudged the Packard onto the highway.

Though the twilight, the lights on the HOLLYWOODLAND sign already twinkled in the distance. It took 4,000 bulbs to illuminate the 13 white letters atop Mount Lee, each over 50 feet tall, flashing, in turn:

HOLLY   WOOD   LAND

A dispute over the sign's electric bill raged between the city and the developer who originally erected the sign. Many suspected the landmark would soon go dark. Basil had no feelings either way.

Though hours remained until their mysterious appointment, Basil's foot pressed heavily on the Packard's gas pedal. He loved speed, but tonight it was speed with a purpose. He wanted to reach his bank before it closed. Everything pointed toward blackmail. But no dollar amount or other demands had been given. Either they were dealing with an amateur or something stranger was afoot. Both possibilities unnerved Basil.

It would be lying to say he had no concerns for himself. Or for Ouida. But Mina was the one in real professional, and personal, jeopardy. Knowing how the system worked, he cringed. It wasn't having the affair that would ruin Mina. It was the getting caught.

There were, of course, means for procuring cash after banking hours. But, reflecting that they increased risk of the very publicity he wished to avoid, Basil rode his accelerator even harder.

With minutes to spare, he sloppily double-parked the Packard at the bank's entrance. Normally, such a parking job would have driven him to distraction but time was of the essence. Already halfway out the door, he turned back to Mina. "Will you be alright waiting here?"

She nodded. Striding toward the bank, he heard her whisper after him "Thank you, Baz."

Five minutes later he was back in the car. In absence of specific instructions from their blackmailer, he had discretely withdrawn funds sufficient to cover any price the maligner would likely ask.

Basil drove southeast through the deepening dusk. As natural illumination dimmed, the city's million electric lights winked to life. Looking around, it was difficult to believe that the world had been in flames just a year ago. Sure, this city experienced some war nerves in those dark, final days of 1941. And, throughout the duration, L.A. had been America's great arsenal. Of airplanes. Of vehicles. And of morale. Hollywood had gone to war, too. But L.A. never looked back.

Like magic, new ribbons of concrete highways, and legions of speeding new cars to fill them, spilled across the map. At every off-ramp, new neighborhoods swelled with returned GIs and their young families. With much of the world still in recovery, Basil found something unseemly yet alluring about it all. The future was being made in L.A. And it fell to Hollywood to properly instruct the rest of the world about what the future looked like.

Finding the silence uncomfortable, Basil asked Mina how

she'd been keeping busy.

Her last screen role had been *Girl on the Spot,* a crime drama mixed with a musical which Universal released, amid not much fanfare, earlier in the year. From the beginning, Basil had been skeptical about its dubious mix of genres. Mina relayed how, after being signed for a small chorus role, she had been bumped down to a non-speaking extra. Until she landed another film role, she was keeping body and soul together with catalogue modeling; her most notable coup as a swimwear model for Broadway Department Store.

Basil suggested she audition for *Little Miss Big.* The upcoming frothy, family-friendly comedy would play to Mina's strengths. As would its director, Erle Kenton. The Missourian was known to have penchant for hiring supporting actors who shared his middle-of-the-country origins. Knowing a little of the man, Basil offered Mina some suggestions for getting on Kenton's good side.

After their awkward discussion of Mina's modest successes, she visibly relaxed while talking about her family in Illinois. But, after running out of things to say to about her parents, the grocery they owned, and her eight brothers and sisters, she lapsed back into silence. For lack of anything else to say, Basil shared his feeling about leaving *Dressed to Kill*, and Sherlock Holmes, behind.

"I will miss Nigel Bruce," he confided, regarding the Scotsman who had been his Watson through all 14 Holmes pictures. As a light went on in his mind, Basil slapped the steering wheel. "That's something I should have told the reporter. He would have appreciated it." Basil recounted his interview with the *Motion Picture Magazine* reporter. "As wooden as Doyle's writing can be," he expounded to Mina "the interplay between Holmes and Watson always had real life. Real feeling. That's hard to do. It's a very tricky chemistry. You might think you have it when you don't. Or, when you're not expecting it at all, suddenly it's there."

Basil showed more enthusiasm discussing his previous film, *Heartbeat.* "I played Professor Aristide, a Fagin-esque character operating a school for pickpockets in Paris." He could hardly blame Mina for showing greater interest in Ginger Rogers, who played the film's ingénue protagonist, than Basil's role as her foil. Still, in defense of his pride, he added "Though hardly high art, at least Professor Aristide was role with some meat on it!"

With his thoughts brought back to Sherlock Holmes, Basil made a candid admission, "Mina, I fear Holmes will cast a long shadow over me. He is someone I must not and will not play again, regardless of circumstance."

Though Basil had not recognized the addresses 3627 Mission Road, in the Lincoln Heights neighborhood, he instantly recognized the destination: the Los Angeles Alligator Farm. Ostensibly an aquaculture business with an educational sideline, everyone in L.A. knew what the alligator farm really was. A tourist trap.

Finding its parking lot empty, Basil wondered if their man might be more professional than he had thought. At least he avoided the amateurish mistake of making his means of transportation obvious…and allowing his victims to note his car's make and model. Taking the lead into an unknown and possibly dangerous situation, Basil felt like thirty years had fallen away and he was once again leading patrols in the Great War.

Approaching the alligator farm's white faux-Greek Revival main building and gift shop, they passed signs proclaiming "Over 1,000 Alligators" and "See the Trained Alligator Show" intermixed with paintings of strapping young men and buxom young women wrestling the creatures.

Finding its front doors locked, Basil peered through the building's windows. The darkened interior appeared depopulated. Whomever they were meeting wasn't inside. Making their way around the farm's outer wall, Basil discovered a side gate left ajar…a gate leading directly into the open area containing the farm's toothsome exhibits. The gate creaked. Mina jumped as Basil pushed it open.

Tensely, they searched the immediate area for their

blackmailer. "Please tell me you have some funny story about being in a movie with an alligator to take my mind off this," Mina said hopefully.

"Me personally? No." As Basil responded, he began purposefully scanning the area near the main entrance until he found a circular tank occupied by a single, massive alligator. "Billy" proclaimed a sign at the tank's edge. "But I'll bet this fellow could tell you a story or two. Would you believe I'm jealous of this reptile?"

"Why?" asked Mina, perplexed.

"Because he's been in more movies than I have. Almost any time you see an alligator or supposed crocodile on the big screen: jungle movies, swamp movies, horror movies, it's been played by Billy here."

The reptile regarded the pair with lazy indifference. Not too different, Basil thought drolly, from what most other big Hollywood stars would give their fans. "I hear he's even trained. After a fashion. Dangling a bit of meat above him, just off camera, he always opens wide. You would expect other alligators to do the same. Apparently they don't. Supposedly, he even lets his trainer ride around on his back. I don't suggest we put that to the test."

Fascinating as it was to meet the world's most famous reptile, Billy wasn't why they were here. But they had yet to find any sign of the person who had summoned them. Apparently, Basil and Mina were expected to work for the privilege of being blackmailed.

They picked their way along paths winding past concrete ponds and through replica bayous hung with faux Spanish moss as they sought their mysterious host. Deserted and dark, the alligator farm possessed a surreal, almost nightmarish quality. Shadowy shapes floating in the water remained so silent and still it was difficult to believe they were alive. Occasionally, one became agitated, splashing furiously about while uttering their distinctive primordial bellow. Basil couldn't say whether the statue-like stillness or the sudden bursts of frenzied activity unnerved him more. As Mina reached forward to take his hand in hers, Basil expected he felt as comforted as she did.

"I've been thinking," he said as they crossed a narrow causeway between two reptile-infested ponds "If this place operates without its attractions eating its visitors on a regular basis, they must keep their animals gorged to the point of gluttony. I suspect our danger is actually minimal." Basil knew his reasoning was entirely sound. He didn't know who he was trying to convince. Mina? Or himself?

His fondness for animals did not extend to the beasts surrounding them. And had not since he was very young. Involuntarily, against his better judgement in fact, Basil shared a story. "I think I told you that I was born in South Africa? We lived there until I was three, when the local Boers started suspecting my father was a British agent and we had to flee on short notice.

"One of my last memories of Africa was a country outing with my parents. While picnicking by a stream, a reedbuck appeared. I don't know if you've seen a reedbuck, Mina. It's an antelope. With elegant, inward curving horns and beautiful, nearly human eyes. Normally they're quite skittish. But this one, after taking our measure for a few moments, walked confidently past us to drink. For a child, there was something magical in that moment. But, mid-drink, a crocodile shot from the stream, took the reedbuck's neck in its jaws, and dragged it into the water where several its fellows appeared and joined in tearing the poor animal to pieces."

"Thanks, Baz. I feel so much better now," she replied with sarcasm so thick that even the alligators could have detected it.

"Sorry," Basil replied, slightly embarrassed. "It's just such a vivid memory. It made quite an impression on me. For whatever it may be worth, I've heard alligators are not as aggressive as crocodiles."

In the end, it was Mina who spotted the Manila envelope taped to the property's rear wall. Opening it, Basil discovered the photographs and negatives, accompanied by another letter. To his surprise, the missive was written in Greek. As a young man at Repton School, he'd studied the language. Basil was the first to admit he had not been a diligent student and, anyway, that was 40 years ago. Still, he could fumble his way along.

> *Dear Mister Rathbone,*
> *I hope finding a Greek Interpreter has not taken*
> *overlong. Thank you for coming. Please excuse this*
> *theatrical means of getting your attention. You have*
> *the once in a lifetime opportunity to play your greatest*
> *role...in reality. Unless you stop me, at sunset next*
> *Friday I will unleash calamity upon your city. Please*
> *do not go to the police or otherwise publicize this*
> *matter. Otherwise, I shall be forced to move up my*
> *timetable or take other drastic action.*

"I am sorry, Mina," Basil said, shaking his head as he handed her the envelope and its contents. "Your worry and our wasted time were for nothing. I, not you, was the target all along."

"What is it?" she asked looking, uncomprehending, at the Greek letters.

"Only some deranged fan playing an elaborate prank."

SATURDAY, APRIL 27TH

Putting the bizarre incident behind him, Basil dove into finishing *Dressed to Kill*. Studios didn't stop for weekends. At the commissary, over an unenviable lunch of pea soup with ham, Basil caught a bit of conversation from a nearby table.

"The alligator farm? Can you imagine?" said the blonde.

"And at night. It would have given me the creeps," her redheaded friend, with hair precisely the color of an Irish Setter's coat, replied.

Basil recognized them, vaguely, two of Universal's regular stable of extras. Men and women who, while not fast-tracked for stardom, had not been shown the door either. Instead, they existed in perpetual limbo while the studio evaluated their potential. Though there could really be only one story they were recounting, that he had previously seen

30

both women in Mina's company clenched it.

Realizing Mina had been discussing their adventure, Basil felt ambivalent. But when the Setter-haired actress added "I don't care how handsome he is. I wouldn't go," it definitely appealed to his vanity.

"But a secret admirer? How romantic! Who do you think it is?" her friend replied, leaving Basil confused.

"I don't know. But Mina said the letter at the Alligator Farm promised she'd get further clues about him."

Finally, Basil understood. Mina had taken liberties polishing the story, removing both Basil and the incriminating photos while creating the character of a mysterious secret admirer. No doubt she hoped a bit of gossip would bolster her career. Well, Basil wished her the best.

As it turned out, all the well-wishing in the world couldn't help Mina. After filming ended for the day, Basil sat in his dressing room leafing through *Variety*.

After a knock at his door, Basil bade his visitor to enter. He looked Jane over as she stood in the doorway. To his assistant's enigmatic gaze had been added a hardness, a distance. He thought he detected a quiver in her upper lip.

"Jane? What is it?"

As that quiver became a tremble, Jane found she couldn't answer. Shaking her head, Basil's assistant deposited a newspaper beside him, departing without another word.

Picking up the day's copy of the *Daily News* that Jane had dropped, it didn't take long to find the blurb.

ACTRESS RUN DOWN

His hand trembling as he held the paper, Basil read.

Mina Reeves, 23, originally of Peoria, Illinois, died during a hit-and-run collision in the 3900 block of Fountain Avenue. Reeves was on her way to an audition, her roommate informed police. While crossing the street to reach her appointment, a vehicle struck Reeves while traveling at an excessive rate of speed. Police pronounced her dead at the scene.

While witnesses did not get a good look at the driver, several described the car as an older Buick Roadmaster. One witness alleged the original wooden paneling of the driver's door had been replaced by a newer metal version. Members of the public with information relating to the incident are requested to contact the LAPD.

Basil threw the paper down, losing himself in thought. The story didn't feel right. Fountain Avenue was a strange place for an audition, especially so far out.

Requiring a moment to compose himself, Basil exited the dressing room. At her desk, Jane had likewise put herself back together.

"I'm sorry about Mina," she told him.

"Thank you, Jane. The rest of your tasks for the day can wait. Instead, call the usual places. Find out who had an audition on Fountain yesterday," he instructed. "If anyone did," he added as much to himself as to her. Returning to his dressing room, Basil made a call of his own. Jane wouldn't know who Mina's agent was. Basil did. He dialed.

"Lawrence, this is Basil. Did you get Mina that audition yesterday?"

"Hell no," the agent's New York accent boomed through the receiver, "You're her big benefactor. I figured you lined it up."

Basil returned the phone to its cradle. No, this didn't feel right at all.

Later, Jane poked into the dressing room. Basil understood the meaning behind her shaking head. To be honest, he had expected it. Nobody had an audition scheduled at that place and time.

Jane looked at Basil curiously. Only after a moment did he realize that, at some point, he had subconsciously placed the prop pipe from *Dressed to Kill* in his mouth while turning the strange circumstances of Mina Reeves' death over in his mind.

32

"Should we notify the police?" Jane asked as Basil sheepishly sat the prop aside.

"No." The strange letter stipulated 'no police.' He grew inclined to take it seriously.

As news spread, several people dropped by Basil's dressing room to extend condolences. Some simply knew Basil had been close to Mina. Others knew, or suspected, the truth. Despite the heavy shadow cast by her death, Basil and Jane managed to push through day's tasks. Ready to be home alone, Basil locked his dressing room.

Walking through the studio backstreets toward the parking lot, Jane and her boss reviewed tomorrow's schedule. Even at the advanced hour, the paths between studio buildings buzzed with activity and every form of studio life. Runners carrying messages. Gaffers, their belts heavy with electrical implements. Grips carrying more traditional tools. Personal assistants on errands for somebody who was, or believed themselves to be, important. Even the occasional bona fide studio executive rushed along. Democratically, carts full of costumes hanging on racks and larger pallets loaded with scenery flats or props impeded the progress of high and low alike.

Especially striking were the costumed extras. Basil never tired of a sight creating the illusion that, somehow, all of humanity's cultures and eras had been thrown together in one place: men in djellabas and fezzes from *Tangiers*, women donning brightly-colored Latin dresses with ruffled sleeves for the musical comedy *Cuba Pete,* fedora wearing hoodlums from the crime thriller *Inside Job*, *Canyon Passage's* buckskin-clad pioneers and painted natives, as well as smartly-attired professionals populating *Lover Come Back.*

Basil and Jane raised their voices to hear one another over the din, until a new voice overpowered them both. "Well, if it isn't the great Basil Rathbone!"

The man interrupting them called to mind the English stage of a generation ago. Its owner staggered toward them with a gait as sotted his breath soon proved. He wore his coal-black hair, with snow-white streaks at the temples, boldly long. A pencil-thin moustache, curled at the ends, hailed from earlier decades. His age approximated Basil's and, likewise, retained the grace and athleticism of a younger man. The overall effect would have been distinguished, had an aura of dissipation not clung to him.

Getting too close, the intruder looked at Jane. "Has Ratters been telling you how extraordinary he is, my dear?"

"My conversation with Mr. Rathbone is none of your business."

"Please, Gil," Basil said with forced patience, "Today is not a good day."

"It must be wonderful to confront one's demons at leisure," the man replied caustically, becoming visibly agitated as he looked Basil over. "I see you're still banking off those hack detective films. How many credited roles for you since coming to Hollywood? Four dozen? Five?"

Basil looked away, "You're making a scene."

"Do you know what I was doing here today, Ratters?" Gil shouted "Hoping to get picked as an extra for an Abbott and Costello film!"

Security guards arrived, each taking the man by an arm they escorting him off. Though Gil did not resist, he looked over his shoulder while being walked away. "I could have been one of greats, Basil. Together, we could have made Tinsel Town tremble."

"Ratters?" Jane asked after the man vanished. "And who was that?"

"Gilbert Talmidge," Basil shook his head sadly. "During the twenties, we were peers, and friends, on the London stage. My friends and fellow actors called me 'Ratters' back then."

"And, because you became successful and he didn't, Gilbert blames you?"

"I fear there's some truth to what he says. *Peter Ibbetson* was my breakout role. To get it, I had to beat not only Gil, but two other fine actors, Peter Daniell and George Ralph. It wasn't only my audition that secured the role. I told the company I'd play Ibbetson for ten pounds a week. An absurdly low sum. But, even if it meant eating beans every night, I swore the part would be mine.

"Gilbert believes if he'd gotten the role, he'd be the famous one now. I can't tell you he's wrong. After failing to make a splash in England, he landed in Hollywood convinced that swashbuckling, seduction, and bad behavior would make him a star. Instead, it made him a second-rate Errol Flynn...about which he should be grateful."

"Why?"

"Because it means *he* will be alive tomorrow. With Errol, you never can be certain!" Basil said, elevating his voice to be heard over a distant, but loud car.

Past the studio buildings, the crowd thinned as they neared the parking lot. Though Jane continued discussing his schedule, Basil, lost in thought, barely registered her words. Only the growing din of an engine interrupted his memories and regrets about Gilbert Talmadge. Someone was driving too fast. Almost certainly an executive or an actor. Basil's thoughts once again turned to Errol...and his custom-built peach-colored Packard convertible.

Resuming his brooding over Gilbert, Basil failed to notice people ahead of him dodging out of the way. And the motorcar bearing down upon them. Awareness dawning, he became, literally, like a deer in headlights. Blinded by the car's high beams he could make out only its tall, narrow grill. When he took a few steps to the side, the vehicle not only swerved to follow him, it accelerated.

Launching herself at Basil, Jane wrapped him up like an American footballer just as the lights and noise reached a crescendo. Hitting the ground fast and hard, for a moment Basil was uncertain whether he had escaped or been struck. Only when he registered the rush of wind, the smell of exhaust, and the engine's Doppler roar diminishing behind him did he completely accept that his assistant had tackled him out of the way in the nick of time. As they rolled over the pavement, Basil watched the car turn a corner and vanish. No, not just a car. A Buick Roadmaster. With one door replaced.

Basil looked at his savior. Jane's expression said she noted the distinctive vehicle, too.

"Thank you," he said after rising and dusting off.

She brushed gratitude aside. "Do you think this is connected to that letter you got? The one threatening the city?"

"How do you know about that?"

"It saw it on your dressing room table."

"You read Greek?"

"My parents gave me the best education money could buy," she said guardedly. "So, are we going to find that car?"

"What do you mean 'we'? This is dangerous business. There's no reason for you to get caught up in it."

"I'm your personal assistant and this is my first job in Hollywood. If I let you get killed, my career is pretty much over."

SUNDAY, APRIL 28

Basil and Jane cruised Hollywood and Universal City. His narrow escape from a vehicle identical to the one ending Mina Reeves' life gnawed at Basil's mind. He cleared his schedule, even, over Jane's protests, the day's filming on *Dressed to Kill*. Instead, Basil shanghaied his assistant into hunting the lethal Roadmaster.

After prowling the lots and alleys of Universal and other studios, they'd widened their search to Hollywood's nooks and crannies. Hollywood wasn't a Buick town. They'd seen a few Roadmasters but none with the distinctive door.

"Do you really think Mina's death is connected with the Greek letter?" Jane broke their silence.

"It might be coincidence," Basil acknowledged. "But the audition seems like a setup. And Mina had been talking. Exactly what the letter's author said not to do."

"And his threat to the city?"

"That…" He paused. "Is hopefully the ravings of an imbalanced fan."

"It must be scary knowing that people can react that way to your work."

"You get used to it. You wouldn't believe how many people don't understand Basil Rathbone *isn't* Sherlock Holmes. Almost weekly, I get letters asking me to solve actual mysteries. This fan is simply more delusional than most," Basil said, admitting as an afterthought, "and more dangerous."

Basil reflected how little he knew about his assistant. Hardly unusual in Hollywood. Jane Westin was the daughter of some big Universal investor back east. She aspired to become a screenwriter. Waiting to see how that panned out, she paid her dues in one the studio system's most thankless roles.

Rosy-checked and honey haired, her wholesome "all American" appearance contrasted with dark, inscrutable eyes. That piqued Basil's interest but Jane had politely yet unambiguously rebuffed him. Only a cad would have tried again.

Broadening their patrol to Hollywood Hills, Los Feliz, and East Hollywood produced no better results. As shadows lengthened, they returned to Universal. While Jane checked her desk, Basil visited his dressing room to collect messages.

"Where the bloody hell were you today, Basil?" Roy William Neill, *Dressed to Kill's* director and producer, fumed in Basil's chair.

"I had things to do," Basil offered nonchalantly, adding, "And I'd like to know exactly when my dressing room and my chair turned into the village common."

His fellow Englishman tried a softer approach. "I know you're upset about Mina's death. We all are. But people depend on you. I covered for you today but I really need you there tomorrow."

"I have things tomorrow, too."

"Don't push me, Basil. The Laemmles lost control of Universal because they tolerated prima donnas. The men running this studio now don't. You'll be on set first thing in the morning. Or there will be trouble." Neill stormed out.

Jane accompanying Basil to his car while reviewing the next

day's schedule had become a ritual for them. With the recent unpleasantness, Basil insisted upon reversing the ritual. Walking with her to the studio's other, more remote and plebian parking lot, he split his thoughts between Jane's reminders and the stack of messages he would examine at home. As they threaded their way among rows of automobiles, a horse-faced figure emerged from between two vehicles. Basil barely registered the dirty undershirt, chinos with suspenders, Panama hat, and cigarette clenched tightly between his teeth before the man laid him out with one punch.

On the ground, eyes still swimming with stars, Basil looked up. The assailant flicked a business card onto his chest and strolled casually into the evening. Regaining his wits, Basil examined the card.

LES STRAD
Private Detective
3160 Scotland Street   LA5-5702

The drive to Bel Air and his Bellagio Road villa soothed Basil. Halting at the entryway mirror, he examined the face staring back at him. The face was an actor's trademark. Fortunately, the hit he taken had not marred his long, almond-shaded visage; its strong brow and chin suggestive of a forceful personality. Sensitive eyes and lips, hinting at refinement, were neither blackened nor busted. The pugilistic detective had done him no real harm. Basil wished the same could be said of Father Time.

At 54, the face now looked distinguished rather than dashing. Having once made women swoon on both sides of the Atlantic, that evolution brought more than a trace of wistfulness. Before Ouida there had been Esther, Cynthia, Marion, Marie, Juliette, Kitten, Tallulah, and June. Basil always had an eye for the ladies. He still did.

After dinner, Basil retired to his library. Ambrose, their English butler, had laid his mail on the table. Amidst financial documents and personal correspondence, one envelope stood out. It lacked a return address, but the elegant handwriting addressing it to Basil screamed familiarity. He cursed himself for leaving the Greek letter at the studio and allowing the original correspondence to remain with Mina. Basil would swear the same hand had penned all three.

Opening the envelope, Basil found a mystery. Five rows of unfamiliar symbols filled the crème-colored stationary. Most of them consisted of two lines of different lengths radiating from a central point. Single vertical lines of differing heights and lengths comprised the rest. The marks resembled no alphabet he'd seen, excepting perhaps some distortion of Mesopotamian cuneiform or the Aegean's mysterious Linear B script. Yet something seemed maddeningly familiar about them. The Rathbones' library had a few books on archeology and linguistics. He hoped he wouldn't have to pull them out.

Letter to Basil

Scrutinizing the letter closely, Basil counted 22 distinct symbols comprising 316 total characters. Twelve characters were underlined but otherwise identical to other marks. Basil suspected, rather than separate symbols, underlining represented grammar or punctuation. English had 26 letters. Greek had 24. Both came close enough to 22 to presume it was a simple substitution cipher.

Considering the recent letter, Greek might be the safer assumption. Basil, instead, decided to try English. If that failed, he could attempt Greek instead.

In the Great War, during a night of drinking with signal corps officers, Basil learned that E was English's most common letter. Unfortunately, he couldn't remember the frequencies of letters after that. Basil wrote E above the message's most common symbol and hoped he could go somewhere from there.

Basil stared at his first fumblings toward a solution, putative Es scattered across the page, for over an hour. Closer to two hours, to be honest. He nearly gave up before noticing a six-letter word ᴿᴱᴱᵀᴱ⅃ While few words met that arrangement, "Reeves" was one of them. Perhaps the message alluded to Mina? The word's first letter had been underlined. If he was correct about it being "Reeves", perhaps underlines represented capital letters.

Basil worked through the message again, filling in potential Rs, Vs, and Ss. The word in front of "Reeves" now read ᴵˢˢ , with the first symbol underscored. If underlining did equate capitalization, "Miss" seem a plausible translation. He filled in the message's Ms and Is. Noting every I that formed a complete word by itself was underlined, he accepted his capitalization hypothesis.

Basil focused on the partly revealed word, ᴴᴱⱽᴱᴿ Thinking it more likely to be "however" than "forever," he filled in Hs, Os, and Ws. Left with no definitive place to go, Basil concentrated on the capitalized word ᵀᴵᴹᴱˢ Technically, it could be "Dimes," "Limes," even "Mimes." Only *Times*, referring to the paper, made sense. Basil proceeded, replacing the symbol with T.

Stuck, Basil looked the document for a while. Not a trained cryptographer, he verged on quitting again when his phone rang. Despite, or perhaps because of, the advanced hour, he expected it to be Ouida.

"Basil, I'm sorry about our words at the studio earlier," Roy William Neill sounded conciliatory.

Focused on the letter, Basil barely heard him. "Mmm, yes," he replied absently before moving the earpiece back toward the receiver.

"Don't hang up on me," Neill said intuitively. "Don't test me Basil. Don't..."

Basil ended the call. Something bumped his leg. Leo looked up playfully, rubber ball between his jaws. Unable to resist any member of the Rathbone menagerie, Basil played until the red cocker spaniel was exhausted before returning to his chair.

Fresh eyes noticed two words he'd overlooked. REMEMBER had to be "remember," just as SAVE became "save" The latter proved especially valuable, A filled in lots of spaces.

TOWARD then became "toward" and CHATTER was "chatter." Basil spotted another overlooked word, INVITE should be invite. While he strongly suspected that SERIOUSLY was "seriously," he resisted making the risky three letter leap in favor of single letter progressions. It pleased Basil that his next success came from context rather than substitution. Occurring between "demonstrate" and "earnestness," MY could only be "my."

With Y, Basil could identify the reoccurring word YOU as "you." One more letter down. That gave him FRIDAY revealing the F. Just as PURITY became purity, SUSPECT became "suspect." Where he once hesitated with that, he confidently deduced L from SERIOUSLY Only two words remained. Basil deciphered both of them from context. First, "...purity of the GAME we play." Clearly, the symbol was G. With that, only "not TAKING this contest seriously" remained, making the final symbol, K.

Breathing deeply, Basil examined the full translation.

Please understand I bore no personal ill will toward Miss Reeves but her indiscreet chatter threatened to undermine the purity of the game we play. You, however, I suspect of not taking this contest seriously. I invite you to pay attention to tomorrow's Times. *It will demonstrate my earnestness and ability. No police. Remember, you have until sunset Friday to save your city.*

Wondering as to the hour, Basil glanced at the clock. Barely noting it was after midnight, he was thunderstruck. One of the mysterious symbols stared him in the face. Clock hands. The symbols depicted in the message showed clock hands, lacking encircling numbers or hash marks, either on the hour or at half past the hour.

On blank paper, Basil listed the 24 half-hours on a clock face, beginning with 12:00 and ending with 11:30. He then assigned a letter to each half-hour, A for 12:00 and all the way through to Y for 11:30. The rarest letters, X and Z, were omitted.

a	12:00	(stroke)	m	6:00	(stroke)
b	12:30	(stroke)	n	6:30	(stroke)
c	1:00	(stroke)	o	7:00	(stroke)
d	1:30	(stroke)	p	7:30	(stroke)
e	2:00	(stroke)	q	8:00	(stroke)
f	2:30	(stroke)	r	8:30	(stroke)
g	3:00	(stroke)	s	9:00	(stroke)
h	3:30	(stroke)	t	9:30	(stroke)
i	4:00	(stroke)	u	10:00	(stroke)
j	4:30	(stroke)	v	10:30	(stroke)
k	5:00	(stroke)	w	11:00	(stroke)
L	5:30	(stroke)	y	11:30	(stroke)

Using that as a key, he perfectly decrypted the letter. It, he noted, lacked symbols depicting 4:30 or 8:00 on the clock, corresponding to the letters J and Q on his key. Like the much scorned X and Z, those letters did not appear in the translated message.

Basil cursed so loudly that Leo, now roused from slumber, looked on with concern before darting from the room. If only Basil had taken time to consider the big picture, he might have cracked the cipher in minutes rather than hours. Instead, the evening was spent. Little remained but sleep.

Slumber came uneasily. Three times Basil got up, checking that his doors were locked and windows shut securely. Though loath to admit it, anxiety ate at him. The letter in Greek, which he'd thought peculiar at the time, called to mind Doyle's story, "The Greek Interpreter." The missive's unknown composer had even used that phrase. Likewise, the clock-face code resembled the dancing men from the Sherlock Holmes mystery of that name. The letter's writer wanted to manipulate Basil into becoming Holmes for some twisted game. He had killed Mina. How much credence should Basil give his threat to the entire city?

Basil was dealing with no ordinary obsessed fan.

MONDAY, APRIL 29TH

Next morning, meeting Jane for coffee at the studio, Basil summarized his struggle decrypting the clock-face letter and the bizarre message it revealed. Jane glanced at the day's paper in front of Basil. "What about the writer's claim about 'demonstrating his earnestness and ability' in the *Times?*"

"I've looked through the paper all morning. Nothing stands out," he scowled. "For all I know, it's a hoax after all. Why don't you take a look?"

"No hoax." Jane said minutes later. With her pen, she circled an item in the Police Blotter, pushing the *Times* back toward Basil.

Police discovered the body of Sherman Laverock, 27, of Newton Rd., Van Nuys, after another laborer from

*Laverock's jobsite stopped to check on him. While
cause of death remains undetermined, foul play is not
immediately suspected.*

"What makes you think this is our mystery man's demonstration?"

Jane ripped a tiny section from the paper, taking her pen to it. The dead man's name now read:

Sher~~man~~-Laver~~ock~~

The remaining letters neatly spelling "SherLock."

"I'll get my keys," Basil announced.

Another scene with Roy William Neill unfolded as they attempted to leave.

Walking toward the actors and executives' parking lot, a voice called after them "Basil. Basil!" Glancing over his shoulder, he spotted the director chasing them. By unspoken agreement, Basil and Jane increased their pace.

"Damnit, Basil! Look at me when I'm talking to you." Neill finally caught up with them as they were about to drive off. He stood stubbornly in front of the Packard, blocking their departure. Red-faced and left breathless from pursuit, the director rested his hands on his knees while drinking down big gulps of air. Thinking his director resembled a woodchuck with a mitten-moustache and gray Homburg hat, Basil couldn't suppress a laugh.

"Everyone's on set..." Neill took another hard breath. "They're...waiting."

"Roy, you're a bright fellow. You'll simply have to figure out a way to carry on without me."

"I can't," he explained. "You've already been out for a day. At great inconvenience, I already changed today's schedule to shoot the remaining scenes Holmes isn't in. At this point, all I can do is sit around burning Universal's money."

"I'm sorry. I have more important plans today. Plans that don't involve me playing Sherlock Holmes," realizing the irony of his statement, Basil was uncertain whether to grin or frown. He compromised with a grimace.

"I don't know what you're up to, Baz," Neill tried the chummy approach. "But you're a professional. You've made it no secret that you're sick of Holmes. Did you ever think I might like to be directing something else as well? But you have too much regard for your fellow actors to let them down like this. Nigel, Patricia, Edmund, Fredrick, they're all waiting for you. The show must go on."

"Sometimes the show is elsewhere."

After continuing in a similar vein for a quarter hour, begging, pleading, and cajoling, Neill tried a tougher approach. "You may think you're untouchable. You're not. Your assistant certainly isn't. If you won't think of yourself at least think of her."

Sitting beside Basil in the passenger's seat, Jane remained silent as her face became a stony mask of resolve.

"I suppose that is a chance we'll have to take. And Neill," he continued, switching to the director's last name, "you know I don't respond well to threats." Basil threw his car into first gear, nudging the Packard forward. Eyeing him coldly, Neill attempted to call his bluff. When the Packard's engine revved and shot forward another foot, the director understood Basil wasn't bluffing and hastily stepped out of the way.

A glance in the rearview mirror as they drove away revealed Neill shaking his fist after them as he shouted "I'm bringing down the thunder on you, Rathbone. The thunder!"

Pulling onto the main road, as if a silent cue had been given, Basil and Jane broke into laughter. True, much of their exchange with Roy William Neill had been comical. But an edge of nervousness fueled Basil's laughter as well. Neill had been right about one thing, Basil was a professional. Whether stage or screen, he had never tested a director like this before. And he really liked Neill, not just professionally but personally. When this was over, Basil would do what he needed to mend fences. But, for now, as he had told the director, the real show was elsewhere.

Driving northwest, Tinsel Town's glitz and glamour

slowly gave way to increasingly blue collar neighborhoods. Occasional green fields hinted at the farm country which stood here just a generation ago.

The late Sherman Laverock's Newton Road address proved to be in an unincorporated part of the county outside Van Nuys. Flanked by police cars and other vehicles, Basil and Jane had no difficulty spotting the property. From the road, its yard sloped downward. Laverock's house, though shack was more apt, sat in a kind of basin. Rain must have made the structure downright unpleasant.

"Shall we talk to the police?" Jane asked.

More than ever, Basil anxiously sought to avoid interacting with police or giving the appearance of doing so. He told his assistant as much.

"Are you sure?" she said doubtfully.

"Yes. First there are the letters' warnings, which I am increasingly tempted to consider credible. Second...let me tell you a story. In 1926, I was in New York appearing in *The Captive*. The play examined same-sex relationships, a theme as underexplored then as it is today. That we touched it at all apparently made someone unhappy. One night, police showed up at the Empire Theatre, arrested everybody, from the stars to the stagehands, for obscenity, and carted us downtown."

"I'm sorry. That's terrible," Jane commiserated.

"Actually," Basil grinned, "I had a fabulous time. The police had also brought in the show Mae West was headlining. With her coarse wit and earthy charms, Mae commandeered the police station. Even the beat cops defected, joining the drunks, thieves, and streetwalkers rallying around her while the precinct captain and his cronies could only look on with despair.

"I later learned the police had been goaded into the arrests by a politician wanting to be seen as protecting the tender sensibilities of New York City's families come Election Day. Since then, I have believed there is an inherent tension between those sworn to uphold social norms...and artists, broadly defined, who by their very nature flout and challenge such conventions."

His pretty speech didn't get them any closer to information about Laverock's death. On the periphery of activity, Basil spotted a man wearing a khaki trench coat, a cardboard "press" tag protruding from the band around his trilby.

"Hot story of the day?" Basil called as he and Jane approached.

"Sure is," the reporter turned and did a double-take. "You're Basil Rathbone!"

"Guilty."

"I'm Woody Hollings. I love the Sherlock Holmes movies!"

"Thank you." Normally, Basil preferred to be praised for any other accomplishment. Today, it offered the perfect opening. "It's macabre, but visiting crime scenes gives me a better handle on Holmes."

Woody nodded enthusiastically.

"What can you tell me about this one?"

"The doors were locked from the inside. Windows shut. No indication of forced entry. No signs of trauma or other marks on the body. Mr. Rathbone, it really is one worthy of Sherlock Holmes!"

"And what of the deceased?"

"Joined the Corps in forty-two. He saw heavy fighting in the Pacific and had trouble transitioning to peacetime. No real friends or family. Difficulty keeping any sort of job. At least until he got work with a road company working on the Coastal Highway."

"Anything else peculiar?"

Woody looked over his notes. "I almost forget the strangest part. See the chicken coop behind the house? All Laverock's hens were dead as him."

"Suspects?"

"Neighbors saw an odd looking truck outside the house last night, but can't give a better description. Police are trying to get a lead on that."

"Thank you," Basil said courteously, "We must be moving on, but you've been a great help."

"Well," Jane said as they returned to the Packard, "What

49

do you think about our mysterious letter writer now?"

"I fear for this city." More than that, Basil berated himself. Not taking his adversary seriously, he'd forfeited much of his allotted time. Friday was May third. It had been April twenty-fifth when he and Mina went to the alligator farm and the twenty-eighth when he'd received the coded letter. Now only five days remained to stop whatever menace the man planned.

Back in Universal City, they tried something new. With hunting the Roadmaster going nowhere, they shifted to interviewing those who knew Mina. What about her mysterious audition? Nobody knew anything. How had her mood been? Any new friends or enemies? Old friends or enemies reentering her life? Jilted lovers? Had she borrowed money, posed for blue photographs, or otherwise gotten into trouble?

For their pains, they encountered little that proved helpful. And, often as not, more than a trace of suspicion regarding Basil's motives. Such individuals often mentioned a private detective who visited, asking similar questions. Descriptions of the detective rang a bell. Near the end of a long day, Basil turned to Jane. "I think time has come for a tête-à-tête with Detective Strad."

Like the narrow block it occupied, the two-story commercial building containing Lester "Les" Strad's office appeared to have been wedged between Hyperion and Griffith Park Boulevard as an afterthought. Master of his dingy one-room lair, the detective reclined on a third-hand office chair. Kicked up on the desk, his feet were surrounded by food wrappers from grab-and-go joints, an overflowing ashtray, and stacks of girlie magazines.

"Lookie what the cat dragged in," Strad said, yanking his feet off the desk and leaning forward with anticipation. His accent suggested the industrial Midwest. Chicago, Basil guessed. "It took guts coming here after I marked up your chevy chase," he said, indicating Rathbone's face, "Not so sure about bringing the skirt, though."

"The skirt does what she pleases. Don't forget it." Jane put the detective on notice.

Reaching into a drawer, Strad produced a Colt pistol, placing it on the desk's corner.

"Are you threatening us?" Basil demanded.

"Just making sure you know I got a heater. More than one, actually."

"Have you ever killed a man?"

The detective's eyes darted away. Not with deception but with the look of a man confronted by memories he preferred stay buried. Strad had served in the latest war, Basil realized. He had seen combat. And killed.

"I have as well," Basil continued. "I commanded scouts for the Liverpool Scottish during the Great War. Remember that before waving around your...heater...again."

"What's your game, Rathbone? You here to confess?" Les asked. He dumped a tin of tobacco on the desk and began rolling a cigarette. Whether through instinct or practice, his fingers knew what to do without Les looking.

"Confess to what?"

"Bumping off Mina Reeves, of course. Everyone knows you did it. The family in Peoria even got an anonymous call saying as much. They're paying me to bring in their daughter's killer. My gut tells me that's you."

"Big as that hunch must be," Basil replied, emphasizing the first word, "it is incorrect. I do want to admit one thing, though."

"What's that?" The detective asked while lighting a cigarette.

"I studied boxing under Jack Miltern."

As Strad tried to work out what Basil meant by that, the actor planted three quick jabs on the detective's nose. Blood streaming from his nostrils, Strad fished a handkerchief from his pants and tried to stanch the flow.

"If you really want to find Mina's killer, don't look at me," Basil said. "Whatever you do, stay out of our way." Exiting, he noted the office's torn couch had a blanket and pillow on it. He wondered if Strad was living out of his office.

Feeling they had spoken with everyone who might know about Mina, they resumed looking for the Roadmaster. Basil and Jane checked parking lots, side streets, and open roads in Hollywood and beyond.

"Where's the one place nobody would think to look for a car that runs?" Jane said suddenly.

"I don't know."

"Someplace where cars don't run."

"You're thinking some sort of garage or body shop?"

"A junkyard."

Basil's eyes lit up. It make sense. The Doyle-esqe flourish seemed consistent with their unknown adversary; calling to mind the steam launch *Aurora's* concealment in *The Sign of the Four*. His assistant had proved herself quite an asset.

Checking the directory, Bakersfield's Junkyard & Repo was the closest junkyard both to where Mina had been killed and Basil nearly run over. A promising start. As Basil drove, Mina held the map. "In a couple blocks, turn right at John Sloat Middle School. The place is about a quarter mile beyond that," she navigated.

"Elementary, my dear Jane."

"What?"

"Elementary. I have some familiarity with this neighborhood. John Sloat is an elementary, not a middle school."

Basil parked his Packard outside the sprawling eyesore of Bakersfield's Junkyard. Bypassing the shack serving as its office, Basil and Jane entered through a service gate in the junkyard's corrugated tin fence, next to a section painted *BE WARE OF DOG* in large, sloppy red letters.

They made their way up and down rows of derelict vehicles stacked two and three deep. Some had simply aged beyond usefulness. Others had been badly damaged or totaled. Spring blooms, attended by butterflies and bees, pushed their way out among wheel wells and chaises.

"What are y'all doing?" A haggard man, a little older than Basil, waved his shotgun at them. Not since the Great War had someone pointed a firearm at Basil. He didn't like it any more now.

"Just looking around."

"Lot's closed. Get out." By his speech, Basil imagined the proprietor indeed came from Bakersfield, but not originally. His thick diphthongs were those of a Dustbowl refugee. Oklahoma, probably. Maybe Texas.

"Surely, you want people coming in to purchase parts?" Jane ventured.

"Lot's closed. You're not supposed to be here."

"Lot's closed," Basil repeated, looking at Jane with mock surprise as they departed.

"You gave up awfully easily," she chided after reaching the other side of the street safely. "Didn't want to get shot by Tom Joad?"

"Not at all. I just think this will be easier tonight. Once he's gone home." He winked.

They drove around, killing time by half-heartedly watching for the Roadmaster they hoped hid at Bakersfield's. A leisurely meal followed at a neighborhood restaurant to which Basil was partial.

Only well after dark did the Packard return to the junkyard.

Approaching its fence, Basil paused. He frowned at a pile of cigarette butts under a tree before continuing. Scrambling over the tin fence with some difficulty, they dropped into the junkyard.

Eerie majesty hovered over the lot by night. The final resting place of hundreds of vehicles, each with its own story. How long had this place been here? Some wrecks, notably a magnificent Rolls-Royce two-seater, stretched back to the century's turn. Basil felt an uncomfortable kinship with the Rolls, a once grand machine with its best days behind.

Another vehicle soon piqued his interest. The Roadmaster was a recent addition, having neither rusted nor grown foliage around it. Examination revealed three wood-paneled doors and one of steel. What looked like dried blood marred the dented hood and front fender. Shivering in the mild evening, Basil turned away.

Baritone baying cut through the night.

Basil froze, a chill traveling up his spine. Ferocious barking followed, coming ever nearer. Too late he recalled the warning painted on the junkyard fence.

The nocturnal guardian offered an unforgettable sight. Part mastiff and part blood hound, its pedigree heavily favored the former. Rapidly closing the distance between them, its jaws spread.

The Roadmaster's doors proved stuck. Hopefully not locked. Both of them pulling desperately, they pried open the passenger's side door. Shoving Jane inside, Basil closed the door behind him.

But not quickly enough.

Teeth sunk into his hand. Flesh tore as he yanked it from the beast's mouth. After shutting the door with his other hand, the hound ran into it with a clang.

As it endeavored to smash the glass with its head, its barking was deafening. Finally, the frustrated animal began circling the vehicle, growling.

Basil's hand bled. Concerned, Jane produced a white cotton scarf from her handbag and wrapped the injury, applying light but constant pressure.

"What do we do?" she asked. "Run for it and get eaten by the Hound of the Bakersfields? Or wait until its shotgun-toting owner appears tomorrow? If you've got enough blood to last until then."

Basil had his old service pistol in one pocket. Escape was as a simple as shooting the beast. But, looking at it, he didn't see a monster. He saw the playful Leo; as well as Rags, Great-Uncle William's fox terrier; Sans Souci, the greyhound Ouida owned when they'd begun courting; and Moritz, his beloved German Shepard, now a decade gone. Basil loved dogs. He could no more harm a dog than a child.

"I think we should call for help."

"Help? How long will that take?"

"Not as long as you think." Cracking the window, Basil shouted. "Hey, detective, a little assistance?"

Les Strad's distinctive Panama hat appeared above the

fence. "Rathbone, what'd you get yourself into?"

"That should be obvious, even to you. And, if you think I'm responsible for Mina's death, then you wouldn't want this charming canine to eat your reward money, would you?"

The detective scowled. "Okay, but I ain't shooting no dog." Silent, he appeared to be thinking. "Gimme me 15 minutes."

"Fine."

The detective disappeared.

"How did you know he was there?"

"The cigarette butts we passed outside. Visiting his office I observed, unlike everything else about that slovenly man, he is fussily precise about rolling cigarettes. When I saw that pile of neat little butts under the tree, I concluded we'd been trailed."

Half an hour later, Strad returned. "You still alive?" he called, in jest. Mostly.

"For now," Basil responded.

"When I say 'go,' you two run like the wind!"

The detective threw several objects. Basil heard them land nearby. After a moment's hesitation, the hound trotted in that direction. The detective's "Go!" proved superfluous. Basil and Jane already sprinted toward the fence.

Running, Basil saw Strad had tossed chunks of meat. The hound hesitated, torn between the easy meal beneath it and its escaping quarry. Predatory instinct won as the creature bounded after them, barking hungrily. Extending a beefy hand, the detective helped them over the fence…with only seconds to spare.

"Clever, Strad," Rathbone said, noting the strip of tape across the detective's bruised nose. "My compliments. How did you know it would work?"

"I didn't. I seen it on a cartoon once. So I drove to this 24-hour greasy spoon I know. After a cup of coffee and a piss, I ordered four raw chops."

"Charming. What do I owe you for the meat?"

"Nothing. When you're in jail, I'll bill the Reeves for the expense."

Acknowledging he had nothing on the pair, for now, Strad let them go. Examining Basil's hand, Jane encouraged a hospital visit. Basil didn't want anything that might put his name in the papers or irritate their unknown antagonist. In exchange for acquiescing, Jane insisted on cleaning the wound herself.

At her Orchard Avenue apartment, much closer than Basil's villa, Jane washed the wound thoroughly before dousing it with iodine. As Basil bore the iodine's sting, Jane nodded approvingly. She produced needle and thread. He watched, fascinated, as she stitched him up.

"How did you learn to do that?"

"I volunteered as a nurse during the war."

With the late hour and both of them exhausted, Jane showed Basil the couch.

WEDNESDAY, MAY 1ST

"I'm sorry last night was a bust," Jane said over coffee and a simple breakfast.

"I wouldn't say that," Basil produced what appeared to be a small piece of rock, irregularly shaped on one side but with a distinctive curve on the other.

"What's that?"

"Bitumen. 'Asphalt' to you Americans. I discovered it near the Roadmaster's pedals. Note the curve? That shape comes from clinging to the outsole of a shoe or boot. The driver had stepped in hot asphalt recently. Concrete is used for many things, including city streets. But asphalt is common for highways. And the nearest highway construction is..."

"The Pacific Coast Highway," Jane interjected. "Remember what that reporter said Sherman Laverock did for a living?"

"Road construction, I believe," he replied as she nodded.

It took much of the day to contact Woody Hollings. When they did, the reporter sounded pleased as punch at hearing from Basil again. Even over the phone, the actor could hear the journalist falling over himself.

"What can I do for you?" he finally got around to asking.

"You said Mr. Laverock did road construction," Basil began. "Do you know anything about the company he worked for?"

"Let me check my notes," Hollings' voice trailed off. Minutes later, it reappeared. "Lodak Canyon Asphalt and Road, northwest of the city on the Pacific Coast Highway between Point Dume and Oxnard. Owner's name is John Smalls. I tried calling him for a quote about Laverock. Never heard back."

"And has there been further word on the man's cause of death?"

"I wish someone would tell me. I keep calling the coroner's office. They keep reminding me L.A. isn't the safest place and say they'll get to him when they can. Hell, I wish I'd grabbed one of his chickens. I'd pay someone to take a look at it."

Star-struck, Woody never asked why Basil wanted the information. Basil ended the call before the question occurred to him.

The day was perfect for driving. Northbound along the coastal highway, golden afternoon sun warmed their skin as fresh springtime scents filled the air. The azure blue sky, dusted with white cirrus clouds, matched the crashing surf visible to their left.

On a lonely and mostly unpaved stretch between Point Dume and Point Mugu, they found Lodak Canyon Asphalt & Road. Across the highway was the Lantern Club, an outsized roadhouse whose marquee proclaimed *Dance Dance Dance*.

A chain-link fence surrounded the asphalt operation. Parking, Basil and Jane looked around. Inside, enormous piles of sand, pebbles, and aggregate piled around large open-sided metal sheds, vats of tar, and a fleet of asphalt trucks. Seeing the distinctive vehicles, Basil thought of the "odd looking truck" seen outside Sherman Laverock's shack the night he died.

Basil approached a weary, grime-covered man clocking out for the night. "Excuse me, I'm looking for your employer.

Where might I find him?"

The man, his expression proclaiming Basil to be out of his mind, pointed across the highway. Presumably, the man was drinking at the roadhouse. Basil and Jane pulled the Packard across the highway to the Lantern Club's sprawling parking lot.

With its remote location and considerable size, Basil would have wagered his Packard the Lantern Club's popularity once owed more to serving liquor on the sly than dancing. But the busy parking lot testified that cutting a rug while enjoying a legal drink could still pack the place.

Inside the cavernous, dimly lit venue, he and Jane were overwhelmed by a fifteen-piece band noisily pushing through Louis Prima's "Just a Gigolo," driven by furious brass and drums. The musicians donned black tuxedo jackets with white polka dots. Except the bandleader, who wore white coat and tails with black spots.

In front of the bandstand, the large and rowdy crowd was jitterbugging or, as Jane called it, "swing dancing." Sailors from the naval station. Oxnard townies. Fisherman. Farmhands. Even some savvy couples escaping the big city for an evening of rug-cutting.

On the dancefloor's far side was an ample bar and several dozen tables. While youth and vigor gravitated toward the dancefloor, this area held an uneasy mix of barflies and well-heeled older couples. Cigarette girls, wearing pillbox hats and skimpy red dresses with scandalously short hems, orbited the room and wandered among the tables peddling their wares.

"Ladies and Gentlemen," a ferret-faced emcee took the mic as the polka dotted musicians finished, "Let's make some friendly hand-music for Roy Lott and his Speckled Band." The crowd cheered. "Remember, we've got the big jitterbug contest later. Until then, we'll cool things down." The band slid into Sinatra's "Full Moon and Empty Arms," as the crowd shifted from swing to slow dancing.

Among the crowd, one figure was unignorable. Surveying the club with an aura of ownership, the human fireplug wore a black pinstriped zoot suit and matching broad-brimmed fedora. His melon-shaped head was clean-shaven, save for a tiny, dark mustache. A heavy cane, thick as a sapling, offset his pronounced limp. A war wound, Basil presumed.

Jane's nose crinkled disdainfully.

"Know him?" Basil inquired.

"I think I know his type," Jane said. "Wears the zoot suit to stick it to society and show he's edgy. But woe to anyone actually from Watts or East L.A. who crosses his path."

As if his ears burned, the fireplug rounded to face them. Snapping his fingers, two similarly attired men appeared at his side. As they approached Basil and Jane, the man's cane thumped thunderously on the floor with every step.

"Mr. Basil Rathbone," he roared, winking unpleasantly. "I had a feeling I might see you here."

"You have the advantage of us. For now." Basil replied neutrally.

"I'm Johnny Smalls. This is my place."

So Smalls was not just grabbing a drink. He owned the roadhouse as well as the asphalt operation. "I wanted a word regarding an employee of your paving business, Sherman Laverock."

"Yeah, a shame about Sherm." Smalls shrugged. "Bad things happen sometimes."

"The letters in his name are just coincidence, then?"

Another shrug. "I don't know what you're talking about. But I don't like being accused of things in my joint."

A cocktail waitress brought drinks to Jane and Basil after Smalls gave a nod. "This round's on the house. Enjoy yourself. But don't get out of line. I mean it. I've got eyes on you and my word is law here."

After Smalls and his flunkies strode away cockily, Basil looked at the drinks. "What are the odds of these being safe?"

"Better than doing shots with Socrates. But only just." Jane pushed her glass aside. "So, is Smalls our guy?"

"Does Mr. Smalls strike you as someone who dashes out notes in Greek or invents cyphers?"

"No," she admitted.

"Our mastermind is still out there," and, though Basil

reviled at the notion, he added, "our Moriarty."

"So, is this a dead end?"

"Hardly. I'm certain Smalls is in on it." Seeing Jane's questioning look, he continued, "I could point out the coincidence of someone like Smalls expecting to see someone like me in someplace like this. Instead, I'll give you something more concrete.

"Early in my career I had the fortune to study under the eminent actress Madge Kendal. She drilled into me that hands were a true actor's mark because they are the most difficult body part to control. And she was right. Think back to our overbearing host. Speaking with us, his hands moved uneasily. Like they belonged to another person altogether."

"What's the plan, then?"

"I would love to check out Smalls' office. If we knew where that was."

"We do," Jane smiled coyly.

It was Basil's turn to look perplexed.

"The paving operation didn't have an office. I can't see an office from here and the Lantern Club doesn't have a second story. Ergo, his office must be down those steps behind the dance floor."

Basil eyed the stairwell. "Let's go."

"Don't we need some kind of plan?"

"Keep a low profile. Don't move too fast. Don't move too slow, either. Hope we don't encounter anybody."

"Gee, thanks."

Waiting until Johnny Smalls and his men appeared distracted, they descended the stairs into a lounge crowded with mismatched, threadbare chairs and couches decades out of style. Empty beer bottles covered battered wooden tables. An ancient Victor radio sat silent near the only other exit, a hallway with several doors on each side.

Two doors led to restrooms. Most others to storerooms. One stood vacant. Another, marked with a tarnished brass plate reading "Jerry Bing" contained an elderly man passed out upon an open ledger, snoring loudly. At the hallway's end, a shut door bore a gleaming brass plate proclaiming "John W.

Smalls, Owner."

Kneeling beside the lock, Jane grinned slyly and removed a bobby pin from her hair.

"I don't wish to steal your thunder, but time is of the essence. I doubt an arrogant creature like Johnny Smalls locks his office," Basil said, pushing open the door.

They rummaged quickly through papers, files, and log books. Especially intriguing was a bundle of papers Jane found on the desk: invoices for several weeks of daily trips to the Port of Los Angeles. On each trip, one of Smalls' trucks picked up unspecified cargo from the *Stella Solitaria,* a freighter out of Bari, Italy.

Basil doubted Smalls was brewing up exotic European asphalt. Unloading cargo one truck at a time rather than all at once made sense only to avoid attention. Smuggling, then. But smuggling what?

Concluding their search, Basil slipped the papers into his pocket.

At the top of the stairs, they encountered Smalls and his men waiting for them. Not just two. This time, Basil counted a baker's dozen.

"Well, boys. Our guests don't know manners," Smalls looked at Basil and Jane. "What did I say about not getting out of line?"

Behind them, the jitterbug contest kicked off on the dancefloor. The Speckled Band roared into Louis Jordan's brassy "Choo Choo Ch'Boogie." The sudden crescendo taking them by surprise, several of Smalls' toughs flinched.

Seizing the moment, Basil tossed the papers into the air. He need a distraction more than he needed evidence. With the thugs momentary confused, Basil and Jane rushed past.

"After them!" Smalls bellowed. "Neither of them leaves."

The gang spread out, searching. One man climbed onto a table near the dancefloor. From that vantage, he could spot two people heading toward the exit. And gesture to the others to intercept them.

"Blend in," Jane said, taking Basil by the hand and dancing.

Basil was twice the age of the other rug-cutters. They regarded the "old" man in their midst with youth's inevitable disdain for age. But it worked. The thugs were not seeking dancers. More than one pair of searching eyes passed over them unaware.

Basil had never danced like this. But he had studied dance extensively. The society dancing expected of an English gentlemen, of course, but also numerous period dances for productions from Shakespeare to Selznick. With that broad base, it took little time to master swing's basic moves by observing those around him.

Quickly Basil became…not the best dancer in the room, not by a mile…but better than average. Seeing the oldster knew what it was about, the dancers' attitudes shifted from derision to curiosity. Onlookers swarmed around Basil and Jane. He cringed. Sooner or later that would draw dangerous attention.

And it did. Spotting them, one of Smalls' gangsters shouted the alarm. Mercifully, he remained unheard over the Speckled Band's din.

Throwing a punch, Basil and Jane leaned away from his fist. It sliced through the space between them, connecting with another dancer's face. The pretty young woman's heavy makeup didn't hide her hard expression any more than her blouse concealed that, even after months of peace, she retained her Rosie the Riveter biceps. Turning her steely gaze on the goon, it was even money whether she or her sailor boyfriend would finish him off first.

The resulting spectacle diverted attention from Basil and Jane. They melted into the crowd as the band moved from "Choo Choo Ch'Boogie" to the even more frenetic strains of Benny Goodman's "Sing, Sing, Sing."

Their problem was the man on the table. If they neared the exit, he'd spot them and alert others. Getting rid of him, the others could be sidestepped or dealt with piecemeal. But they couldn't get near the man without giving him time to observe and react.

Or could they?

Moving as close as they dared, Jane and Basil danced, using other dancers as cover, and waited for their moment. They imitated a move other dancers made. As Jane lay on the floor, Basil took Jane tightly by both hands. Spinning her around him, Jane's skirt reduced friction to nearly nothing, Basil kept one eye on their unwelcome watcher.

As "Sing, Sing, Sing" moved towards its climactic syncopated bass drumming and wall of horns conclusion, the band could no longer remain seated. Standing, they blasted their instruments until the building shook with swinging fury.

When the path became clear, Basil loosed Jane toward the watcher. On her skirt, Jane slid across the dancefloor. Twenty feet away. Fifteen feet. So far, luck kept other dancers out of her way. Ten feet. Five feet. As she slid under the table, Jane kicked up ferociously with both legs. The powerful blow sent both table and its occupant flying upward, over, and crashing back to the hard floor. The man wouldn't be alerting anyone tonight.

Basil leapt the overturned table and caught up with Jane as she shook herself off. Taking her by the hand, they rushed through the crowd toward the door. Two men posted at the exit spotted them. Before the toughs could react, Basil punched one in the stomach, doubling him over. Jane shoved the other away. A dancer accidently struck him, knocking the goon deeper into the chaos. Basil and June sprinted out the doors and into the night.

"I think we won the contest," he panted as they ran.

"I'm not going back for my prize."

In the Packard, Basil observed, "It will be very late by the time we return to L.A. Anyway, after all that, I'm too tired to drive."

"Me too. It's okay, my Aunt Winnie lives near here."

Aunt Winnie's Spanish-Colonial style home stood just outside Oxnard's city limits. Peeking into the enormous backyard, a Quonset hut intrigued Basil. And there was the long, narrow line of short-cut grass. Like a landing strip.

Answering her door in a wine-colored nightgown,

Winnifred Adams was tall and slender with her thick silver hair bobbed. She shook Basil's hand with a grip at once elegant and firm. And, if Aunt Winne questioned what her niece was doing so late at night with a man twice Jane's age, she didn't ask. Instead, she invited them into the kitchen and uncorked a bottle of red wine.

Over glasses of wine and games of Rummy, Jane and Basil relaxed as Aunt Winnie entertained. Dawn would bring the penultimate day before their adversary's plot unfolded. Sacrificing sleep to indulge in frivolity was irresponsible. But Basil needed it.

With Jane winning more than her share of hands, Winnie looked at Basil. "She cheats, you know." As Jane protested and Basil laughed politely, their host continued. "I'm serious. She always has. Playing hide-and-go-seek with her older sisters, little Jane would leave the area of play entirely. Those poor girls spent hours hunting her."

Winnie had her own stories. What Basil had taken for a landing strip was exactly that. An aviatrix since adolescence, Winnie married an ace from the Great War. Before Pearl Harbor, he returned overseas with the 1st American Volunteer Group, the celebrated "Flying Tigers," and trained Chinese Air Force pilots.

When war came, Winnie joined the Women's Army Air Corps, piloting newly built aircraft from aviation plants to airbases before transfer overseas. Ostensibly, the WAACs freed male pilots for combat missions. But Basil suspected Winnie wouldn't hesitate to tangle with any Zero or Messerschmitt unlucky to come her way.

"Poor Alfred never came back to me," Winnie added melancholically. "Fever. Not enemy action." Her eyes glanced out the window to the Quonset hut. "After the war, to have something to remember him by, I had his Warhawk shipped here."

Basil recounted stories from the Great War. He told of the night he led his scouts into no-man's-land between the trenches, hid there all day, and infiltrated enemy positions at night. Obtaining invaluable intelligence, they returned to their own lines. They got away with it because the Germans couldn't imagine anybody being so reckless.

Aunt Winnie had been candid regarding her husband's death. Feeling it appropriate to make a similar disclosure, Basil talked frankly about his despondency watching his regiment suffer heavily from German gas attacks late in the war. Giving a happier coda, Basil discussed his active involvement, following the Armistice, with efforts to outlaw such weapons and ensure the destruction of all remaining stocks.

After another cry of "Rummy!" Jane slapped down her cards, announcing "I'm off to sleep." Perhaps it was the wine or his exhausting day. Either way, Basil's decorum slipped, observing Jane's swaying curves as his assistant departed. His musings were interrupted by Aunt Winnie pointedly clearing her throat.

"Mr. Rathbone, there is a reason I did not place you and my niece in adjoining rooms," she proclaimed. "If you want directions to my bedroom…that is another matter entirely."

THURSDAY, MAY 2ND

It was midmorning before they left Aunt Winnie's for the Port of Los Angeles. Basil regretted the relaxation that seemed so essential last night.

Though America had been at peace over half a year, wartime protocols still prevailed at the West Coast's busiest port. Sneaking in proved an impossibility. After many hours, it became clear security did not let just anyone wander around. Not even Basil Rathbone. Spirts dampened, he cursed the port authorities for wasting most of their day as he pointed the Packard toward Bel Air.

Back home, Basil phoned Les Strad. Again, the detective proved a surprisingly useful nuisance. "Strad, what can you tell me about a man named Johnny Smalls."

"I already done you one favor. I ain't a soup kitchen, Rathbone. Why would I do another?"

"You know what they say about 'keep your friends close and your enemies closer'?"

The detective grunted. Presumably an affirmation.

"I thought you'd be thrilled at the chance to keep me close," Basil replied.

"You saying you're my friend…or my enemy?"

"I am afraid you'll have to work that out on your own."

After a pause, "Okay, Rathbone, gimme a couple hours."

The detective called back late in the day, "I found out a little. Nothing you'd call a ringer," he began. "Your guy's a smalltime operator out of Ventura County. A few legit business as covers for smuggling, extortion, loan sharking. Maybe a hit or two. He mostly stays away from the city to avoid trouble with Bugsy Siegel's outfit. But he's been in town recently and, word is, he's making free with his cash all of a sudden." Strad paused. "That help?"

"Nothing revelatory, but it confirms I'm on the right track."

"I'm still watching you, Rathbone."

The trail of clues continued pointing to the *Stella Solitaria*. Sitting in the library, over sandwiches the butler prepared, they schemed how to get into the port. As the phone rang again, Basil presumed Strad had forgotten some tidbit. He looked at Jane, "Get that for me, please."

"Rathbone residence," she spoke into the phone. The color drained from her face. "Yes. Yes, sir."

Basil questioned her with his eyes. Putting one hand over the mouthpiece, she whispered "John Cheever Cowdin."

If Universal's president was calling, it couldn't mean anything good. "What does he want?"

Relaying Basil's question, she then transmitted Cowdin's response. "He says if you're not on set first thing tomorrow morning, you're fired."

So, Roy William Neill had escalated. He couldn't blame the man. But Basil had bigger concerns. Besides, the threat pricked his ego. "Tell Cowdin that if he thinks audiences will accept someone else as Holmes, he's welcome to try."

Repeating Basil's remark, Jane pulled the phone from her ear, eyed it curiously, and hung up.

"What did he say?"

"Two words I'd blanche to use separately. And never imagined putting together."

Basil presumed he'd kept his job. For now.

Relief proved short lived. He heard the front door fly open hard enough to strike the wall with a thud. A crash followed as someone knocked over the entryway table.

"What now?" Basil groaned.

Gilbert Talmadge staggered into the library, the actor's eyes bleary from drink. "You ruined my life, Ratters."

"I'm sorry you think that, Gil. But you should go."

"You ruined my life and I demand satisfaction."

"What are you talking about?"

In answer, Basil's uninvited guest grabbed one of two swords hanging above the Rathbones' mantle. Aside from its fancy gold-plated guard, the blade was utilitarian, its single-edged blade gently curving to a terrible point.

"Gil, you're inebriated. You don't know what you're doing. Put that down, I'll call you a cab."

The sabre slashed through the air. Drunk though Gil might be, nothing lacked from his reflexes or aim. Fortunately, Basil owned good reflexes as well. The blade passed where his face had been instants before. As Gil continued his offensive, Basil reluctantly accepted his rival was in earnest. Snatching the other weapon, he parried Gil's blows with a jewel encrusted longsword, making an occasional counterthrust.

Jane fled the room. "There's another phone in the kitchen," he called after her. His assistant could alert the authorities. Or at least escape the madman.

As the duel progressed, an unfortunate truth revealed itself. Basil's sword was a display piece. Gil wielded the genuine article. That kept Basil on the defensive. Finding his back to the wall, Basil jumped onto the sofa before leaping atop the marble table. Gil slashed at his legs, Basil jumping clear each time. He wondered what Felix Grave, their old fencing instructor at the Salle d'Armes, would say if he saw Basil and Gil now.

With his free hand, Basil pulled paintings from the wall, lobbing them at Gil. Hopefully, the sabre would penetrate a canvas and make the weapon too unwieldly to use. Oh, yes, Basil would get it from Ouida when she got home. If he lived that long.

Jane reappeared, swiftly approaching Gil from behind. Raising her hand, Basil barely had time to note the syringe it held before she jabbed Gil's neck. An instant later, a warm, dreamy expression washed over the actor's face. Basil soon overpowered his practically unconscious opponent.

As they carried Gil to a turquoise divan, Basil quizzed his assistant. "What was that?"

"Sodium Thiopental." Jane replied breathlessly, struggling with the unconscious actor's bulk.

"Where did you get it?"

"Stitching you up after the junkyard, it seemed pretty clear our investigation wouldn't be open-and-shut. The next day, I went to a studio doc for a few things we might need."

Every studio kept a few so-called "studio docs" or "lot docs" on the payroll. Physicians, of a sort, their primary value resided in writing prescriptions for stars' real or imagined medical needs. No questions asked.

Waiting for Gil to come around, Jane inquired about the swords. Basil looked to the now battered ceremonial piece he had used. "George V knighted my friend, Frank Benson, with that. After Sir Frank passed away the sword came into my care. As for the cavalry sabre, improbably, my great-great-uncle took up the cause of the American South during your Civil War. His blade, too, eventually passed into my hands."

Gil stirred. Confused, his attention drifted to the swords on the floor as his eyes filled with tears. "Ratters, I'm sorry, I…"

"It is alright, Gilbert," he replied. "Maybe I'm the one who should apologize. I didn't know you felt so strongly."

"Strongly, yes. But not like that. You don't know how bad things are. Nobody does. I'm nearly destitute. A week ago a man offered me $1,000 to make your life difficult. Ten thousand, should I hurt you badly enough to lay you up for a week. That's why I made that big scene at the studio. It's why I'm here tonight. And I'm the one who told Mina's family you were connected to her death."

Asking about the man, Basil nor Jane were unsurprised when Gil perfectly described Johnny Smalls. From his wallet, Basil laid out ten $20 bills. "Will that get you through for now?" he asked.

Gil nodded, eyes proclaiming gratitude. "Thank you, Ratters." For the first time in years, Gil made the nickname sound affectionate rather than accusatory. "What can I do to make this right?"

"Just one thing. A little thing, but very important," Basil handed Gil the business card Les Strad "gave" him upon their first meeting. "Call this man," he continued, "tell him you're the one who told Mina's family about me and that there's nothing to it. That will give me some breathing room. You do that, and we're square."

As it turned out, they were more than square. The man proved an inspiration. Around midnight, Basil sprung from his bed to the phone. His animated conversation must have woken Jane. Replacing the receiver in its cradle, he found his assistant standing in the living room.

"Who was that?" she asked.

"Seeing Gil reminded me of our early days on the London stage. Jane, nobody gets their part right the first time. Our adversary plays his role masterfully. He's rehearsed somehow. And I had a suspicion regarding when.

"You're probably too young to remember, but from the third until the fourteenth of December, 1926, the mystery writer Agatha Christie vanished. Where she was and what she was doing has never been satisfactory explained. Rather suggestive in light of recent developments, wouldn't you say?"

Jane nodded.

"Fortunately, I have the pleasure of being acquainted with Mrs. Christie," Basil continued. "I called and, under promise of keeping her answers from the general public, she confided to me what transpired during those eleven days. A mysterious man forced Agatha into the shoes of her own creation, Miss Marple, challenging her to thwart his plot to embarrass the monarchy: a complex scheme involving the stolen Condé

Diamond and rigging Nobel Prize selections.

During the adventure, Agatha conversed with her mysterious adversary three times. Twice over the phone and once, at the case's conclusion, in person at the Swan Hotel in Harrogate. Though the man kept his face in shadow during the encounter, she swears that, by his speech, he was Italian, and by his elocution and bearing, unmistakably aristocratic."

Basil kept Agatha's final observation to himself. "The man is clever. A genius, I'd say," the mystery writer offered. "But he has a flaw. He sees the character he wants you to play, not the person you are." Basil had seen that already, with his adversary's presumption Basil needed a translator to read Greek. And he saw how to make that blind spot work against their opponent...

"I'm tired of chasing his clues like rats through a maze," Basil proclaimed to Jane. "We're running out of time. The city is running out of time. With what Agatha gave us, we can go straight for the head."

Seeing Jane's confusion, he continued. "Only a handful of hotels in this city would appeal to the person she describes."

"What if he's rented private lodging? Or staying with friends?"

"Let me tell you another story. At one o'clock on June fourth, 1918, I was in the trenches. Suddenly, I thought of John, my brother, and grief overcame me. I wept openly. Later, I learned John had been killed in action exactly at the instant that fugue came over me.

"That pales compared to incidents I could recount about my mother. Sherlock Holmes may solve mysteries exclusively through deduction. That's what our adversary expects from us. Rathbones do not work that way. I'm certain our man is in a hotel. If I'm wrong, we'll check other options. But we start with hotels."

The list of possible hotels proved lengthy, testimony to the City of Angels' opulence and ostentation. The Ace, Ambassador, Bel-Air, Beverly Hills, Biltmore, Casa del Mar, Figueroa, Garden of Allah, Georgian, Hollywood, Huntington, Normandie, Roosevelt, and Wilshire. Fourteen in all.

"Let's not overthink this," Jane cautioned. "Our man is particular about the rules of the 'game' as he calls it. He does everything for a reason. If you're correct, I suspect there's something about the hotel that will clue us in. A connection to you. A connection to Holmes. Something like that."

They revisited the list. The infamous and improbably named Garden of Allah Hotel in West Hollywood was the first match. In 1936, Rathbone starred in a movie of the same name. Next came Santa Monica's Georgian Hotel. Doyle wrote about a quarter of the Sherlock Holmes stories during George V's reign. While neither Jane nor Basil recalled if ambassadors figured in any Holmes' mysteries, diplomats certainly did. So downtown's Ambassador Hotel went on the list. Finally, as Jane noted, their opponent was Italian and Casa del Mar, another Santa Monica hotel, had been built in an Italianate style.

"Going any further requires waiting for morning," Basil concluded. "I suggest we get what sleep we can."

FRIDAY, MAY 3RD

Basil woke with a sour taste in his mouth. His mind screamed. Today was *the* day. The sun would set at 7:40 PM, he'd been unable to resist checking the almanac. In about 12 hours something terrible would happen. Unless he and Jane stopped it. It terrified him he still didn't know what. Or where.

Basil phoned the four hotels he and Jane listed. Identifying himself honestly, he asked if a friend of his, an eccentric and aristocratic Italian gentleman, stayed at the hotel. Nobody of that description resided at the Garden of Allah. Nor could Italians be found at the Georgian. Yes, the Ambassador Hotel's desk clerk acknowledged, a group of Milanese businessmen stayed there. But the clerk found nothing particularly eccentric or aristocratic about them.

When he inquired at Casa del Mar, however, the manager's voice grew chummily conspiratorial. "Yes, sir, I know the gentleman."

"Wonderful," Basil replied. "I wish to surprise my friend.

Kindly say nothing to him, would you?"

"You're awfully chipper," Jane observed as Basil whistled during the drive to Santa Monica.

"Indeed. If I truly was Holmes, I might say 'the game's afoot.' For the first time since this affair began we are closing in on our man, not just following the trail of breadcrumbs he's left. This feels good. This feels right. I can't help wonder if he and I waged similar contests in previous lives."

"Do you really believe in that?" Jane asked, curious. "Reincarnation, I mean?"

"Of course. What are souls if not old actors eternally treading the boards across one stage after another, embracing one role after another?"

Casa del Mar resembled a Renaissance palace dropped on Santa Monica's beachfront, tall palm trees swaying all around. With its six-story wings and seven-story main section, the luxurious hotel appeared far larger than the 129 rooms it contained.

Doormen opened the heavy glass and copper double doors for them. The mosaic floors, expensive furniture, cream-yellow walls with white trim, and, above all, the sweeping double staircase flanked by enormous twin pillars, gave its interior the feel of a wealthy doge's palace.

As Jane approached the front desk, Basil stayed her with a hand upon the shoulder. "If I inquire after my 'friend' and then don't immediately go to him," he reasoned, "it looks suspicious. I want to reconnoiter first. Splitting up, we can cover twice the ground." Basil looked at his pocket watch. "Meet back here in half an hour."

Leaving Jane to explore the lobby, grounds, first floor, mezzanine, and basement, Basil took the upper floors. To be honest, he expected to find their adversary there and wanted Jane out of harm's way. Leaving behind the fancifully decorated corridors and chambers of Casa del Mar's well-to-do guests, Basil accessed the hotel's other half, the part used by staff. Ascending a utility staircase to the seventh floor suites, he carefully made his way down the hall.

A door opened. One of Johnny Small's men emerged. Spotting Basil and scowling, he went for his gun. With too much distance to close and nowhere to hide, Basil ran. Turning the corner before the man could fire, Basil discovered he'd gone from frying pan to fire. He smacked into two thugs coming the other direction. Struggling to escape, he had a chance until the first man arrived and the trio overpowered him.

"Escorted" into the Presidential Suite, Basil found Johnny Smalls and his henchmen there. But Basil had eyes only for the man in a leather chair, staring out the panoramic window at the beach and ocean beyond. The gentleman wore an elaborately tailored white suit at the height of continental fashion. His snowy hair was shaggy. Moustache long and bushy. One hand bulged with an enormous gold ring set with a ruby and a pearl, both the size of a child's marble.

Basil had encountered him before. In the Universal Studio commissary, over cups of tepid coffee. "I presume you're not really a correspondent for *Motion Picture Magazine*, then? A shame, I thought I gave a good interview."

He stood. "Mr. Rathbone, this is a true honor. I am Giacomo Colleferro, Count di Otranto." With a sweeping, debonair gesture, motioned for Basil to take the seat beside him.

Smalls intercepted Basil. The gangster patted him down and removed the service revolver. Smalls looked at the trio who had seized Basil. "He was alone?" A henchmen nodded. "Then the girl's around here somewhere. Find her."

Stepping away, Smalls allowed Basil to take the seat next to Count Otranto.

"Basil. May I call you Basil? Forgive my little imposture at Universal. A conceit. I wanted to meet you face to face before we began our game. I am impressed. Nobody has ever found me before I wanted to be found. But here you are. You're worthy of Sherlock Holmes himself!"

"So, that's it? I'm Holmes? And you fancy yourself Moriarty?"

"Heavens no," The Count protested. "For all his brilliance,

avarice motivated Moriarty. At the end of the day, no better than a common criminal. I, sir, am an *artiste*.

"From my youngest days, I devoured mysteries. I never identified with the detectives but, rather, with their nemeses. Yes, especially James Moriarty. I wrote my first mystery at ten, continuing throughout my teens. Even I had to acknowledge they were no good. But a man of my resources and vision has the opportunity to concoct great mysteries…in real life. If only he could find sleuths worthy of the effort. Even before coming of age, I poisoned my father's valet. Young and timid, I made it look like an accident. But nobody suspected foul play and that emboldened me. To my regret, Italy has no tradition of great mystery writers. Perhaps, after I am gone, my accomplishments will become public and inspire such a legacy.

"Instead, I started my work in France with Gaston Leroux. Today, people remember him for *Phantom of the Opera*. But he wrote one of the great locked-room mysteries, *The Mystery of the Yellow Room*. So, I created a similar puzzle for him. The poor laborer I hired under pretenses of serving as my accomplice, instead became the mystery. He was discovered shot, stabbed, hanged, and poisoned. The man's faithful hound appeared the only possible suspect. But I forgot Leroux was a journalist as well as a writer. Looking beyond the locked room, he sent me fleeing Paris one step ahead of the gendarmes.

"But I didn't stop. Six months later, I returned to the City of Lights. You've heard of the Mona Lisa's theft? I was baiting Maurice Leblanc. In the end, he proved no Arsène Lupin. I bested another Frenchman, too. Though he had the last laugh. I signed my taunting letters to Marcel Allain as 'Il Fantasma'…the Phantom. Later that year he published his first story about the arch-criminal and antihero, Fantômas. And I learned a lesson about not inserting myself directly into the mysteries I created."

In his seat, Basil shifted. Attempting to appear aloof he was, admittedly, both horrified and fascinated.

"During the Great War, I turned my talents in another

direction," the count continued. "Orchestrating the theft of orders from Austro-Hungarian headquarters, I forestalled a major offensive along the Southern Front. Following the Armistice, I cast my eyes my eyes across the Channel.

"Chesterton? I call him a draw. The plot was humble: the disappearance of subscription money to erect a monument to fallen soldiers in the parish churchyard. Perhaps such iconoclasm marked my own Lost Generation phase. Chesterton pieced my machinations together, but not before I plunged a small Essex village into chaos.

"In the 1920s, came Agatha Christie's turn. As Miss Marple, she bested me. But only just. She never understood how close the monarchy came to falling.

"Afterward, I took time off. My father died and I became Count di Otranto. Don't look at me like that, it was natural causes. Well, that and his fondness for cream sauces and Cuban cigars. All the while, I schemed for my greatest match of all. Against the master. Arthur Conan Doyle. But I waited too long, trusting that such a robust man, and a physician at that, would enjoy a long life. His death, before we could enjoy our grand contest, sent me into deep depression.

"Clearly, it didn't last," Basil observed. No longer feigning indifference, against his better judgement, he had been pulled into the man's tale. More importantly, the longer he could keep Count di Otranto talking, the more likely Jane was to realize something was wrong and get help. "What happened?"

"It was Nero Wolfe who pulled me out, actually. Perhaps I jumped too soon onto Rex Stout. He was far greener than other writers I challenged. But his Wolfe, born in Montenegro and with a shady, mysterious past, called to me. I felt like Stout, by writing a character so like but so unlike myself, was challenging me. Coming to America for the first time, I abducted a controversial socialist writer with whom Stout was acquainted and then framed the writer for embezzling funds from a construction company. Then I dropped clues about the writer's whereabouts to both Stout and the gangsters who used the construction company as a front. Unlike the corpulent and rather agoraphobic Wolfe, Stout had no compunctions about leaving his house, displaying boundless energy chasing down leads. But he was determined to solve every puzzle before drawing a conclusion. Regrettably, for him, the mob reached his friend before Stout could.

"My last opponent, before you, was Erle Stanley Gardner. A charming and fascinating man. At first, however, he hardly seemed a worthy opponent. Trying to clear a poor but well-liked pensioner whom I framed for murder, Gardner's methods relied upon on the same coincidences and personal glad-handing as his Perry Mason. By the time it came to trial, I believed every advantage was mine. But Gardner insisted upon representing the pensioner. And, like Mason, once in the courtroom, Gardner was the devil himself. He knew every technique, trick, and obscure precedent. Only my cocktail of bribes and blackmail kept the state's attorneys committed to prosecuting the case. In the end, Gardner's creative lawyering and the defendant's age kept the pensioner out of California's new gas chamber. But he received a considerable prison sentence. So I consider that a hard earned victory. Perhaps the one I am proudest of. So far.

"My years back in Italy during the next war were difficult for me. Lifting valuables from under *Il Duce's* massive nose and looting museums using the American invasion as misdirection barely felt worth leaving bed for. But it gave me time to think; if I couldn't match wits with Doyle, I would seek out his protégé.

"And that was me?" Basil asked. The count had revealed himself as an amoral fiend. But Basil could not doubt that the man was also an artist. Not just an artist, but a master of his craft. "Everyone else you've challenged has been a writer, someone who creates mysteries. Why the sudden switch to someone who merely acts them out?"

"A very perceptive question. And you are right, at first I thought that protégé was John Dickson Carr. No living writer is so directly indebted to Doyle's style. Plus, Carr is a great scholar of the man. He's writing the definitive biography of Doyle, you know. But, late in the war, I attended a screening of *Sherlock Holmes Faces Death,* shown using a smuggled print. So perfectly did you bring Holmes to life as I had always pictured him that I instantly understood you, not Carr, represented Doyle's true heir. I began preparations for our little competition. A competition in which I now proclaim myself 'winner.' Despite your cleverness in finding me, you carelessly got caught."

Indignantly, Basil stood. He should have paid less attention to Count Otranto and more to Johnny Smalls. Dimly aware of Smalls' cane smacking the back of his skull, Basil's world darkened.

He had the sensation of riding in a car, finally opening his eyes as a quartet of sweaty thugs manhandled him into the Lantern Club. Hazily, he noted the marquee proclaiming *Cheryl & The Cowboys*. Apparently, the swing band had been jettisoned for a country act. Basil lapsed back into unconsciousness.

Coming to again, his cheek registered sharp pain. Johnny Smalls loomed over him in the club's vacant cellar room.

"Just checking you were still alive," Smalls mocked, backlit faintly by a single high window.

"The Count wouldn't like it if you died. See, he wants you to see him win. He's got a personal touch like that."

"Yes, a real prince," Basil spat. Struggling, he discovered he'd been tied securely to his less than comfortable chair.

"You should be grateful," Smalls retorted. "Unlike a lotta folks, you'll still be alive when the sun comes up tomorrow."

Straightening his fedora, the gangster prepared to leave. Basil became serious. "Johnny, what's going to happen tonight? There's 'bad' and then there's 'evil.' It's not too late to help me stop this."

"I'd love to stay and chat," Smalls grinned, "but I gotta go help the Count with some things. After tonight, I'll be a very rich man." Smalls backhanded Basil once more before departing, leaving one of his goons behind to watch the battered actor.

The following hours gave Basil time to work things out. Italy had been with the Allies during the Great War. With his personal interest in the matter, having seen his men suffer horribly from the weapons, Basil knew that after the war Germany's remaining chlorine gas had been shipped to an Italian chemical company for destruction. A scandal erupted when some of that gas "disappeared." The company had been owned by an Italian count. Basil didn't specifically remember it being Count di Otronto. He didn't need to. Everything else fit.

Gas perfectly explained Sherman Laverock's strange death. And his chickens'. Yes, there would have been telltale signs. Ones, fortunately, America's policemen and physicians never needed to learn. Otranto, a born mastermind, had arranged for the gas to go missing, knowing he'd one day find a use for it. The *Stella Solitaria* sailed the chemicals from Italy to California and Johnny Smalls' waiting trucks. Basil expected the well-sealed asphalt trucks could be modified to handle deadlier cargo.

Putting the pieces together, he shivered. Thousands would die in a major gas attack. Actually, it would be lucky if *only* thousands perished. Compared with contemplating the city's fate, he welcomed sinking back into unconsciousness.

Basil woke again. The sunlight through the tiny window had waned. Smalls' goon leaned against the open doorframe, brandishing his pistol with machismo. Still groggy, Basil noted someone approaching the henchman. A cigarette girl. Lit cigarette in one hand, she carried her trade's ubiquitous tray full of tobacco products, matches, and anything else a smoker could want.

"What are you looking at?" the gunman challenged her. "This ain't no free show."

"I'm sorry," she stammered. "It's my first day."

That melted the goon a bit. "Okay, dollface, walk down the hallway. Find Mr. Bing. Give him your cut and you're good to go."

Thanking him, she exhaled a cloud of gray-white smoke directly into his face. Basil took satisfaction at the guard's coughing fit. But he had not expected the girl to crush out her cigarette on the goon's hand. Hissing in pain, he dropped the gun. Before he could react, she slammed one heel onto the henchman's foot. Raising the injured foot instinctively, he balanced precariously upon one leg. Grasping her tray with both hands, she brought it crashing upward into his face. The thug lay, unmoving, on the ground.

The cigarette girl rushed to Basil, loosening his bonds. Disoriented, he required a moment to recognize Jane's face. "Wherever did you get that outfit?"

Jane turned cagey. "Let's just say he isn't the only person I've knocked unconscious today."

Before leaving, Jane scooped up the pistol and handed it to Basil. Creeping down the hallway and up the stairs, Jane explained what happened after they separated at Casa del Mar.

"When you didn't show up after thirty minutes, I went looking for you. Smalls' men found me and locked me in the boiler room. I banged on the door for hours. Bruised up my hands good. I got so exhausted that I fell asleep. But I woke with my head screwed on tighter. Instead of banging on the door, I banged on the steam pipes. That got two custodians down there in fifteen minutes or so. The Lantern Club was the obvious place for them to stash you. So I jumped in the Packard and sped here."

Patrons packed the club, awaiting the country band. Fortunately, aside from the man unconscious below, Smalls seemed to have taken his hired muscle with him. Rushing to the Packard, Basil reprised what happened to him at Casa del Mar.

Sliding into Basil's motorcar, Jane prodded, "Where to? We can't have much time."

Basil shared something else he'd worked out. With chlorine gas's high specific gravity, to have the effect he wanted, Otranto needed to release the gas from an elevated point. True, Mount Lukens was the city's highest point. Other viable options existed, too. But all were too prosaic. For the Count, panache and the grand gesture meant everything. In his heart, Basil knew the adventure would end almost where it began: Mount Lee and the HOLLYWOODLAND sign.

"Let's get moving!" Jane exhorted.

Checking his pocket watch, Basil's heart sank, 6:45. Dusk fell in less than an hour. It was about 60 miles from the Lantern Club to the HOLLYWOODLAND sign. "That's two hours," he announced. "Even driving to beat the devil himself, it's an hour and a quarter. We're too late."

"Not if we fly..."

They stood in Aunt Winnie's foyer at 7:00, pouring out their tale and pleading their urgent need to get to the city. Listening, hands on hips the entire time, Winnifred Adams accepted their story.

"We don't have time to spare, follow me. There used to be an aerodrome a mile or so northeast of the sign," she continued, leading them across the well-manicured lawn to the Quonset hut hanger. "It closed before the war, but the runway still exists. We can land there."

Inside the hanger, the aviatrix prepared her machine. The Warhawk was not as elegant or artful as the fighters America produced later in the war; a reliable workhorse not a dexterous thoroughbred. With its stubby fuselage, the straight-winged, single-engine craft resembled a giant olive-drab thumb. Only the shark-mouth and predatory eyes painted on the fuselage behind the propeller lent the machine character.

Struck by inspiration, Basil dashed back to the house. Grabbing Winnie's phone, he made a call. "Strad, you want to catch Mina's killer? Meet us outside the Hollywoodland sign in one hour. And bring every heater you've got."

Basil returned to the hanger as Jane asked her aunt "How long will flying there take?"

"The two-seat trainers aren't as fast as regular Warhawks," she replied distractedly while prepping the aircraft. "The manual says she'll do 275. These days, I wouldn't push her much beyond 200."

Basil did quick math. "That's about 20 minutes."

"Eighteen to be precise," Aunt Winnie corrected.

"Then jogging a mile to the Hollywoodland sign, that's ten or 15 minutes," Jane calculated. "About 30 or 35 minutes total. Giving, at most, ten minutes to stop Otranto and save

L.A."

That wasn't good. But it was the only option on offer.

Preflight preparation completed, Aunt Winnie stepped behind a canvas screen. She reappeared a minute later, changed into her blue WAAC flight suit accented with leather pilot's jacket, goggled helmet, and a set of custom leather boots that had never been part of regulation anything.

"It's time for this bird to fly."

Sliding glass panels allowed entrance and exit to long glass canopy covering the trainer's two cockpits. Before climbing into her cockpit, Winnie guided Basil into the student's seat, strapped him in, and sat Jane on his lap. Not safe, but neither was stopping a criminal mastermind from unleashing chlorine gas.

Taking to the sky just after 7:10 P.M., Winnie pushed the Warhawk as hard as she dared. In the time they'd been airborne, shadows had lengthened. The increasingly soft, golden light of late afternoon bathed cityscape and hills alike. Except for the Santa Monica Mountains' stony tendrils, the web of streets and buildings stretched as far as they could see. Through the cockpit window, one summit grew ever larger.

Overhearing Winnie muttering about "damnable headwinds," Basil cringed. That, combined with hiking from aerodrome, left him skeptical about their timetable. He fought the urge to look at his pocket watch.

Either they would make it. Or they wouldn't.

In the gathering dusk, the HOLLYWOODLAND sign's letters cast legible shadows just south of the summit. Long rows of modified asphalt trucks lined the summit itself, ready to disgorge gruesome death onto the city below. A few cars scatted around a lone construction trailer. Enviously, Basil eyed a plum-colored Isotta-Fraschini Type 8. Though unfamiliar to most, the name of Italy's Isotta-Fraschini joined Rolls-Royce and a handful of others in embodying the pinnacle of automotive excellence. A vehicle fit for a count.

The old aerodrome's runway remained visible amidst the expanding Rodger Young housing development. In unison, the trio sighed. The distance look longer than the 'mile or so'

Winnie recalled. Worse, rugged terrain separated the landing strip from Mount Lee. It seemed impossible they'd be in time to stop Otranto.

"Is it over?" Jane wondered aloud. "Is Otranto really going to win and gas L.A.?"

"Never give up," Winnie replied, circling the Warhawk back toward Mount Lee. "The summit looks flat, wouldn't you say?"

Basil and Jane exchanged looks. Still, from hundreds of feet above, the summit, long east to west and narrow north to south, did appear fairly level. "How much room does the Warhawk need to land, Mrs. Adams?"

"A single-seater could do it in 800 feet. The trainer needs about a thousand."

"And how long is the summit?" Jane asked nervously.

"About a thousand feet...give or take."

Touching down, Mount Lee's top proved neither so level nor free from debris at it appeared from the air. No matter how hard Winnie fought the stick, her Warhawk drifted farther left. And nearer the sharp drop-off to the summit's south.

"We're not going to make it!" the aviatrix yelled. "Bail out!"

Observing how Winnie slid open her canopy window, Basil did likewise. "As you hit the ground, roll," he shouted in Jane's ear while helping her onto the wing. Then came his turn. It had been a decade since Sir Guy of Gisbourne leapt from a galloping horse to avoid death at the hand of Robin Hood and his Merry Men. True, Basil was older now, but this was basically the same thing, right? He dove from the Warhawk, tucking into a roll before landing.

As he stopped just feet from the summit's lip, Basil watched the Warhawk tip over the edge and roll down the steep slope, bouncing over rocks and plowing through brush, toward the HOLLYWOODLAND sign. The plane's wing clipped the bottoms of the sign's final "D" and the "N." Like breaking waves, the wounded letters toppled slowly forward and smashed apart on the rocks below them. Impact with the

"D" and "N" turned the Warhawk directly into the "A," obliterating both plane and letter as a column of golden fire and black smoke erupted into the sky. The explosion's force blasted the adjacent "L" onto its back.

For the moment, city promoters would have to be content with a sign proclaiming HOLLYWOOD.

In *Robin Hood*, not only had Basil been ten years younger, but he landed on springy turf. Not hard-packed earth and stone. He would feel this tomorrow. If he survived to see it. Just now Basil felt too terrified to care, he had looked at his pocket watch…7:39 P.M.

Blood marked Jane's shins. Either a bruise or some dirt graced her left cheek. Aunt Winnie hadn't faired so well. Laying prone, she moaned and clutched at a leg bent unnaturally. In the trenches, Basil had witnessed enough terrible things to recognize a broken leg.

Standing amidst the trucks, Count Otranto and Smalls' gasmasked goons had been stunned into inaction by their opponents' dramatic entrance. Recovering from his shock, the Count raised his mask, screaming "Get them! Get them you fools!"

Wielding an assortment of pistols, knifes, chains, and other weapons, even a baseball bat, the henchmen advanced toward Basil, Jane, and the wounded Winnifred. Tiny clouds of dust and the sound of ricocheting bullets kicking up around their feet brought them to a halt.

"You mugs get those ham hocks up where I can see 'em!" From the summit's western side, Les Strad advanced holding an army surplus carbine. Reluctantly, the thugs complied. "Okay, Rathbone," Strad hollered, "it's your show."

Using the distraction of Strad's arrival, Otranto bolted between two trucks. As the detective prepared to fire at him, Jane and Basil cried "No!" in unison; fearful what errant bullets might do to a truck full of chlorine gas. While Strad kept his carbine trained on Johnny Smalls' men, Basil and Jane pursued Otranto as the mastermind took refuge inside the construction trailer.

Advancing on the structure, Basil turned to Jane. "No. This

time you're staying behind."

"Remember what I said about you dying ending my career?"

"Have you considered that *you* dying would end your career just as effectively?"

Gazing groundward, Jane said nothing.

"Look after Aunt Winnie," Basil advised. "Otherwise, cut off Otranto if he tries to escape."

The trailer was dark inside but his ears detected shuffling sounds to his right.

Lashing out, he connected.

By sound of gasping and someone falling to the floor, he'd struck the henchmen's solar plexus.

"Really, Otranto? I expected better."

Lights flicked on. The Count sat behind a desk at the trailer's end. Johnnie Smalls lurked in front of him. Straightening his zoot suit, Smalls raised the ironwood cane and stalked toward Basil.

"I'll crush your skull," he breathed.

A powerful swing, barely ducked by Basil, left a metal filing cabinet with a dent bigger than a man's head.

Basil cursed. At close range, he couldn't lower his defenses long enough to draw the pistol. Instead, he had to continuously dodge and weave, landing the occasional punch but, mostly, just staying out of Smalls' way as he destroyed the trailer. As Basil debated whether to wait for the crook to tire himself or attempt to grab his cane away, a third option presented itself.

Another wild swing punctured the trailer's thin metal sides. Smalls struggled to free his weapon, now half inside and half out, giving Basil time to produce the gun and pistol-whip his opponent. A solid crack to the temple left Smalls unconscious and possibly concussed. Or worse. Rathbone was not in the mood to be concerned.

Otranto flew through the trailer's rear door. Giving chase, the setting sun blinded Basil briefly. A moment later, he spotted the count climbing into the Isotta-Fraschini's rear while yelling and gesticulating at his driver.

Basil caught up, slipping into the luxury vehicle from the other side. One hand on the door handle. The other gripped the pistol now pointed at Otranto.

"Do something!" the Count pleaded with his driver.

The figure in the chauffer's cap turned around.

"Today's not your day, Otranto," Jane said, smug.

"You've beaten me, Basil," Otranto admitted. "Decisively. For these few days...I believe you've truly been Sherlock Holmes. After I confess our story to the authorities, the whole world will marvel."

Basil shook his head. "I didn't best you by being Sherlock Holmes. I bested you by being Basil Rathbone. And if you had listened to the interview I gave you with the same zeal you read Doyle's mysteries, you would know that, before Holmes, I specialized in roles villainous and vengeful." Pulling the trigger, his bullet struck the Count between the eyes, exiting the back of his head.

fNDAY, MAY 10

Today would be the final day of shooting on *Dressed to Kill*. Basil still looked forward to moving on to new roles, but now with a touch of regret at leaving behind a character he had come to respect strongly. Having patched things up with Roy William Neill and John Cheever Cowdin, he'd even pulled strings to get Gilbert Talmadge a small speaking part in the upcoming Universal thriller, *Temptation*. It wasn't much, but it was a start.

In his dressing room, Basil read a letter from Winnifred Adams. Off her feet for a couple weeks, she was expected to recover fully. Though saddened by the Warhawk's loss, she wrote excitedly about buying a new Aeronca Chief.

Setting down her letter, he picked up the *Times*. Wishing to avoid publicity, Basil, Jane, and Aunt Winnie gave Les Strad full credit for foiling the gas plot. Their presence on Mount Lee, and the unfortunate fate of four-thirteenths of the HOLLYWOODLAND sign, had been portrayed as an unlikely but unrelated accident. Strad could be seen on every front page, while the city had feted him with a tickertape parade. For his part, the outpouring of gratitude so moved the detective that he changed his shirt.

Already frustrated with the cost of maintaining and illuminating the landmark, both the city and the sign's owner refused to replace to the destroyed letters. Visitors and new arrivals would henceforth be welcomed to HOLLYWOOD.

As Jane entered, Basil smiled, tossed the paper aside, and took out his pocket watch. "You're early. Or is there something scheduled that I've forgotten?"

"Actually, I'm here to give notice."

"I hope I haven't displeased you," Basil offered, taken aback. "Or that our recent adventures traumatized you."

"Actually, the opposite," Jane looked disdainfully at her clipboard. "It showed me what I'm good at. And it's not this Hollywood crap. I've been accepted into medical school, starting this Fall."

"Congratulations," Basil glanced at the healing scar where Jane had sutured the dog bite. "I can testify you'll make a fine physician." He paused a moment. "In many ways, Ouida and I are giving our notice, too. Los Angeles is a little too exciting for us. While I will continue working in pictures, we're selling the Bel Air home and moving back to New York. But, I will write you, Jane Westin."

"Actually, I'm changing my name back."

"You real name isn't Jane?"

"My first name is real. But father's studio friends thought 'Westin' sounded better than our actual family name, 'Watson.'"

"Really?" Basil guffawed as she nodded. "And you're giving up on screenwriting completely?"

"Oh, I don't know," Jane winked, "I might have one good story in me."

NICE WORK IF YOU CAN GET IT

Nicole Petit & James Bojaciuk

One night, after a hearty meal at Barney's, the boys took us back to their apartment. Everything appeared very romantic, as the lights were turned down low and soft music played in the background. Before Lucy and I knew what had happened, we were danced into the kitchen to wash a week's worth of dirty dishes. So much for romance; maid duty was uppermost in their minds.

~Ginger Rogers, *Ginger: My Story*

The ideal date: candles, slow music, his arm soft around her back and leading her into the sway.

Ginger's date: elbow deep in caked-on dishwater. She scrubbed rough, sliding the suds away.

Lucy huffed. "Ginger, next time I sign up as maid, I'll go to the Waldorf. They pay."

Ginger pulled a dish out, and she flicked it. Suds landed all over Lucy's face.

"They pay for dinner."

"They *paid* for dinner. *Once.*" Lucy pointed at Ginger's open mouth. "Don't deny it."

"No. They haven't."

Two steps away, just outside the kitchen and into the hall, Jimmy was perched by the door. "Shhhhhh," he hissed. "Rebellion is in the air. How much do we have in our socks?"

"Four-eighty, if you didn't steal some for lunch."

Jimmy nodded sharply, barely out of sight. "Four-fifty now. Grab it. If we want to keep our dishwashers, we're going to have to treat them."

Hank screwed his face up. "We'll take them to Joe's. Four hot dogs, three cents apiece…"

Jimmy peeked into the kitchen to find Ginger and Lucy

splashing suds at each other.

"No, no. All of it. We let things deteriorate. We have to take them *out*."

"We can't—"

SMASH—SMASH—SMASH

Plates clattered everywhere.

Hank grimaced. "I'll get the money."

Hank and Jimmy pulled open the Arabian doors (they were neither Turkish nor Ottoman nor Syrian, but had emerged from fairyland unscathed; they were not Arabic, not quite, but refuges from Arabian Nights). The Ambassador passed away into its stodgy halls and the four emerged into a harem. A slim Persian carpet escorted them down rows upon rows of tables; a tent was above them, briefly, and then the fairy-lights of false stars.

"The Cocoanut Grove, m'ladies." Hank smiled like a man duty bound to enjoy his new bankruptcy.

A man in a plain-cut Tuxedo glared.

"There's old Fritz." Jimmy raised his hand. "Table for four!"

The glare descended into a scowl.

"Will you be dining?"

"We will take it under advisement." Hank waved the air.

The scowl became an expression so hateful no man had named it, but Jack Warner had probably copyrighted it. "Right this way."

Fritz led them on gossamer strings to a far-off, badly cornered table. "Your table, sirs, madams." His grin, Ginger was sure, was also copyright Jack Warner.

When Fritz left, Hank didn't waste any time. He leaned forward with his most charming Hollywood smile. "Lucy, can I just say you're looking stunning tonight?"

Lucy didn't hear Hank's schmoozing, she was staring at something past his shoulder. To be more specific, staring at someone. "That's Roth."

"Roth who?" Ginger asked.

"Roth, Big Shot Director Roth, Mr. 'No First Name' Roth.

That's *who*." She gestured to a table meant for patrons who could afford to pay. Down near where the carpet gave way to a glossed-up dancefloor. Ginger gave him a glance. Fat. Middle-aged. Uproariously pink. Fingers curling around his drink in a death grip. Typical Hollywood.

"Talk around town is he's starting on an epic filmed right under the Sphinx's nose. If we make baldy giggle, tickets to Egypt are as good as ours. And no, he hasn't cast leads yet. He's 'looking for the right legs," she glanced at Ginger, "the 'right laughs'," and she pointed at Jimmy, "and the 'right beauty.'" She pointed to herself. "I'm sure he's looking for the right whatever the hell it is you do, Hank."

Hank made a face somewhere between a smile and a scowl. "Well, *thank you*, Miss Ball for that *kind* assessment of my talents. I'm sure with your charm you'll be able to sweep Mr. Roth right off his feet. Why don't you just go right up there and introduce yourself to him?"

"I'll go and do just that." She rose, her tone saying *I'd stick my tongue out at you, but I'm the picture of refinement and grace.*

Jimmy grabbed her right arm, Ginger grabbed her left, and both pulled her back down into her seat.

"Strategy," Ginger whispered.

Lucy brushed them away, yawned with a pantomime that vaudeville would have found broad, and strode off after Roth. As she went she patted herself down, straightened her dress from "refugee from the costume department" to "second-stringer, background division," and arranged her hair up and out (but nowhere near up and out enough to invite comparisons to the Bride of Frankenstein). She tap-tap-tapped out across the room, threading the edge of the ballroom without so much as the first syllable of a "How do y'do" to the people she bumped and rocked. With every tap her face grew a little bit sweeter, and her smile a touch more genuine. By the time she was near his table, underneath a metal palm tree, she looked like money. Not a million, not by any means. But decidedly more than a buck-fifty.

"Mr. Roth—"

"No." He didn't so much as look her way.

"But—"

"No." He stirred his drink.

"Mr.—"

"No." He touched the edge of his fork, never looking up. "Do you have any idea how long it takes for the entrées to arrive?"

She tried to punch him.

She really did.

But between the wind-up and the blow, something snagged. She tried again, then again.

"This is the hell I'm good at," Hank whispered. He gripped her arm tighter and hauled her back, far back, very far back. When she was seated again, storming profanity, Hank held her there by the shoulders.

Ginger patted her knee. "Like I said, sugar, strategy."

A man in full white-tie affair took careful steps toward Roth's table. He was young, with close cropped brown hair and wide doe eyes. The Mickey Rooney type, exuding youthful charm that every studio loved to milk dry. Lucy watched him with a predatory glare. From that day on, Jimmy insisted she growled. More sensible accounts only include the way her lips parted and her fangs inched past her lips. "If he gets that—"

But he didn't.

Roth shoved his hand up. The apathy he had shown to Lucy evaporated in favor of exhaustion. The lithe man pulled a book from his breast pocket, turned it to a fresh page, and presented it to Roth.

"Autographer, see." Jimmy held Lucy's hand down on the table. "No-one to steal your part."

Roth grabbed the book. He rifled through it, then tossed it down. Roth grabbed up a glass of water, waiting on the table for the drunk or the destitute, and poured it out over the booklet. His jowls shook with the wild turns of his head, then he returned to the slow, steady stir of his drink.

The lithe man walked away.

Lucy grinned, then chortled, then laughed.

Now the music boomed.

Now the back-up dancers sashayed out along the stage.

Although the visitors to his table didn't grab Roth's attention, a little strawberry blonde that took the stage kept him riveted. Peaches Latorre, the talent for the night. Freckles weren't in vogue, but no man, especially not Roth, seemed to fault her for it. Their gaze was directed elsewhere.

Hips swung drunk under the gale of horns; she swished, the cadence of her femininity catching up the audience, and she faced the rising bass. She raised her arm and breathed, a nymph splashing out from water. She peeked across her shoulder and winked out at the audience. "So kiss me and say you understand."

Roth missed no move, wide-eyed, tracking the sway of her well-built buttresses. He didn't even move his eyes when he drank.

"Typical. Goes for the dark meat." Lucy huffed.

Drums pat-pat-pattered up into a gale.

Lucy clamped her palms up over her ears. "Oh, what a headache."

Horns died down, swings slurred into a whisper; through this, Peaches stepped from the pedestal and slid down the stairs. Dressed in red and sequins shifting over ample curves, she slid across the dance floor with more sways than a cobra. Men sucked in breaths with soft hisses as she passed. They were looking too low to notice the sly smile on her painted lips.

If Roth's eyes were only for her architecture, she only had an eye for business.

Peaches stopped by his side and slid her arm around his neck in the way of a lounge singer, with an ease that only comes with practice and an eagerness that only comes with a desire for tips. She slid down into the chair beside him—very near beside him, and leaned across the back of the seat.

"Need to hear a secret, sugah?" The Georgia drawl was thick, saccharine.

Lucy pantomimed a gag, then gripped Jimmy's arm, "Time for you to leave." She walked quickly, now, dragging him toward the back of the club.

"Now just a minute—"

"Time to leave. You don't even have the money to buy me a drink. So maybe, just maybe, you *should get a job*. Don't get back until you *have one*."

"Ah, but, ah, Lucy—"

"A job. Maybe as a *waiter*."

He stopped incredibly still. "Now—now—wait just a minute. We spend all night trying to get his attention, and now I have to get a job as a waiter? I—I—I won't do it, no sir."

Lucy pinched the bridge of her nose. "No."

"Yes, darn right, 'no.'"

"*No*, you're only going to work for one night, then straight back to acting with you. Step outside, through the back door, then show up for work. Put your jacket on a 'in' peg, take a white jacket off the 'out' peg, pick up a tray of drinks, then come back in and schmooze. Give Roth a drink, give the hussy a drink, impress them with your range. We aren't getting close without you. Now go. Out. Out. Out."

She propelled him toward the door.

"Out," she finished. "I mean it."

And out he went. The alleyway was your typical Los Angeles alleyway, with all the perks you could ever wish: a cat, growling low from behind a garbage can; a stench that refused to be waved away; a broken-brick walk that tripped over itself, falling down cracks. He trailed the walkway, then arrived at the other, *smaller* backdoor. He rapped on it.

It swung open on agonized hinges. A man peeked out. He was a cook, certainly.

"Do you think I can just go and open the door every time some moron wants in?"

Jimmy opened his mouth.

"No. Don't answer that. What is it?"

"I-I-I'm here for work."

"Fancy dress for a workin' stiff. Get in, get in."

Jimmy stepped in. The kitchen was a cramped affair: sixteen stations (oven, fryer, stove) shoved into a foot and a half wide work-area. A go-fer held a central position in the room, handing out ingredients as needed. The generous could call it "art deco," but all that really meant in this case was that if something could be constructed by steel, it was. If it made clean-up easier, the owners could afford to be stylish.

"Go on." The cook shooed him out toward the service hall.

The hallway was no less spacious: as he walked, the metal gave way to an unadorned hint of the outer decor. The wallpaper picked up its rich, Arabian hints and, as he neared the end of the hall, the flagstaff floor gave way to lotus carpet.

A young brunette with her hair tied back in a ponytail, slumped over on her elbow and bored the way only a young woman could be, stared at him from behind her counter.

"New guy? Jacket."

"Yes, um, yes." He tumbled his buttons apart, shook his shoulders, and slid the jacket down. He put it on the counter.

"Don't dress up so much. Nobody's impressed." She snapped her bubblegum. Picking up his jacket, she took advantage of her rotating chair and kicked herself off into a whirl. In the midst of her spin she picked up a white jacket and swiveled around back facing him.

"No stains. *Ever*. Report over there."

Jimmy supposed she waved him over to the left, but it was hard to tell. It may have been a sneeze.

"Do you suppose he got lost?" Ginger sipped her drink.

"With that head on his shoulders," Lucy paused, "I suppose he got Shanghaied. He's halfway to China."

Jimmy found himself fighting for his life. They had given him a tray, very well, he could handle a tray. Then they had placed two glasses of champagne on his tray. Very well, he could handle that, two cups are nicely balanced and don't fight back.

Then they had placed two more, and he shivered.

Then they had placed two more, and he shook.

Then they had placed two more, and he quaked.

Then with a grin even Jack Warner would've found too reminiscent of Satan, they give him a final glass. It tottered in his hand like W.C. Fields. As he brought up his other hand to support the tray, he was met with a glare from the service chief.

"One hand, sir, one hand!"

"Yes, and I suppose I have to walk straight too!"

The service chief smiled divinely. "Of course!"

It's just walking, just one foot in front of the other.

So he took a step.

And another.

And another, and another, and another, and another. The resultant motion was nothing at all that could be likened to *just one foot in front of the other*, instead it was a wild fairy reel that left the right foot sticking out left, the left foot sticking out right, side steps, panicked balances, all the more panicked counter-balances, and in desperate straits, a spin.

The service chief leaned into the kitchen. "Mark, make a note to order more champagne glasses."

Roth was pink. The light didn't help, certainly, yellow and thick light that hung like candle wisps. But what sealed the deal was Peaches. She said something, while smiling in Jimmy's general direction, and Roth laughed himself into a breathless squeal that dyed him pork-rind pink.

Jimmy slowed.

Far across the room, Lucy hit Ginger and Hank on the arms. "There's our boy!"

He put one foot out, gingerly as Cinderella stepping into her slipper, then followed with the tiniest step in the world. His confidence exploded, so he put his foot down and took the next step—

—But his toes got caught on the carpet and he stumbled once, twice, thrice, adrenaline and panic the only things that kept the tray upright, sloshing but never spilling.

He stopped still, breath ragged, composing himself. Scattered applause broke out across nearby tables. The applause died down and died out until Peaches was the last person clapping. Slow, deliberate claps, covering her giggles.

"Nice effort, honey. One day, if you work really hard, you

might even be able to carry *hors d'oeuvres.*"

He smiled, he nodded, then he took a careful step up to their table. "Complimentary, uh, champagne, for sir and madam." He eyed the nearest glass stem and calculated his grip with the suave grace of an ungreased Ford production line. He settled this one in front of Roth, smiled ever so slightly too wide, and repeated the process for Peaches. She couldn't stop laughing. Good Lord, this was the best response his acting had ever had. She buried her hands in her face and she shivered with laughter.

"I, uh, my friend, see—" Jimmy ventured.

"No."

"But, uh, now see—"

"Your friend is not the type. Too pale. Too blonde. Now if she had been a redhead, like Peaches here, she'd've been perfect." He waved Jimmy off. "No to you too. No-one would ever believe you're Egyptian. Or Roman. Or Hebrew. Or— what are they—Philistine. You're too American. No." His waves became frantic. "Simply wrong."

"I—"

"No."

Now it happened. He took one step—just one fateful step—and once again his foot caught in the thread of the carpet. He left foot came slamming down, but it was too late. He tumbled, the glasses tumbled, the champagne tumbled all into a sopping wet pile. He rolled off the tray. Well, glory be, nothing was broken (glass or bone). The gentle drum of dancer's feet approached.

"Mr. Roth, I'd really like to discuss what happened between us because you know—" The autograph hound brought such a gale of words that Jimmy tuned them out, simple as switching away from the radio ventriloquist. He hauled himself up to his waist, sitting upright, staring up from below.

The autograph hound leaned down over the table. He passed over the menus and over the drinks to get right near Roth's face. "Mr. Roth, please, think of my friends who—"

The tray, though soaked and mildly bent, would still serve.

He took it up, settled it comfortably in his lap, and set to scooping up the glasses. When he glanced up again at Roth and Peaches, he found they were still weathering his hot air fairly well. Nothing too unusual, just another touchy fan. The autograph hound seemed ready to remonstrate. He seemed almost ready to slap Roth, the way he moved his arms. Then he turned.

"I'll leave you to your evening."

The hound threaded between the oncoming storm: Jimmy's friends.

"Did you get us the parts, Jimmy?" Ginger asked, oh so sweet.

"N-no."

"Told you he wouldn't." Lucy stuck her tongue out at Roth. "Strategy is for dopes."

Hank extended his arm, grasped hands with Jimmy, and pulled him up.

Back on the table: Peaches reached over to Roth's glass, swirling it listlessly as she thought. She sprinkled her fingers over the table, busting herself awake. "This is boring. Wanna dance?"

Peaches tucked her hand in his and waltzed him out to the dance floor—up the stairs, across the carpet, and into the dance. They slid across the floor and nearly out of sight.

Ginger grinned. "May I?" She butted Hank out of the way. "Jimmy, your hand."

She slid her arm up behind his back and whirled him back along the dance floor, just fast enough to keep him off-balance. "When we stop, grab the rotten peach. I'll handle Roth."

"That's not exactly sporting." Jimmy leveled his body weight away from Ginger and regained control, leading them backward, past other dancers.

Ginger flinched out of the way of an oncoming elbow. "Jimmy, stop, I know what I'm doing, so don't you try to lead."

Jimmy led them backwards, unaware, until he crashed into the back of tall, curly-haired man in a velvet jacket. The blonde in his arms, dressed in a masterpiece, laughed. "You still insist you can dance?" He boggled at her. "Did you see who you were cheek to cheek with?"

Ginger hooked her hand around Jimmy's waist and yanked him back with her. "Just dance with the lounge singer." Ginger put on the world's sunniest smile, glared at Jimmy over that sun-dipped goodness, and Lindy Hopped side-by-side with Roth and Peaches.

Jimmy released Ginger. "Em." He wasn't sure what to do with his hands, now. "Ma'am. Uh. Ma'am." Peaches' chin has not left its perch on Roth's shoulder; her lips moved in the pitter-patter of sweet nothings. "Miss Latorre. Uh. Miss Latorre. It'd, uh, be my pleasure to—"

A gentle tap on the shoulder and Peaches looked his way. "Miss, uh, Miss—"

Ginger gripped Peaches' shoulders and plied her off Roth. She shoved her at Jimmy.

"Now Mr. Roth," she purred, sliding into his vacant arms, "Don't you think it's time for a turn with a *real* dancer?"

Mr. Roth was gasping for breath.

"I'm so glad you agree." Ginger waited. Roth did nothing, still gasping like a fish. His breath smelled like almonds. She tilted her head and swayed back and forth. He followed her waves.

"So about that film you're about to shoot, I've heard you need a woman with class and I've got that in spades."

Roth's eyes began to bulge and his skin went from pink to purple-red.

"Or maybe you need more of a rough and tumble kind of woman, I can do that too. I know, I know, everyone thinks I'm attached to Fred's hip, but I'm a crack shot with a rifle—"

Roth slumped over on her.

"I am *not* that kind of—!"

And then he slid down her onto the floor. He convulsed, foaming at the mouth. By the time Ginger had called for help, he had already gone still. Peaches untangled herself from Jimmy, and made her way to Ginger's side. She looked down at Roth, then patted Ginger on the shoulder.

"Oh honey, I didn't think your dancing was *that* bad."

As the crowd massed around them, Peaches slipped away from the commotion to her dressing room.

The police always come.

Just when the party's getting wild, or just when the kisses are getting hot, the police, without fail, will knock up on your door and break up the fun. So here they were, the boys in blue, standing around Roth's body and while they stood around, they asked questions.

"Who was he talking to?"

"Who touched him last?"

"Who was he dancing with?"

None of those answers boded well. With each new question, Ginger took a step back, and took a step back until she was up against a metal palm tree and shrinking against it.

Someone tapped her shoulder.

"Were you the young lady dancing with the deceased?" said an official voice. It's always an official voice with the worst news and questions.

Lord. He didn't even wait until I had turned around. As she turned around, she asked, with a steeling breath, "If I need to answer, yes…"

If you've only read comic strips, you expect police to be moderately handsome with jaws a lazy stoneworker had cut straight from granite. Pale blue eyes that shine in the dark. Fists as big as milk cans. Yellow trenchcoat optional. But when confronted with the real police—exemplified by the little figure tapping on Ginger's shoulder—she found an officious little man, suit better than his build, his full height sagging somewhere below her chin. His jowls were borrowed, half-price, from a bulldog. He was distinctly ferret-like, despite his winding, expanding middle. His fists were, at most, were the size of mugs at a cheap diner. His eyes were muddy, and weary, and distinctly not blue. He couldn't even get the yellow trenchcoat right.

"Yes, I'm afraid you do. Let's start with your name…?"

"Ginger. Ginger Rogers. Um. And yours?"

"Inspector Lestrade."

"Like the de—"

"Don't. No relation."

She raised her fist to her mouth and coughed. "Yes?"

"Now what do you know about Mr. Roth?"

"Oh, lots of things. He's directed *Singin' Scarlet*, which was quite a challenge for a silent movie, then he's moved up to epic talkies. Caesars, Manchus, little redheads running around the old west—"

"Very cute. What do you know about Mr. Roth's death?"

She put up a wall of silence while looking for an honest answer that didn't point at herself, shouting *I did it! I killed him! It was me the whole time!* She frowned. "My friends and I approached him for some uncast parts in his next film, that's a—"

"That's *not* all. Fact, he died of orally ingested cyanide. Very obvious, very messy, very painful. Fact, you and your friends have been hounding him all night. That waiter, Fritz, was very helpful. Fact, everyone saw the two of you…inappropriately close shortly before his death. Lip to lip, some say."

He left no room for a question, or for explanation.

"I. Um, no, *yes*—but that's not quite right."

"We'll be in touch, Miss Rogers. Don't think of leaving the club." He began to walk away, then turned around and added. "Might be wise to splurge tonight. They won't have such fine chardonnay where you're going." This would have been more threatening if he didn't pronounce it *shar-donnies.*

Ginger sagged against the tree once more, when another voice spoke in her ear. "What's Little Boy Blue want?"

"He's pinning it on me. Cyanide. Lucy, what are we going to do?"

"Cyanide? I'm going to pin it on the hussy. You just wait here and I'll give her hell."

If Lucy had a talent, it was leading people where (she thought) they needed to go. She hooked her arm through Hank's and lead him through the thinning crowd and deep into the backstage They stumbled through the press of the technicians (all stripped down out of jackets, all sweating), down under the lights, and weaving around the dancers and musicians and comedians (all gossiping).

"Step faster, Hank." Lucy smiled at the workmen, and at the dancers, and at the producers as if she not only belonged, but as if she was the biggest star and their lives—to say nothing of their jobs—depended on stepping out of her way.

They stopped at a door with a big, fat star emblazoned across the surface. Lucy gripped the handle, and shoved inward.

Ginger sat by their table, hands running down her skirts. "This is bad, Jimmy."

"Yeah, yeah, no work for us." He sat beside her.

"*Worse*, Jimmy."

"Now why's that?"

"Look. Roth keels over dead." She watched him nod. "Do you follow?"

"Un-huh, yeah."

"And who is near him?"

"Us."

"And who faked being part of staff to *be* near him?"

"Us."

"And who did he tell to beat it several times?"

"Us."

"Now who does that make the police think killed him?"

"U-Us."

"Big problem."

She leaned back in the chair, staring at the ceiling.

As they threw open the door, Peaches eyed them from the mirror of her boudoir. She studied them with a rather absent air as she continued to fix her makeup. "So, any leads from our detective friends?"

"Pretty cocky of you, letting that man drop dead in front of God and everybody and just waltzing back to your dressing room like that. Almost like you got away with murder." Lucy growled.

On one hand Peaches rapped her nails against the boudoir. *Ratta-tat-tat. Ratta-tat-tat.* She flashed a welcoming smile, her Georgia drawl sugar sweet. "Lucy, right? The one tryin' to meet Mister Roth while he was otherwise engaged…with me? Now why would you insinuate such a nasty thing? You saw the same thing I did; we danced, I traded him off, and he keeled over. In *your* friend's arms." She rolled the tubes of lipstick back and forth with her other hand.

"Then you up and left," Hank said.

She picked up one of the darker tubes of lipstick and held it up to her own pink lips. "Honey, the show must go on. I have to do a number in a few minutes. Club might be closing thanks to Mister Roth, but we have a practice number for tomorrow, and there's no way they'll let that be delayed by something so small as a dead body."

They stepped into the room, Hank shut the door behind them. They stayed near the door, neither one too keen on getting close to what might be a dangerous dame. The buzzing from the crowd outside grew louder, pushing in on the silence of the dressing room. Weighing down on the lungs. One of Peaches' hands dipped down to a drawer of her boudoir, and she gripped the handle tight.

"Well, don't keep me in suspense. What'd the detectives say?" She asked, laying on the accent a little too thick and a little too saccharine.

"Poison, they think. Cyanide."

Peaches gave a little dismissive wave. "Yeah, yeah, I *know* that." They stared at her, she paused. "The foaming. What *else*?"

Lucy was taken aback by the casual tone. She frowned at Hank.

"Oh, just that they think, uh, someone slipped something in his drink. Now, you wouldn't have happened to see anything like that, being so attentive to his table, would you?" Hank asked.

Peaches shot a glare at his reflection. "All I saw was you lot hovering around like some kinda vultures." She opened the vanity drawer and rummaged, pulling out options for eyeliner.

"You're really calm for someone who saw a murder."

"This ain't the first time I've seen a stiff."

Lucy and Hank grew silent, trying to unpack that sentence. Peaches laid the liner thick around her thin lashes.

"What were you even doing with him anyway?" Lucy snapped. Her voice was sharp, slicing through that heavy silence like the crack of a pistol. Peaches flinched, eyeliner pencil clattering to the floor.

She gave a rather melodramatic sigh and twisted around in her chair to face the two, draping her arm over the back. Leaning down as much as her tight dress allowed, she picked up the pencil and dropped it into the drawer with little ceremony. Her hand hovered over the open drawer, forgotten, and answered, "It was business, and not pleasure if that's what you're asking. Too old for my tastes."

Hank grunted. "Business? What kind of business?"

"The regular kind. You know, the kind that insures my prompt service." Peaches drew out the words as slow as that obviously fake accent allowed.

Lucy huffed. This is the part in the movies where she'd tell the hussy they have ways to make her talk, and then the camera would turn away because the Hayes Code didn't approve those ways. But this wasn't the movies, and she had no desire to play detective any longer.

"Well, how's this for prompt?" Lucy grabbed Hank by the shoulder and hauled him out the door while he continued to glare in Peaches' direction. Peaches flashed a coy smile and waved them off.

As the door slammed shut behind them, Peaches turned back to the vanity to give her makeup one last once over. Satisfied with her work, she glanced down into the open drawer. Barely discernible under the make-up kits was a gun. She patted it and closed the drawer.

"No more stiffs tonight."

All around the club gossips banded together in clumps, sing-songing all the press' favorite words. "Murder," one whispered, "Jilted lover," said another, just ever so much louder, "I heard he tried to press himself on her and she murdered him to preserve her honor," and then, at last, they looped through "Poison," "Horrible way to die," "Cyanide," and then back around to the most pressing questions of all: "Doesn't the murderess have a picture out? Think we can make the last showing?"

Amid this gale, Lucy glared hot enough to burn the world to cinders. "She's a cagey hussy," is all she could bring herself to say for quite some time.

"How do we know she did it?" Hank asked over his bourbon. "I was thinking…"

"Because my feminine intuition trumps your thinking. Now hush. How am I going to get back at…how are we going to clear our names?"

Hank never lowered his drink. "She has a show in ten minutes. If the police refuse to interfere, and think of where our fine drunks would be without her show, we can sneak into her dressing room. There has to be evidence. Haven't you seen Charlie Chan's pictures? Murderers leave evidence within easy reach. Inescapable law of reality."

Jimmy asked, "Who's breaking and who's entering?"

"The women have taken point all evening, save for your adventure in the white suit service. Shall we?"

"Oh no. I'm the least mixed up in this crazy business. I've made no death threats," he looked at Lucy, "Haven't kissed him right before he dropped dead," he looked at Ginger, "And I haven't—"

"But you did bring him the drink, Jimmy. And you can't go to prison just yet. You need to pay your half of the rent."

Hank rose to his feet and Jimmy followed. They followed the same path Lucy had trailblazed: up around producers, down under lights, around the dancers resting for the next set, through the saw-dust and stuffy back rooms until at last they arrived before Peaches' door.

"So far so good," Hank whispered.

He tried the knob and it gave way. "Step inside. Hurry."

The music from Peaches' number played loud.

The room was ultimately nondescript. It had all you'd expect from a dressing room: lights, mirror, chair, clothes rack, dressing table, and make-up. But it was so nondescript, so void of all personality, that it felt like a hotel room: a small box people check in and check out of but never leave a trace of themselves behind. They quickly rifled through the dresses hanging from the rack, then through a small bag they supposed to be her purse.

"It's easier in the movies," Jimmy said.

Hank had to lean near to hear. The band was in full swing, and had they been a bit more aware of this new number, they'd know it was rising to a climax.

Then they came to the drawers in the dresser.

The first drawer revealed make up: foundations, paints, mascaras, all the tools for deceiving the eye.

The music dimmed.

The second drawer revealed more makeup, and under it a gun. A hefty, full-sized .45. Blue steel. Round in the chamber, magazine full.

The music dimmed down to silence, but they carried on, never noticing.

The third drawer revealed clothes, stacked carefully, more carefully than any of the rest of Peaches things suggested.

"Little too neat, there," Hank said.

They pulled things out, leaving them much less neat.

At the very bottom they found a pill. It was an oval capsule, fashioned from glass and about the size of a malnourished pea. It was wrapped in a thin strip of rubber, end over end.

"*Welllllllllll*," Hank asked, "What's this?"

"You need to watch more spy pictures. That's a cyanide capsule." Jimmy stared at it.

Now, in the dead-gap of music the door swung open and a smoky, barely Georgian voice said: "Has anyone ever told you you know too much?" Her heels clomped up to them and, short as she was, she stared right into their eyes.

"Let's have it. Now. And I won't—"

Hank stepped up in front of her. "Run! Get to the—"

Peaches pushed him back and took off after Jimmy. He held a good lead, at least for the first two dozen steps. The steps that took him back past the technicians and through the dancing girls by the props.

Step by step, leap by leap, she caught up right behind him. She was a preternaturally quiet runner, without the thuds of the strongman or the dancer's patter; all Jimmy heard was the rush of the wind around her, and he pressed faster, his heels sometimes getting caught up in the hem of her dress.

That was the beginning of his undoing.

Next time his foot was behind him, in what was to be the launch of a great jump that cleared the stairs down to the dance floor and carried in sailing to freedom, she twisted her heels around his ankle.

Down he went.

Down she went.

All thumping face first down the stairs. They stopped, groaning, at the base of the dance floor. The police—as always, looking to bust up any fun—made their way to them.

Peaches leaned down to his ear and hissed. "That's not the murder weapon, idiot."

The gap closed from twenty feet to ten.

"I'm one of Uncle Sam's girls."

Then it closed further, down to a handful of steps.

"I'm a spy."

Suddenly blocking his vision: big black shoes draped by the blue pants of law and justice. "And what's goin' on here, then?"

Her drawl was back and sugar-coated, she giggled. "Oh, hi there, honey, always happy to see a man in uniform." She snapped a salute. "Just an overzealous admirer, here, tried to sneak backstage and catch an…autograph. Nothin' for you to worry your pretty little head over, I was just givin' him a good little chase. Not so good with that in heels though."

Jimmy just stammered.

The officer looked her over, looked Jimmy over, looked her over again. She was combing through her hair with her fingers, face screwed up with great intent. He grunted something about a "brain-dead broad" and walked away without even offering her a hand.

She didn't seem to need it. Before Jimmy had even thought of sitting up she was on her feet. She sighed, placed one hand on her hip and held the other out to him.

"Ah, thank you, ah, miss."

He went to grab onto her arm and she pulled away a fraction. "Not your hand. What's in it. Come on, let's have it." She laid her hand out, palm up. She waved her fingers in a *gimme* motion. As he laid it in her hand, she glowered. "Maybe you'll stop gumming the works if I explain myself. Fetch your girls and bring 'em back. All will be revealed." She waved her fingers like some carnival mystic. "*Alllllll.*"

"Ah."

"Just do it, okay? You need your names cleared, don't you?"

When she was nearly out of Jimmy's sight, and out of sight of all on the floor or the stage, she stopped and muttered "And let's put you some place no-one will ever get to." And she slipped it down the front of her dress.

This time as she sat at her boudoir, the gun was in plain sight. She had snatched it from Hank with a hiss. "Give me that. You'll hurt yourself." And then rested it securely in her lap. All traces of southern hospitality were gone, her words now slow and measured.

"This was supposed to be an easy, in and out, sort of a mission. Roth needed information. I have information. I do a little song and dance, I spill my beans, he flies off to Cairo and does something heroic. Off I go to harvest more beans."

Lucy huffed. "Great spy you are, leaving your pill here for some enterprising sleuth."

Peaches pinched the bridge of her nose. "Like I said, this was supposed to be easy, I didn't think…I just didn't think. I never claimed to be Mata Hari. I'm just a presidential secret."

"Just?" Ginger echoed.

"Wars. Clandestine rendezvous. Spy stuff. Not really my forte. I mean, I do look good in a dress and have a lovely singing voice like every femme fatale should. But what I really am is an expert on the supernatural. Something *certain* governments are very interested in." She held her pinky finger under her nose, imitating a certain dictator's mustache. "Very, *very* interested in."

"Wars? Unless I slept through a newsreel, Uncle Sam isn't in any," Hank said.

Peaches leaned back and held out her arms. "And now you see my problem." She pantomimed tapping someone on the shoulder. "Oh. Yes, hello, Mr. Officer. I'm in a bit of a bind. You know that big mess of a war brewing up overseas? The one we're doing a great job of ignoring over here? Yes, well, Mr. President isn't ignoring it. And that man who died? Well he was going to shoot a film in Cairo, but it wasn't actually a feature. It was intelligence gathering. But now he's dead and I'm the only one with intelligence left to gather. I'm not really a nightclub singer, I just moonlight as one."

"Yeah that's about as convincing to the boys in blue as it is for me," Lucy growled. "What's in Cairo that'd have Adolf chomping at his bit?"

"Oh what I wouldn't give to have Boris Karloff around and not you. Pyramids. Curses. Ancient artifacts of unspeakable power. A friend of mine—Professor of Archaeology, skips his own classes to travel around—is on assignment over there, and Fritz and his Kraut-boys are keen to snag him. *I* have his preliminary findings right here." She tapped her head. "And I'm not going to get them into some living fellow's head until we get this all solved, put away, and put so far out of my hair that I'm not a *person of interest* anymore. So, since you all fancy yourselves Charlie Chans, tell me, who knocked off Roth?"

Ginger shook her head. "No clue. To be honest, you seemed like the most likely suspect."

Hank nodded.

Lucy picked up in the middle of his nod. "Really, honey, you're still the most likely suspect. You should sell that story of yours to Republic. They'd snap it up and showcase it in twelve parts, right between Mickey Mouse and Porky Pig.

Might even get Crash Corrigan to star as you, gorilla suit optional."

"Or you, if they can't get the gorilla."

Lucy was going to say something.

But she was spooked out of it by the sound that came next...

"AHA!" Jimmy shouted, rising. "So Ginger didn't kill him, even though her lips were all over him; you didn't kill him, Lucy, as much as you wanted to; you didn't kill him, Peaches, even though you touched him all night and sprinkled your fingers over his drink; and I definitely didn't kill him, and I carried the drink that killed him over to that table. Only one other person touched it between the time I set it down and when he, uh, died."

Everyone sat forward.

"The autograph hound!"

"The little one with that whiney voice?" Lucy asked.

Jimmy nodded. "The same. He brushed the drink." He pressed his palms together. "Maybe he dropped something in, maybe he had powder ringed around his palm. But it was a neat enough trick. I think I'm the only one who even saw his hand there."

"Great," Lucy moaned. "We know who did it. Doesn't exactly unstrap us from the electric chair, now does it?"

"Well, hrm." Ginger tilted her head. "I might have a plan. A very dangerous plan. This is what I was thinking: Peaches fetches our killer and leads him over to a table. It's one of the ones on the ledge over the dance floor, so Lucy and I can get the detective and lead him over, and we can crouch under the overhang and listen. Once he says something damning, Jimmy and Hank can come up and grab him until the police get there. Hank, you'll need to get a white coat too, because there aren't enough people left to blend in."

"And if he says nothing incriminating?" Lucy asked.

"Then, well, either we've blown it or he might kill us for knowing too much." She paused, looked up at them all, then asked her question.

"Shall we try it?"

Peaches slipped her arm up through his, purring. "Well, hello there. I believe we have something to discuss."

He was oh so thin and oh so short with just the merest slice of hair. He looked handsome enough, if your tastes ran to the conventional. His eyes widened as he put on his most innocent face. "With me? I thought you and Roth didn't want anything to do with your adoring public."

Peaches ran her tongue over her teeth, screwed up her face in a thoughtful look. "Well, he sure didn't, especially after you made him foam at the mouth like that. But he didn't pay too well for my *services*. Maybe you'd give me a better deal."

His innocent gaze grew a bit colder. "Perhaps you could tell me how Cairo is this time of year?"

"Oh, fer sure. I could tell you all sorts of things about that." With a hip-wiggle she usually reserved for the stage, Peaches led their way to a table in an obscure corner. It overlooked the dance floor, beside the railing separating the restaurant section of the club's affairs from the dance section.

Behind him were the six sharp steps to the dance floor below.

The table was pristine, silverware in order, cloth starched, glasses unfilled and untouched: murder cases, with all their rope and stern faces and "You can't go there, sir, nothing to see, ma'am" have the inevitable result of scaring off club-goers. Even the promise of a first-rate stiff, frothing mouth and purple skin, can't quite revive business.

Peaches smiled at him.

"Now, it's appropriate for a gentleman to give a lady his name."

"I am—"

"Now if you're afraid to use your German one, well, your Yankee one will do fine. I thought Nazis were supposed to be, ya know, blonder."

"Such a petty understanding! No, I only have the one. We're not *all* Germans, you know. Good sense transcends nations. I am Adrien Paget."

"And you know me. Everybody does." She tossed a

coquettish little nod. "So, I was thinking…money. Enough money to get me somewhere the coppers aren't."

"It's adorable. You think money will help you. But, very well. Enough money for the new life you are so likely to enjoy. Anything more?" While she wrote her wishlist, his face became increasingly thoughtful: crinkled-up nose, squinted eyes, tilted neck, the perfect picture of consideration. Below the lip of the table, his hands softly rooted through pockets. His hand rested upon the handle of a dirk but rejected it as too messy, and upon a slimline automatic which was, unfortunately, too loud—but he had just enough cyanide left, and why not leave the cops a messy, confounding present…

And while Peaches listed everything from *a new Ford* to *a telephone of my own—none of that party-line business*, Jimmy and Hank bartered at the far, far back of the restaurant where the patrons fear to tread and white jackets reign. Jimmy began, "We need another jacket."

"We need another *white* jacket," Hank said.

Her bubble gum snapped. Her face, otherwise, stayed perfectly still. "You got a stain, new guy. Bunch of stains. You going to apologize for making me do laundry, or do I have to wrestle off your jacket, suspend you, and give it to your friend here?"

"I, uh—"

Jimmy's stutter was cut off by Hank leaning down closer to her. "We're special agents, and if you hand us that jacket we'll make sure the papers give you all the credit. *Girl Detective Catches Killer. Nancy Drew Returns. Cocoanut Grove Detective Sells Life Story, Movie to Follow.* Who knows who might play you. How does that sound?"

"Sounds like a load of wash. But I'm liable to melt for flattery." She kicked her chair back into the threads until only her lower half was visible among all the coats. Then she stood. "No stains, no rips, and I get to watch. Always good if I can describe some punchin' to the movie executives. There *will* be punching, right?" She held out a white jacket to Hank with an eager grin.

Hank shook his head as he slipped his fingers under hers (all the better to pry her grip off) and took his new jacket. "Modern police work, you know, almost entirely precludes violence. Sherlock Holmes would be proud. We're great brains who think our way to solutions. But if you were to cast us in your movie…Jimmy here has a great right hook."

They arrived back at the table, hovering at the distance waiters call their home: just near enough to lightly impinge on the conscious, but far enough away they can be mocked, teased, and ignored.

"And that should be just about it," Peaches finished. "And delivery by tomorrow, so I can take it to Argentina with me. That won't tax Adolf too much, will it?"

Paget ground his teeth. "*Certainly*. That can certainly be arranged." He snapped his fingers in the vague direction of Jimmy and Hank. "Drinks. In honor of a successful evening."

Hank and Jimmy laid out two champagne glasses, and Paget smiled and leaned across the table, his hand extended and snaking toward Peaches. "To us," he said, as he took her gloved hand and shook it, calmly, above her glass.

While things heated up for Peaches, Ginger and Lucy were far across the dance floor to where Inspector Lestrade (no relation) hunched with his blue-coats. His bulldog jowls jiggled when he looked up at them. "Come to confess?"

"No, dear," Ginger responded. "Just duck down. We'll clear it all up."

He grunted. If such grunts could have supported punctuation, it would have ended with a question mark.

"Just crouch down," Lucy said, "And we'll show you. We can even hold your hand if you get scared."

And Lucy did just that, grabbing the Inspector's hand and pulling him down and after her. She duck-walked him to the low wall, and pulled him along behind her. "Just listen. No talking. I imagine that might be hard for you," she hissed, pulling him roughly along.

They passed along silently, save for the susurration of their skirts along the floor.

When they got near enough to catch Peaches eye, she had lifted the glass of champagne. She held it close to her lips, smiled at Paget, then turned in her chair to the Inspector. "Hello, copper, caught your killer for ya. If you take a look in this here drink you'll find the same nasty stuff that offed Mr. Roth. This twit tried to sing the same tune twice."

Paget moved to grab her, but he found two hands on his shoulders. The one on his right belonged to Jimmy, the one planted firmly on his left belonged to Hank.

Paget raised his right fist, capped it with his left hand, and drove his elbow back into Jimmy's stomach. Latching onto the momentum of the blow, Paget stood and rounded on Hank. One blow (blocked by Hank's forearm), two blows (caught in Hank's hands); Paget lashed out with a kick, knocking Hank down to the ground beside Jimmy. Paget leapt over Hank and toward the stairs. All the while, the jacket girl applauded.

She took a seat next to Peaches, who had snatched up the champagne meant for Adrien and was sipping it as she watched.

By this time, Paget had come to the top stair, gun drawn. Lucy had come to the bottom stair, and wound up for a punch.

Lucy wound back her arm. As Paget rounded down the stairs, he would arrive on the dance floor just as her fist graced his face, knuckles dusting from jaw to cheek to nose in a single blow; it would take him off his feet.

She wound back all the way as he mounted the first stair.

She released as he made halfway down the steps.

And just at the moment when she would hit him a blow which could send Kid Chocolate into retirement...

She realized Ginger was below her.

She realized Ginger had thrown her arm out across the bottom step.

She realized Ginger had caught Paget's leg, in passing, and knocked him down to his belly. His head smacked against the dance floor.

But it was too late.

Lucy's punch still flew out, true to the mark where her target should have been, and without the impact to balance her she tumbled herself. She thudded right down onto Paget's back.

"When you get up," Peaches waved from above, "I have a drink for you." She swirled the drink Paget had prepared.

The jacket-girl looked down at them all, laughing. "Modern police work!"

Jimmy could only groan.

The drawn-out night concluded with a rushing thunder of activity: statements collected, events reconstructed, names cleared.

"You're free to go." The Inspector nodded carelessly, happy to have sealed up the case before breakfast. They stepped out past palm trees, past carpeting, past the big glass doors. And the four friends walked out into the pre-sun morning, smiling. Hank took Lucy's hand, smiled, and leaned in. . .

The perfect ending: a drawn-out kiss as the sun woke up, the magic of his lips blending into the kaleidoscope skylight.

Lucy's ending: Her date bent over, coughing (or as Lucy would insist, *retching*) down into the gutter. When he stood, still coughing, her cinder-burning eyes were on him.

This time, she got to finish a punch.

Well, we went dancing. and actually Miss Ball and I were having a great time together....But you may notice that I'm the only one on the podium that calls her Miss Ball, I was never intimate enough to call her Lucy. That's the point of the story....Both girls looked ravishingly lovely in the soft lights, and we danced 'til dawn. But when we came out into the harsh glare of the daylight, the girls' make-up looked about an inch thick and it was—well, what it was—was ugly. It's simply untrue what Miss Ball has been telling people all these years that I went to the gutter and retched. I was just coughing a lot. I'd like to take this opportunity, after all these years, because it was a very ungentlemanly thing to do, to apologize. Miss Ball, Lucy, I love you.

[Breaks down into a coughing fit.]

~Henry Fonda, *The Dean Martin Celebrity Roast: Lucille Ball*

THE UNFILMABLE

C. L. Werner

"The script was bad, but I didn't think it was rotten enough for someone to do this."

No one in the crumbling wooden shack seemed to hear the sardonic comment. They were far too mesmerised by the ghastly scene into which they had stepped to pay attention to the grim gallows' humour of the beetle-browed grey-haired actor. A touch of grim levity was the only thing that kept George Zucco in the room, however. If he were to allow the full measure of the horror he was looking at hit him with all its force he'd probably turn around and not stop running until he was in Bakersfield.

The thing that was strewn about the shack amid a patina of blood and less agreeable fluids had been the writer H. Marrion Stanhope. There were enough recognizable pieces to be certain of that much. It was his shack, after all. So it made sense it would be his corpse. Nobody else had a reason to be in the tumble-down shanty where Stanhope had been slaving away on revisions. Except, it appeared, for the man's killer.

An awed silence gripped the other members of the cast and crew as they gawked at what was left of Stanhope. Zucco was the only one who maintained an air of detachment. Less rattled than the others. Perhaps he was simply better prepared mentally to accept the reality of such horrors. Not quite five years earlier, he had been considered for a role in a remake of *The Lodger* and did some research on his own in preparation for the project. What had been done to Stanhope reminded Zucco of the ghastly photographs taken of Mary Kelley, the last victim of Jack the Ripper.

"Police." The word was muttered by Avery Pierce in little more than a whisper. Gruff and grizzled, 'Two-Take' Pierce had a reputation as a hard and demanding director. Now he was ashen-faced, one foot stamping absently against the plank floor in a nervous tremor. "Police," he repeated, his voice louder. "Someone call the police!"

Charles Stone, the heavy-set film producer tore his eyes away from the grisly remains and snarled at the technician who had first discovered Stanhope's body. "Take my car. Get down to Victorville and get some law back here."

The technician nodded, but continued to gawk. "Go get the police!" Stone snapped at him, spurring the man into action.

As the technician left the shack, Zucco noticed someone else trying to enter the crowded room. He stepped over and blocked the newcomer's path, trying to hide from her eyes the havoc that had been visited against Stanhope. Gripping her shoulders, he turned her around and pushed her back outside.

"There's nothing in there you need to see, Miss LaRue," Zucco stated. He blinked as he stepped out from the shack, his eyes dazzled by the high desert sun after the gloom inside.

"But what has happened, George?" she asked, worry in her tone.

Zucco tried to give her a reassuring smile. "We're not certain. Perhaps some kind of terrible accident. Brace yourself, but Mr. Stanhope is dead."

Monique LaRue gasped. She pressed one hand to the breast of her costume, a beaded buckskin dress that was some Hollywood costumier's idea of what Indians wore. Zucco noted that her hand, unlike her face, was not caked in make-up but instead retained its naturally dusky colour. Monique was a Creole from Louisiana, though the studio's publicity department had decided to make her a Polynesian from the mysterious island of Ponape. She was being billed as "Tara," no surname, and ballyhooed as the most exotic beauty to ever appear on the silver screen.

Zucco did smile at the absurdity of the publicity department. Here was an actress from Louisiana being passed off as a Polynesian while playing an Indian half-breed, her skin caked in what amounted to white-face. Monique's film debut was already confusing enough without throwing a murder into the mix.

"But…but I was speaking with him…only last night."

"That, I fear, is the way these things happen," Zucco told her. He turned her away from the shack. They started down the dusty road that stretched between the weather-beaten wooden buildings. "Come along, I'll see you home. I don't think Mr. Pierce will be shooting any scenes today."

"They won't…I mean they aren't…" there was a trace of genuine fear in Monique's voice now.

Zucco gave her a reassuring pat on the arm. "Only a delay. They don't cancel a picture simply because the writer dies." Monqiue's inexperience was endearing. Maybe it was likewise naïve of him, but he hoped the studio system didn't make her too cynical too quickly. He doubted if Charles Stone appreciated it, but it wasn't her pretty face that gave Monique such an exotic air, it was her innocence. Maybe he'd thrown a bit too much of himself into his current role—he was playing Monique's father in the film—but he felt protective towards her, as though she were in fact his daughter rather than only acting the part.

Monique shook her head. She glanced at Zucco with an embarrassed look. "I know it is awful, with what has happened, but this could be my big break. If everybody packed up and went back to Hollywood…"

They were passing the larger of the three saloons that fronted the street. The little western town had been built to scale in the high desert just the other side of the San Bernardino Mountains back in the 30s for Tom Mix and Bob Steele oaters. Over the years it had been neglected and much of it now resembled an actual ghost town. Some of the buildings had been gussied up with new paint and a few repairs, but such improvements had been carried out only sparingly. Stone was determined to bring the picture in under budget.

The tight purse strings extended to the amenities for cast and crew. Except for the producer's own trailer, everyone had been billeted in one of the set's buildings. The prop department was in the school house, camera equipment was being stored in the jail when not in use. Pierce was viewing the daily rushes in the back of the blacksmith shop and the general store was doing service as a commissary when scenes weren't being filmed there.

"Home" for Monique was a little building with a tin roof and a doctor's sign hanging from its awning. Perhaps the one touch of consideration Stone had extended towards his "discovery" was setting her up in the only place that had four solid adobe walls and a ceiling which didn't leak.

"You should get some rest," Zucco assured Monique. "There won't be any more work today. Even Pierce isn't going to try to get any footage with everyone thinking about the…accident." He pointed across the street to where he had been established. In a grim gesture he'd been set up in the undertaker's parlour. "I'll be in there if you need anything."

Zucco waited until the actress was inside before making his departure. He started towards the undertaker's but then stopped in the middle of the street. He glanced back at the shack where Stanhope had met death. Contrary to what he'd told Monique, he walked back towards the violent scene.

Stone was forcing people out of the shack. With him was Curly Becker, the studio cop who had been brought along to act as security. Zucco noticed that for the first time since he'd met the man, Becker had a gun hanging from his belt.

"Nobody gets in," Stone was telling the crowd of cast and crew. "I've sent Jake off to get the police. They won't be happy if we're tromping around in there and messing up any evidence."

"Then you do think Stanhope was murdered?" The challenge came from Douglas Irons, the former rodeo bronc-buster who was playing the film's hero. Since production started, the cowboy had been butting heads with Stone's high-handed attitude.

Stone glowered at the Texan actor. "I think Stanhope drank like a fish and it was finally too much for his ticker," the producer declared in exasperation. He licked his lips anxiously and looked across the crowd. "Not to speak ill of the dead, but we all know Stanhope lived in a bottle."

Zucco shook his head, stunned at the producer's audacity.

"You expect us to accept that Stanhope drank himself into such a state he slashed himself to ribbons? Don't forget, quite a few of us saw his body."

"Coyotes," Stone replied, his tone surly. "Stanhope died and coyotes came slinking into the shack for a free meal." He again cast his gaze across the crowd. "The police will explain everything when they get here. Until then there's no use in everyone making up wild stories."

"And if there *is* a murderer around here?" Irons persisted.

"Surely a sharpshootin' Texan can handle himself?" Stone retorted.

Irons' hand flashed like lightning, whipping the Colt .45 from his gun holster. Stone blanched as the cowboy aimed the weapon at him and fanned the hammer. Smoke and flame flashed from the barrel while the crack of gunfire echoed down the street. When the smoke cleared, an unharmed Stone glared at Irons.

"Not going to do much with blanks," Irons observed, tucking the pistol back into its holster. He pointed at Becker. "He's got the only live ammo in the whole place."

Bill Weaver, the propsmaster, objected to Irons' remark. The short, thin-faced man turned on the cowboy. "That's so there aren't any accidents. So some damn fool doesn't go and forget what he's loaded his gun with! Only person who has any reason to have real bullets is the one who has no reason to be carrying blanks."

"Has it occurred to you that the murderer might be thinking the same thing?" Zucco asked. The question sent frightened whispers through the crowd. Stone's face turned bright crimson.

"We're getting worked up over nothing," Stone insisted. "When the cops get here, they'll take stock of things. I'm telling you, Stanhope drank himself under and then coyotes started picking at him." He fixed his gaze on Zucco. "Maybe you should be more worried about your performance. We're shooting your big scenes tomorrow." He glanced aside at Pierce. Director and producer shared a look and then Pierce broke away from the crowd. Clapping his hand on Zucco's shoulder he guided the actor away from the shack.

"Not good to provoke the boss like that, George," Pierce admonished Zucco. He gave the actor a stern look as they walked through the ghost town. "You know his first choice was Bela Lugosi."

"Then I am to be thankful Bela got hired by Universal to play Dracula again," Zucco quipped. It was his turn to give Pierce a hard stare. "That man is playing with all our lives. You saw Stanhope. That wasn't the result of too much bad liquor and a pack of hungry coyotes. He was murdered and his body defiled in some obscene ritual."

Pierce shook his head. "You've been reading the script too much," he told Zucco. "That kind of thing happens in horror pictures, not real life." There was an uneasiness in his eyes.

"There's something you aren't telling me," Zucco said. "*You* know it was murder."

The director glanced up and down the street. "I don't know anything, George. If you want to keep getting a paycheck around here, you'll do the same." Pierce stalked off, heading towards the general store and the commissary.

Zucco watched the director walk away. "Stone isn't paying any of us enough to stand around waiting to be murdered," he muttered before turning back towards the undertaker's parlour. He paused on the boardwalk and looked up at the coffin-shaped sign. If the shop had been real, he suspected it would be doing a good business soon. Because what had been done to Stanhope was more than simply murder. It was the work of a maniac.

A maniac Zucco didn't think would stop at one killing.

"For he is the key and the gate. Yog-Sothoth…" Zucco stared more closely at the jumble of letters that followed. It was meant to be an infernal incantation in an ancient tongue but to him it looked like Stanhope had tried to transliterate the sound of a cat choking on a hairball. He set down the script and glanced over at the little table which stood beside the army cot that served as his bed. Resting atop the table was a battered pulp magazine.

"Of all the things Stanhope took out of that story, why on earth did he see fit to leave that gibberish in?" Zucco wondered to himself. He set down the script and walked over to the table. He thumbed through the magazine until he reached the story he was looking for. "The Dunwich Horror" by H. P. Lovecraft. He squinted at the print, the feeble light shining through the parlour's dusty windows not exactly the best for reading a decades-old pulp.

"I'm surprised Stone even bothered to pay for the rights." Zucco abandoned his perusal of the story and replaced the magazine on the table. It was more than simply his opinion, in Stone's production very little remained of Lovecraft's story beyond a few of the names. "The Dunwich Horror" had become "The Ghoul of Gunsight Gulch," the narrative transplanted from Prohibition-era New England to the American Southwest as only Hollywood could. Cowboys rode into town with sixguns on their hips while radios blared big band music in the saloons. It was a hodge-podge mixture of Wild West and modernity that had become an accepted conceit of the bijou and weekend matinees.

A few of the parts at least bore a semblance to what was in the story. Zucco was playing Ike Whatley, a rancher who had converted over to a mysterious sort of Navajo devil-worship. Monique was playing his half-breed daughter. His adversary was Preacher Armitage, a former Texas Ranger who had become pastor of Gunsight Gulch. That was Doug Irons' role, at least if he didn't push Charles Stone so far as to get himself fired. Stone was tight enough with the studio's money that Zucco didn't think there was any great danger of that happening, at least not when it would mean considerable re-shoots.

The tightness of the budget was something of a mixed blessing as far as Zucco was concerned. It was thanks to his willingness to work for less than Lugosi that he'd gotten the job. With a wife and daughter to support, and most of the Poverty Row studios closing up shop, Zucco had not dithered about his salary. The end of the War had also brought an end to the horror boom. Even the picture Lugosi was making at

Universal was some sort of a comedy. The steady stream of mad scientist roles paying Zucco's rent the last few years had dried up. Always anxious about where his next job was coming from, he was particularly worried now.

Even so, Stone was proving to be a miser worthy of Scrooge. It might be cynical of him to think it, but Zucco wondered if Stone's handling of Stanhope's death wasn't simply the producer being worried about how much such a complication would add to the movie's bottom line.

Knocking at the door drew Zucco away from his dour speculations. "Five minutes Mr. Zucco," a voice called from outside. He could hear the speaker walking across the street and a few moments later heard the faint sound of him knocking at Monique's door.

Zucco sighed and retrieved the wide-brimmed hat that was part of his costume. He couldn't decide if it was supposed to make him look like a pilgrim or a pirate, but he was certain it looked out of place in this western-horror hybrid. Pierce had yet to let him see any of the dailies, so he couldn't be certain his performance was strong enough to offset the ridiculous hat.

"A big step down from Professor Moriarty," Zucco told himself as he looked in the mirror. He smiled as he remembered that role, a hallmark of his career as a heavy in much bigger films. There was some talk about Basil Rathbone doing some kind of Sherlock Holmes radio programme. Maybe Zucco's agent could see if there was a part for him on the show.

"May as well get along with it," Zucco declared. Tucking the hat under his arm, he emerged from the undertaker's and started down the creaky wooden walkway to where they were filming today's scenes. Squinting in the sunlight, Zucco could just make out members of the crew gathered around the rundown barn at the edge of town. The building had been redressed to serve as the Whatley ranch, the walls adorned with cattle skulls, hex signs, and other macabre flourishes. There was even a fog machine that had been dragged up from the studio. After all, no horror picture was really complete without copious amounts of dry-ice floating about.

Pierce spotted Zucco walking towards the set. He motioned to Weaver. The propsmaster hurried over to intercept the actor.

"For this scene, Mr. Pierce wants you to act like you're referencing passages from this," Weaver said. He held out a huge dark-covered book to him.

Zucco started to reach for the volume, then his brow crinkled in surprise. "This isn't the prop we rehearsed with," he said. The book they had used earlier was about the same size, but its leather cover was far rougher and not nearly so dark. Neither did it have the heavy, musty smell of the one he now held. There were small ornaments embedded in the cover, bits of coloured stone and tarnished metal that might have been silver at some point. The prop had been obviously new, the extreme age of this one was equally obvious.

"Mr. Pierce didn't like how the prop looked," Weaver explained. "He wants us to use this one instead." He laughed nervously. "At least until I can get the prop to look good enough to pass it off for the real thing."

Zucco was barely listening. Instead he was concentrating on the book in his hands. The cover wasn't leather, it had a pebbly texture to it that made him think of lizards and reptiles. As if that discovery wasn't eerie enough, when he opened the book he found himself staring at a title page that bore a name with which he had recently become familiar.

"*Necronomicon*," Zucco read. He gave Weaver a puzzled stare. "That is the same book of witchcraft in the story." He looked again at the volume, flipping through the wisp-thin pages. What was written on those pages had been copied by hand, at first a crabbed scrawl and later a cramped script that tended to gradually lift to the right before the end of each line. Leafing further, Zucco found still a third and fourth hand at work. No one man had put those words down. It had been the effort of a team of writers.

"This isn't your prop?" Zucco asked, even though he knew the answer.

"No," Weaver replied. "I'm not sure where it came from,

but Mr. Stone gave it to Mr. Pierce. He thought it would lend an air of authenticity to the film."

"Authenticity," Zucco repeated. He studied the page he had turned to. The words were Latin, but a jumbled kind of Latin that made little sense. There was a diagram as well, a circle with strange glyphs and sigils. "This might be the real thing, the very book that inspired Lovecraft to write his odd little story." He gave Weaver another curious look. "Do you know where Stone got it?"

Weaver shook his head. "*No sir.* And not my place to go asking him either. I'm not so bold as Doug Irons. I can't afford to get fired."

Zucco slowly closed the book. He put it down to imagination, but it felt unclean in his hands. What he wanted to do was throw it to the ground and walk away. Instead he sighed and shook his head. "I can't afford to get fired either, Bill. So I think both of us should try to keep our noses clean."

As Weaver walked away, Pierce came over to speak with Zucco. He nodded at the book. "Ghastly looking thing, isn't it?" the director stated. "Try and be careful with it, George. It looks to be damn old. I really wanted to use a prop, but Weaver didn't get it ready in time."

"I understand this…volume…belongs to Stone," Zucco said.

An uneasy look came into Pierce's eyes. "Yeah…well he doesn't need to know we're using the real McCoy for these scenes. For all he knows, we're fooling around with the prop." He gave Zucco another anxious look. "Not that you should be goofing off with it. Be careful."

"I'll treat it like the family Bible," Zucco vowed. The instant he said the words he felt a shiver run through him. It was hardly the sort of sentiment to be evoking under the circumstances.

Pierce pointed across the way to where the barn stood. The doors were tied shut with heavy ropes and across the frame a large hex sign had been painted. "Now you understand this scene, George. You'll be off to the side near the corral and start reading from the book. That will call up the monster hiding inside the barn."

Zucco looked across at the doors. "Don't I have to undo the ropes so it can come out?"

Pierce smiled at that. "Your daughter will take care of it." He turned around and watched as Monique walked through town towards them. She was wearing the same buckskin costume as before. "See, she's going to have to stretch up to undo those ropes…"

"And when she does her skirt is going to creep up and let the audience gawk at her legs," Zucco said, not quite able to hide a touch of disapproval.

"Have to give the audience something to look at," Pierce stated. "There are two things the posters are promising. One is a monster and the other is a lissome damsel. Well, Stone is too cheap to do the monster so Monique is going to have to make up for it."

The director's statement surprised Zucco. "I understood that Stone had hired this Harryhausen kid to animate a monster."

"He did," Pierce agreed. "Willis O'Brien was too expensive, so Stone hired this guy who makes short subject fairy tales with clay figures. Anyway, the arrangement was to be $500 for each minute of animation. Harryhausen took it and started making his models and everything. Only thing he didn't do was check his contract. It promises $500 for each minute, but doesn't say how much animation Stone is paying for."

"I'm seeing why Stone picked a story about an invisible monster," Zucco groaned.

"Yep, that's exactly what he's planning," Pierce said. "The monster stays invisible until the end. Stone wants ten seconds of animation, and if we need to use more we will have to loop the footage. All Harryhausen gets is the pro-rated cut, $75. He'll be lucky if it pays for the models he's built."

Zucco looked down the street to where Stone's trailer stood. "The kid gets something else out the deal. He learns what it means to deal with men like Stone."

"Just as long as my paycheck doesn't bounce," Pierce said.

He turned back and gestured at the barn again. "So we're going to film all of the scenes where you let the monster out to murder people in town." He pointed across to where Doug Irons and a group of extras in cowboy costumes were idling around. "Once we have those in the can, we'll shoot the last bit where the townsmen have finally had enough. They gun you down as you try to call out the monster one last time." He glanced down again at the book Zucco held. "Just remember not to knock the book around when you fall."

"I'll clasp it my breast and guard it with my dying breath," Zucco swore. He looked aside to where Monique was getting a final application of make-up. She had a strange expression in her eyes, staring at him and the director with a troubled gaze. "Is Harryhausen animating the monster's escape?"

"No," Pierce said. "We're doing it in one take. The crew has rigged up a set of pistons that will slam the doors from behind and throw them open from inside."

Zucco thought he understood why Monique was worried. "That sounds dangerous for your star. The script says she is killed when the monster breaks free. There is such a thing as too much authenticity."

Pierce smiled. "I've already hashed it out with Monique. She's excited and wants to give it a go. There's not much risk. She has more chance getting banged up riding a horse. The pistons only open the doors. It is going to be up to her to sell how hard then hit when they fly open."

"I don't like it," Zucco repeated. "She might have said she was okay doing her own stunt but I rather think she is having second thoughts."

"Then she can talk to Stone about it," Pierce growled. "If they can find a stuntman who will fit into her costume, then they're welcome to swap. In the meantime I have a movie to make." The director turned away from Zucco. Cupping his hand against his mouth, he shouted to the rest of his cast and crew. "Places, everyone! We're starting with Scene 40!"

Zucco marched over to his mark near the edge of the corral facing towards the barn. Slowly, Monique came forwards to join him. She still had that haunted expression in her eyes. He could feel the intensity of her gaze on him.

"It'll be fine," he whispered to her. "Just think about this scene. Worry about the rest when you need to."

She didn't respond. It took Pierce snapping at her to get Monique to recover something of her composure. She was almost sheepish as she assured the director she was ready to shoot the scene.

Zucco held the book in front of him, brandishing it towards the sky the way he'd seen revival preachers hold the Bible aloft. Drawing it back towards him, he leafed through the pages, picking a spot at random and then recited the occult doggerel from Stanhope's script.

"Cut!" Pierce yelled. The director came out from behind the cameras and motioned to Monique. "You're doing it up too much! Tone it down some. Remember, George is supposed to be your father. The way you're looking at him, you'd think he was Tyrone Power!"

"I'm sorry Mr. Pierce," Monique apologized. She gave Zucco an embarrassed smile. "I wasn't concentrating, George."

Zucco wasn't so sure about that. If anything it seemed Monique was concentrating too much, but not on her acting. He glanced down the street, surprised to see a coup parked beside Stone's trailer. A large, heavy-set man was standing there talking with the producer. It was only a suspicion, but he felt the man was a cop come up from Victorville or Hesperia to investigate Stanhope's death.

No wonder Monique was so distracted. Despite her pretensions to the contrary, she didn't have the calloused attitude of an industry veteran. A dead body and a possible murder were not so easily put out of mind. Zucco and the others might be able to forget by throwing themselves into their jobs, but newcomers like Monique were a different story.

"It'll be alright," Zucco promised as he helped Monique back to her mark. When both of them were back in their places, Pierce called for the next take.

Between takes, Zucco was able to watch Stone escort their

visitor around the town. When Becker let them into Stanhope's shack, he was more convinced than ever that the stranger was a police detective. The three of them spent considerable time in the shack, then proceeded to prowl across the town from building to building. The detective was thorough, checking both those buildings being used by the film crew and those that were still derelict.

"Cut!" Pierce called out the command and waved his arms at Zucco and Monique, motioning them both away from the barn. "Okay, Reese, let's see how that contraption of yours is working today."

Connel Resse, the film's stuntmaster, walked over to the small door at the side of the barn. He disappeared into the building's interior. It was a few minutes before he reappeared. "All set, Mr. Pierce."

"Okay, Connel. Let's see how much oomph it has." Pierce kept a keen eye on the stuntmaster as he approached the double doors. At the director's signal, Reese reached up for the ropes. There was a lever hidden behind them that was his real target. Throwing the hidden catch would activate the machinery behind the doors.

What followed happened so fast that Zucco would have missed it if he'd blinked. Reese touched the lever and a loud bang sounded from inside the barn. The heavy door was flung outwards, catapulted by the pistons behind it. The force of the machine nearly ripped it from its hinges. The stuntmaster was a big man, close to three hundred pounds of beer and cheesesteak. The door slammed into him with such momentum that he was thrown back a dozen feet. Reese staggered back, pinwheeling his arms in an effort to stay upright. It was a useless gesture and in a moment he was flat on his back in the dirt. Blood streamed from his nose where the door had smashed into his face. Even from a distance, it was obvious Reese's nose was broken.

Pierce muttered a livid curse under his breath. "Somebody help Connel!"

Zucco put his hand on Monique's shoulder. "You might want to rethink doing your own stuntwork," he suggested.

Monique didn't turn towards the barn as crew rushed over to help Reese. She gave Zucco an intense look. He wondered if his sardonic remark had struck a little too close to home. This was, after all, her first picture.

"They'll get it working right." Zucco pointed to where Pierce was already yelling at Reese's assistants. "They can't let anything happen to you. You're already on all the posters."

Monqiue shook her head. She started to say something, but then her gaze was drawn to the town's main street. Zucco turned and saw that Stone and their visitor were headed towards them. Drawn by the commotion around the barn, Zucco thought.

Stone and his companion made their way to where Pierce was filming. The producer walked in front of the cameras. "That's a wrap for the day." He gestured to the heavy-set man. "This is Sheriff Cameron. He's here to look into Stanhope's death."

"Was it murder?" Doug Irons asked. Stone gave him a black look, but the damage was already done. Barely suppressed fears came bubbling up in a babble of concern that rippled among the cast and crew.

Sheriff Cameron ran his forefinger along the thin moustache he affected. "Stanhope didn't cut himself up like that."

"And it wasn't the work of coyotes," Irons persisted.

"No, not unless the varmints have started carrying around knives," Cameron quipped. His gaze swept across the movie-makers. "Somebody had it in for Stanhope. Somebody who must have hated him a whole lot to do that kind of work." His gaze lingered on Zucco.

Stone waved his hand, trying to ease the mounting alarm. "The sheriff is just speculating. It could have been a drifter, some maniac who is long gone." He turned towards Cameron. "You did say the shack looked like it'd been ransacked. Anybody who knew Stanhope would know he didn't have anything worth stealing."

Cameron tucked his thumbs under his gunbelt. "Maybe yes, maybe no. You Hollywood people are a funny bunch.

Lots of skeletons in your closets. Maybe Stanhope knew where some of the bones were buried."

"So what will you do now, sheriff?" Zucco asked, unsettled by the attention Cameron was showing him.

"I'll start by interviewing each of you, one by one," Cameron said. "Ask a few questions. Find out how things sit around here." A cheerless grin spread across his face. "Somebody around here isn't what he seems. Somebody around here is a murderer." He turned and pointed at Pierce. "Next to Stone, you're the big-shot around here, so we'll start with you. The rest of you can go back to your bunks. I'll send for you when I want you." Again, his gaze lingered on Zucco. The actor felt relieved when Pierce left with Cameron and drew the sheriff's attention away.

Weaver walked over to Zucco as the cast began to leave the set.

"I'll take the book back."

Zucco didn't need to be asked twice.

"Here, and you are welcome to it," Zucco said. He looked back at the barn. "Too bad we didn't finish the shots Pierce wanted. My big sendoff and then you wouldn't have to worry about my dropping the thing when they kill me off."

Weaver nodded and tucked the book under his arm. "Maybe you won't have to worry about that. If I work all night, I think I can have the prop looking as good as the real thing."

Zucco clapped Weaver on the arm. "Then I will leave you to it. I have certainly seen enough of *The Necronomicon* for today."

Zucco watched the propsmaster head off towards the schoolhouse. When he turned around, he found that he wasn't the only one with an interest in Weaver. Monique was observing him with the same kind of fascination she had shown Zucco during filming.

"If you are worrying about the killer, I don't think Weaver is anyone to be worried about," Zucco told her. "I am sure that for once Stone is right. The murderer was some vagabond who is far away now."

Monique suppressed a shudder. "I wish I could believe that." She continued to watch Weaver as she spoke. "It isn't…well I don't think…" She gave Zucco one of her uneasy smiles. "I don't think he's the murderer. I'm worried about him is all. He's been so nice."

"That is a relief to hear," Zucco stated. "You were looking at me the same way earlier. I might play maniacs and murderers in my films, but I'd hate for anyone to think I was serious about it."

Monique smoothed the front of her costume. "I think you are a good man….That is why I am worried about you."

"Don't be," Zucco assured her. "I'm a tough old bird who will put up more of a fight than might be expected." He laid his hand on her shoulder. "And don't go worrying about that man Cameron. Just tell him the truth and you'll have nothing to worry about."

Monique nodded and started to walk away. "Oh, I know that, George," she said as she moved down the street.

Zucco wished he could share Monique's sentiment. The way she'd looked at him could have been chalked up to excessive concern, but Sheriff Cameron's attention had been nothing if not hostile.

Why the lawman should be so antagonistic to Zucco was a riddle he didn't have an answer for. Had Cameron found something in Stanhope's shack that implicated the actor?

"Think that guy is on the level?" Doug Irons asked. The Texan pointed at Cameron.

Zucco hadn't heard the cowboy walk up beside him. When he wanted to, the cowboy could make less noise than a snake sliding across glass. "I'm going to tie a bell around your neck if you keep sneaking around like that," he snapped at Irons.

The cowboy shook his head. "I would have figured somebody making all these horror pictures wouldn't be so jumpy." Irons looked down the street to where Stanhope's shack stood. "Then again, maybe you've got the right idea. Fella can't be too careful with everything happening around here. Now I think…"

"You don't have to think,' Zucco told Irons. "In case you

didn't notice, there's a new sheriff in town. Cameron will get this sorted out in due time."

"You really think so, George?" Irons slapped his hand to the holster hanging from his belt and whipped out the Colt .45. His acting skills might be questionable, but Zucco had to concede the Texan had one of the fastest quick-draws he'd ever seen. "Think Cameron can match that?"

Zucco rolled his eyes. "Do you actually believe all it needs to be a policeman is a fast draw? Surely even in Texas that sort of thing went out with the horse and buggy. A policeman has to use detection and deduction to uncover the culprit. He can't just whip out his gun and start shooting on the off chance he hits the guilty party."

"That's what I'm getting at," Irons explained, ignoring Zucco's acerbic tone. "I've figured out who knocked off Stanhope."

Zucco gave Irons an incredulous stare. "And how did you come by this remarkable discovery?"

"Laugh if you like, but I saw Weaver hanging around Stanhope's shack the night he was murdered." Irons nodded towards the schoolhouse. "He's been slinking around quite a bit and keeping strange hours."

"I dare say you must have been sneaking around a good deal yourself if you've been keeping tabs on Weaver," Zucco pointed out. "Of course, if his hours were odd, then so are yours if you've been watching him."

"Like I said, laugh if you want," Irons said as he started off towards the commissary. "But if you get carved up like a Christmas goose, don't say I didn't warn you."

Zucco watched the cowboy swagger off down the street. He smiled as he considered the fantastic accusation. Bill Weaver had been employed at the studio for almost fifteen years. He was a veteran of the industry and in a town like Hollywood, if there had been anything unsavory in Weaver's habits it would have been picked up by the gossip grapevine a long time ago. The thought that Weaver could be a murdering fiend was absurd.

The smile faded from Zucco's face as he stared more

closely at Irons. Unlike Weaver, Irons was new to Hollywood. What did anyone really know about him aside from his claims to being a rodeo star back in Texas?

If Irons was the killer, then he might be trying to stir up suspicions towards Weaver to divert attention from himself. A bold if not terribly clever ploy.

"Maybe I should speak with Sheriff Cameron about Irons," Zucco mused. He glanced back towards the barn where the crew was tending Reese's broken nose. The stuntmaster wasn't hurt so badly that he was kept from muttering a stream of vulgarities. While a crewman applied plaster to his nose, Reese directed his assistants to reset the door mechanism.

"Then again, maybe I should just concentrate on finishing this picture and getting out of this place as quickly as possible." Zucco looked in the direction of the schoolhouse, then back at Irons. Zucco had been in enough whodunits to know that the murderer was always the person the audience least expected.

"If only real life was so tidy," Zucco grumbled as he walked to the undertaker's parlour.

"Iä Cthulhu!"

Zucco woke with a start, the semi-coherent words still echoing through his room. He pressed his hand to his forehead, surprised to find his brow damp. He looked at the disarray of his bed clothes, the way they were twined about his body. It was apparent that his slumber had been anything but restful.

Snatches of dream lingered at the edge of his awareness. Cloaked figures swarming around sacrificial stones. Crooked knives stabbing down into helpless victims. The book was there, that hoary old volume that purported to be *The Necronomicon*. Through it all there had been that eerie chanting, the invocation Zucco thought he could still hear when he awoke.

He glowered at the tattered pulp magazine which contained Lovecraft's story. Between it and the script, it was small wonder that Zucco's mind was awash with nightmares!

The actor rose from his bed. Through the dusty window he could see the silvery glow of moonlight. He picked up his watch from the table. He was surprised to find it wasn't even midnight. Cameron had only finished questioning him at ten. At best he'd only had an hour of sleep.

Strangely, Zucco didn't feel exhausted. A kind of nervous excitement gripped him. Jumbled thoughts raced through his mind, darting and weaving around, refusing to let him focus on them and make some sense of their pattern.

The dream. Something about that dream. Zucco felt there was a note of warning there, something his conscious mind hadn't recognized.

He looked again at his watch. It was clear to Zucco he wasn't going to get any sleep unless he did something to burn off the excited energy that held sway over him. A walk around the town might help. Certainly the exercise would do him more good than sitting around the ghoulish undertaker's parlour. With first call at seven in the morning, anything that would help him get back to sleep was worth trying.

A few minutes found Zucco dressed and walking down the deserted street. If the old movie set had looked like a real ghost town in daylight, at night the resemblance was complete. Wisps of curtain danced about empty windows, splintered doors creaked in the desert wind. Bats flitted through the air chasing moths. Lizards scurried about the tumbleweeds.

"If Stone wasn't so cheap, Pierce would probably try a night shoot." He started to chuckle when a faint sound struck his ears. He might have dismissed it if not for Stanhope. What he'd heard sounded like a muffled scream.

Taking a firmer hold of his walking stick, Zucco dashed towards the source of the sound. Briefly, he considered turning around and trying to alert the rest of the crew. Becker and Cameron were the only ones with loaded guns, after all. Zucco rejected the idea. Time might be of the essence. Any delay might be enough for a killer to finish his grisly deed.

Another muffled scream spurred Zucco onwards. He pushed his aged frame to the limit, dashing with an urgency he'd not felt in many years. The sounds were coming from the schoolhouse. "Weaver," he hissed under his breath as he rushed into the yard and threw himself up the short flight of steps.

The door was unlocked, swinging open freely as Zucco pressed against it. Moonlight cascaded into the school, revealing before his horrified gaze a scene of carnage even more monstrous than what they'd found in Stanhope's shack.

Weaver was dead. Butchered. He was sprawled across one of the desks, his mouth stuffed with a crude gag. There was a look of utter terror frozen on his face. The rest of him was almost unrecognizable. Great gashes and cuts had been carved into his flesh, his blood strewn all around. Zucco gripped his walking stick tighter, his eyes roving across the room, peering into every shadow for some sign of whoever had done this to the propsmaster.

He saw no trace of anyone and after a time Zucco found his attention drawn back to the body. He stared at the horrible wounds with something more than morbid fascination. There was something about those cuts…

With a shock Zucco realized what it was. *The Necronomicon*! The mutilations were like the weird glyphs he'd seen in the cursed book!

Zucco swung around, looking not at the body or the shadows, but at the rest of the schoolhouse. The place was a shambles. Props and furniture had been tossed about in what appeared to be an exceedingly violent search. At last he spotted something lying on the floor. Something with a dark cover. He started to walk over to it.

"My God! Bill!" The cry came from the entrance to the schoolhouse. Zucco swung around, his stick raised above his head like a club. Standing in the doorway was Pierce. The director's face was ashen, his eyes gaping in horror at Weaver's body.

"He's dead," Zucco declared. "Just like Stanhope." He stared closely at Pierce. There was no blood on his clothes. The terror in the man's face wasn't the kind of thing he'd expect from a murderer who fears capture but rather from someone who expected to be the next victim.

"You know something about this," Zucco accused.

Pierce didn't seem to hear him. He just kept looking at the body. "My God. Bill…"

"He's been more than just killed," Zucco said. "He's been sacrificed in some obscene ritual." He pointed at the battered book lying on the floor. "Something copied out of *The Necronomicon*."

"Nonsense," Pierce mumbled. "It is all ridiculous! Cthulhu and all the rest…so much rot!"

Zucco nodded towards Weaver's body. "Somebody doesn't think so. Somebody believes it. Believes it enough to kill!" His brow knotted with concentration. "Why Weaver though? Why Stanhope?" He glanced around the room. "And what was he looking for?"

A moan of despair rose from Pierce. "*The Necronomicon*," he shuddered. "That is what the killer was looking for. Stanhope was using it to spice up his script. Weaver was using it to make a prop…"

Zucco reached down and retrieved the battered book. It had been savagely mangled, assaulted with a nigh unbelievable fury. It also wasn't *The Necronomicon*. It was the prop Weaver had been working on.

"At least if he has the book, maybe the killing will stop," Zucco muttered, letting the prop fall back to the floor.

"But *The Necronomicon* wasn't here," Pierce said. "Stone learned we'd been using it in your scenes and demanded it back."

"Then whoever did this is still looking for the book," Zucco gasped. "Quick! Rouse everyone, let them know the danger they're in! I'll go and tell Stone!"

Zucco hurried down to Stone's trailer. Behind him he could hear Pierce pounding on doors and alerting the rest of the film crew.

It was too much to hope that the murderer would be content with the atrocity he'd already perpetrated. Zucco had a feeling that Cameron's arrival had brought things to a head.

136

With the sheriff present, the killer wasn't going to stop at half-measures. It was a final brutal ploy to steal the book and slaughter whoever had it in their possession.

There was a dark object lying just outside Stone's trailer. It took Zucco a few moments to recognize it as Becker. The studio cop's head had been smashed in, his face a gory mess. The actor paused over the body and removed the gun from Becker's holster. Tossing aside his stick, he held the snub-nosed pistol at the ready as he pushed open the trailer door.

Stone was laid out on the floor, his mouth stuffed with newspaper and his outstretched limbs tied to the furniture. The producer's chest was bare and already bleeding from a number of vicious cuts. Standing over him was a heavy-set man with a knife and the leering visage of a human gargoyle.

"Drop it!" Zucco snarled at Cameron. The maniac glared at him, but let the knife fall to the floor. "Now your revolver," Zucco demanded, keeping Becker's weapon trained on the supposed sheriff.

Cameron started to comply, but before he had more than started to reach for the revolver the situation was suddenly reversed. Becker's gun fell from his hand as a heavy object smacked against his wrist. Cameron finished his reach for his own weapon, but instead of letting it fall to the floor, he turned it on Zucco.

"Quick thinking of you," Cameron said to his confederate.

Zucco looked to his side and found Monique standing just within the doorway. There was blood all over the dark robe she wore and in her hands was the brandy bottle she'd used to strike Zucco's wrist.

"None of the unbelievers will stand in our way," Monique affirmed. "They will profane the sacred text no longer." She threw down the bottle and folded her arms across her chest, palms outward. "In His house of R'lyeh, dead Cthulhu waits dreaming."

Zucco's mind reeled. Straight out of Lovecraft's crazed fiction! It was insane! One look at Monique and Cameron told him how true that last estimation was.

"It is too bad we cannot make a proper offering of these

two," Cameron stated. He turned and pointed the revolver at Stone. The bark of the gun was almost deafening within the confines of the trailer. Stone jerked in his bonds as the bullet smashed into his skull.

Zucco seized the brief instant before Cameron could turn the revolver back on him. Without warning he threw himself backwards, pitching through the doorway and into the street. He struck the packed dirt and scrambled onto all fours. He knew he had only a second before Cameron came plunging out of the trailer after him. Sure enough, he heard the angry bellow of the madman an instant later.

"Stay down, George!" The cry came from further down the street and was punctuated by a rapid burst of gunfire. Zucco looked up to see Doug Irons fanning his pistol and putting round after round into Cameron's reeling form.

"Iä! Cthulhu!" Cameron shrieked as he crashed down into the street.

Zucco stared at the dead murderer, stunned by the nearness of his own escape. Then he heard a scream rise from inside the trailer. He gestured at the doorway and shouted at Irons and the men with him. "Cameron wasn't alone! Monique was working with him!"

Zucco ducked his head down as a bullet smashed into the street beside him. Monique leapt down from the trailer, Becker's gun in her fist, *The Necronomicon* clenched against her chest. The men further down the street scattered as the crazed woman came running towards them. Irons dove into a doorway, cursing loudly as Monique sent a shot his way.

"After her," Zucco cried out. He took the revolver from Cameron's dead hand and ran after the fleeing woman. Irons and a few others soon fell in with him as they dashed down the street.

"I emptied my gun into Cameron when I saw him aiming at you," Irons stated.

"For which you have my thanks. Everyone should have known better than to think a Texan would carry a gun without bullets."

Irons shook his head. "I felt there was something off about

that sheriff, but how is Monique tangled up with him?"

Zucco felt a shiver course down his spine. "They're both members of the Cthulhu cult. Just like in the script."

"That's insane!" Irons swore.

"Of course it is," Zucco replied. "But that doesn't make it any less real."

The film crew pursued Monique to the very edge of town. Along the way she'd fired a few wild shots at them before casting aside Becker's empty gun. The cultist was now like any hunted thing, wild with the impulse to escape. As her pursuers closed the distance, Monique darted aside and ran towards the barn.

"No! Not that way!" Pierce shouted.

The director's warning had the opposite effect of what he'd intended. Monique hurried straight towards the barn doors. She reached for the ropes that bound them together and gave them a pull.

The next instant the doors exploded outwards, driven by the pistons the effects crew had prepared for the final scene. The mechanism didn't work exactly as planned. Instead of opening the doors, it merely punched gaping holes in them. Slivers of wood were sent spraying in every direction. One especially long splinter drove itself through the book Monique was carrying before stabbing through her chest. Skewered by the jagged splinter, she sagged against the barn in a bloodied heap.

Zucco hurried forwards, arriving in time to hear the dying cultist moan a last invocation to her god. "Iä! Cthulhu!" A stream of blood bubbled up in her throat and Monique collapsed against the building, her mangled body folded almost protectively around *The Necronomicon*.

"Madness!" Pierce wailed as he walked over beside Zucco and stared down at Monique. "Madness," he said again. "They had to know it wasn't real."

"It was real enough to them," Zucco corrected the director. "If Lovecraft based *The Necronomicon* on a real book, perhaps he based the cult of Cthulhu on a real cult."

"But…but you're not saying Cthulhu and all that junk is

real," Irons objected.

Zucco drew the hood of Monique's cloak down over her dead features. "Cthulhu was real enough to her." His eyes focused on the blood-soaked book fixed to the dead woman's chest. "Real enough for her to kill for. Real enough for her to die for."

"Maybe that is what they meant back at the studio," Pierce muttered. "Maybe that is why they call Lovecraft's stories unfilmable."

Screen Time

M.H. Norris

May 15, 1949

Even with the lowering of the blockade a few days earlier, the room Shirley Temple Agar walked into felt divided in more ways than one.

A String Ensemble played the Sleeping Beauty Waltz. Couples danced to the music in a way that made that area seem the least divided in the room.

On her right were groups of tables, each able to seat eight. The centerpieces were made up on a blue flowers that Shirley discovered this afternoon. She wondered if the cornflower would grow well at home. Germany's national flower was really quite beautiful. There seemed to be an invisible line, the front half went to East Berlin and the Soviets, the half closest to Shirley to West Berlin. The line seemed to continue through the dance floor.

"Is everything alright, Mrs. Agar?"

She turned to see Axel Reichleitner, special assistant to the Governing Mayor Ernst Reuter. He handed her a glass and she smiled when she realized it was a Shirley Temple. Chuckling at the drink, she took a sip.

"Quite alright, just enjoying the music and these flowers. Has the Soviet delegation arrived yet?"

"Some of them have. If it weren't for the fact that Governing Mayor Reuter wants to maintain a semi-working relationship with his East Berlin counterpart, I doubt they would have been invited. As you can see, tensions are still high."

"But better since they lowered the blockade?"

"Yes. There are some that believe that someday Berlin, and Germany as a whole, will be united."

"You're not one of them?"

"I don't think it will happen in my lifetime, Mrs. Agar. If it happens, maybe my children or their children will see that day. I merely hope to keep them in a world that's not under the Soviets."

"Mr. Reichleitner?"

Someone pulled him a few feet away and launched into a conversation in German. After a second, he apologized. "I apologize, Mrs. Agar, but I need to attend to an issue elsewhere. I will check on you soon."

"Thank you."

Shirley circled over to the far side of the room heading for the buffet table. Making her way there, she realized she entirely sure what everything on the table was. Taking a plateful regardless, she made her way to one of the empty tables to eat.

Out of her corner of her eye, she saw a curtain-offed area in a side room just off the ballroom. Curtains closed the opening, though two were partially open.

Wandering over, she took a look. Inside the booth were small television screens. But these weren't like the ones she'd seen on a couple of visits to New York, they were a bit smaller, though she suspected that there might be more behind the wall. On that wall beside them were telephones. A small bench took up much of the space in the booth. Faintly, she could hear someone speaking German in the booth on the far end.

"Magnificent devices aren't they?" a middle-aged man said. He stood by the machines. "Dr. Gregor Feulner. It's a pleasure to meet you. "

"A pleasure sir. What am I looking at?"

"Fernsehsprechstellen. One of the greatest triumphs of Germany." Dr. Feulner waved at the booth. "These devices use cables, similar to telephones."

"To do what?"

"Allow us to communicate with video as well as audio."

Shirley stared at the device. "I'm sorry, it does what?"

"For a not-so-modest fee, you can call people and see them while they talk."

"But that's impossible!"

"Not quite, Miss Temple. We are a bit protective on the how. Sadly, this is one of the projects that came to a standstill during the war. Hopefully we can continue to develop it. Before the war, this facility helped doing most of the research for the project. I used to work here. Well, I still do. But it was a more...scientific capacity. Hopefully Governing Mayor Reuter will allow for us to advance with science as we establish West Berlin."

"Wait, you're telling me that this device lets you interact with moving pictures?"

Dr. Fuelner paused. "More, it allows an image of a person to be transported from one location to another almost simultaneously allowing an unprecedented connection between two parties."

"And you want to expand this? Connect more than Germany?"

"That is our goal. Perhaps someday, Miss Temple, these devices will reach all the way to America."

"How can you run cables across the Atlantic Ocean?"

Dr. Fuelner laughed. "I didn't say I had all the answers."

"Fair enough, thank you for telling me about this..." Shirley struggled with the severely unfamiliar word.

"Fernsehsprechstellen."

"Yes, that."

"Dr. Feulner!"

Both Shirley and Dr. Fuelner turned to see Axel Reichleitner rushing into the annexed room. "Dr. Fuelner! You need to come quickly. There's been a robbery in the laboratories downstairs."

The discreet exit of the various dignitaries didn't go completely unnoticed. From where she sat, she watched people gossiping like school girls in the movies. Soviets were glaring at the East Berlin guests and vice versa. The string quartet continued, this time playing something upbeat she didn't recognize

Taking a sip of her drink but almost choked on it when she

felt something move by her feet. Peering under the table, she found herself face to face with a little girl who couldn't have been older than six.

"And who are you?"

The girl peered back out at her, her blue eyes filled with tears.

Shirley patted the chair next to her, slowly coaxing the girl out. "What's wrong?"

"I can't find Papa." The little girl sniffled. "He was there and there were people and then he was gone and I can't find him."

Shirley took the little girl into her lap, comforting her. "What's your name?"

"Larissa."

"Well, Larissa. I'm Shirley. Can I help you find your Papa?"

Wide eyes nodded at her.

Sitting the girl back on the floor, she took her hand. "What do you think of the party?"

"It was fun, until I lost Papa. He even danced with me for a bit." Larissa gave her a small smile.

Shirley wandered towards the main entrance, taking care not to let go of the little girl's hand. Picking the girl up, she scanned the room. "Do you see him?"

Larissa shook her head, her sniffling starting up again. "No."

"Shhh, there there. We'll find him. Does your Papa work here?"

"Yes, ma'am."

"Do you know where his office is?" Shirley smiled at the little girl, trying to life her spirits.

Her question earned her a nod.

"Can you take me there?"

Another nod.

Shirley took Larissa's hand, letting her lead her out of the ballroom and down one of the halls. The sounds from the party faded as they wandered deeper into the facility. After a couple of turns, the little girl stopped in front of a door, opening it and going inside.

Fresh tears formed and Shirley stepped in to find an empty office—no sign of Larissa's father.

"We'll find him." Shirley turned to head back towards the party, and perhaps to find someone who knew the small girl when she heard someone coming down the hall.

"Du hast gesagt, du würdest die Dokumente heute Abend bekommen."

A second voice, another man, answered him. "Ich konnte sie nicht aus dem Gebäude holen. Mit dieser Gala ist die Sicherheit der amerikanischen Schauspielerin hier enger. Ich bezweifle, dass sie finden werden, wo ich sie getroffen habe und ich kann morgen gehen und sie rausschmuggeln."

The two were coming closer, Shirley didn't recognize either voice nor did she understand German. Shutting the door most of the way, she turned to see that Larissa playing with a doll she must have left in the office.

She paused, looking at the gramophone on a table near the window. "Papa got us a gramophone!"

"Mach es heute Nacht. Stalin möchte sofort mit dem Projekt beginnen. Tun Sie dies für uns und Ihre Tochter wird alle Chancen haben, die unsere Welt bieten wird. Selbst mit dem Fall von Berlin wird sie umsonst sein."

One set of footprints seemed to stop outside the door, the other continued down the hallway. Shirley turned to Larissa, ready to return to the party when the door opened behind her.

"Miss Temple?"

"Papa!"

Larissa ran into the arms of the man. He quickly picked her up.

"Larissa!" The rest of the sentence was in German. Larissa answered him in German and the talked for a minute exchange before the man turned to Shirley.

"Thank you for taking care of Larissa. Frederich Vogel." He held out his hand.

"Shirley Temple Agar."

"I have to say, my late wife was a fan of your films."

"I'm sorry for your loss."

"It's been a couple of years and at times it's hard. A business associate pulled me to the side to ask me a question and when I turned back, I was frantic. I came here to grab a picture, security would ask for it."

"Shall we head back to the party?" He smiled at his daughter. "Would you like another dance?"

She giggled and nodded. The trio made their way into the hallway and headed back into the ballroom.

"Thank you again, Mrs. Agar for helping my little girl."

"My pleasure. She's a sweetie."

They entered the ballroom and a man crossed from the Soviet side of the room to meet them near the door. "What is the meaning of this, Frederich? I knew I should have fought for those plans before you let the disappear."

"I did no such thing, Frank." Frederich turned to Shirley. "I apologize for my former colleague's attitude. This is Dr. Frank Pohl, he was my partner on the project until he left to join his comrades in East Berlin."

"I went where I would have the most success, where those plans are most valuable."

"Those plans are more valuable helping bring Germany back to where it was on the world stage before this war tore us apart."

"It was a pleasure to meet you, Miss Temple." Dr. Pohl shook her hand. "I must go and salvage what I can of my research."

"It's not your research anymore." Frederich called after him. As he walked away, Shirley couldn't help but feel like his voice sounded familiar.

There was a slight break in the music not long after Shirley returned to the ballroom. Dignitaries from both West Berlin and the Soviet-occupied East Berlin were introduced as well as scientists from the facility.

"It is our honor that the great Shirley Temple came to join us to celebrate this momentous occasion. Miss Temple, would you like to say a few words?"

Shirley stepped up to the microphone, smiling at the

applause she received. "I want to thank all of you for the warm welcome I have received during my first visit to your beautiful country. It is an honor and a privilege to be able to join with you tonight and celebrate." She looked at the room, standing on the Soviet side of it for the first time, something she would be perfectly content to not do for the rest of the night. "West Berlin, may you enjoy your new-found freedom. In America, we often take such things for granted, but you have earned it. Both of our countries lost too many lives in this war. Now we all have to rebuild. May your rebuilding go smoothly as you embrace the freedom you now have, and your place in our hearts."

Towards the back of the room she saw Larissa and her father. As she finished statement, a couple of people came and led them away. Smiling and waving as she left the stage, she made her way to the back of the room, pausing to talk with some people who stopped her.

When she made it to the back of the ballroom, she stepped out into the hall to see several four officers talking to Frederich Vogel. It seemed like there were a mix of them, judging by the emblems they wore on their uniforms.

"I'm afraid I don't know what you're talking about, officer. I stepped away to talk with a colleague and went to my office but I've been at the party the whole time. What research was stolen?"

"Fernsehsprechstellen relay plans."

Shirley stayed out of sight, curiosity getting the better of her.

"Frederich, we're just trying to get to the bottom of this." Axel Reichleitner spoke up. "Governing Mayor Reuter wants West Berlin to resume its rightful place and lead in innovation. Those plans are supposed to help us."

"Axel, I'll help with the investigation, but I don't know where the plans are."

"The police have to hold everyone involved until we figure out who did that. Is there someone you can call to take care of Larissa while we sort this out?"

Walking away from them, Shirley made her way

downstairs, eyeing the hallway where the police were gathered. Telling herself it wasn't her job to look into this, she tried to walk away but Larissa's teary eyes came to mind and at least looking into a bit might help her sleep tonight.

Rule out Frederich Vogel and call it a day.

The lab in question was one floor down and on the opposite side of the building from where the party was being held. Considering she was just down the hall with the police investigating, she could easily assume someone could get to the lab to commit the robbery.

Getting into the lab, that was another story.

Shirley went back down the hall but searched for another staircase. The one she'd come from led directly to the main lobby. If the robbery occurred during the gala upstairs, whoever did it would know the building well enough to know a second way out.

After a series of turns, Shirley found another staircase and took it, going upstairs she found herself in a hall, the gala sounded close. Walking one way, she opened the door to find the video booths. The third booth was now empty, she ducked her head in out of curiosity.

This way couldn't be used either. The only way out was right through the ballroom.

She ducked back into the hallway, wondering where else it led when she heard footsteps. She rounded a corner and almost ran into Dr. Frank Pohl who looked as surprised to see her as she felt.

"Dr. Pohl, did you get turned around as well?"

"No, I knew of this short cut to the kitchens. I used to sneak out back to get some fresh air when I needed to think. I wanted to thank the chef for the magnificent food they provided."

"It was quite nice."

Perhaps she should go pay her respects to the chef as well.

Wandering back into the ballroom, she saw Dr. Fuelner sitting at a table, filling out paperwork.

"Dr. Fuelner?"

"Ah, Miss Temple. I'm sorry our conversation ended as abruptly as it did."

"It's quite alright, you had other things to worry about. I was wondering if you had time for a quick question, though."

"I can make a minute."

Shirley took a seat next to him. "Why is this device so important? Frederich Vogel and Frank Pohl just fought over it. If Frederich's daughter wasn't there, I'm fairly certain they might have taken it further."

"What you have to understand, Miss Temple is that this project means a lot to not just Germany but possibly to the world."

"How so?"

"Your husband and daughter are both back in America, correct?"

"Correct."

"What is you could talk to them? See your daughter— Linda isn't it?"

"Yes."

"It would make travelling for your work a lot easier, wouldn't it?"

"It would."

"And that's just on the personal side." Dr. Fuelner stopped a waiter who was walking by and grabbed two glasses, handing one to Shirley. "Imagine what this war would have been like if Adolf Hitler had been able to contact the Axis Powers, see what the front lines were seeing instantaneously. What if Stalin could do it today? Telegraphs, radio reports, and telephone calls can only do so much. This adds a new layer. Even beyond video. It's high-capacity information exchange. You could send photographs of a document, or pass information across the world faster than a phone call."

Shirley took a long sip of her drink. "The Soviets want it."

"The only reason Hitler didn't use it is because it was too expensive and time consuming to lay the fiber optic cables. It was shoved to the side. Part of me wonders if he didn't see the potential as the Fernsehsprechstellen couldn't have changed the way this war was fought. It could change the way the

Soviets communicate with all of their holdings. It could make it better, faster, easier, more effective."

"It could help them spread, cover more ground..."

"Exactly, Miss Temple."

Shirley learned at a young age that sometimes one didn't have time to eat when you were out and about mingling with people at movie premieres. She remembered one of her co-stars taking her into the kitchen so that she could get a bite to eat.

Over the years, she could be found in the kitchens at various events. After being stopped a handful of times to talk, she slipped back and into the kitchen to get a moment of peace.

Someone yelled out something in German as a waiter walked by Shirley, their tray full of cake. "Can I?"

The waiter nodded and Shirley took a piece and an offered fork. Taking a few bites, she closed her eyes in satisfaction. She wandered off to the side, near where a boy washed dishes and took in the scene.

"Is everything okay, Miss Temple?" A woman came up to her.

"It's fine. I'm hiding in here to have some of this amazing chocolate cake." She took another bite to prove her point.

"Alright." The woman smiled. "You are not the first to hide in here."

"Oh?"

"One of the scientist's little girls hid in here. Took her dad ages to find her."

"You must mean Larissa. We met earlier."

"Sweet girl. She hid in the dishes. I thought her father was going to crawl in there with her." The woman laughed. "Stay as long as you need to and let us know if you need anything, Miss Temple."

"Thank you." Shirley finished her cake before handing it to the boy doing dishes, the stack beside him quite large. Yet, the rack where they kept them looked like it was full. She walked over, chuckling at the idea of the girl hiding in a dish rack when she noticed that the dishes had been pushed to the front of the shelves.

Peering behind, she was surprised to see that the shelf wasn't empty like she expected. Sitting behind a couple of rows of dishes was a briefcase.

Axel Reichleitner followed her into the kitchen and to the dish area and she pointed out the briefcase, slightly relieved it was still there and she wasn't crazy. Axel grabbed the briefcase and laid it on the counter.

"How did you find it?"

"One of the chefs told me how Frederich Vogel's daughter Larissa hid in here and her father got her out. It looked weird with all of the dishes towards the front of the shelf considering there are some on the table outside, a pile over at the prep station for dessert and yet another stack at the dishwasher's station.

"Alright there, Nancy Drew."

"That's Bonita."

Axel tried to get the case open. "It's locked."

"Combination or key?"

"Combination. Let's take it to the police and let them investigate. What made you look here?"

Shirley went to a door in the corner she'd seen earlier and pushed it open. Just as she'd suspected, it lead to the back hallway she'd been in earlier. "I ended up downstairs by accident and got lost and ended up in this hallway. Another door is to the room with the video booths and that leads to the ballroom. I also may have read a bit too much of Sir Conan Doyle's work."

Axel laughed at that. "Fair enough."

"Plus, I could get some quiet in here to eat chocolate cake."

They entered the lobby, an older woman joined Larissa and her father. When the little girl saw them, her face lit up and she ran up to Shirley. "Shirley! My Oma is here!"

"Oma?"

"Grandmother." The older woman smiled. "It's a pleasure to meet you, Miss Temple. My son tells me you helped my granddaughter out today."

"It was my pleasure."

"Herr Reichleitner? Why do you have Papa's briefcase?"

"Your father misplaced it and Miss Temple found it. Frederich, if you wouldn't mind opening this."

"It's just some papers. I must have set it down when we were playing hide and seek in the kitchens."

The lingering officers moved to join the group.

"Frederich, open the briefcase."

Shirley stood towards the back of the room, watching the party continue as if nothing happened. She sipped on a drink, not quite in the mood for a party anymore.

Eyeing the booths, she saw Axel exit one, and she approached him. "The Steward said they cost money. Who monitors that?"

"We have a switchboard, just like the telephones."

Shirley looked at the booth. "Could they tell us who is in that third booth during the time of the robbery?"

"Is it relevant?"

"It could be."

"I can put a request in. Why does this matter to you so much?"

"Larissa. It's just rubbed me the wrong way since I saw how her father reacted when he found her. To think he would risk losing her like this? What makes a man betray everything he knows and loves?"

"I'm sure it will be revealed in the coming days."

"I'd just sleep better tonight if I knew why."

Shirley wasn't actually sure if that was the case. Nor did she know why she was letting herself get so invested in this. But some small part of her hoped that maybe she could make a difference during her time at this German gala.

And that one little girl didn't lose her father if she didn't have to.

The party wound down and Shirley was exhausted. Looking around, she searched for Axel, hoping to arrange her car back to her hotel for the night. Larissa went home with her Oma a couple of hours previously and at this point, the string quartet and some of the scientists remained, the latter pouring over something at one of the tables.

She wanted to know the cornflower's secret to not wilting because she was dangerously close to doing so.

"Mrs. Agar."

Axel came over to her, several papers in the air, his face grim. "There's a call for you."

Shirley's heart raced, if John was calling her across the Atlantic, something must have happened. Not many people knew about her trip to Berlin, a result of this trip coming together at the last minute. She headed towards the lobby, taking a few deep breaths.

"Not that phone."

She turned to see Axel standing by the doorway that led to the video booths, she'd given up trying to pronounce their name. He nodded to the first one and she walked in to see a woman looking at her. The woman smiled from the screen waving at her, the motion causing her image to freeze slightly before resuming normal pace.

Shirley looked around, she was in a curtained room, a screen in front of her with the girl who continued to smile.

The woman couldn't be much older than her and a wide smile grew on the girl's face as Shirley picked up the receiver.

"Miss Temple, can I just say that I'm a huge admirer of your work? My mother used to take me to the cinema to see your films."

Shirley chuckled. Here this girl was talking to her about her films when Shirley was basically interacting with a film. Unlike her films where the same lines were said every time it was played, this changed with whoever was on each end.

She was interacting with a moving picture. A real live person.

Shaking off her bewildered thoughts, she turned back to the matter at hand. "Thank you. Mr. Reichleitner mentioned you wanted to share something with me?"

"Yes." She straightened some papers in front of her, her image freezing slightly and then suddenly moving faster for a second before returning to normal. "There have been six calls from the booths there tonight. The longest was the call in question. It was placed between Dr. Frederich Vogel and someone on the other side of Berlin, to the Wolff residence."

"East or West Berlin?"

"East."

"What happened?"

"He placed the call and I monitored it, seeing how long it lasted, they went back and forth, primarily a Kurt Wolff talking. After about ten minutes, they hung up."

"It was him on the call."

"It was. They were talking about the advancements made recently on the Fernsehsprechstellen system. After the first few minutes. I stopped paying attention to the video feed because the audio was giving me so many problems."

"Problems?"

"Dr. Vogel's audio was loud, and it popped and crackled almost constantly."

Shirley paused, a statement from earlier coming to mind. "Thank you for your help, and for helping me have my first conversation on one of these. I still can't completely wrap my mind around them."

"I think they're brilliant. Could you imagine chatting like this with people around the world? The potential there?"

"Perhaps someday it will happen. Thank you for your time."

"Of course."

The screen went blank and Shirley sat there for a second, holding the receiver.

"What did you learn?"

"I have a feeling you already know, Mr. Reichleitner." She took a seat at one of the tables with a sigh. Part of her felt like she betrayed Larissa, part of her knew there was nothing she could have done, after all, she wasn't the one to betray her daughter and her country.

154

"Miss Temple?" She looked up to see one of the officers holding some papers. "I need to take your statement."

"Of course."

"What happened here tonight?"

She stared at the man for a second. "I was talking with Dr. Fuelner when Axel Reichleitner came and told him about the robbery. I stayed in the ballroom until I ran into Larrisa Vogel who was hiding under a table. Her father had gone to take a call in one of the motion picture booths. I'm sorry I struggle to pronounce its proper name."

"That's quite alright, continue."

"We went down to her father's office…" Shirley paused, making a connection she hadn't earlier. "I heard Dr. Vogel talking with Dr. Pohl. Unfortunately, it was in German and my understanding of your language isn't great, so I cannot tell you what they were discussing."

"Are you sure he was talking with Dr. Pohl?" Axel came over.

"Fairly certain."

"Because Dr. Pohl works for Dr. Yohannes Wolffe."

"Dr. Vogel was talking to someone at the Wolffe residence."

"He came into the office, mentioned that Larissa wandered off while he was in a conversation. We rejoined the party where I met Dr. Pohl. I saw Dr. Vogel get accused and all I could think about was little Larissa. Her mom was a fan of my pictures and if she loses her father, well she has her grandmother but no little girl should grow up without a father. So I poked around. Found the hidden back hallway that connects the moving picture booths to the kitchens to a stairwell that can lead to the lab. What I'm still trying to figure out is the why."

"I can help with that, Miss Temple." Dr. Fuelner walked into the room carrying a file folder police following him. "There was a locked drawer, Dr. Vogel gave us the key after we convinced him cooperating was in his best interest. In there, we found this agreement."

He handed it to her and after looking at it, she looked back up. "For those of us who can't read German?"

"The Soviets promised him a position of power in their research centers in Moscow. In exchange for the plans to the Fernsehsprechstellen as well as his expertise, he and Larissa would be kept safe when they retook West Berlin."

Shirley scoffed at that. "If it were not for the facts that he sold the secrets to the Soviets, I would perhaps feel some sympathy. As it stands, he knew how important these plans could be to establishing free Berlin's place in this world, for restoring their reputation on the world stage? To sell those for the promise - a probably fake promise I might add - of comfort in safety in a regime that may or may not have happened. He gave up his freedom—and he's depriving an innocent girl of her father for what?"

"There's still the matter of Dr. Vogel claiming he was on a call."

Shirley nodded. "The switchboard operator confirmed that. She did also say something interesting though. The audio as loud with a lot of pops and crackles. Officer, if you go down to Dr. Vogel's office, I believe you'll find a gramophone that wasn't there earlier today."

MAY, 1999

Shirley Temple Black walked along where the Berlin Wall stood just ten years previously. Before that, it had been both a barricade and a war zone. Slowly but surely, Berlin was becoming the city its residents remembered from before the war.

"Shirley!"

She turned to see a middle aged woman walking briskly towards her, a wide smile on her face. Larissa hadn't needed a fake promise to succeed in this world and Shirley was proud to say she'd paid for this woman to go to college and go into science, just like her father. Shirley's smile widened as she saw that Larissa Vogel-Schmidt brought a couple of her grandchildren with her.

Larissa approached and Shirley hugged the woman. "Hello, Larissa."

One of the grandchildren walked up, a small bouquet of cornflowers in his hand. He held it up before retreating behind Larissa. "Thank you, young man. You know, I met your grandmother when she was about your age. Just a few miles from here."

Errol Flynn starring in...

GHOSTS DON'T LEAVE FOOTPRINTS

William J. Martin

There was a girl in Mr. Flynn's dressing room. This was not an unusual occurrence, nor was it something that Mr. Flynn tended to complain about. Some would argue it was an unspoken perk of a job like this. Unexpected, gratuitous adoration was rarely worth turning down. It didn't hurt that most of the girls that came to see him also happened to be stunningly beautiful.

A wry smile. She didn't seem to have noticed him yet, and he never missed the chance for a grand entrance. He crossed the threshold, clearing his throat.

"Forgive my intrusion." The smile shifted into a wide, mischievous smirk. "But I'm afraid I'm something of a regular when it comes to that seat."

Before his second word, she was up, spinning on her heel, grabbing the back of the chair. She stared—eyes wide, mouth agape.

"Y-yes…" Eyelids flickered as she glanced down at the floor. "You're here. Thank goodness!"

With a few clicks of her heels, she reached the door. Holding it ajar, she cast a furtive glance out into the corridor. The door snapped shut. She held herself against it.

"Well, you certainly have made yourself at home. Although I must admit I like to at least know somebody's name before we move in together."

"Ah. Yes. Excuse me…I'm afraid it's frightfully important that I speak with you, Mr. Flynn." He was fixed with a firm, blazing stare. "I have something terribly important to tell you."

"Oh?"

"I'm afraid that I have reason to believe your life is in danger."

He almost laughed.

"Yes, now, I'm sure you probably think I'm insane. To be perfectly honest, I would likely feel the same. But I swear, there will be at least one attempt on your life. Soon."

"Oh, yes, naturally."

"Mr. Flynn, I swear!"

"Of course, of course. And do you have any pieces of helpful advice for this supposed threat I'm going to be dealing with?"

She paused, biting her lip. "I'm afraid I can't…"

He reached for his coat and fedora.

The girl jerked forward, taking hold of his hands.

"You can't tell me you don't see it! This film! There's something wrong with this film! Tell me you don't find it odd that all your co-stars—Brenda Marshall, Ralph Bellamy, all of them!—tell me you don't find it odd they've all been taken off of the production! Tell me you've heard of any of their replacements! Please, Mr. Flynn! Tell me! You aren't even the only one in danger! I'm putting myself into it just to tell you this! I'm risking my life! Please, just—"

"Yes, yes, and I'm sure that now we've all been saved from the madness of Jack Warner's business management." Finishing with his coat, and with his hat waiting in his hands, he opened the door. With his other arm he outstretched his hand, only to let it swing over until it pointed through the empty doorway. "No doubt thanks to your timely intervention."

They barely made it out of the room before Mr. Flynn collided with a small man. He had been waiting on the other side.

"Oh, ah, good evening, Mr. Flynn!" The young man beamed, nodding toward the girl. "I wasn't getting in the middle of something now, was I?"

"No, there's nothing the matter, George, don't worry." He held out his hand, urging him away. "This young lady and I had just about finished our business, wouldn't you agree?"

Her hands tightened into fists.

"Well, Mr. Flynn," George continued, "I've just been sent

down here to tell you that some of the boys have organised something of a party. I know Mr. Isaacs is already on his way over there."

"Ah, and we should never keep our fearless director waiting now, should we, George?" A flash of teeth, followed by a strained sigh. "Yes. Yes, I'll be right there. Just lend me a moment."

With an eager nod, George headed off down the hallway. Mr. Flynn turned back to the girl.

"Now then, as for you."

"Mr. Flynn, you can't—"

Eyes closed. A deep breath, fingers moving to grip the bridge of his nose.

"Miss, I'm rather afraid that I'm not going to lock myself into my apartment until I'm free of this…danger that you're so concerned about." He patted himself down, producing a small notepad and pen. He quickly signed his name, ripping off the page and handing it to her. "There. Now you've got something to show for your time. Now please, if you'll excuse me…"

He strode down the hallway, adjusting his jacket. The girl stood back, forlorn. She crumpled the paper in her fist. Then after a moment, she sighed, and straightened it back out. Now neatly folding the autograph, she tucked it into her bra, turned, and ran in the opposite direction.

Two figures stood at the corner of a hallway. Their backs touched the walls, yet neither one could see their counterpart. This would not be the first time they would meet in this location, nor would it be the last.

"Is he moving?"

"Almost. The Green Light was going to make contact as I left him."

"Good. You know I don't like leaving it until this late."

"It was necessary. The Blood Captain demanded that we allowed him to continue with his work as long as possible."

"The Blood Captain is an excitable child. We all know he shouldn't have been give the position he—"

"Watch yourself, Prince. You know how words can

sometimes carry in these corridors."

"Yes, Pauper. I…apologize."

"As you should. Now, be about your business. We cannot allow ourselves any missteps this close to the Hooded Hours."

"Yes, Pauper. Give way, little man."

"Only to a better man than myself."

Soundlessly, they were away.

"Say, Bart!"

A young boy perked up, grinning at the sight of who was calling for him. "Yes, Mr. Flynn?"

"Head down to the garage, I'm going to need a lift rather soon."

"Sure thing, Mr. Flynn!"

"Oh—say, Bart?"

A different voice. The young boy halted in his tracks. His smile wavered slightly. He felt George's hand on his shoulder as the two men caught up with him.

"Make sure Mr. Flynn gets to his party on time, understand?"

Shaking off the man's hand, Bart nodded, and dashed off.

"You know how it is." George's grin somehow managed to get even wider. "They always end up managing to get the slowest drivers, and always when you really need to be somewhere."

The two men left the building. In the harsh evening, the lots appeared to be coated with rust.

"I find that they seem to do a decent enough job on their own, personally."

"Well, Mr. Flynn, you have a fair bit more experience than I do."

"Not to worry, George, we were all a rising star at one point or another." They paused at the curb, a short, black car pulling up in front of them, and Mr. Flynn moved to open the back door. "Now, let's see if old Gerry Isaacs can stop fawning all over me when he isn't being paid to."

"Oh, no, Mr. Flynn, I—" Protesting hands urged him away. "I've still got a bit of work to do back in the lot. I'll be along in a little while. Please, don't worry about me, I'm just happy to be giving you the message."

"Suit yourself, old man." With a farewell tip of his hat, he pulled the door closed. "Take me home, would you, driver?"

The car pulled away. Only a few minutes later, it was invisible amongst its fellows.

"Who knows? Perhaps the people from the Northampton Rep have finally grown a bit of backbone."

His mind drifted, eyes glazing over as he became consumed by his own thoughts. The studio car continued on. When he returned to his senses, the buildings that passed them by were unfamiliar. A quick glimpse through the window, and it was clear they were heading out of town.

"Driver?" He leaned forward, not quite tapping the man's shoulder. "You do happen to know where you're going now, don't you?"

The driver didn't answer. Mr. Flynn kept his position, leaned forward, expecting an answer.

"I say, driver?"

The tiniest movement caught Mr. Flynn's eye: the driver's hands tightening on the wheel.

"Driver…" His voice carried a wary edge as he shuffled across to the opposite seat, hoping to catch the man's eye. "There's nothing wrong is—*Woah*!"

The driver slammed his foot down on the accelerator. The car jolted. Mr. Flynn regained his balance, gripping the front seat as he leaned forward.

"Are you alright, man? You seem to be trying to get the pair of us killed!"

The driver still didn't respond, still staring dead ahead as they careened through the streets. His neck glistened with sweat as he stared forward, too nervous to focus on anything besides reaching his destination as fast as possible. A commendable trait, in other circumstances.

Mr. Flynn looked about the cabin, weighing his options. He tried the door, only to find it locked. The windows seemed to be jammed shut. A quick reach across the back seat returned the same result. He looked down to the footwells for anything that may be useful, cursing as he found them empty. He looked up, before having to blink in surprise as he saw…

A horse.

Pulling up beside the car.

"Mr. Flynn!"

He looked up at the horse's rider, only to see…that girl!

She flicked her hand upward, urging Mr. Flynn to join her. Without a thought, he leaned back, lying across the car seat. Shoes slammed against glass. A few heavy kicks, and the window shattered outward.

With a bounding leap, he launched himself up, out of the window. His arms wrapped around the girl just as she flicked the reins. The horse galloped.

The car's engine snarled. It turned into the next lane. Launching forward, it began to charge its target.

"I must say, I'm not exactly used to being on this side of the situation."

"I'm afraid that I'm not exactly used to being in this situation at all, Mr. Flynn. Something of—of an impulse, really!"

The harsh growl of the engine echoed through the street. The girl leaned forward, legs tightening.

Hooves clattered against tarmac as they began to cross the intersection.

All around them, tires screeched. Swerving cars ground to a halt.

They hadn't made it halfway across. The first crunch of metal. Glass shattered. Rubber screeched.

A cacophony as they reached the intersection's far side.

The studio car crashed through the snarl. Its body crumpled as it battered its way between cars.

"You don't happen to have any more of those impulses on hand, do you?"

Desperate glances scanned the road. Tightly packed buildings hemmed them in. Ahead of them, cars began to slow, lining up at the next intersection, blocking their path.

The girl tightened her grip on the horse. Mr. Flynn tightened his grip on the girl. The ravenous roar of the studio car tightened its grip on their breath.

Flynn looked back. The body of the car was crooked. The passenger door collapsed inward, the window shattered. The hood distorted, half of it bent upward. The engine, laid bare, popped with spluttering, sparking flames.

Ahead, a flash of green caught her eye.

"There!"

She pointed out toward the edge of the block. Far ahead of them, at the point where the buildings fell away, lay a park. Narrow, tree-lined paths weaved through the grounds. The problem: the park was protected by a sturdy, metal fence. They only caught a glimpse before the approaching cars of the opposite lane began to pass in front of it.

With a quick tug of the reins, the horse swerved into the oncoming lane. The rush of cars engulfed them. Screeching tires and panicked horns.

Any space that presented itself, any time a car moved forward faster than the rest, they moved in. Grinding, the studio car followed.

Headlights flashed as a car almost crashed into them. With a fierce screech, the horse reared back. It kicked out. The scream of rubber. A burst of air—the car swerved around them.

The horse turned. The park was still a hundred feet away. They stumbled forward, moving sideways across the road. A car flew past them, and they leapt into the space behind it.

Further along the road, Lights changed. The flow of cars began to dwindle. The studio car smashed through the dying squall. A sedan was knocked aside, pinwheeling out of control as the studio car barged past. An empty stretch of road was all that lay between it and its target. It charged.

The horse's hooves were inches away from grazing the bumper. Just as the studio car gave a final, triumphant roar, they swerved to the side. They galloped back across the lane. Another car passed behind, the horse's tail brushing against the edge of the windshield.

The park stretched out beside them. One last burst of speed, hurried them toward the fence.

The horse reared up.

It leapt.

They were almost weightless.

With a soft crunch, they came to land on the grass.

The studio car careened through the park fence, the windshield shattering. Behind them came the searing, grinding crack of twisting metal. Wrought iron scraped against the paint, long fingers of silver rending the remains of the hood.

Through sheer momentum, the car continued onward. For a few feet.

Black smoke sept up through the hood.

Through the cracked windshield, Mr. Flynn could make out his driver. He slumped against the fractured glass. Blood wept from his forehead.

Cold, white electricity lit the streets by the time they came to a final stop. Mr. Flynn climbed down from the horse, before reaching to help the girl do the same. Above them loomed the towering citadel of the Hollywood Roosevelt.

"Now that's something I'm far more familiar with."

The pair of them worked to catch their breath.

The girl shared in his laugh for a moment, before leading the horse away. The main entrance to the hotel drew closer, and they caught the sight of a rather bemused usher.

"M—Mr. Flynn!" He scrambled to attention.

"Evening, my good man." He thrust the reins into the usher's hand. "You couldn't find a decent spot for my friend here? I want him well-fed and ready for me to pick him up tomorrow."

"You do…?"

"I wouldn't expect anything less. If he isn't in tip-top condition tomorrow morning, I'll see to it that your employers have a new opening. Now then…"

They hadn't even reached the door before he lost interest.

"Any chance you could tell me where you got that horse?" A slight melodic lilt in his tone. "Or, for that matter, why we just happened to be chased across town after my driver suddenly ended up possessed? Actually, for starters, how about you give me something to call you?"

"Lilian. Lilian Hartford. Lil." Even as he directed them toward the front desk, fighting through the bustling lobby, she was already prepared. "This way, Mr. Flynn."

Effortlessly striding through the room toward the hushed interior corridors, they moved through a maze of doors and stairs. Occasionally they came across a lone bellhop, but otherwise, they were alone.

Reaching for his hat, he found that he had lost it sometime during the chase.

The main room of Lil's suite was a sumptuous lounge. Openings in the walls lead to a master bedroom, along with a dedicated dining room. Instead of doors, enormous, shimmering silver curtains hung on either side of each entrance. Creamy-white walls ended with a dark, wood-panelled floor. Two sofas faced each other. A coffee table, made from a block of solid glass, stood between them.

Lil quickly lit the main room, before attending to the wet bar tucked away in one of the walls.

"Make yourself at home, please. You know, they say I came up with a new type of rum in this place. In a bathtub down the back of the barbershop downstairs. Though this completely disregards the fact that a man creating his own strain of drink should have the good sense to do it in the privacy of *his own* bathtub."

Lil returned with a pair of warm whiskeys. Handing one of the glasses off to him, she took a seat opposite. She took a long sip from her own glass. Her eyes squeezed closed for a moment as she swallowed. A deep breath, and she opened them again.

"I'm afraid that I wasn't completely honest with you this morning, Mr. Flynn."

"I find that all too easy to believe."

"The men that are after you right now, are working under the orders of my father."

His eyes narrowed, head tilting as a narrow frown crossed his face.

"I really had no idea it would go this far. Father always seemed somewhat involved with his interests, although never to this extent…Father has been the chairman of a fan club—one of your fan clubs, in fact—for a number of years. I, too, share something of a fondness for your work, as you might have guessed, Mr. Flynn. Although I must say I was never really one for clubs of that sort."

"I'm flattered, although I'm not sure how that extends to kidnap and murder."

"Exactly how it got to this point, I'm not sure. After all, I was under the impression that Father's weekly meetings were purely innocent social gatherings. I'm sure I'd still believe that to this day if I hadn't seen—

"Just a few weeks ago, no more than two or three months. That's when I saw it. I was minding my own business when I heard some sort of scuffle coming from the basement. Naturally, I went to see what was going on, and when I did…Father, along with two of his club members. They had someone there. Tied up. He was beaten, bruised. Whatever they were doing to him down there, it was terrible. Before I knew what I was doing, I ran and stayed at a friend's house for a few hours. When I got back, everything was gone. Everything. Father, that man, even all my things…As if we never existed there."

Mr. Flynn stared at his drink, before bringing it up to his nose. He took a deep breath, before swallowing the glass' contents.

"Tell me about your new film, Mr. Flynn."

He blinked, letting the drink warm him before answering.

"It's a comedy. Something a bit lighter than all of those rousing adventure pictures, you understand. I'm a writer, who every so often dabbles in being a gumshoe. Though I'm not sure why this is so important."

"I was hoping to hear more about the goings-on behind the scenes."

"Ah yes, you mentioned this, didn't you? All of my co-stars being suspect because they haven't had their names up in lights."

"But it's more than that, isn't it, Mr. Flynn? Isn't this supposed to be a sequel to your *Footsteps in the Dark*? Everybody was on board at the start of the production, but now, where are they? What sort of a sequel replaces all but the leading man, hmm?"

He swirled his empty glass. The line of his jaw tightened.

"And it goes deeper, doesn't it, Mr. Flynn? It isn't just your co-stars that have been replaced. It took me a lot of searching, but eventually I found something. That man I saw, the man that my father kidnapped, is the man that's currently directing your new film."

He found himself standing on the sun, alone, amidst an unknowable darkness.

He didn't dare to look above him. The light that shone down from the ceiling was far too bright, especially considering the darkness that filled the rest of the chamber. A mural lay beneath his feet, and so he admired that. Though the image that he currently disgraced with his presence was not a depiction of the celestial body, it was certainly one of the brightest stars he had ever known.

"You know why you have been brought here this night."

The voice echoed out from the outskirts of the room. Its origin was unclear. He span on his heel, desperate to address it.

"Y—Yes…I—I…"

"You failed us, Prince. You failed us all."

"Yes, my Lord. I tried my best, I—"

"Do you know how many Princes would have killed to have the honour I bestowed upon you? Of all the lower castes, I chose you. You could have risen to the rank of Pauper, if only you succeeded. Yet, this is what you have given me?"

"It was going according to plan, my Lord!"

"My plans are revealed to me by the Shining Star himself. They are perfect, just as he is."

"There was something I did not expect! A girl!"

To his right there was a scrape of rubber against the cold, stone floor. He took a hesitant step toward the darkness, toward the source of the voice.

"Excuses. Nothing more. This close to the Hooded Hours, any setback is unforgiveable. I must apologize, Prince, but I cannot allow this mistake to go without chastisement."

A sudden glint appeared behind him, the light reflected from the dagger piercing the darkness. He stepped back, hands raised in desperation. Then there was a choked, gurgling scream, and a stain of red seeped out onto the face of his god.

"Ghosts Don't Leave Footprints. Scene Thirteen. Take Four. Action!"

A dull crack and he was in his element. Practiced feet crossed the floor. A hand moved down to caress the cold, broken corpse. After a moment, his mouth began to work, spouting deductions and hypotheses that weren't his own.

"Nothing seems to be broken…If it were poison then there would have to be some sort of sign or smell…"

The room around him was false. The walls were painted a dull yellow, yet he was one of the only people that would ever see them as such. Bright pink carpets were positioned around him, some coming with their own small, round coffee tables. After today, they would only appear as a deep, dark red. Behind the closed curtains, there was little more than a backboard.

Beyond that, empty, echoing space—and that was the wall that was actually complete.

In the corner of his eye, he could see where the world ended. The floor dropped away, and was replaced by an unknowable void.

"It's just that it happened so fast. I was barely talking to him just fifteen minutes ago, and now something's happened to him….Murder surely, but…it can't be…"

He was being watched. That was why he was here. Kneeling down in the centre of the room, continuing his examination of the body. A woman stood behind him. His wife, but also a near-stranger.

"So, what is it, Francis?"

"Seems like nothing more than a heart attack. Although…"
In a moment, he was on his feet.

"There's something about this that doesn't quite sit right with me…"

Curious fingers gripped his chin, eyes glazing over as his mind worked. The woman drew nearer, clasping his arm.

"He seemed perfectly well on the phone, just now." She cast an inquisitive glance down at the body. "You make it sound as if he died of fear."

"Perhaps…"

She glanced around the room, pausing on each item of furniture. "There's something about this room…I don't like this, darling. There's more to this than meets the eye."

"I know what you mean, dear. I feel as if we're being watched. As if there's something here with us. Something that we can't quite see…"

They paused, the woman glancing around, fearful of the unknown that they were on the verge of discovering.

"Cut!"

They held their positions for a few seconds more before allowing the tension to leave their shoulders. Almost forgotten, the corpse climbed to its feet, stretching out his limbs with a welcome sigh. The woman gleefully wrapped her arms around his waist, beaming up at Mr. Flynn.

"How was that, Errol?"

Despite her eagerness for an answer, she didn't seem to be getting one. Instead, his attention was focused on the man approaching them from behind the cameras.

"Wonderful stuff, Errol, wonderful stuff! Got it in one again!"

"You sure, Gerry? There's a couple of lines near the end there that I feel I'm taking too long on…"

"Nonsense, nonsense, absolute nonsense!" He gave Mr. Flynn a reverential pat on the chest. "You're doing just perfectly. There's hardly anything I need to tell you, you just get it! Isn't that right, Angie?"

The woman gave a few frantic nods.

"If you say so."

He began to disentangle himself from the woman's arms, as she did her very best to foil these efforts.

"Alright." Gerry Isaacs clapped his hands together, turning back toward the cameras. "Everyone, take five! When you get back, we're going to be running Scene Sixteen! Angie, you're doing good. George, nice job being dead. Errol…" He took a moment to consider his next words. "I'd say keep it up, but I know you will."

Angie's smile somehow managed to stretch even wider. With considerable effort, Mr. Flynn wrenched himself free. George followed him off the stage, the woman accepting defeat. For the time being.

"Didn't see you at the party last night, Mr. Flynn."

"Yeah, sorry, George. I found myself taken for something of a ride, as it were."

"Ah, not to worry, Mr. Flynn. I already hear the boys are planning something for tonight anyhow."

"I'm not sure I'll be in the party mood tonight, George. Nothing you can do, I'm afraid."

The pair made their way over to the catering stand. Over a coffee, he was vaguely aware of George chattering away. Through the steam he watched his director talking with one of the stagehands. He couldn't help but notice how well he seemed, for an abductee.

The investigation continued in the victim's room. A perfect square, with a double bed against one wall. It was smaller than the living room; bookshelves were lined up opposite the bed, and a door to a bathroom stood in the middle. A window opened out, with cold, sunless light pouring in.

His wife stood at the entrance to the bathroom, half of her visible in the frame. Meanwhile he examined the shelves. All of the books were empty covers, but that did nothing to quench his interest.

"I'm not entirely sure what we're supposed to find," he called out, "I doubt there's anything here that we couldn't find in the man's study."

"Now you're just sulking." The woman turned, poking her

head out through the door. "Say what you might about the stomach, but I've found that the bedroom can be a much easier way to the inner workings a man's heart."

"Oh, is it now?" He broke off his examination, turning with wide eyes and an open smile, "Not that you would know from experience, I'm sure?"

She giggled, before disappearing back into the bathroom. He continued along the shelves, tracing his finger along the row of spines.

"Well, whatever the inner workings of his heart, our man certainly has a curious taste in books. An Aleister Crowley here, a John Dee there...Oh, and one of mine!"

"At least you're in good company." His wife began, her voice trailing into silence. After a moment, she emerged. Any sense of levity had vanished from her face, along with much of the colour.

"Francis, darling, look at these." She walked over, carrying a collection of small sheets of paper. Upon each of them was a series of unique designs. Twisting, jagged lines contained with perfect circles. The designs all marked in brown ink. Holding them in the light of the bedroom, she noticed that each design was visible through multiple layers, so that they formed new, complex patterns when placed on top of each other.

He did as she asked, closely examining one of the sheets.

"Blood." His voice was a murmur, yet loud enough to be heard throughout the house. "Blood in a...Rita, dear, I think you may have been right about the man's bedroom..."

The world came back into being with a sudden crack. A window opened out onto nothingness, yet light still poured in from the unknowable outside. Three men stood around a large, wooden desk. Two of them wore a uniform, the other a light suit. Badges hung from the uniformed men's pockets. A bundle of papers slammed down, onto the desk, the man that held them rising up from his seat.

"Now I know you've gone too far, Pettijohn!" Inspector Mason, the largest of the three, crossed his arms in a huff.

"Warren," said the tallest, the man in the suit.

"Hey, the chief can call you whatever he wants, Pettijohn!" Detective Hopkins poked him in the chest.

When he heard the name, there was no immediate reaction. Mental springs wound up for less than a second, an eternity longer than any instinct. A mouth opened, already knowing that it would not be given time to speak its piece.

"It doesn't matter what I call him!" Mason shouted over the other two, "Now, Pettijohn…I know you've been laughing at me ever since that Fissue business—"

"Oh, don't be ridiculous, Inspector, I've been doing that since long before then."

"What I mean is, when you come here telling me that my trained and experienced band of detectives is off the mark, simple, old-fashioned murder is the least I expect."

"And not—"

"And not that Emmet Carmichael, one of the foremost bankers this side of the Mississippi, died because he saw a ghost!"

"Come now, Inspector, it's a little more involved than seeing…"

There was a moment of quiet, the Inspector's words echoing through the room. The man in the middle caught a glimpse of movement outside the edge of the world.

From out in the void, two men stood together, watching the tableau. They leaned toward each other, their mouths moving soundlessly. Unknown eyes fixed on him, just as he held them in his own gaze.

"Uh, what are you getting at, Pettijohn?" Hopkins jeered, his eyes skittering between the man and the void.

"Hm?" he blinked, "Oh, uh—Well, clearly, Hoppy, I—No, no it's gone. Excuse me, but I've lost it."

A frustrated sigh cast around the little universe.

"Cut!"

A weary hand raised to Mr. Isaac's eyes.

"Errol, you alright up there? Is there anything we can do?"

"No, sorry, Gerry, this one is on me. It's just—" He looked back out into the void, only to see that it was empty,

173

"Something must be stuck on my mind."

"Everything alright, Miss Gerhardt?"

Looking up over his lunch, he greeted his co-star, inviting her to take a seat nearby. She slunk down into the chair, her face downtrodden.

"Oh, no, I'm…I'm just dreadfully sorry, Errol. Sorry for mussing up your work…"

"Excuse me?"

"It's just that you handle all of this so well, and so smoothly. I'm just in the back doing…" She held out her hands in a wide gesture, before mechanically bringing one up to her wide, gaping mouth.

"You know?"

"Oh, no, come on now. There's no need to worry." There was a brief pause as he chewed on a mouthful of chicken. "Think about it, how long have you been in this job?"

The woman looked down at her lap, then back up at him. A long breath, her voice catching in her throat before she answered.

"Not long."

"And, might I ask as to your experience in this line of work? If it's not too secret."

Another moment of hesitation.

"I was…in something for…Paramount. Yes. I'm sure you wouldn't have heard of it, I'm afraid. It was far too small to go anywhere, but still, I wanted to work, and so I got picked up here."

"And there you have it." Hands were held wide, before returning to his meal, "All you're really lacking is time."

"Of course. Coming in a bit late doesn't help."

Giving her a thoughtful nod, he continued the thought. "Truth be told, I'm probably still just used to working off of Brenda. It's hardly your fault that you've been thrown into a production halfway through, now?"

She nodded.

"I suppose it is a bit of a shock." Her smile grew to a more familiar size, "It isn't every day that a girl is suddenly the leading lady next to Errol Flynn after all. A few of the guys that work the lights feel just the same!"

"There you are, see. Back to normal already. Now, you'd better run along and get ready for that scene again. I know that's what I need."

With a stilted giggle, she was off. Mr. Flynn watching her go.

"The lighting men…" His brow furrowed. "I wonder just how many people on this picture have found themselves replaced recently…"

A small figure made its way through the darkened hallway, self-conscious of every click of her heels. Linoleum floors were not her friends. The doors here were dark, characterised with a large, glass pane inset into each of them.

Names had been pressed into the glass, though she didn't bother to read any of them. Light seeped out from underneath.

Mr. Flynn had seemed so confident in the plan when they were deciding upon it. Even going over it once again, it seemed to make sense. Whatever her father's plan was, it hinged on this film, *Ghosts Don't Leave Footprints*. The only thing that seemed to have slipped Flynn's mind was that he *wasn't* the one going to trespass in the Warner Bros. offices.

At least they knew who they were looking for. Finding a film's writer wasn't difficult when their name was on every copy of the script.

Walter Cartwright, the man responsible for this film, and the man whose name was on this door.

This was it. Casting an eye up and down the corridor, she took a deep breath. The lock was a simple matter, quickly solved with the judicious use of a few hairpins.

"Clearly the movies are good for something."

A self-satisfied smile. She slipped through the open door, with a small click as it shut behind her.

Soft, yellow light seeped in around the closed blinds. It wasn't perfect, but it was enough to see.

Now her steps were lost in the carpet. The office was painted in dark shades of blue. Bookcases lined the walls, their contents likely for show. A row of dull, grey filing cabinets was tucked into the back corner. A glint of light caught her eye—a silver picture frame perched on the desk, just off centre. It was difficult to resist a closer look. The grinning face of Errol Flynn looked up at her from inside the frame, and her heart sank.

Filing cabinet locks were no harder than the door's, and their contents equally bare. Most of the drawers were practically empty, as much for show as the bookcases, but there was one folder that proved to be of great interest.

"Mr. Cartwright—an emerging writing talent. Good fit for Flynn's mystery sequel. New writer necessary following Cole and Wexley's removal."

Before she had even finished, she was panicked, clearing her traces. The letter was already folded. She had barely tucked it away when she was blinded by a harsh, white light.

There was a shrill, terrified scream as the door clicked shut.

"Oh, Francis! Oh, my darling!"

The woman darted across the room. Her hands shook as she rushed behind the steadfast silhouette that stood in the doorway. Mr. Flynn stepped forward. Angie peered out from behind him, gripping his arm. He raised his other hand up, demanding the oncoming threat to halt in its tracks.

An invisible pillar of flame stood before them. Wind rushed through the room.

"Don't you dare come any closer, fiend!"

The flame twisted in response.

"You may be able to work your powers on your little followers, but not on my love! And certainly not me!"

The wind picked up, the flame seeming to grow even larger.

"You seek to defy me, Francis Warren?" A booming voice cascaded across the set. If Mr. Flynn focused he could just make out the man curled around a microphone in a nearby soundbooth.

"I do, and I shall until the end of days!"

The wind picked up one final time.

"No!" yelled the voice, "I cannot—I must not! My connection to this world is weakened!"

"Oh, Darling, you're doing it!" Angie squealed. Unable to contain herself, she pressed a kiss to his cheek. Taken off guard, he paused, attention snapping back to reality.

"Y-you…You shall—" He stammered for a moment, his rhythm broken. His next words were projected outside the room, into the void. "Look, I'm sorry, but could we take a moment, please?"

"Oh, alright. Cut!"

A low murmur of commotion buzzed through the set as production fizzled to a halt. Angie let go of Mr. Flynn, taking a few steps back. He couldn't remember ever seeing her look this sheepish.

"Everything alright, Errol?" Gerry Isaacs called from his perch beside the camera.

"Yes, it's just…This scene, there's something up with it." Jumping down from the set, he began a quick search for a script, "It doesn't sit with me at all."

Angie shot a look at Gerry.

"W-was it my fault, Errol?" She offered a weak smile.

"No, it's not you, Miss Gerhardt…This is one of the new scenes, isn't it? I don't remember it being in the first few run-throughs."

"Yeah, I'm pretty sure. Is that important?"

"I'll say. Just look at it. I know I'm the star of the picture, but there's a fair difference between that and outright propaganda. It's nonsense, the lot of it!"

With a flick of his wrist, his script went flying. Wayward pages drifted down around them.

"Am I supposed to believe that our man Francis goes from having a few troubles with his mother-in-law to fighting the damned devil?"

"Now, come on, Errol, this isn't something I'm responsible for. If you have a problem, you take it up with Mister…err, what's his name—Cartwright! If it's written, then you act it!"

"It hardly seems to have been written at all!" He took a

step toward his director. "If I wanted to put out a half-baked fantasy, I think I'd ask for one! Wouldn't you? Even Robin Hood didn't fight Satan!" A fierce stare. "Tell Mr. Cartwright that I signed up for a good, honest comedy! If you want somebody to act out this drivel, then *you'd* better sign up for it!"

Mr. Isaacs watched him go. After a moment, he nodded toward the set. "Alright boys, we have to clean this place up before we run it again. Get to it."

Canvas stretched as he took his seat. His mind was racing, though its thoughts were sluggish, tired.

Sighing, he closed his eyes. He focused on the sounds around him. Gofers and backstage workers moved across the studio floor. Footsteps in the dark.

"Need anything, Mr. Flynn?"

"Oh..." A slow, gentle nod, "Hey there, Bart."

"You look like you could do with a bit to drink, Mr. Flynn!" The boy stood to his full height as Flynn pulled out a cigarette.

"I'd say you have a good eye, there." He sucked in a lungful of smoke. "Fetch me a coffee, could you? I feel like I could drop dead."

"You got it, Mr. Flynn!"

Mr. Isaacs crossed the room ahead of him, coming together with a group of Flynn's co-stars.

No doubt they were still going along with this preposterous spiritualist angle.

"Here you are, Mr. Flynn!"

Pulling his attention away from his colleagues, he turned to the boy.

"Thanks, kid." He raised his cup in a playful toast, before taking a sip. Leaning back in his chair, he was still aware of Bart's presence nearby. His eyes drifted back over to the group, widening as he saw that they were now staring at him.

"You're welcome, Mr. Flynn."

Looking up at the boy, he attempted to rise from his chair. He made it to his feet, only to collapse back down.

"Kid...Bart, what's..." he held up the coffee, dropping it

as a few scalding drops spilled out onto his hand.

"Don't worry, Mr. Flynn. I got you exactly what you needed."

The entire production team was staring at him. Cameramen, lighting and sound operators, each one of them. He looked forward to see his director start toward him.

Mr. Isaacs mouth began to move, and then the world started to sway.

A laugh passed over the desk of Walter Cartwright. Behind it sat the man himself, opposite him there was a young girl. Lilian Hartford gripped the chair with white knuckles.

"I just had no idea your dad was gonna send you around!" Mr. Cartwright chuckled. "I mean, we've been so busy sorting things out, getting a few things finished. But, hey, everything is nearly done, and it's been so long since any of us have seen you!"

"I hope you didn't miss me too much, Mr. Cartwright."

"I know a few of us certainly did, your dad especially. And please, you've known me long enough to call me Walter."

"I know. That doesn't mean it doesn't feel strange."

"Not to worry, Lilly. That's a pretty common feeling around these parts. I mean, look at us, for Pete's sake. Thanks to your dad, we're all doing exactly what we've always wanted, and with our Shining Star walking amongst us at that."

"Oh, Mr. Cartwright, I'm sure it couldn't get any better for you!"

"Lilly, dear, I'm afraid it can. And it will."

Her smile faltered.

"And…how is that, Mr. Cartwright?"

"The Hooded Hours, Lilly. All of this, all the planning. The years of carefully positioning ourselves in the right spots at the right time. Soon we're going to receive our reward."

"I…I've heard about this. From my father. Something about Mr. Flynn, am I right?"

"Exactly right, my dear. Thanks to my masterful additions to the original script, *Ghosts Don't Leave Footprints* contains just enough of our Shining Star's essence for us to use."

"When you say your 'Shining Star'...this is still Mr. Flynn we're talking about, yes?"

"Ah, of course. Mr. Flynn, as you put it, is indeed our Shining Star. He is the one we hold above all others, even your father, or the Hooded Robin, as we know him now."

"And this so-called 'essence' of his?"

"Yes, yes. That's this film, Lilly. For weeks, we've been locking out Shining Star away, capturing him on celluloid. Soon, we shall release the potential in this film of ours, and we shall become like him. There's so much you've missed out on, Lilly. I'm honestly so glad that you've decided to come back and finally join us."

There was a creak behind her, and muffled footsteps began to move toward the two of them.

"Oh, and speak of the devil!" Mr. Cartwright gestured toward the new arrival. "Lilly, this is Green Light. I'm sure you both remember each other."

Despite her reluctance to turn and greet their visitor, she found herself going through the motions regardless.

"Good afternoon, Lilly. My, it has been a while."

George looked down at the girl, his smile thin, twisting at the edges.

"Hello, Mr. Cavallo. It does feel like it, doesn't it?"

"Blood Captain," already his attention had moved on, "The time is upon us. A number of Paupers are preparing to move. As we speak, the Hooded Robin is preparing the grounds. Soon, my friend...soon we shall all be as Shining Stars."

The only sound in the room was that of their breaths.

"I do hope you feel like coming along and enjoying yourself. We'd all be thrilled to have you back."

At first there was darkness. And a dull, throbbing pain.

There was noise, somewhere. Somewhere close. The pain continued.

He cracked open his eyes. The light hurt, so he closed them again. The sound began to come into focus. Rhythmic chanting surrounded him.

Again, he opened his eyes, slower this time. He allowed himself a closer look at his surroundings.

He was in the center of an enormous, circular room. In another time, Mr. Flynn supposed it could have been a ballroom. Fragmented scraps of wallpapers littered the walls, grey plaster underneath. A narrow staircase snaked around one edge of the room, leading up to balcony. On the other, a small library's worth of bookcases. Numerous pairs of broadswords were mounted around the room. Although, the most striking part of what he saw was the sheer volume of film posters. *Captain Blood*; *The Charge of the Light Brigade*; *The Adventures of Robin Hood*. Wherever Mr. Flynn looked, he found his dazzling grin shining back at him.

A congregation of chanting, hooded figures stood in a circle around him. Two of them crossed his gaze, separate from the main group. These two were nearer, moving in the space between him and the outer circle. He watched them as they moved, their path leading him to notice the strange stacks of metal containers that lay around him. They were film canisters, and they were labelled.

Ghosts Don't Leave Footprints.

Letting his head drop, he finally saw the room's hidden centrepiece.

The painted face of Mr. Flynn stared up at the real thing. He almost gasped, taken aback by the sheer detail. Dried blood stained his false face. The stain drooled across "his" eye.

He tried to move. His hands were bound, as were his ankles. The broadswords on the walls gleamed, painfully out of reach.

The chanting around the room began to quiet.

"And now, my friends!"

The voice came from the two circling figures. They had both stopped circling the stacks of canisters. One held out his arms. The other turned, moving toward Mr. Flynn.

"We look upon ourselves in our lesser forms one final time!"

The figures around the room reached up, pulling off their

hoods. Underneath each of them was a painfully familiar face.

My god...Angie! He looked from face to face. *And Gerry! And...that damn kid, Bart!*

A shadow fell across him. Lil glared down at him, her hood falling away. His jaw tightened.

A small bowie knife was produced from inside Lil's robes. Leaning down, the knife was placed within Flynn's bound hands. She turned away.

One man remained hooded. He spoke.

"My friends!"

The knife twisted in his fingers. The blade scraped against the ropes between his wrists.

"When we first found each other, we were imperfect beings."

The knife chewed through the rough fibres.

"We each recognized a failing in ourselves. Like reasonable men and women, we sought to resolve those failings."

Restraints loosened. His movements quickened.

"It is my honour to tell you all that at long last, we shall be rid of our earthly faults!"

A reverential murmur.

The rope fell away as the knife finished its meal.

"With the captured essence of our Shining Star, we shall become as one in his light!"

With a few heavy, slicing cuts, the pinion around his ankles fell apart.

He rose to his feet.

"I hope you're all enjoying the evening's entertainment. Mind if I join you?"

All eyes were on him.

"I hear you're all rather interested in getting a hold of me."

Heavy footsteps thumped behind him. A pair of arms reached around him, pinning him back against a cultist. He twisted in the other man's grip. He bent over, jerking the other man forwards. At the same moment, he jabbed backwards with the knife. Blind stabs sunk into soft flesh. The man screamed as Flynn cut into his side. He pulled the knife free as the cultist fell away.

Using the stacked canisters as a springboard, he vaulted away from the cultists behind him. Momentum carried him forward. Approaching the wall, he took hold of a broadsword.

It took a slight effort to pull it free. The cult did the same, arming themselves.

The hilt felt familiar in his hand. The broadsword was smaller than usual. The handguard seemed to be missing. Yet, as he looked, he realised that was simply a part of the design. Without a handguard, the wielder would be forced to defend through attacking. As he tested the balance, there was a moment of realisation.

He always wondered what they had done with all the swords made for *Robin Hood*.

Twelve of what had been his film crew advanced toward him. They loured at him, wielding swords of their own. He held out the sword, the knife in his other hand. A steady step forward, body leaning into the movement. The tips of opposing swords crossed each other.

Eyes narrowed, a confident smirk.

"Hold him, my brothers! I must continue the ritual!"

The clash of metal on metal. With each swing of his sword, he connected with at least three others. Slashing downward, he picked out a target from the crowd. His blade sliced through a microphone operator's arm. The man screamed. A few days ago, the pair of them had shared a joke about brunettes.

Matching each of their blows with one of his own, his opponents' swords clanged away. Every moment a cultist swung down at him. Every moment he swung his sword up at a new angle.

Walter Cartwright stabbed at Flynn's chest. A sudden counterattack knocked him away. The air sang as Flynn swung, faster than Cartwright could comprehend. The writer stumbled, almost losing his grip on his weapon as he fell back into his fellow cultists. Regaining his balance, he pushed forward. With a clumsy sideward swipe, he swung at Flynn. But Flynn dodged backward—Cartwright's sword sailing harmlessly through the air. Flynn darted forward. A blow pierced his leg, sending him to the floor.

The crowd paused. Six of the armed figures lowered their swords. A low murmur passed between them. They stood transfixed at the sight of their fallen friends. Eyes unable to leave the growing pools of blood.

Four remaining cultists pushed forward through the crowd. Together, they formed a line. A moment later, their swords flashed toward Mr. Flynn. With every blow meant for him, his sword twisted, weaving through their attacks like a needle through cloth.

His arm was low, tight toward his body, ready to react to the onslaught of blows.

One of the four aimed a fierce blow at his head. Another swung a swipe at his legs. He parried the first blow.

Still recoiling from the clash, he sprang back. The second sword shot past him. It cut out a chip from a cuff on his trousers.

Flynn paused as he landed. He glanced down at the rip in his clothes. Glimpses of his skin could be seen underneath, less than an inch from where the blade sliced through. He took a single step backward.

He began to retreat.

The cult pursued.

He ducked into the maze of bookcases. Weaving in between different rows, he reached the back wall of the room.

He looked around as the muffled clamouring of the congregation worked its way through the mass of bookshelves. Lone cultists wandered the aisles, making their steady path toward him. One final row of bookshelves stood against the wall. He stepped into the final aisle, waiting. He turned, the sounds growing louder.

Rushing the bookcase in front of him, he pushed it over.

The bookcase fell onto another. Then another. The bookcases smashed into each other; each smash reverberated like a rifle crack. Screams and the sound of falling books. He rushed into the aisle, pushing past a group of confused cultists. Several were knocked into the path of a falling bookcase.

The bookcase crumpled one's legs. Another screamed from somewhere deep underneath.

The crowd parted around the fallen bookcases. The four leading figures had barely faltered, continuing their pursuit. Behind them, the main congregation began to scatter, enervated as their fellows continued to fall.

He made for the staircase. The same four cultists followed. He turned to face them. Mr. Flynn gave a wild stab forward with his blade. His targets ducked away, leaning just over the banister.

"Rather persistent bunch, aren't you?"

One split away from the group, rushing forward. A metallic crack. Another slash, another parry. With every blow levelled at him, Flynn took a step backward. Hurried swings glanced off of his sword, each one quicker than the last.

One of the enemy's blades rushed down a final time. He leapt back. The sword lodged itself in the stair. As he tried to pull his blade free, the cultist's arm was wide open. Flynn stomped on his wrist. A wet crunch. He stepped down, momentum carrying him, and swung sideways. Blood splashed onto the banister as the body collapsed down onto it.

Mr. Flynn carried through with his momentum, rushing down another two steps. Before the next cultist had time to think, Flynn's own blade sliced across his neck. He fell away as Flynn ripped the sword out from his body.

As his two remaining attackers took their comrades' places, he withdrew. The pair of them leaned forward, raising their swords in a defensive stance before taking a decisive step toward him. Pushing himself forward with strong legs, Flynn dashed up the stairs. He emerged onto the balcony. He made for the edge.

He vaulted over the railing.

Knees bent, arms wide. Barely a sound as he hit the floor. He rose back to his full height. The two cultists on the stairs turned to face him. They rushed down the stairs, ready to strike.

The first cultist swung her sword down toward his head.

His own rose to meet it. He backed away as they clashed, the second cultist moving in next to his accomplice.

The second cultist sliced upward. Flynn swung his own sword across, deflecting the attack. Continuing the rebounding movement, he aimed his sword at the first cultist. She blocked, sending him back towards that of the second cultist.

His sword bounced between the cultists'. His parries flew faster with every incoming attack. Everything they threw at him was pushed back further than the last.

Flynn's eyes narrowed as he looked back and forth between his two enemies. Already they were forcing him backward.

The first cultist launched a sudden swipe. Flynn's blade jerked across to block it. Metal clashed at a wild angle. Flynn stumbled backward, holding tight onto his weapon. His opponent was knocked against the banister. She hurriedly fought to regain her balance, taking an offensive stance as she did so. Her counterpart swung in retaliation as Flynn darted forward. The second cultist's blade sailed sideways, and Flynn caught it with his own. He pushed to the side as it moved, the other's blade swinging across.

She hardly had time to react to her own brethren's sword. A deep gash cut through her stomach. Blood rushed along the polished metal. As they collapsed, the sword fell from the astonished cultist's hands. Flynn shot forward, punching him to the floor

"You think you can stop us?" A voice rang through the room, "Soon, we shall be all that you are, and more! Come on, my brothers! It is time to earn our impending godhood!"

Flynn's chest heaved. His face glistened with sweat, skin flushed and red, as he surveyed the last few people that wanted him dead.

The four remaining cultists began to regroup. Three had gathered together on the far side of the room, while one straggler made to circle around the Hooded Robin. Charging forward, Mr. Flynn made for the lone cultist.

Turning at the sound of approaching feet, the cultist

hurried to raise her sword. Two blades clashed together. Both fighters recoiled from the blow. Flynn circled the woman, cutting her off from her fellows. His target took a step to the side, and he swiped across with his sword.

The first note of an overture whistled through the air. Metal clashed against metal, the sound changing into a first chorus. The blades played against each other. The reverberating scrape of crossing blades became verses. Variations on a theme.

Mr. Flynn launched a hard strike downward. The cultist defended, swinging up, knocking his blade away. A crescendo began to rise.

Her arm flew backward, out of control for just a moment. Allowing the movement to continue, Flynn stretched his arms out. He stood defenceless, a mischievous, taunting grin on his face.

The enemy swiped. The sword sang as it flew across from the side. As it did so, Mr. Flynn jumped backward, out of reach. The sword continued on, momentum sending it out of the cultist's control.

Her arm swung back, one hand losing its grip on the weapon. Darting forward, Mr. Flynn rammed his own sword's pommel into the woman's stomach. Winded, she bent over. The sword swung downward, slicing into her leg.

The final three cultists stood apart from each other, across the room. As one, they began to move toward their target. Mr. Flynn stepped away, jumping up onto the fallen bookcases. Someone attempted to crawl from under it, before their arms gave way under his weight.

The first man swung across, and Flynn jumped over his slash. The rush of air flew by his feet. Once again, he dodged, stepping to the side to avoid an upward blow. He swung his own sword, metal clashing, before leaping upon the second man.

A volley of blows forced the cultist back. The swords glimmered in the light. A downward blow clashed against a defending blade. The two swords slid across, rolling to the side.

A swipe flew toward his head. He ducked, a leg sweeping out. The other man had his body knocked from under him. Balance gave way at the force of Mr. Flynn's kick. Winded, the man collapsed to the ground.

His sword fell from his grasp. He began to climb back up onto his feet, only managing to balance on all fours before Mr. Flynn knocked his sword away. Flynn followed with an upward slash, cutting open the man's side. He turned from his fallen enemy to face the final two cultists.

Three swords crossed. Once again, they reeled to the side. They broke apart. One by one, the two men slashed at Mr. Flynn. Sleek scrapes slid through the air as he was forced to step back. They directed him, skilfully moving him with aimed blows. As he defended his right, so they focused on his left. Together, they pushed him nearer to the room's center.

Flynn's eyes snapped between them, hoping to find any possible hole in their defence. With a sudden twist, he pushed toward one of his attackers. The other cultist's sword sailed downward, the air just disturbing the back of Flynn's shirt. The man on his left moved to defend, not expecting the sudden manoeuvre. The man's sword was knocked away, too slow to stop it.

Flynn threw himself between the pair of them. He spun on his heel, slashing up just as the right man's blade came crashing down.

As Mr. Flynn focused on his other attacker, the left man raised his sword, and swung down, slicing the air as readily as it would the star's head.

But at the last moment, Mr. Flynn turned. Flynn's knife, almost forgotten, swung around in his off-hand. Catching the blade, the knife's hilt gnashed down its length. The sword bit into the hilt's cheap metal, and locked. The left man tugged. Mr. Flynn pulled—and flung both away. Two blades clattered to the floor. With his hand now free, he grabbed a hold of the left man's robes.

Flynn dragged him around as his shield. Flynn's body pressed against his back. Before him was Flynn's sword, the star deflecting blows from the final armed cultist.

The final sword slashed across from the right. Then again, and again. Flynn clashed against the blows. Yet another blow came in from the right. Flynn released a sudden attack of his own. The opposing sword was knocked aside, just as he threw the unarmed cultist at his brother. A heavy thunk.

The two cultists stumbled backward. Flynn stepped forward, leaning back and kicking them down. He swung his sword towards them as they fell, piercing one's back. With a cry of horror, the final two bodies collapsed to the ground.

Groans of discomfort already sounded throughout the room. Some cried out in pain, others in anger.

Mr. Flynn turned to the Hooded Robin, his sword already slicing downward.

When he saw the knife, it was a moment too late. Already, his body was going through the motion of a swing. Reflexes worked unconsciously. The only thing he could do was watch as the Hooded Robin stabbed sideways, the knife piercing his clothes. Blood began to flow out from his side, a stain of red growing across his shirt.

The sword continued on. It sank into the Hooded Robin's collar.

A fresh pool of blood. Hesitant, unconscious steps pulled him back. The sword fell with an echoing clang.

"Yes…"

A low wail, steadily increasing in pitch.

"Yes!"

"I have captured both your image and your essence! Thank you, my children…" he held out his arms, thanking each of his fallen followers in turn. Dumbfounded, Mr. Flynn watched as he revelled in his triumph. He reached out pulling down the final hood to reveal…

The chanting stopped. In its place, there was a confused murmur. The wail continued.

"Is…is something supposed to have happened?"

The Hooded Robin, no longer hooded, turned to face Mr. Flynn. Looking at him, Mr. Flynn could recognize Lil's features in his face.

"What do you mean?" The Hooded Robin's eyes widened,

he turned to his followers for validation, "Am I not the image of our Shining Star? Am I not the result of all that I promised?"

Police burst into the room. A swarm of figures surveyed the remains of the congregation. Half went to examine the groaning cultists. As they moved further into the room, their attention shifted to the last two men on their feet.

"I…" the Hooded Robin stepped backward, collapsing to the floor as he fell over a stack of film canisters. "I became the Shining Star…I did it…I'm the hero now…"

Lil rushed in, wearing the same cowl. Aware of the pain, Mr. Flynn also moved down to the floor. In a moment, she was at his side.

"I kept them busy for you." He almost laughed.

Margaret Rutherford starring in...

Death Among the Marigolds

John Linwood Grant

London, September 1941

There were two explosions near the Piccadilly Theatre on that warm September evening.

The first one was caused by a homeward bound Heinkel, shedding the last of its load. It was a token effort only, for the Blitz itself was over. Proving that God loved a show, the bomb missed the actual theatre. Unfortunately the building had already been weakened by a raid some time before. The management decided to have the damage surveyed, and gave strong indications that further performances would have to wait.

The director was furious—his '*Blithe Spirit*' was capturing the capital. The cast, on the other hand, were grateful for even a day or two off. Plans were made to see families, to drive out of the city for a relaxed break, and in general to take their feet off the boards.

The second explosion was less usual, and quite localised. As the actors sorted out their belongings and considered this unexpected freedom, the stage door was the scene of a much smaller blast.

"But I have to! I have to see her!"

The speaker was a mass of wild blonde hair and smudged make-up, barely over five foot tall and dressed in a black velvet cape which would have suited any revival of an old romance. The doorman, who looked like a doorman, was being slowly beaten back into the Piccadilly. He held out his large hands to ward off small fists until relief arrived.

"I told you, miss, you can't go in the—"

"Is there a problem, George?"

He turned, managing a grateful smile. "Miss Rutherford, it's this 'ere girl. Insists she sees you."

"I'm not a girl," said his assailant. "I'm Lily Maunsey, and I really, really, need to talk to Miss Rutherford. Really."

The actress, whose own cape was of a more sensible tweed, stepped up to the firing line. "Now now, dear. Why don't you come inside and tell me what the fuss is about? Yes, George, it's all right."

The theatre bar was still open. A reluctant barman found a brandy for the girl, and Margaret steered them both to a table, wiping away the fallen plaster with her sleeve.

"I'm an enormous, enormous admirer." said Lily, large brown eyes fixed on the actress's face. "I saw you in Hull, and Leeds, and Manchester, and I've been to absolutely loads of performances of *Blithe Spirit*, and you were wonderful in *Rebecca*, far better than that Judith Anderson, and I saw you in—"

Margaret held up one hand. "That is most gratifying, dear. But the fuss at the door..."

"I'm in awful trouble, Miss Rutherford."

The older woman's somewhat crumpled face crumpled more in concern.

"Goodness. Why on earth is that?"

The girl leaned forward.

"There are dreadful things happening at home." She sat back again. "And you are the only one I can trust."

It took two brandies for the girl to deliver the story. Lily, only surviving child of Sir Cedric Maunsey, eighth Baronet of Kelwich, was rather emotional.

"Miss Rutherford, it's my older sister, Alice—she's trying to talk to me about some awful problem, but she won't make things clear."

"Is it a very personal matter perhaps? Family can be difficult. Or is she unwell?"

Lily blinked at her half-empty glass. "Oh, nothing like that. She's dead"

"Good heavens!"

"I mean, she died a couple of months ago, but I can sense her. Like you do in *Blithe Spirit*, you see?"

192

"My dear, I—"

"I'm sure our house is doomed, or cursed, or that sort of thing. Alice is—I don't know—hovering over me, trying to break through." The girl was not to be halted. "Daddy's useless, and since most of the staff joined up to fight, the place is falling to pieces, and I really, really don't have anyone to talk to apart from nanny, who's lost most of her marbles anyway…and we can't even get decent butter any more."

Lily drew in a deep breath, and stared expectantly at the actress, who was as bereft of words as the girl seemed full of them. Margaret felt much as she did when presented with a script for the first time. The words were there, but not the meaning.

Lily took advantage of the pause.

"I've seen *Spring Meeting* three times. You were so wonderful in that film! I'm staying with my aunt in Pimlico this weekend, but she's an old biddy and half-deaf, and absolutely no one listens to me, and I have to go back home. My sister is trying to warn me of something terrible, but I don't know what it could be. Please, please help me!"

It was Margaret's nature to be attracted to waifs and strays, but this situation seemed beyond common sense. She knew nothing of troublesome sisters, dead or otherwise.

"It sounds most distressing, but I'm not sure how I could help."

The girl sat up straight. "You are Madame Arcati."

"But that's merely a part I play, dear."

"Oh, I do know that, but you believe—I can see it when you're on stage. I've read about you. I've read everything about you, Miss Rutherford. You're sensitive to these things. You're kind, and decent, and you're so determined, and I'm very confused…"

If the tear in the girl's eye was theatrical, it was very convincing. Margaret softened.

"What did you want me to do?"

"Come home with me, just for a day or so?"

"I don't think I could possibly—"

"I know, I just know that you won't let me down." One tear became two, accompanied by a wild stare. "Would you rather I turned to strangers?"

The actress was about to point out that she was a stranger, but hesitated. The girl's huge eyes, set above a small nose and a determinedly-pointed chin, were awash with genuine distress—and a certain blind faith.

It seemed that somewhere between a first and second act, on one stage or another, Lily had decided that Margaret Rutherford was to be her saviour.

"Please, darling Miss Rutherford."

Margaret was a poor liar, and when pressed, she admitted that she could, technically, come away for a short time. One by one her arguments were beaten down. Nor did it escape her that here was a young woman in need, at the only point in a long run when the theatre would not be requiring its actors.

Some bombs fell on one by chance; others, perhaps, had a purpose.

So it was that Margaret, still confused about her role, agreed to take the train to Yorkshire the next morning, accompanied by the baffling Lily. She had barely time to make enquiries about the Maunseys amongst the theatre people, but was fortunate enough to find Noel Coward himself, working late in his office.

Noel assured her, in between complaining about the perfidy of actors, that there was a genuine eighth Baronet of Kelwich. Sir Cedric was gouty and glum, and once an occasional patron of the arts. He had removed north to a place called Selby Hall when the War Office requisitioned the family seat down south.

"An old dodderer. His ancestral pile in Suffolk is a convalescent home for our boys at the moment," said Noel, scribbling furiously over some lines in a script.

"And his children…"

"Children?" Noel frowned, though she couldn't tell if it was directed at her or the lines. "I believe his eldest daughter died in a car crash, with her husband. Some dashing young officer, Mountford or Mountforth. I knew the chap's mother, vaguely. Danish. I'd hoped to have a production at the Royal Theatre in Copenhagen, in their rather droll annex. All very Art Déco, you know—"

"The couple," asked Margaret, trying to redirect his flow. "Did they die in Denmark?"

"Who? Oh, the Mountforths. No, in Yorkshire, I think. Can you imagine it? 'Death in the Wolds.' How terribly, terribly dreary."

Which seemed a tasteless thing to say, but she was growing used to his dismissive style.

"Yes, well, thank you, Noel."

"Back by Wednesday, mind you, old girl. I simply will not be made to find another Madame Arcati."

Selby Hall was not that far from York, less isolated than she had feared. The train journey up was a mixture of silences and sudden barrages, both supplied by Lily. Margaret managed to discover that the girl was twenty years old, and lived off an allowance from her father, who had been widowed many years ago.

"I paint, you know," said Lily. "I'm absolutely dreadful."

All had been well in recent years, apart from the baronet's gradual decline. Lily's older sister Alice married Gerald Mountforth not long before the war, and they had seemed happy. Then three months ago the couple took a private yacht to Occupied Denmark, apparently to see Gerald's maternal family. They left their two year old son, little Cedric, at Selby Hall.

"Rather odd, don't you think, dear?"

"Was it? I suppose so. Alice and I weren't so close after she married. I've no idea why she dashed off like that—and to somewhere full of those dreadful Nazis, of all places. Then the car over-turned, on the road from Bridlington." Lily fretted with her purse, momentarily slowed. "I mean, they'd docked safely, and were coming home…but the police said that the road was wet, and they took a bend too fast."

Margaret felt for the girl, whose face had lost much of its

animation.

"Was it…quick, dear?"

"Gerald was killed instantly, they told me. Alice…a passing farmer drove her to the hall, to die a few hours later. I was away—I didn't even get to see her before…"

"I understand. Such a shock for you all."

"Daddy hasn't been the same since. It was such a mess. Little Cedric has his nanny, of course, and I do what I can. He'll be the next baronet, you know, poor baby, and…" Lily paused as the train slowed. "Gosh, we're almost at Selby."

Whatever else the girl might have added was lost in the scrabble for their luggage, most of which was Lily's. They were picked up at the station by a flustered youth called Carter, who had come for them with a horse-drawn carriage. Apparently it was easier to feed the beasts than it was to get hold of petrol.

"I phoned daddy to say we were coming," said Lily. "It's going to be a sort of house-party, seven or eight of us. I do hope that you don't mind."

Margaret forced a smile. "Not at all. Nothing like a jolly company."

After half an hour the carriage juddered to a halt on a gravel drive. Selby Hall seemed a dilapidated chunk of history, a three-storied house of white stone, set in neglected grounds.

Lily whisked Margaret down from the carriage and up the main steps.

"No butler, I'm afraid. Peters joined up, and is in North Africa, along with most of the gardeners. It's all sand out there, you know, not an inch of loam. You'll have the Blue Room, Miss Rutherford. It's where daddy usually keeps his fishing gear."

A brief glimpse of the main hall, dominated by a broad staircase, was succeeded by entrance into a large reception room. Grey light toyed at the French windows, but a chandelier fitted with electric bulbs made up for the day's shortcomings.

Afternoon tea was under way, and mouthfuls of scone or sandwiches precluded any concerted chorus of welcome. The gentlemen rose, and were introduced. A red-cheeked man in his thirties, with a thin moustache, was Lily's cousin, Edward Maunsey. His friend, far paler but with the same dark, slicked-back hair and moustache, was a Mr. Godfrey Colne. And there was a third man, Arthur Connaught, who kissed her hand and said how marvellous she had been in *Rebecca*.

"Your Mrs. Danvers was terrifying, madam. Quite terrifying."

It seemed that Mr. Connaught and his wife Gertrude, sitting next to him, were family friends, also up from London. Margaret accepted a seat, a cup of tea and a small, hard currant scone.

"Sir Cedric's twinging again," said Edward, offering her sugar.

"I'm sorry?"

"His gout. He'll be down for dinner." Narrow eyes considered her. "Very kind of you to visit us, of course. I suppose Lily pestered you into this—she has a bit of a thing about you."

"Really? I only met her yesterday, to be truthful. She's...full of energy, isn't she?"

"Full of fancies." Edward laughed and lit a cigarette. She couldn't quite hear what he murmured to Godfrey, but it sounded dismissive.

The conversation was predictable. A smattering of weather and the war, followed by a rush of curiosity about acting, theatres, and whoever was in vogue. Had she met Margaret Lockwood on the set of *Quiet Wedding*? What was Noel Coward really like?

"I do so dislike gossip," she said, when pressed by Mrs. Connaught. "Dear Noel is quite a character, and a fine director, of course."

And she explained the situation at the Piccadilly. Having gained their attention, she regaled them with talk of the opening night, and how one unfortunate member of the audience had fallen off planks laid over the rubble in the foyer. It served well enough to distract them from more personal enquiries.

When enough pleasantries had been exchanged, and sufficient tea drank, Lily showed the actress to her quarters in the west wing.

"It's not as…blue as I expected." Margaret contemplated the bright green room, set around with various looming pieces of dark oak furniture.

"Daddy's colour-blind. We humour him." The girl sat down on the edge of the bed, feet swinging in the air. "This was Alice's room before she married. Do you mind?"

"Not at all." Margaret had decided to be brisk and business-like. "And you feel her presence?"

"In a way. Things move, you see. Last week, I went to my little desk, and Alice's letters—I kept them all—were in a different order. She was trying to tell me something. I told Mrs. Barton the housekeeper, and she said it was my imagination. No one else has noticed anything. I was sure it was Alice, trying to contact me. Perhaps I'm going mad."

"Nonsense. Ten to one there's a perfectly natural explanation."

Before Margaret could answer, the boy arrived with her luggage. He was pink-faced as he placed her cases down by the bed.

"Sorry, madam. I had to bring your things up the back stairs, and I got confused about—"

"Please don't worry about it," said Margaret.

He was eighteen or nineteen, with widespread acne which spoiled what was essentially a broad, pleasant face.

"Argyranthemum," he said suddenly.

The two women stared at him.

"Marguerite, the flower. Miss Marguerite Rutherford."

Pink turned to red, and he almost ran from the room.

Lily sighed.

"Carter's a bit odd. Been a gardener's boy since he was twelve. He knows everything about plants—all the Latin names and everything—but I don't think he's cut out to be the general help. Still, with the war…"

At Margaret's suggestion, the girl helped her unpack, which punctuated Lily's stories about her supposed haunting with cries of delight at costume jewellery and this or that piece of clothing. Picking out a diamanté broach, the girl told of the time when a locket of hers had been opened and moved from the dressing table to the night-stand.

"It was a memento of Alice, you see."

Margaret could see how a young, impressionable girl might begin to worry—and yet it seemed so unlikely. Although she hated to think ill of people, it seemed more feasible that a maid had been prying. She teased out more about the staff, but the information wasn't promising. Mrs. Barton, the housekeeper, was a brisk woman in her fifties; the two maids had come up with them from Suffolk. Cook was as obsessed with baking as young Carter was with plants, and had no obvious motive for interfering.

"And is this Mrs. Barton a pleasant sort?"

That brought a frown. "Oh, she's a monster! Strict, and keeps to herself. Even Daddy's afraid of her."

"Heavens." She made a note to study Mrs. Barton at the earliest opportunity. After all, she had 'been' Mrs. Danvers to great acclaim, as Arthur Connaught said. "And you mentioned a nanny."

"We shall go and see little Cedric."

The nursery, airy and smelling of lavender, was in the same wing on the ground floor. In one corner a bundle of lace and blankets cooed over a smaller bundle.

"Nanny Fletcher," said the girl. "She was Daddy's nanny, and mine, and Alice's."

The face under the mob-cap was a history book, containing some eighty years of nurture and service. Margaret would have made a pleasantry and slipped away, but when Nanny Fletcher's eyes opened, she saw intelligence—and enquiry.

"I seen pictures o' you," said the old lady.

"Yes, um, you may have."

"Actress. Not a proper job."

Lily giggled. "Nanny, really. Miss Rutherford is our guest."

There followed a reluctant showing of little Cedric, a fat-faced two year old asleep in his nanny's arms, clutching a battered tin rattle. He had the same disordered blonde hair as his aunt, and Margaret imagined that he would have the same large brown eyes. Sensing a lack of welcome, she suggested that they leave the two and have a walk in the grounds.

"So how will you start?" asked Lily as they strolled through what might once have been a small orchard.

"Start? Oh, I see. Well, I shall have to have a jolly good look round, and get the lay of the land. I'm still not sure that there's anything I can do, but if it makes you feel better having me—"

"It does, honestly it does. At least I have someone to talk to. Will you hold a séance?"

"No, dear." Margaret frowned. "I know you've seen me as Madame Arcati, but I'm absolutely sure I don't understand half enough of it to do any such thing. You will have to settle for a sympathetic friend."

Anything Lily might have said was stalled by the sound of a gong from inside the house.

"Time to dress for dinner."

The dining room was too large for the small company, as was the table, a huge dark thing. Margaret, in green chiffon and broaches, was floated to a seat of honour next to the eighth Baronet, a thin man who eyed her as if she were an approaching pirate ship. Arthur Connaught, cousin Edward, and his friend Godfrey were distributed strategically around Lily and Mrs. Connaught.

It was a modest meal, good food tinged by war-time shortages. Margaret wrestled with her mutton and tried to engage Sir Cedric, but as Lily had warned her, he was a gloomy man. His one active contribution to tell her that she was older than he had expected, to which she had no answer.

Conversation fluttered and flapped around the table throughout dinner—a sudden burst of Lily, a sarcastic mutter from Edward, and then silence before Lily began again, or Arthur Connaught tried a pleasantry in the actress's direction. No one spoke of the late Alice Maunsey or her husband. The occasional comment about the war was shot down by a look from Sir Cedric, heavy-browed and silver-haired.

Margaret was curious as to Godfrey Colne's role. He said

little, and moved less, a man seeking not to court attention. It was possible, of course, that he and cousin Edward were 'special' friends—Margaret had met other such couples in theatrical circles, and was relaxed about such things.

"And what do you do, Mr. Colne?" she asked in a lull.

He looked surprised to be addressed directly.

"I manage the Maunsey estate in Suffolk, Miss Rutherford."

"Only since last year," said Lily.

He nodded, as if the girl's sharp remark was quite reasonable.

"Indeed. I am a…newcomer to the family."

An estate-manager with ambitions, thought Margaret, but said no more.

Biscuits, cheeses, and fruit followed the main meal. As the food was laid out by the maids, Gertrude Connaught made various complimentary remarks about the house. The second of these, concerning the magnificence of the dining table, brought a smile to Edward Maunsey's lips.

"Haunted, of course."

Lily paled; Mrs. Connaught looked interested. Edward put down the knife with which he'd been paring at the cheese.

"Grandfather bought the whole place—lock, stock, and barrel—for a song, just before the Great War." He leaned forward, fixing his cousin with what Margaret thought was a touch of malice. "They say there used to be séances here, all sorts of nonsense, around this very table. One of them went terribly wrong, and the lady of the house, a countess, went mad. They had her in High Helmsley Asylum until she died."

"Perhaps not ideal talk for dinner," said Margaret.

He shrugged. "It's history, madam—over thirty years ago. And the count, an Austrian or German chap, he had been—"

"Port." Sir Cedric slammed his hand down.

"You're only allowed one glass, daddy," said Lily. "Ladies, shall we retire and leave the gentlemen to their nasty tales."

Sherry with Lily and Gertrude Connaught was a bore. Margaret was tired, and after half a glass she excused herself. Lily insisted on following her to her room, and as the girl showed no signs of leaving, the actress sat on the bed, patting the counterpane next to her.

"Why don't you sit here, and tell me every little incident since you lost your sister. We'll see if there is any sense to be made of it."

'Every little incident' took half an hour to recount. Sounds in the house after Alice's death—the mention of her name in the night—and a shadow in the gardens where her sister used sometimes to sit at night. The locket, and numerous trivial misplacements.

"Almost a Gothic tale, my dear." Margaret thought over the many scripts and plays she had seen. "This may seem silly, but is there any doubt over the inheritance?"

"No. The baronetcy goes to little Cedric, or to Edward if anything happens to Cedric. It's ever so simple."

"And Edward—is he…reliable? Trustworthy?"

Lily's brow creased.

"He's all right, I suppose. Gambles, of course—all his set do. I wouldn't lend him money, mind you."

"He seems close to Mr. Colne."

Lily's frown deepened. "Yes, I don't understand that at all. I don't even think they like each other that much, to be honest."

"Um." The actress stood up. "I shall give the matter some thought, my dear. We should both rest. I shall see you at ten o'clock in the morning, I think, and we shall find somewhere private to talk more."

"No one goes to the orchard except me. We could meet there. But Miss Rutherford—"

"Tomorrow."

Ignoring Lily's look of disappointment, Margaret ushered the girl out of the Blue Room, washed, and undressed for bed. Years of being on the stage had taught her how to cat-nap, and she lay down and closed her eyes.

She woke a few minutes before midnight. Slippers and an old towel dressing gown were to hand, comfortable companions. If there were strangers, or even spirits, abroad in the old hall, then she would at least dare a glimpse, for Lily's sake.

A new moon shone through the many large windows of the

hall and made navigation of the main corridors a simple matter. Armed with a small electric torch, just in case, she found the attic stairs easily.

Where servants had once slept in busier times, decay and the occasional rat dropping prevailed. Someone had been up there before her, though. Footmarks in the dust, too indistinct for her to say anything about the owner—or owners—and a stubbed-out cigarette, a discarded match. And she spotted a smudge on one bare wooden window-seat. Someone had sat there in recent times.

In the farthest room she found what had been kept of Alice Maunsey's belongings after the fatal crash. Half-open cases of clothes, and small items of furniture which had perhaps held some personal significance. The clothes were mostly sensible and practical—jodhpurs, climbing woollens, nothing of fashion.

And a trunk full of memorabilia and letters. It felt wrong to look, though she did pass her torch over a single, unframed photograph which was surely Alice, Lily, and their mother. Alice must have been thirteen or fourteen; Lily four or five. They were both pretty children, which struck her more when she saw their mother.

"Oh, Lily," she sighed. For Lady Maunsey had been a stocky woman with a double chin and a beady gaze. No vanity could let Margaret escape the resemblance between herself and the dead woman. "I just know that you won't let me down," the girl had said when they met.

She laid the picture aside, and was trying to imagine what a real detective might do when she heard a noise.

Footsteps on the attic stairs.

Margaret dodged into the next room, which held only a rusting bed-frame, and closed the door behind her. The footsteps came nearer, muffled by the door.

"There's no point," said an indistinct voice. "We've been through everything up here, I tell you."

"It's here, in this house. It has to be, but we're running out of time." The second voice was fainter. Both were male, she was sure. The second man's voice held anger. "We'll try something else. Something more direct."

The voices faded. After crouching there for as long as she could bear, she emerged, stiff and trembling slightly. Her slippered feet made little sound as she crept down the stairs, trusting to moonlight. Once back on the main landing, she would be within sight of…

"Are you lost, madam?"

The actress dropped the unlit torch. Before her stood a severe figure in a starched black linen dress, full-length and tight to the neck. White skin and the moon gave her face the look of a stage Elizabeth, harsh and regal.

"I…I…"

"I am Mrs. Barton." Expressionless, the woman looked over the actress's towelling gown and fluffy slippers. "The housekeeper."

Margaret tried to recover, as if the script had been changed last minute.

"I don't sleep well," she said, waving one hand vaguely. "Sometimes take a stroll, you know?"

"No." Mrs. Barton picked up the torch and handed it to her. "I sleep when required. You would be Miss Rutherford."

"Um, yes."

"Do you wish for some hot milk, Miss Rutherford? To help you sleep."

Margaret began to breathe calmly again. "No, I'm fine now, thank you. A short constitutional around the house has done the trick, I'm sure."

"Very well. Goodnight, madam."

The housekeeper moved away with the smoothness of a stage device, along the landing in the opposite direction.

"Goodnight, Mrs. Danvers," murmured the actress, and made for the welcome comfort of the Blue Room. "Enough adventures around Mandalay for one night, I think."

The Maunsey breakfast drifted through the morning, with people coming and going. Margaret went down at nine and found some overcooked kidneys to accompany a few slices of toast, followed by a confection which was some wartime substitute for marmalade.

"Carrots and apples," said Gertrude Connaught. "So very clever."

"Yes, indeed." The actress forced down a slice of toast. "Have you seen Lily this morning, Mrs. Connaught?"

"I think she went for a walk." Her normally vapid face took on an air of concentration. "Through the woods, someone said."

"Capital idea. I shall have a stroll myself."

"Lovely."

It wasn't lovely. The clouds were back, driven across the heavens by a stiff breeze. Margaret, congratulating herself that she had her tweeds with her, muffled up and set out for the orchard, where she sat down under an apple tree and waited.

Ten o'clock passed, and the half hour. At eleven, there was still no sign of the girl. Puzzled, Margaret headed back to the house. She found Edward Maunsey and Arthur Connaught playing snooker in the games room.

"Mr. Maunsey, has Lily been back?"

"Not that I noticed. You should ask Barton." Edward looked a touch drunk.

"Who I would find…where?"

"Around the house, dear lady. She keeps track of absolutely everyone."

She hurried to the breakfast room, where a maid was cleaning up. The maid, Hetty, directed her to a small office at the back of the house, where Mrs. Barton apparently did the accounts.

She must have taken a wrong turning, because she found herself in a study. Ink, blotter and pens out, as if ready for work, but much like the attic, a thin layer of dust lay on desk and books.

"Mr. Gerald worked here."

"Oh my goodness!"

She turned, hand to her chest, to face Mrs. Barton.

"My good woman, you have a habit of startling me."

The housekeeper's cold blue eyes met hers.

"Sir Cedric is resting. Mrs. Connaught is on the terrace,

but will retreat soon from the cold wind. Mr. Colne has motored to Selby to shop and send a telegram; Mr. Maunsey and Mr. Connaught are in the games room."

"And Lily?"

An eyebrow flickered.

"Miss Lily is late back from her walk."

"I was to meet her over an hour ago."

A second eyebrow showed signs of life.

"I shall inform the gentlemen, and Carter," said Mrs. Barton, gliding away. A black queen crossing the chessboard, thought the actress.

By lunchtime others began to accept that Lily was missing. The carriage was untouched; Colne had gone in his own car, and there were no other vehicles apart from the Connaught's unreliable Austin.

"I'll take a spin along the road, keep my eyes open," said Connaught, whilst Edward went to tramp the woods. Carter, being local, was instructed to drive the carriage along some of the unmarked back lanes. Mrs. Barton organised a search of the house and outbuildings, to no avail.

All they could do was to wait. By four o'clock everyone was in the drawing room, including Godfrey Colne, back from Selby, but there was no word of Lily Maunsey.

"Young Carter isn't back," said Margaret.

"Well the carriage is," said Edward. "I could see it as I walked back."

"Carter would always come through the glasshouse to enter the hall." Mrs. Barton sniffed, and led the way through the house and down a short corridor. A door there opened onto a glasshouse which clung to the back wall of the main house. The far door of the glasshouse opened onto the courtyard, where the carriage could be seen, the horses still in harness.

"That can't be right," said Connaught.

Two large cast iron stoves were flanked by trestle tables, some supported by bricks. These tables held a range of plants in troughs and pots. A few appeared to be tender refugees from the coming autumn; others were garden plants which might be induced to extend their flowering season in a bright spot indoors. Marigolds still bloomed freely here, orange and yellow gaiety odd beside tall, sickly-looking cacti and late geraniums.

Margaret, at the housekeeper's side, had something else on which to concentrate. A body lay sprawled face down on the wooden flooring, close to a table of potted plants.

"Carter," said the housekeeper. She gave Margaret a hard stare, and then slid over to the prone form, bending to feel at the wrist.

Margaret knew there would be no hope. Above the collar of the patched jacket, the back of the boy's head was a mass of blood and hair.

Gertrude Connaught shrieked. Edward went pale.

"The body is warm. I shall telephone for the police," said Mrs. Barton rising to her full height. "Mr. Maunsey, in Miss Maunsey's absence, it would be best if you informed Sir Cedric."

"Absolutely."

"I'll keep an eye on the body," said Colne. "Best not move anything."

Margaret thought for a moment that Edward was going to speak, but he bit at his lip and walked away. She had no stomach for such things, but if it had anything to do with young Lily, then she had a duty to be strong. She looked around. There was no obvious 'blunt instrument' as the crime stories would have had it. Everything was where she imagined it should be, except…

Two pots lay by the body, quite out of place. One was on its side, and the dead fingers were an inch from it. A spatter of compost leading from the table indicated the plants had been moved quite recently. She might have thought he had been surprised in his work, but that didn't hold water. Surely he would have been coming in to report on his search?

She made herself go closer. There was nothing special about the plants. One was a dark green rosette which she recognised from its pretty red flowers—an avens—and the other was a bushy potted marigold.

"Avens and marigold," she said, not meaning anyone to

hear.

Gertrude Connaught, still standing in the doorway as if frozen, looked at her.

"AM," said the woman. "Alice Maunsey. Lily was right!" And she fled into the depths of the house.

An ageing police inspector was sent out from Selby, along with a sergeant and a constable. The actress was considered above suspicion, and was barely questioned. She sat in the drawing room and sipped at strong tea with Gertrude Connaught whilst interviews were held elsewhere.

"What did you mean dear, when you said that Lily was right?"

Mrs. Connaught looked around, eyeing the tall windows and the half-open door. When she spoke, her voice was low and far more serious than previously.

"Miss Rutherford, I don't think this is the best place for you at the moment. You might consider going back to London."

Margaret frowned.

"Are you talking about—"

"Secrets." The other woman leaned closer. "You will have to trust me, Miss Rutherford. The closer you get to anything connected with Alice Maunsey, the more danger you may be in."

"There's no haunting, surely? No restless spirit at Selby Hall."

"There may be—I wouldn't know about that sort of thing. Lily was always over-imaginative." Mrs. Connaught had a humourless smile on her thin red lips. "But I do know that there's a war on." She rose, and her voice returned to its usual airiness. "I simply must ask the police what is happening. Such a shock..."

Baffled, the actress went onto the terrace. The air was fresh, almost bracing. A young woman was missing; a boy had been killed. She had always avoided roles which brushed too closely upon the gore and mechanics of death. They disturbed her—and there was enough in her past that disturbed her already. And yet, there was Lily. It always came back to that. To go home now was unthinkable.

Rooks cawed in the trees, and she set her jaw at them.

"We shall see what we can do," she told them, and went back inside.

She found the police sergeant in the glasshouse.

"Are you a local man, sergeant?"

He looked surprised.

"Uh, yes, madam."

"Do you remember Miss Maunsey's—I mean Mrs. Mountforth's—accident?"

A florid man, he eased his collar with one finger.

"The missus and I saw you in Hull, Miss Rutherford. It were a good evening, that. Madame Arcati, very funny. I said to the missus—"

"Thank you, but please, the accident?"

He shifted from one large boot to the other.

"Tragic, it were. Lot of rain that night. We had a couple of nasty jobs—someone nearly went in the Ouse, where the bank had slipped, and there was a crash by Brayton…"

"So you didn't suspect foul play?"

He looked surprised. "No. Not to speak ill of the dead, but they must have been going at a fair rate, far too fast for these roads. That Mr. Colne checked the car as well, said it was fine—"

"Mr. Godfrey Colne?"

"Aye. He were at the hall that day. Knew about motors, thought he should make sure. Nothing mechanical amiss, he said, and he was right—the inspector had one of our people look at it after it was towed." Understanding dawned. "Thinking it was one of these plots, like your plays, Miss Rutherford?"

"Idle thoughts, sergeant, idle thoughts."

She must have a plan of action. Others were searching for Lily, and she prayed that the girl was safe. There were things Margaret could do, as a member of the house-party, that the police could not: quiet things. She had her wits, and she knew people. Suspicion did not come easily to her, but she must take the bull by the horns.

Mrs. Barton was in her office. It was as Spartan as the woman's clothing, with everything neatly labelled and shelved.

"Can I help you, madam?"

"What was Alice Maunsey like?" She had decided on the direct approach.

The housekeeper gave one slow blink.

"I'm not going away, you know," said Margaret.

Mrs. Barton closed the ledger on her desk.

"Difficult. Headstrong. And over-involved in her husband's activities."

"The Army?"

"Military intelligence." Mrs. Barton fixed her with eyes of ice. "Sir Cedric, Miss Lily and Mr. Maunsey know nothing of this. I, on the other hand, see most things that happen at Selby Hall."

Margaret leant back against the door-frame.

"Then the trip to Denmark was a cover of some sort, for dangerous work."

"No doubt." Mrs. Barton moved the ledger a half inch, aligning it perfectly with the rectangular desk top. "But I wasn't privy to any of their secrets. I have nothing to add. Miss Alice and her husband are dead—"

"And so is Carter."

"Yes." She gave that measured blink again. "That is a nuisance. Will that be all, madam?"

Margaret went to her room and rummaged through one of her cases. Pulling out a notebook in which she sometimes wrote difficult lines, trying to fix them in her head, she made a series of entries:

> *Lily Maunsey—Missing. Thought AM trying to warn her of s'thing.*
> *Edward Maunsey—Sly. Weak?*
> *Godfrey Colne—Too involved. Not right.*
> *Connaught—What he seems, pleasant young man?*
> *Mrs. Connaught—Playing a part. Why?*

Mrs. Barton—Controlling.
Sir Cedric—Self-involved. Grieving. Too old.
Carter—Knew something. Murdered.

Margaret shivered at that last word. It was still tempting to leave this to the police. She wished she had Stringer with her, but he was far away overseas, doing his bit. At a time like this she needed a confidante. She closed her notebook and slipped it under her mattress. That poor boy—only the day before he had brought her luggage up to her, and made that silly joke. Marguerite. She was fond of marguerites, such pretty white flowers, though he had used the Latin name…

"Oh!"

A brief visit to Sir Cedric's library gave the answer she needed, enough to make her bold enough to search out the housekeeper again.

"I need to make a private telephone call, Mrs. Barton."

"Mr. Mountforth's study has a telephone, madam."

"I'm not sure I should—"

"It is more private than the usual apparatus. Under the circumstances."

Mrs. Barton's eyes flickered in the direction of the police constable by the main entrance.

"Ah, yes. Thank you."

Under the circumstances. This time when she entered the dead man's study, it seemed to have more meaning. He and his wife had gone to Occupied Denmark to do something, presumably for the war effort. The Danish Resistance? Or to make contact with someone else? She saw the telephone, set on a small table in the corner, and made her call.

"It is most urgent," she said into the receiver. "If you could please just fetch Mr. Coward, even for a moment."

A pause, and then the Master's unmistakable voice, tetchy and bored. Margaret made a hasty apology, but she knew what she had to do.

"Noel—I have some dreadfully important questions for you."

"And I have a dreadfully important dinner to attend, Margaret. Did you know that we continued performances, using a couple of understudies? Heaven knows why, but the masses don't like our replacement Arcati, not at all. Fay's had a terrible row with Quartermaine—I predict a scene and divorce—and will be back soon. I simply must have you all together again—"

"Please. You have certain, um, connections I need."

"I rather thought you had an agent, darling."

"Not those sort of connections. Your 'other' work."

"Ah. I did not realise that you knew. And I doubt that you should, given the importance—"

"A girl's life is at stake," she said, daring to cut across him. He sighed dramatically.

"If you must ask, do hurry. There is a difference, you know, between being fashionably late and being a bore."

Almost stammering, she rattled off her questions, muddling names at one point. When she had everything right, she drew a deep breath.

"You see?"

"The Mountforths again? I shall do what I can, dear lady, though I'm sure I shouldn't. There is a dear boy at the Ministry who owes me a favour—and a drink—or two. Expect a telegram in the morning. And have your bags packed, remember. The Piccadilly is waiting."

The dressing gong sounded almost as soon as she placed the receiver down. To go through dinner with Lily missing and Carter dead seemed almost macabre, but she supposed it had to be done. On her way to dress, she slipped into the nursery. Little Cedric, the young heir, was in a playpen, enthusiastically hitting wooden alphabet blocks with his rattle. The battered tin toy made no noise, and Margaret suspected that some sensitive soul had wisely removed the beans, or whatever had been inside.

"Is he well?" she asked the venerable nanny, who was knitting by the playpen.

Nanny Fletcher looked up.

"Eh?"

"Master Cedric. I do hope he's not upset by all this business."

"It's the war," said the old woman. "It took my Alice, and now my Lily…" She wiped one eye. "I was the last to speak to her, I was."

"Lily?"

"Miss Alice. Such a mess she was, and she had to see him…" She tipped her mob-cap towards the playpen. "But I did right, and he loves his rattle, he does."

Margaret smiled. "I'm sure you did right, nanny. He seems a happy boy."

But the old lady's chin was down on her chest.

Margaret slipped away.

Dinner was what might have been expected. Sir Cedric refused to come down, leaving five people to make an indifferent job of the courses. Gertrude Connaught talked brightly as if all would be right, and the men, in the eighth Baronet's absence, discussed sport and the Russian front.

Police and the estate workers were searching the woods on foot, and volunteers were on the nearby River Ouse in a rowing boat, checking the banks. The only progress was that a bloodied brick had been found in the glasshouse, presumably the murder weapon, though there was little hope of fingerprints. Inspector Tolliver had asked the family to stay where they were, and await news.

Alone with Mrs. Connaught after the meal, Margaret felt a certain impatience.

"You know something," she said, fixing the other woman in her sights. "About what is happening."

Gertrude Connaught slid one expensively-stockinged leg against the other.

"Not exactly. Arthur—my husband—is simply Arthur, you know. Works for the Ministry of War Transport, making sure we have sufficient lorries for food transport, and so on. Worthy and dull. I was jealous of Alice Maunsey, frankly."

"Why would that be?"

"She dropped enough hints that she was doing something wild. That she and Gerald were living life to the full, and taking risks—unlike the reliable old Connaughts."

"Denmark?"

"Oh that, and other things. Hints, as I said, not details. Free French, the Resistance—goodness knows what Gerald was involved with." The woman's laugh was bitter-edged. "I even suggested I might help, but Alice said it was too dangerous. Gerald had relatives on the continent, and connections."

Margaret refilled their sherries.

"You felt left out?"

"I suppose so. We argued before they went abroad. And I'd been spending more time with Lily. I'm little Cedric's godmother, by the bye."

The actress sipped her drink.

"How does Edward Maunsey fit into all this?"

"I suspect he's in debt to Colne. Oh, I think he's harmless—believes himself a smart gadabout—but it wouldn't surprise me if Godfrey Colne had lent him cash from the Suffolk Estate. Arthur, naturally, thinks no evil of either of them." She looked up from her sherry. "Edward couldn't hurt a dead fly, if that's your angle, Miss Rutherford."

"No, perhaps not."

They subsided into a more comfortable silence, until Gertrude's husband popped his head into the room and said the men were going to play snooker.

"Nothing else to do," he said to the actress, apologetically.

Gertrude put down her glass. "A book and an early night. Let's hope to God that the police find Lily, unharmed."

Margaret decided that she could risk one more investigation of her own. While the men were occupied, she visited the bedrooms of Edward Maunsey and Godfrey Colne. And found something which puzzled her.

Coming out of Edward Maunsey's room, she met the housekeeper. There was no way she could conceal where she had been.

"On one of your constitutionals, madam?"

Margaret drew herself up to her full height, which still wasn't a match for Mrs. Barton.

"We all have our part to play," she said, with as much dignity as she could muster.

The woman nodded, almost imperceptibly.

"Mr. Maunsey has forgotten his cigarette lighter, and will be up here very shortly. You might wish to use the servants' stairs. Madam."

Margaret was at a loss.

"Um, thank you, Mrs. Barton."

Once safe in her own quarters, she considered that she had done all that she could. The trail led back to whatever Alice Maunsey had been up to, and she wouldn't be surprised if both Lily's disappearance and the boy's death were a result of that. She would have to tell the inspector, as soon as she had things clear in her head.

Sleep was elusive. Twice she imagined footsteps in the attics above, and the sounds of the old house settling disturbed her. At around one in the morning she drifted off, still fretting that she wanted to be up and ready early.

She awoke suddenly, unable to breathe. No, she could breathe, but there was a soft weight on her face, a pillow being pressed down over her mouth.

"This is not the stage," said a man's muffled voice. "If you stay here, your only role will be as the body in the corner. Remember Carter, and go home."

The weight diminished. When she dared push the pillow aside, there was no one in the room. Shaking, she reached for her handbag, and pulled out the small flask of brandy she kept there. One, two gulps.

The warning had been received, loud and clear.

Everyone was there around the same time at breakfast, as if summoned by some silent gong. Appetites were poor, though the police sergeant in the hallway was munching his way through several rounds of toast. The search had moved on towards Selby, and they were told that constables were stopping local cars, asking if they had seen anything.

As for the murder of the boy, the official line was that he must have surprised a ne'er-do-well, tramp—or even burglar—trying to sneak into the hall from the rear. Even the inspector seemed uncomfortable about such a weak conclusion, and was prowling the glasshouse again in person.

She picked at half a plate of scrambled eggs.

"I think," she said, with a tremor in her voice, "That I should leave. My nerves are quite shot by these terrible events, and I saw Inspector Tolliver a few minutes ago. He says that he has no further questions for me. There's nothing an old woman can do here."

"Barely middle-aged, Miss Rutherford," said Arthur Connaught. "Don't be so hard on yourself."

"So kind. No, really, I must be off. I expect that the organised Mrs. Barton will have the times of trains from Selby."

As if summoned by her name, the housekeeper was in the doorway.

"There is a telegram for you, Miss Rutherford."

"Goodness me. That will be dear Noel, from the theatre." She looked at the other guests, an apologetic smile on her lips. "I expect he will want me back at the Piccadilly."

She rose and went to receive the telegram. It was more detailed than expected, and she read it twice before slipping it into her handbag. The contents occasioned one more telephone call from Gerald Mountforth's study, and a quiet word with the police in the hall.

Back in the breakfast room she examined the railway timetable.

"The twelve forty-five would seem suitable." She hesitated. "Of course, poor Carter can no longer take me in the carriage. I wonder if there's a local taxicab…"

"I have the Austin." Arthur Connaught rose to his feet. "She's a touch juddery, but I could—"

"No need," said Godfrey Colne. "I was heading into Selby anyway. I would be delighted to see Miss Rutherford off. We have said little to each other, with these unfortunate occurrences."

"Very kind of you, Mr. Colne. I accept, of course." Margaret coughed, unsure what else to say. "I do wish we had all met under better circumstances. Well then—I have time for a turn around the old orchard before I leave. Fresh air is always a blessing when the mind is troubled."

"I shall find you there when the car is ready, Miss Rutherford," said Colne.

She made her goodbyes to the others, pressing Gertrude Connaught's hands, and accepting pleasantries. Edward Maunsey had little to say, which did not surprise her.

A light wind stirred the apple trees, a pleasant rustle which made the place seem peaceful, if sad. Lily's place— contemplation amongst the twisted trunks of the past. The actress kicked a windfall, and waited, breathing deeply of the cool Yorkshire air and the smell of decaying leaves. Twenty or so minutes passed before she heard the crunch of footsteps.

"All is ready, Miss Rutherford." Godfrey Colne was there, in an expensive leather motoring jacket and matching gloves.

"Tell me, Mr. Colne, how well do you know Edward Maunsey?"

A puzzled expression crossed his face. "Why do you ask?"

"Between you and me, I have my suspicions about him." She moved closer, "These dreadful events…I feel sure that Mr. Maunsey knows more than he is letting on. I understand he gambles, and has debts."

Colne blew out his cheeks, looking thoughtful.

"You think he might be involved in Lily's disappearance."

"Possibly. Goodness me, in so many of these books and plays, a family member is at the bottom of it all. Nearest—but not dearest."

He looked uncomfortable.

"I know Edward, of course, but never thought him anything but harmless. Of course, you're right about his gambling. No real head for it, from what I've seen. But the rest…have you anything to go on?"

"A detail or two." She frowned. "It may be nothing…"

He paced, circling a withered tree.

"I'm not the person to ask, really, Miss Rutherford. Perhaps we should tell the police, though it's a poor show, casting suspicion on a man like that."

"Oh, I understand. That's why I wanted to ask you before I did anything."

He nodded. "Of course. A tricky situation. On balance, I

suppose that we must go to the inspector."

"I'm so pleased you see it that way, Mr. Ohnerecht."

He stood silent for a long moment, examining his gloved hands.

"A strange name to use," he said at last. "Should I know it?"

Margaret fixed him with a glare.

"You should, having been born with it. Gottfried Ohnerecht, late of Cologne—or Köln, as I believe you Germans call it. Was that where you had the idea of becoming Mr. 'Colne' from?"

"It seemed appropriate."

"You don't deny it, then?"

He had a tight smile upon his face. "I no longer need to— with you. I did warn you, last night, if you remember, but it seems you are too stubborn for your own good."

"And Lily?"

"She is safe enough, though I found her unhelpful. A bruise or two. Now I must find a way to remove you from this theatre of ours, at least until I have time to think."

She thrust out her jaw. "I am a professional. I stay until the last performance." She raised the whistle she had borrowed, hidden in her left hand, and blew with all her strength.

Cursing, he lunged to dash the whistle from her hand.

"Too late," she said.

Inspector Tolliver was at the edge of the orchard, closing on them, and she was relieved to see the sergeant and the Connaughts coming up at a pace from the hall. It had been rather a mad gamble.

Colne swore again and grasped her, sliding one arm around her throat.

"Come no closer," he shouted, "Or it will go badly for Miss Rutherford."

The men held back, hesitant, but Gertrude Connaught stepped forward. She glanced at her husband.

"Arthur, I love you, but you are very boring sometimes. I always, always, wanted adventure." And she pulled a small revolver from her purse, pointing it directly at Godfrey Colne's head. "I'm not a terribly good shot, Mr. Colne, but there's a fair chance that I'll hit you."

Arthur Connaught looked appalled.

"Gertrude—you carry a gun!"

"A consolation present from Alice, for my birthday last year."

"You would not dare fire." Colne gripped the actress tighter, keeping her between himself and the small revolver in Mrs. Connaught's hand. Margaret, finding it hard to breathe, did the only thing she could think of. She stamped down hard on his instep with her solid, sensible leather heel.

"Ach!" The man staggered, and Margaret threw herself to one side. She heard the crack of a revolver shot, and when she looked up from where she had fallen, Gertrude was standing with the gun still raised, a wild smile on her face.

"I missed," she said, "But I think there are four more bullets."

Colne lifted his arms in surrender, and was grabbed by the sergeant, handcuffs ready. Arthur Connaught helped the actress to her feet, looking confused.

"Thank you, dear. I think your wife might need you."

Gertrude had dropped the gun, and was visibly shaking. He rushed to her side, and they held each other.

Inspector Tolliver came over, out of breath.

"I don't entirely understand, Miss Rutherford, though I did what you asked. Nor do I approve of civilians—"

"Neither do I," said Margaret. "But an act was needed to draw him out, and I am the only actress you have." She looked around at the small company. "Where is Edward Maunsey?"

"Damn, I forgot about him. I should have had him watched."

They made their way back to Selby Hall, Colne cuffed and subdued with the sergeant behind him. The housekeeper stood in the main hallway, her arms folded as she watched the strange procession.

"Have you seen Mr. Maunsey?" asked Margaret.

"Mr. Maunsey is in his room."

"But…"

"There seems to be a problem with the door. No doubt I will find the spare key soon, and will be able to extricate him." Mrs. Barton's face was expressionless. "Your Mrs. Danvers was very effective, if I might say so, madam. Perhaps a trifle overdone. I attended one performance. I found Celia Johnson to be damp."

Margaret smiled.

"I won't tell her that."

Edward Maunsey, brought down and faced with Colne in handcuffs, fell apart. He had done nothing, Edward insisted, almost weeping. It was true, he had borrowed heavily—and without Sir Cedric's knowledge—on the Suffolk Estate, and Colne was blackmailing him. Invitations to Selby Hall at key moments, information about the Mountforths, and so on.

"Nothing illegal, for God's sake!"

"Where is Lily?" Margaret wanted to slap the man.

"He wouldn't tell me, honestly. I told him it was wrong, what he was doing! He threatened me."

Tolliver grabbed the German's collar.

"Come on, Colne! The truth, now."

"His real name is Ohnerecht, Inspector." Margaret brushed leaf-litter from her jacket. "He's a German agent."

Edward paled. "Dash it, you don't think I--"

"No," said the actress. "I don't believe that you have it in you, Mr. Maunsey. You are a foolish and unreliable young man, but not a traitor."

"A spy, eh?" Tolliver whistled. "That paints another picture altogether..."

"I have harmed no-one." Ohnerecht pulled free of the Inspector's grasp and stood stiff-backed, glaring at the actress. "Your precious Lily is confined, merely, in one of your crumbling English cowsheds, some miles away."

"Along one of those narrow lanes that poor young Carter searched, I suppose?" said Margaret.

Ohnerecht shrugged. "He was suspicious. He may have seen the man I hired to watch her—I do not know. When I returned from Selby and saw him in the courtyard, he was going to tell the police..."

"So you killed him. Cold-blooded murder. And yet you say you harmed no-one." Tolliver was red with anger.

Ohnerecht shrugged. "No-one of importance."

"Take him out of my sight." Tolliver turned to his sergeant. "Get the location out of him and have a car sent straight away. If he tries anything, or lies to you, I'll hang him myself."

Arthur Connaught took it upon himself to hand round stiff drinks in the dining room. Edward Maunsey sat alone, cradling a whisky and avoiding everyone's gaze.

Tolliver wiped his forehead with a large handkerchief.

"Why? What is all this really about, Miss Rutherford? I mean, German spies here in East Yorkshire…"

"Secrets, Inspector," she said, accepting a large brandy from Connaught. "Secrets, adventure, and the war." It was the same at the end of any show. She felt exhausted, unwilling to speak to anyone, but it must be done. She took a deep breath.

"I am no detective, Inspector. You must piece things together properly. But it is often the small touches that make a show work. The plants in the glasshouse, for example."

Puzzled stares met that comment. She let the brandy warm her.

"Argyranthemum. That poor boy knew his Latin when it came to plants, and he must, like many of his age, have read those cheap thrillers that one sees. As he was dying, he dragged two pots down from the tables."

"An avens and a marigold," said Gertrude Connaught. "AM. Alice Maunsey."

"No, dear. A Geum and a Calendula. GC, do you see. Godfrey Colne. And then there were the handkerchiefs." She blushed. "I'm afraid that I snooped into these men's rooms. I heard two voices in the attic, and settled on Mr. Colne and Mr. Maunsey as the most likely suspects, though at that time I had no idea what was happening. There were no secret plans or incriminating notes in their belongings, of course. This is not a stage play. I did however find monogrammed handkerchiefs in Mr. Colne's room."

"I have some of my own," said Arthur Connaught. "Quite

common."

"Yes, but these had been altered. I do a little sewing, in between acts. GC they said on them, but the C was the result of stitches being carefully unpicked. You would never notice, normally, that they had belonged to someone with the initials GO, originally. The O had been made into a C."

"How peculiar," said Gertrude.

"One of those tiny mistakes, which would never have been noticed in normal circumstances. But I had enough—Godfrey Colne, whoever he really was, cropped up everywhere. I found it hard to understand his acquaintance with Edward, and then I found that he was the person who had volunteered to check the Mountforth's car after the accident. He was named in plants by the dead boy, and yet he seemed to have another name altogether. Too many puzzles about him altogether."

"But why? What did he seek to gain?" Gertrude clutched her husband's hand. "What was he after?"

"I don't know, exactly, but it was something of Alice's. Something the Mountforths brought back from Denmark."

Edward Maunsey gave a bitter laugh. "He told me that it was to do with the estate. That there was proof I should have the baronetcy after Sir Cedric, not that blasted kid. Documents that Alice had kept from me."

"He fed you total nonsense. I had a telegram from a friend in London this morning. The Mountforths worked for British Intelligence. And although the authorities know nothing of a Godfrey Colne, they did have a file on one Gottfried Ohnerecht, of a remarkably similar description. A Nazi agent believed to be working in England. I was certain then that GC was GO."

Tolliver looked thoughtful. "Information, then. The war effort."

"Oh, yes. Quite important information, I imagine, to take such risks. After searching the car at the time, and then the house repeatedly, for weeks, I think he became desperate. In the end, he took Lily to try and um, squeeze the truth out of her. He assumed that she, as Alice's sister and former confidante, must know where it was, if anyone did."

"Yet Colne didn't leave," said Tolliver. "So Miss Maunsey held out."

"She never knew, inspector. She had no idea what they were after."

"Then whatever it was, it's lost."

"Not necessarily. I have a thought, silly though it seems."

The actress led them into the nursery, where Nanny Fletcher was watching over Cedric. Margaret pulled up a chair, and took the nanny's hand.

"Do you remember the night of the crash? What Alice Maunsey said to you, about something very, very important?"

The old lady looked up, puzzled at the number of visitors to her domain. Her eyes narrowed. "I'm not supposed to tell."

"You can tell me, dear," said Margaret. "I'm only an actress, no-one important."

Nanny Fletcher mulled that over, and then nodded.

"She said I should keep it safe, and not tell until she came for it." Her wrinkled face showed distress. "But then the doctor said…he said that my Alice wasn't going to make it. My poor little Alice…"

"It's all right," said Margaret, patting her hand gently. "The police are here, ready to take what you've been keeping. Inspector, do you have your warrant card?"

She took it from his outstretched hand, and held it close to the nanny's face.

"You see. It's what Alice would have wanted."

Nanny Fletcher blinked back tears.

"He loves his rattle, you know."

"I'm sure he does."

Margaret went over to the play pen and leaned down. The boy was heavy for his age, but she sat him on the nanny's lap.

"Can I look at your toy, Cedric?"

Big brown eyes, which reminded her so much of Lily's, weighed her up, and then he handed the tin rattle to her.

"For you, inspector."

Tolliver took the toy awkwardly, and shook it.

"It doesn't make any noise."

"That's what made me wonder."

Carefully, the inspector twisted the top of the rattle until the head split into two neat halves.

"Blimey."

Inside, along with some dried beans, was a wad of papers, tightly screwed up. He unfolded part of the ball, enough to show that small, neat letters covered every inch.

"Names," he said. "English, French and Danish names, but with other ones next to them. And addresses. Hang on, it's alphabetical." He squinted at a second sheet, and a satisfied smile lit his face. "Colne, Godfrey = Kapitän Gottfried Ohnerecht. Well I never!"

Margaret took back the pieces of the rattle and put them together, returning it to the child. Little Cedric shook it, and a smile as wide as the inspector's filled his chubby face as it rattled properly once more.

"I imagine they're names gained by or through the Danish Resistance, inspector. You might want to be very careful with those, and get them to the authorities as soon as possible."

Tolliver looked at her with admiration.

"You're a regular Hercules Poirot, Miss Rutherford."

She blushed. "Hardly, inspector. Though if the role should ever come up, possibly a Miss Marple. I doubt it, though. I have no head for murder or such unpleasantries."

Lily Maunsey was recovered, safe and only slightly bruised, and returned to great acclaim. She tumbled from the police car into the actress's arms.

"Is it over?"

Margaret kissed her on the forehead, as she hoped Lily's mother might have done.

"All over, and a happy ending, of sorts."

"I knew I could rely on you, darling Miss Rutherford. But Alice…"

"Alice is at peace, and always was, my dear. There were no spirits, troubled or ominous. Sadly a human presence was responsible for everything."

"And that awful Godfrey Colne—the constables said in the

car that—"

"On his way to jail, or possibly worse. I'd rather not think about it. You will need to have stiff words with your cousin Edward, though. He'll be facing charges. He's a fool, but not much of a criminal."

Lily pulled straw from her blouse.

"You will stay, at least for tonight?"

"I will, dear. But the Piccadilly awaits, and a somewhat demanding director."

"You will be marvellous!" Lily beamed at her. "I shall write and tell Mr. Coward what a hero you are, as well."

"Tut tut, none of that. We shall keep this little adventure quiet, I think." She watched as Gertrude Connaught came forward to help. "And speaking of adventure, I suggest you befriend Mrs. Connaught. I suspect that you will find her far more suited to this sort of thing than a bumbling old thespian."

"Bumbling?" Gertrude put her arm around the girl. "Hardly, Miss Rutherford. Hardly!"

DID YOU ENJOY WHAT YOU JUST READ?

If you enjoyed this book, *please* review it on Amazon and GoodReads!

It's the best way to support the author.

For fantastic fiction, in-depth articles by your favourite authors, open submissions, and more, please...

VISIT OUR WEBSITE
18thwall.com/

LIKE US ON FACEBOOK
facebook.com/18thwall/

FOLLOW US ON TWITTER
@18thWall

We'd love to hear from you! You help make these books possible.

Author Bios

Johannes Chazot was born in 1988 in Evry, France, and soon realised they liked to doodle nonsensical things full of colours that made most reasonable adults go "Huh?" 30 years later, nothing much has changed.

Nicole Petit writes because no other job lets her sleep until noon. She writes the Magic Realm Manuscripts series and curated the collections Speakeasies and Spiritualists (Best Magical Realism Short Story; Best Other Short Story; as well as top ten Best Horror stories & Best Anthology—Preditors and Editors Readers' Poll 2017), After Avalon (#4 Best Anthology—Preditors and Editors Readers' Poll 2016), and From the Dragon Lord's Library (Best Story and Best Cover—PulpArk New Pulp Awards 2016). The Preditors and Editors Readers' Poll named her #2 Best Editor overall.

Josh Reynolds has been a professional freelance writer since 2007. His stories can be found in anthologies such as *Sharkpunk* and *Atomic Age Cthulhu*. Besides his own work, he has written for Games Workshop's *Warhammer Fantasy Battles* and *Warhammer 40,000* media tie-in lines, as well as Gold Eagle's *Mack Bolan: Executioner* line. To find out more, visit https://joshuamreynolds.wordpress.com/.

Jon Black is your basic "absinthe and BBQ" guy from Austin. As a child, he listened to Sherlock Homes on audio book during family road trips and watched *The Sign of the Four* movie on cable approximately a million times back in the '80s. Sherlock Holmes has been part of his fiber for a very long time and "A Scandal in Hollywood" is his affectionate, if tongue in cheek, tribute to all things Holmesian. He is the author of the Jazz Age supernatural mystery "Gabriel's Trumpet," voted "Best Short Story, all other genres" in the 2017 Preditors & Editors poll. *Bel Nemeton*, the first book in his series combining 6th century Arthurian historical fantasy with 21st century progressive pulp, is now available from 18thWall. He also writes for roleplaying games and is an occasional contributor to Steve Jackson Game's *Pyramid*. His nonfiction includes extensive work in music history and music journalism. Look for him at JonBlackWriters.com, https://www.facebook.com/JonBlackAuthor, and, when he remembers, on Twitter at @BlackOnBlues.

James Bojaciuk is CEO Duobus of 18thWall Productions. He's also the co-host and producer of *The Raconteur Roundtable*, a podcast dedicated to intimate, in-depth interviews with creators. If that weren't enough, he's written a *Faction Paradox* spin-off story (in *Stranger Tales of the City*), a Sherlock Holmes story which won *Best Steampunk Short Story* (*Preditors and Editors Readers' Poll 2017*), and listened to *Gallifrey* more times than is strictly good for him.

Exiled to the blazing wastes of Arizona for communing with ghastly Lovecraftian abominations, *C. L. Werner* strives to infect others with the grotesque images that infest his mind. He is the author of over thirty novels and novellas in settings ranging from Warhammer, Age of Sigmar, and Warhammer 40,000 to the Iron Kingdoms and Wild West Exodus. His novella *Himalayan Horror* was featured in the Cryptid Clash series. His short fiction has appeared in several anthologies, among them *Rage of the Behemoth, Sharkpunk, Kaiju Rising,*

A Grimoire of Eldritch Investigations Volume I, Edge of Sundown , *Shakespeare vs Cthulhu, City of the Gods, Mech: Age of Steel, Marching Time*, and the first issue of *Tales from the Magician's Skull*.

M.H. Norris recently launched her mystery series, *All The Petty Myths*, which combines forensics and mythology. The first volume featured the premiere story "Midnight," which won #2 Best Mystery Novel in the 2017 Preditors and Editors Readers' Poll.

Her first novel, *Badge City: Notches*, earned her the 2016 Pulp Ark New Pulp Award for Best Novella, and her second novella, *The Whole Art of Detection*, took #4 Best Mystery in The 2016 Preditors and Editors Readers' Poll.

She is co-host and co-producer on *The Raconteur Roundtable*, a popular podcast focused on in-depth, intimate interviews with authors, actors, and other creators.

William J. Martin is a burgeoning writer from Liverpool. His previous work has mostly been for 18thWall Productions, most notably in their award-winning anthology, *Speakeasies and Spiritualists*. A story inspired by his favorite 90s sitcom appeared in the *Doctor Who* charity collection Unbound (FTB). His more mundane accomplishments include maintaining a large collection of *Doctor Who* DVDs, and being too tall.

John Linwood Grant is a professional writer/editor who lives in Yorkshire with a pack of lurchers and a beard. Widely published in magazines and anthologies, he writes strange fiction, including the Mamma Lucy tales of 1920s hoodoo, the Last Edwardian series, contemporary weird stories, and speculative fiction in the Technosophy series. He is also editor of Occult Detective Quarterly, plus forthcoming anthologies. His 2017 collection 'A Persistence of Geraniums'—stories of murder, madness and the supernatural—is now available on Amazon.

Previews
Casefiles of the Royal Occultist
Josh Reynolds

Formed during the reign of Elizabeth I, the post of the Royal Occultist, or 'the Queen's Conjurer' as it was known, was created for and first held by the diligent amateur, Dr. John Dee, in recognition for an unrecorded service to the Crown.

The title has passed through a succession of hands since, some good, some bad; the list is a long one, weaving in and out of the margins of British history and including such luminaries as the 1st Earl of Holderness and Thomas Carnacki.

Now, in the wake of the Great War, the title and offices have fallen to Charles St. Cyprian, who, accompanied by his apprentice Ebe Gallowglass, defends the British Empire against threats occult, otherworldly, infernal and divine even as the wider world lurches once more on the path to war…

The Unwrapping Party

The beast was dead, to start with. It was a good way to start the day, to Charles St. Cyprian's way of thinking. Something hungry and foul had dredged itself out of the muddy bottom of Windermere in Cumbria, and it had taken a week and a day to give it a seeing to, lest it nibble on the day-trippers. Now, the black Crossley 20/25 prowled down the Thames Embankment in the morning fog, Cumbrian mud crusted on its tires and hood, the driver's fingers tapping on the wheel. The car was the same make and model used by the Flying Squad of the London Metropolitan Police, a fact which its owner found amusing.

After all, the Royal Occultist was a policeman of a sort, at least in the Year of Our Lord 1919. Formed during the reign of Elizabeth the First, the office of Royal Occultist (or the

Queen's Conjurer, as it had then been known) had started with the diligent amateur Dr. John Dee, and passed through a succession of capable (or not-so capable) hands since. The list was a long one, weaving in and out of the margins of British history, and culminating, for the moment, in one Charles St. Cyprian and his assistant-cum-apprentice, Ebe Gallowglass.

He looked over at the latter, smiling slightly. Slender and dark, she was quite obviously 'not from around here' wherever she went this side of the Nile. Born in a Cairo slum to the unpleasant former priestess of an equally unpleasant cult and a deranged Gaelic occultist, Gallowglass had her mother's looks and her father's temper. She dressed like a man and fought like, well, a woman, which meant she was deadlier than St. Cyprian was entirely comfortable with at times. While shooting things was a large part of the Royal Occultist's job, there were times when decidedly *not* shooting things was the order of the day. If she lived long enough, she'd have his job, and be welcome to it; the 'job' being the investigation, organization and occasional suppression of That Which Man Was Not Meant to Know.

Vampires, ghosts, werewolves, ogres, goblins, hobgoblins, bogles, barguests, boojums and other assorted unclassifiable entities were the purview of the Royal Occultist, as were sorcerers, both foreign and domestic, and the occasional dragon. In short, if it needed to die and the usual methods wouldn't cut it, the Queen's (or King's) Conjurer was on the case.

The title and its offices, such as they were, were bestowed either by the King or Queen, depending upon the gender of the fundament upon the throne, and could only be removed by the same, though Cromwell, bless his black heart, had given it a go. But even the Puritans had had their Witchfinder General in Matthew Hopkins. A horse of another color, but a horse all the same. The holders of the office had ranged from the heroic to the villainous, with a number of stops at marginal and ineffective along the way. St. Cyprian knew that only time would tell how he'd be remembered.

"Brief, but embarrassing, in all likelihood," he muttered,

pulling the car up along the sidewalk.

"What is?" Gallowglass said, yawning. She stretched, nearly causing him to ride up onto the pavement. Batting her arm out of the way, he stopped the car.

"Nothing," he said, looking at her. "Have a nice nap, did we?"

"Until you started muttering, yes," she said, rubbing her eyes with a knuckle. "Where are we?"

"Home," St. Cyprian said, getting out. The house at 427 Cheyne Walk was a perk of the job and had been since the Regency. Placed perfectly to watch over certain old structures long hidden by the Thames, the house was unassuming, given its surroundings. Some Royal Occultists had employed staff, but St. Cyprian had never been comfortable with batmen, butlers or the like. Besides which, he had an apprentice to take care of the menial tasks.

"Start the tea, would you?" he said, opening the door and stepping aside to allow Gallowglass to enter ahead of him.

"Coffee," she grunted as she trudged down the hall towards the kitchen, running her hands through the sharp-edged bangs of her hair. "Coffee, then tea," she continued, her voice a dolorous moan.

"As long as it's hot," St. Cyprian said cheerfully. He had played the part of dogsbody for Thomas Carnacki before the War, even as Carnacki had done for Edwin Drood and Drood had done for Aylmer Beamish and so on and so forth. While it took a Royal decree to make it official, the Royal Occultists had been given tacit permission to pick their own successors after the Restoration. It made things easier all around, and insured, theoretically at least, that the title-bearers were of an appropriate level of competency.

"Or have a replacement waiting, if nothing else," he said out loud, walking into his sitting room, his hands in his pockets. Pictures of former bearers of the office lined the walls, jostling for space with fetish masks and lurid artworks by Goya, Blake and Pickman. Great bookshelves, smelling of British oak and Puritan fires, groaned beneath a library of occult works. Said library was smaller than it should have been, by about three centuries.

"Ta for that, Mr. Cromwell," St. Cyprian said, pulling an unpleasantly large and sharp tooth out of his pocket and grabbing a small chest off one of the bookshelves. The chest was old and ornate, with brass clasps and hinges. Ancient scorch marks marred the treated wood. The Gothic characters inscribed on the lock harkened back to its original owner, Prince Rupert of the Rhine.

Rupert, nephew of Charles the First, had been as energetic a Royal Occultist as he was a cavalry commander, and had spent his short term collecting and organizing the diverse libraries of the former office holders in between crafting treaties with Faerie and driving back incursions from Those Below. Books by Dee, Strange and Subtle, lost Pnakotic texts and hairy bibles of horrid knowledge had all been combined into one of the greatest sources of occult knowledge short of the Papal Libraries. And when Charles had gotten the chop, Cromwell's men had burned Rupert's home and the library with it.

Some of what had been lost had been replaced. Most, though, was gone. Granted, Royal Occultists past had never been meticulous diarists. Except for Drood, who'd paid a number of penny-a-word men to scribble his accomplishments for future generations, at least when they weren't turning said accomplishments into plays and pulps and writing Drood out of his own story. "Bah humbug," St. Cyprian said, popping open the chest and dropping the overlarge fang within.

"Christmas is months away yet," Gallowglass said, from behind him. As he turned, she shoved a steaming mug at him and he was forced to juggle the chest and the coffee for several unpleasant seconds. Glaring at her, he took a gulp and coughed.

"That's not coffee," he said, making a face. "I thought rationing was over."

"It's the best I could scrounge up. We haven't exactly had time for a shop, what with Windermere and that thing with the thing in Dover," Gallowglass said, sipping her own coffee. She blinked and looked at the cup. "I didn't know it could go bad."

"I don't think it was ever good." St. Cyprian set his cup aside and pushed the chest into her arms, deftly snagging her cup before she dropped it. "Put that back, please."

Gallowglass held up the chest and shook it slightly. "When do I get to see what's in this?"

"When you have achieved the seventh level of enlightenment," St. Cyprian said, folding his hands together piously. Gallowglass stuck her tongue out and put the chest back in its spot on the bookshelf. St. Cyprian watched her and his hand idly scratched at his shoulder. There was still a mark there, a physical reminder of their first meeting, a year earlier. It had been less than friendly, as first impressions went. He took a seat and leaned back, sighing in relief. Being yanked beneath the water by a huge slithery thing was exhausting on several levels.

Gallowglass sat opposite him and stretched out in an undignified manner, her muddy boots thumping on the carpet. "What level am I on now, three or four?"

"Too low to calculate accurately," St. Cyprian said.

The doorbell buzzed. The two looked at each other. "I just sat down," Gallowglass said.

"Yes, bully for you. However, you are also my apprentice," St. Cyprian said and he raised a finger in a chiding gesture. "And apprentices get the door."

"I'm your assistant," Gallowglass said.

"It could be ex-assistant," St. Cyprian replied. He closed his eyes and interlaced his fingers over his stomach. The doorbell buzzed again. They maintained a stubborn silence until the third buzz, when Gallowglass threw up her hands with a disgusted sigh and stomped towards the door. She returned a moment later with a card, which she flicked onto St. Cyprian's chest.

St. Cyprian looked at it through narrowed eyes. It was a business card, embossed and covered with the curved shapes of Egyptian hieroglyphics. "What's this?"

"What does it look like?"

"Something annoying," he said. The card would have seemed so much gibberish to anyone not versed in the formal writing system of ancient Egypt. "Who delivered it?"

"Some posh bloke with a face like a man who eats lemons," she said and sniffed. "Dressed like a valet, smelled like a distillery."

"Curiouser and curiouser," St. Cyprian said and picked the card up gingerly. "It's an invitation, apparently."

"Funny looking invitation," Gallowglass said, leaning over the back of his chair. "Who is it from?"

"The Esoteric Order of Thoth-Ra," St. Cyprian said.

Gallowglass snorted.

St. Cyprian glanced at her. "They're not half as silly as they sound. I know every secret society and occult club in London. We're practically drowning in seekers into ancient mysteries and in less than a year, the Esoteric Order of Thoth-Ra has plucked the pearls from the pigs' ears, so to speak. Every half-wit toff with too much money and too much interest in the spooky set has been invited to join. They've poached members from the Mausoleum Club, the Bell Club, the Drones…"

"So they're not fussy," Gallowglass said, sitting down across from him. She glanced aside at the large fireplace, staring hard at the strange faces carved in the mantle. "Neither was Crowley's bunch'."

"Crowley needed funds. Edward Bellingham, from what I gather, does not." St. Cyprian tilted his head back and scrubbed his palms across his face.

Gallowglass smirked.

"You've been playing detective, then, and without me? For shame, Mr. St. Cyprian," she said.

"Perish the thought, Ms. Gallowglass," St. Cyprian said, still looking at the ceiling. "No, I've merely kept my ear to the ground. I—"

A soft snore interrupted him. He looked down, frowning. Gallowglass was curled up in the chair, her eyes closed and her mouth slightly open. St. Cyprian smiled and pushed himself to his feet. He stripped off his coat and draped it over her gently.

He forgot, sometimes, that she was a few years his junior. It was more evident at times like these, when she relaxed into something approaching softness and the hard edge of her experience drifted away. Both of them had been ill-used by life, and would likely continue to be so. Their line of work wasn't a long one or a straight one. He looked up at the pictures. Painted eyes, sorrowful, arrogant, fearful and mad, looked down on them and for a moment, he felt the weight of ages on his soul.

Some Royal Occultists retired, but most died. By accident or by design, they died and were replaced by royal edict, like stripped out cogs plucked from a machine, lest they damage the mechanism. Carnacki had been one such cog. His eyes found the oil-on-canvas ones of his mentor and friend. He stood in front of the painting, looking up at it, his hands clasped behind his back.

St. Cyprian remembered that first night he'd spent listening to Carnacki's stories in this very room, with Dodgson and Arkwright and the others. Just before Franz Ferdinand had taken an assassin's bullet to the brainpan and touched off a Continental firestorm. He closed his eyes, old aches springing again to prominence, and he felt the trails of old scars beneath his clothes.

The scars, earned at Ypres in the closing year of the War, traced his evolution from a callow youth to a slightly-less callow man. It had been a quick one as such things went; two bullets deep and one long. His thigh ached abominably in the damp, but he was learning to live with the phantom physical pain, if not the spiritual. Carnacki had died at Ypres, blown out of one life and into the next. One moment he'd been there, and the next...

St. Cyprian looked away and his hands clenched so tightly that his knuckles popped. Absently, he stuffed a hand in his pocket. His fingers found the card. He withdrew it and looked at the hieroglyphs. It was a fancy way of playing mysterious. He frowned again, rubbing his thumb across the embossed figures.

What he knew of Edward Bellingham, the self-proclaimed Grand Vizier of the Esoteric Order of Thoth-Ra, read like a patch out of Strachey's *Eminent Victorians*. Bellingham had been at Old College, Oxford for a brief period in the early days of the century before being sent packing under a dark cloud. Something to do with Egyptian antiquities was the rumor. Bellingham had trundled off to the Sudan before vanishing entirely for the duration of the War.

Then, in 1918, he'd come back. He had money and could mumbo with the best of the jumbos and had subsequently founded the EOTR for the high-stockings. In truth, most occult groups were nothing but harmless would-be pilgrims. Even Crowley's lot, despite their growling, were little more than dilettantes. Crowley himself was another story, but he was safely in United States, which meant he was someone else's problem. But Bellingham...there was something there.

He'd received regular invitations to attend the meetings of the Esoteric Order of Thoth-Ra since it had opened its doors. So far, he'd refused. The Royal Occultist couldn't be seen to favor one faction over another. While most of the bookhounds of Olde London Towne were harmless sorts, others were dangerous, especially in groups.

St. Cyprian chewed his lip. In the War, he'd been able to *feel* an artillery barrage before it hit. Like hearing thunder in your bones, or feeling rain in your joints. He had that same feeling now, closing in from all sides. There was a storm gathering, and they needed to be at its eye.

St. Cyprian eyed the card, as if hoping it would reveal Bellingham's secrets. Nothing was forthcoming, however. He sighed and slipped it back into his pocket and then went to make himself some tea.

When evening came and they had rested, bathed and eaten St. Cyprian felt more human than he had in days. Bundling Gallowglass into the Crossley took less effort than he'd feared. Normally, such occult-orientated gatherings held little interest for his assistant, a fact which he blamed on the oddities of her upbringing. Mostly, he was content to leave her be, but tonight he couldn't help but fear he was going to need her. Luckily, Gallowglass didn't require any convincing.

"Of course I want to go to the—what'd you call it?" she said.

"It's an unwrapping party, apparently, mummies and that sort of rot. A bit passé as the modern set judge things, but among the psychical crowd it's still a done thing," St. Cyprian said and fiddled with his tie. His suit was Savile Row, straight from Gieves & Hawkes. "Mostly cats, though."

"Cats," Gallowglass said darkly.

"Cats," St. Cyprian said, nodding. "Barmy for cats, your ancient Egyptian. Whole temples devoted to Ulthar's own, what? Dozens of the poor pusses are found every year, wrapped tighter than a footballer's ankle after a scrum and there's nothing your basic Theosophist likes better than unwrap 'em, preferably over wine and cheeses while singing hymns to Bast."

"I hate cats," Gallowglass said, shuddering. She didn't elaborate, and St. Cyprian knew better than to pry. Gallowglass had grown up in the slums of Cairo, and though the pharaohs were long dust, the gods they had worshipped still had some power in that land, despite the best efforts of Turk and Englishman alike.

"I don't think this is a cat," he said, gesturing with the invitation as they left the flat. The Crossley sat on the street, where they'd left it. "Bellingham wouldn't bother sending me an invitation to see some curried stray being skinned of its linen vestments, I don't think. No, he's got something large in mind."

"Good," Gallowglass said, hunching forward, "Because I bloody hate cats."

"So you said."

"Just reiterating for future reference," she said, glaring around her, as if to remind the world of its place. She shivered and slid into the Crossley. St. Cyprian got behind the wheel and within a few minutes, they were off, heading towards Seven Dials.

Barely more than two decades prior, Seven Dials had been more popularly known as St. Giles Rookery, and had been one of the worst slums that London had to offer. The area had become a byword for squalor and depravity, and had hosted more than its fair share of occult-types—palm readers, clairvoyants, herbalists and the like had occupied, and indeed, likely still did occupy, the crooked lanes and hidden storefronts of the area. There were also Bolsheviks, Anarchists and Mafioso crowding each other in the garrets, taverns and side-streets. Too, more than one esoteric society had settled roots into the coiling streets, including Theosophists, Freemasons and the ever-present Swedenborgians. And, of course, the Esoteric Order of Thoth-Ra.

On the whole, Seven Dials was a tangy sort of stew, and one St. Cyprian rarely visited, unless it was in a professional capacity. Previous incumbents had tried, more than once, to drive the money-changers out of the temple, so to speak, but St. Cyprian had lived through a mundane war and found he had no taste for the occult variety; he acted only when necessary. It was bad enough dealing with foreigners whose knowledge of the invisible far out-stripped his own; going up against the Sisterhood of Rats or the Si-Fan when, by and large, they adequately policed themselves, was not something he looked forward to. If some bunch of amateur, fifth form demonologists wanted to summon Mephistopheles without considering the consequences that was their business. But sometimes…sometimes it spilled over. And that was where the Royal Occultist came in.

The orange sky of early evening had slid into the purple of twilight when they finally reached the house that had been claimed as the ritual center of the EOTR. Around them, Seven Dials woke up for the evening. Bawdy laughter sounded from the open windows of nearby garrets, and cars honked and chugged through the streets.

"Are you sure this is the place?" Gallowglass said, tilting her head to peer up at the house.

St. Cyprian stepped out of the Crossley. "Quite," he said,

as Gallowglass joined him. He glanced at her and raised an eyebrow. "Is that my suit?"

"You only just noticed?" She grinned and snapped the braces holding up her trousers. She wore a man's suit with the trouser and sleeve cuffs rolled up to accommodate the difference in height, and an eight-panel cap akin to the sort newsboys wore. "We might need to run." Patting the lapel of her borrowed suit coat, she said, "And I thought it might be a good idea to hide the lemon squeezer." She twitched the edge of the coat aside and St. Cyprian saw the holstered shape of a revolver.

"I don't recall asking you to bring a pistol," he said.

"You never have to ask," she said, shoving her hands in her trouser pockets and slumping against the Crossley. "Besides, we're walking into a den of iniquity. I might need to shoot a lock off or a light out or something of the sort."

St. Cyprian looked at the house, which was indistinguishable from any other low-rent house in Seven Dials, and snorted. "Oh yes. Practically satanic, that house."

"Hiding in plain sight, the bastards." Gallowglass shoved the brim of her cap up.

"Let's go see if we have the right place then, shall we?" he said, striding towards the house. As he drew close to the door, he saw that there was one difference between it and the others that surrounded it. On the door, just above the knocker, a strange, recursive symbol had been carved into the wood. It was eerily familiar, and St. Cyprian felt a chill as he tried to grasp its shape. Reaching out, he rapped on the door, his rings adding a sharp edge to the sound. The three steel rings were, like the house on Cheyne Walk, part and parcel of the office, though St. Cyprian still had little idea of what they were for, if anything. Carnacki had insisted on wearing them, and St. Cyprian saw little reason not to do the same.

The door swung open and a blast of music washed over them. A man wearing the uniform of a butler and a highly-stylized Egyptian death-mask stepped into view. The butler nodded diffidently and extended a gloved hand. "Your card, sir," he said, his voice echoing strangely from within the confines of the mask.

St. Cyprian extended the card, his eyes narrowed. "I wasn't aware that this was a costume party," he said.

"Ceremonial dress, sir," the butler said tonelessly. He accepted the card, flipped it over several times, and then stepped aside. "Please enter, Mr. St. Cyprian, you and your guest."

At the other end of the corridor, a set of double doors painted in the fashion of an Egyptian temple were pulled open to admit them. The music rose in volume and they stepped into a large room, crowded with figures and furniture alike. More servants, all in masks similar to the butler's, threaded through the crowd with practiced grace, bearing trays and bottles. The music was distinctly foreign, full of the buzzing rhythms of the Arabian Peninsula. Lit braziers decorated the corners, expelling sweetly scented smoke.

Gallowglass took a sniff. "Smells like home."

"As well it should. The smell and the sound of the thing are the surest pathways to the soul of the thing, as they say," someone said. St. Cyprian and Gallowglass turned. A heavy-set man stood behind them, a silk robe thrown over his wool suit and a fez perched on his bulbous head. He placed his hands together and bowed shallowly. "Mr. St. Cyprian, your presence here adds to our web of light. I'm glad you finally decided to attend one of my soirees."

St. Cyprian inclined his head. "Edward Bellingham, I presume," he said.

"None other," Bellingham said. He smiled thinly. "Might I say, sir, that I am an avowed—ah—fan of your work?" He waved a hand to indicate their surroundings. "I am sure that my humble temple of mysteries isn't a patch on what you're used to."

St. Cyprian spared the room a glance. It wasn't humble in the slightest, Bellingham's protestations to the contrary. Expensive tapestries, likely Moorish in origin, hung from walls which were decorated with Egyptian hieroglyphs and Etruscan bas-reliefs. It was a garish nightmare of conflicting cultures, all exploited for their exoticism to English eyes.

When he turned his attentions back to Bellingham, he noted that the man was watching him closely, his dark eyes amused. "A bit patchwork, you might say," Bellingham said.

"By design," St. Cyprian said. It wasn't a question. Bellingham inclined his head.

"Egypt grows more familiar to the jaded eyes of our fair metropolis by the day," Bellingham said. "Dedicated orientalists scour the world, ferreting out secrets." He made a loose gesture. "I simply strive to inject some mystery back into things."

"And extract a bit of dosh in the process?" St. Cyprian said.

Bellingham's smile turned frosty. "A man has a right to make a living. The Esoteric Order of Thoth-Ra is open to all men." He glanced at Gallowglass. "And women too, of course."

"Cheers," Gallowglass said, snagging a glass off a passing tray.

Bellingham chuckled. "I'm glad you came, sir, for tonight is a very special night indeed!"

"Oh?"

"Quite so, quite so! One of our most esteemed members has even now returned from the Valley of the Kings with a prize worthy of…well…a king!" Bellingham's smile threatened to spill past the confines of his cheeks.

"And what's that then?" St. Cyprian said, his eyes narrowing.

Bellingham tapped the side of his nose. "Wait and see, sir, wait and see." With that, he gave another of peculiar bows and then spun and bounded off, like an excited school-boy. Gallowglass watched him go and knocked back her champagne.

"Rum sort," she said.

"The rummiest," St. Cyprian agreed. He looked at the crowd. There were some familiar faces there, men and women whom he'd had contact with at one time or another. In the corner, beneath the gaze of a stone bust of the great god Pan, Dion Fortune—formerly Violet Mary Firth—was arguing in increasingly loud tones with several other members of the Hermetic Order of the Golden Dawn. St. Cyprian wondered whether she was one of Bellingham's newest recruits; by all accounts, Fortune wasn't happy with the Order and they certainly weren't happy with her. They'd kicked Crowley to the curb as well, he recalled.

Near the buffet the young vintner and would-be author Dennis Wheatley was chatting amiably with the writer, Elliott O'Donnell, as well as Rollo Ahmed, who was a fraud, albeit a friendly one. Ahmed, who claimed to be Egyptian but was, according to most of St. Cyprian's sources, actually from Guyana, raised a hand in a gesture of greeting as he caught sight of St. Cyprian. St. Cyprian smiled and returned the greeting. "Before us ebbs and flows a veritable sea of sins and infractions, Ms. Gallowglass. It's a who's who of the sorcerous set."

"Den of iniquity, innit," she said, sniffing. "Glad I brought the pistol now?"

St. Cyprian didn't reply. He made his way into the crowd, Gallowglass at his heels.

"What's the plan?" she said.

"We mingle."

"Mingle? That a code for something?" she said.

"Yes, it's code for mingling," he said, glancing at her. "Try not to embarrass me."

"I can hob with the best of the nobs, no fear," Gallowglass said. "We aren't here for drinks and caviar, are we?"

"No," St. Cyprian said. "Or, at least not entirely; we're here for the show." He gestured, indicating a bandstand that had been set up along the far wall. Heavy braziers had been mounted at the corners, and a wine-red curtain had been tacked to the wall. The curtain bore the same symbol as had been on the front door, albeit larger and splayed across its folds. "Keep your eyes and ears open. Mingle."

"Mingling," she said, giving a two-fingered salute. She snagged another champagne glass as she disappeared into the crowd. St. Cyprian turned back to the stage. He sidled closer, his hands in his pockets.

A large circle had been painted on the stage, its radius extending to each corner. He sniffed and recognized the smell of certain strange unguents; it was a familiar mixture. His predecessor Carnacki had showed him how to mix it, from a recipe recorded in the Sigsand Manuscript. It was a protective circle; a pentacle, in actuality…evil forces couldn't enter it, or, in the event they were inside, couldn't leave it. "Now why would he need that?" he murmured.

Something was off about the whole evening, he thought. He looked around the room and his senses, both physical and otherwise, reached out. There was a pall over everything and he was put in mind of what a hare must feel, as the fox closes in. Something was coming, something vast and terrible and he had no idea where it was coming from or what form it would take, and that made him very nervous indeed.

He was tempted to find Gallowglass and leave. Let the play-actors deal with the consequences of their actions. But he knew that if he did, it would be worse than just a few dead amateurs. As he pondered, Bellingham climbed up on the stage and clapped his hands for silence. It fell in swathes, as the crowd realized that something was happening.

"Ladies and gentlemen," Bellingham said, his voice carrying easily. He held up his hands, his oversize sleeves dropping down to his elbows, exposing his surprisingly brawny forearms. Tarnished bracers that had the look of something pried from an Egyptian tomb decorated his arms. "I am so glad that so many of you could be here tonight!" Bellingham went on. "For a year, we have undertaken an exploration of the Great Mysteries of the East together; we have plumbed the unutterable depths and scaled the remotest heights…" Bellingham gestured for emphasis.

He was theatrical, but then, all the best conmen were. St. Cyprian listened with one ear while he surreptitiously scanned the crowd. Where was Gallowglass?

"But tonight…ah, tonight, we shall all partake of incandescent ambrosia, my friends, as I have promised!" Bellingham said floridly. He flung out a hand. "Come forth, Brother Parker!" he shouted, and the crowd at last fell completely silent.

Heads turned as wheels squeaked. Masked attendants wheeled in a large gurney with a long, covered shape on it. A thin, nervous looking man trotted beside it, his face pale and strained. The hairs on the back of St. Cyprian's neck prickled as he watched the attendants move their burden to the stage. Someone had turned off the music. Everything was quiet, save for the squeak of the gurney wheels.

"Brother Parker, returned from the dim avenues of the Valley of the Kings, with the very prize I promised you all at the beginning of this communal journey to Khem's black shores," Bellingham said, spreading him arms. "Bring it up, gentlemen! Bring it up, lest we waste the night in awestruck wonder!"

The attendants hefted their burden, gurney and all, and carried it up onto the stage. They deposited it dead-center in the pentacle, and St. Cyprian blinked. The old artillery feeling was back now, and strong. He could practically hear the whistle of incoming shells. What was on that gurney?

Bellingham gestured, and someone dimmed the lights, leaving the only illumination the flickering glow from the braziers. "It is said, by the wise men of the American Indians, that wisdom sits in places," Bellingham said, folding his hands together. "That certain spots soak up the very stuff of history. The Valley of the Kings could be said to be such a place, I'd wager. It houses the sleeping souls of history's greatest monarchs, including a few whose names are unknown save to jackals..." Bellingham snapped his fingers.

One of the attendants whipped the covering off, revealing what lay on the gurney. The crowd gasped appropriately as the sarcophagus was revealed. Bellingham leaned over it, his fingers creeping over its bare surface. "You see it before you, fellow knowledge-seekers. The sarcophagus of one of the greatest men ever forgotten by history. The last pharaoh of the Third Dynasty, whose name was stricken from the holy writ..."

St. Cyprian found himself leaning forward. Attendants gripped the feet and head of the sarcophagus. Parker stepped back, his hand twitching towards his coat. St. Cyprian frowned as Bellingham snapped out a hand to drop a grip on the other man's wrist, holding him in place. With his free hand, he gestured upwards, and the attendants carefully levered the sarcophagus open. He could see that the seals had already been broken, likely in preparation for this big reveal.

"Behold, he who was known as the Doom of All Mankind! Behold, the Black Pharaoh! Behold…NEPHREN-KA!"

A cloud of dust rose from the opened sarcophagus, obscuring St. Cyprian's view of Bellingham for a moment. The name of the sarcophagus' occupant rang through his mind like the rumble of distant guns or thunder playing among black clouds. It couldn't be, could it? But the rush of sheer, black malevolence that swept over him as the syllables of the name settled on his mind like a gargoyle-weight told him otherwise.

This was Nephren-Ka, the Black Pharaoh, one of only a handful of pharaohs ever erased from the peculiar bureaucratic records of the Egyptian dynasties, his name hidden even as those of Akhenaten and Nitocris were. The reasons were lost, but they had likely been damn good ones.

The dust cleared and for a moment, Bellingham's eyes met his own. A chill caressed St. Cyprian's spine. The gleam of triumph in Bellingham's eyes was unmistakable.

"Oh hell," he muttered, looking around for Gallowglass.

Bellingham waved aside the dust and gave a loud chuckle. "Yes, my friends, yes, this is the last earthly remains of him whom a centuries' worth of mystics have sought! And thanks to the dedication of Brother Parker, we have found him!"

As the crowd made appropriate noises, St. Cyprian felt something building beneath his feet. His hair stiffened, like a dog's hackles, and he felt strange electricity prickling along the edges of his consciousness. Something was happening. Something…

The groan, when it came, was so deep as to be almost mistaken for the distant rumble of the District Line passing through Earls Court. It stretched out, reaching every corner of the makeshift temple and bringing everyone inside to abrupt, horrified attention. It was a sound full of weight and pain and color drained from every face in the crowd. Bellingham swallowed, the triumphant glee gone from his face, replaced by consternation.

"Yes…yes, you hear him?" he said, speaking over the deep, dull sound, though with difficulty. "Even in death, his *ka* clings to his body, held by chains of secrets that no man remembers, save me." Bellingham looked at his audience, holding them in silence by sheer force of will. It was impressive, St. Cyprian had to admit.

"But the dead are no threat to the living, not even dead sorcerer kings," Bellingham went on. He motioned to the stage. "Though a bit of preparation doesn't hurt." The crowd tittered appreciatively, but fell silent as the groan rose in volume. It was an almost spiteful sound, like the growl of a tiger in a cage. The sarcophagus shuddered slightly, causing the gurney to rattle. Bellingham licked his lips and stepped back and snapped his fingers.

"It is said, in the Sudan, that unlucky is the town whose wizards are not yet ashes," he said. "There is some truth in that, my friends. For the power of a sorcerer, like a fine wine, only grows stronger as it sits contained. It ferments as the worms grow fat. Nephren-Ka was the equal to the sorcerer kings of the lost antediluvian kingdoms named in the Chaldean Fragments or the Cimmerian Scrolls; imagine, my fellow pilgrims, what rare brew then sits before us in this humble sarcophagus!"

The groan rose in pitch, spiraling up into an angry shriek. Glasses trembled in people's hands, vibrating sympathetically to the sound. St. Cyprian winced. The necessity of the protective circle was plain now. Whatever was in that sarcophagus, ancient pharaoh or otherwise, wasn't happy about the current situation. The braziers flared, spitting embers and smoke. People drew back from the stage. Bellingham raised his hands, calling for calm.

"Pay no heed to his snarls," Bellingham said. His face was damp with sweat. "Nephren-Ka is dead and his ability to wreak harm is dead with him! But his power remains still and as I have promised, it will be ours!"

St. Cyprian realized suddenly what was going on. This was no mere unwrapping party. It was something much, much worse.

"We shall feast upon the very essence of power itself!" Bellingham shouted. With a flourish, he pulled a curvy bladed *kris* knife from within his robes. "We shall do as the ancients did and taste of the flesh of the sorcerer and become as him!"

"Damnation," St. Cyprian said, hands clenching. "Bellingham, you stupid fool!"

"Oi," Gallowglass hissed urgently, squirming through the crowd towards him. "I think we've got trouble!" She had one hand in her coat, ready to draw her pistol.

"Really, do tell," St. Cyprian snapped, his eyes still on the stage.

"Doors are locked. Bellingham doesn't want anybody leaving, and his fancy boys are armed to the pants," Gallowglass muttered.

The flames in the braziers turned blue. There was a foul stink on the air, like ancient damp rising through old stones and it was growing stronger by the minute.

"By their smell shall ye know them," he muttered.

"Smells like the gas has sprung a leak," Gallowglass said.

The gurney was trembling now and visibly. The braziers wobbled on their iron legs. Bellingham was calling for silence as the crowd began to shift and roil. Panic was in the air.

"Nothing for it," St. Cyprian said out loud, moving towards the stage. If Bellingham saw him coming, he gave no sign. The pudgy magus was too busy trying to calm his audience.

"What are you doing?" Gallowglass called after him.

"Getting in on the act," St. Cyprian said. He needed to stop Bellingham before the man did the unthinkable. He pushed towards the stage. He could feel the floorboards bending and breathing beneath the thick carpet. No one was listening to Bellingham. People were beginning to turn towards the doors, primitive survival instincts prompting the herd towards safety. Only those doors were locked, and none of Bellingham's masked attendants were giving ground.

"Friends, why do you rush to leave?" Bellingham bellowed. "Would you forsake greatness? We are all bound to this journey by bonds of aetheric harmony, are we not? Friends! Friends!"

He reached the stage and began to run up the stairs. Gallowglass had been right; he should have brought a weapon. On his hand, the three rings began to grow unpleasantly warm. "Stop right there," a high-pitched voice said. St. Cyprian froze, his foot on the top step of the stage.

"Whoop," he said, looking up into the barrel of a Mauser, clutched in Brother Parker's sweaty hand.

"Who are you? What are you doing?" Parker nearly shrieked. His eyes were wide and showing too much white and St. Cyprian knew that Brother Parker had gone quietly, savagely mad somewhere between Cairo and Seven Dials. What had he heard, trapped aboard a cramped steamer with the thing in its box? What had it whispered to him as it groaned and scratched? "Bellingham!"

"Parker, what are you doing?" Bellingham snarled, turning. His eyes widened slightly as he took in the tableau and then they narrowed in anger. "You...are you responsible for this?" he said, glaring at St. Cyprian. "I should have known! I invited you here to show you that I did not fear you, that your antiquated notions of magic and sorcery held no power over me, but you couldn't have that, could you? What have you done?"

St. Cyprian stepped up onto the stage, hands raised as Parker stepped back. He stood relaxed, ignoring the trembling barrel of the Mauser that lingered perilously close to his head. He reached slowly into his coat and pulled out his silver cigarette case. Taking one out, he made a show of tapping it on the side of the case before placing it between his lips. "Nothing, but then, I'm sure you're well aware of that, Mr. Bellingham."

"He's lying!" Parker said. His face was gray from fear. "He's come to free it! He'll set it on us, the damned monster!"

"Shut *up* Parker," Bellingham barked. The braziers were

moving as if being swung around and around. Smoke and embers scattered across the stage. The tapestries on the walls were rippling as if rats crawled behind them. There were long shadows on the walls and ceiling, stretching like the talons of some immense beast.

"The circle—the markings—they aren't enough, Bellingham," St. Cyprian said carefully. The smoke circles floated around his head. He'd learned the art of blowing protective circles from an Ostyak shaman in Siberia, though he doubted it would do much good against whatever was pressing against the Outside even now. He could feel something, like the buzzing of scarab beetles, in his head. A humming, whispering voice beneath the bestial groaning.

"Quiet!" Bellingham said, licking his lips. "They should have been enough. The books said they would be!"

"Books can be wrong," St. Cyprian said, stepping forward. "We have to close it! Get the top back on it and reseal it! That might stop it, or put it back to sleep."

"Stay away from it," Parker snarled, his Mauser twitching. "Don't let him get near it!"

"Silence, Parker!" Bellingham growled, but St. Cyprian knew he'd lost whatever hold he'd had on the other man. He saw the thread of sanity give way and then the Mauser rose like a cobra's snout.

"No! I won't let him do it—not to me! I won't let it get me!"

The pistol gave a short, sharp sound and St. Cyprian felt a bullet tug at his coat. He dove across the distance between them, driving his fist up into Parker's belly. The air went out of the smaller man in a whoosh and he folded over St. Cyprian's arm.

He let Parker fall and snatched up the Mauser, spinning around in time to see Bellingham sinking to his knees, his face white with shock as he clutched at his bloody arm. Evidently his coat hadn't been the only thing to feel the bite of Parker's shot.

"Damn it," he said, hurrying towards the fallen magus. He wasn't so much concerned with Bellingham's health as he was with the consequences of spilling blood inside a magical circle. He'd seen the results of that more than once, and it was never pleasant. "Get up Bellingham! Get out of the circle!"

"He—he shot me!" Bellingham blubbered.

Shots rang out, plucking at the stage. St. Cyprian skidded to a halt as several of the death-masked servants shoved their way through the crowd towards the stage. One he recognized as the doorman barked an order and pointed at St. Cyprian. They'd seen the gun in his hand and made assumptions, obviously. Gallowglass had hers out as well, and she overturned a table as the servants swung their weapons towards her. Bullets cracked and the crowd gave a communal scream and the doors bucked on their hinges as somebody went at them with a credenza.

The stage squirmed beneath his feet. He heard again the cracking of wood and he felt as if he were stepping on a bed of snakes. A bullet spoke loud near his ear and without thinking he returned fire, old instincts rising to the fore. The Mauser bucked in his hand and there was a scream, but he didn't stop to see if he'd actually hit anyone. He stooped, reaching for Bellingham's arm.

The magus looked up at him blearily, his fez askew. "What?"

"Up, man. Get up!" St. Cyprian snapped. A brazier toppled over, spilling coals and fire across the stage. It seemed as if the whole room was shaking. St. Cyprian jerked Bellingham up even as he realized that the strange groaning that had punctuated the beginning of Bellingham's aborted ritual had ceased. All was silent, save for the crackle of flames.

The hairs on the back of his neck prickled and he turned, still gripping Bellingham. The thing in the sarcophagus had sat up. Brown, leathery flesh rubbed against ancient bone as the narrow, almost vulpine head turned towards him. Eyes like those of a beast just beyond the light of a campfire met his own and he felt his blood turn to ice in his veins.

Nephren-Ka was awake.

Previews
Every *Little* Thing
Anna Maloney

COSMIC HORROR STRIKES SUBURBIA

"You've got to be on your toes. You seem to be the only one who isn't forgetting anything."

There was a slight pause. "How can we be sure of that?" she asked in a shaking whisper.

"We can't."

Lois McCarthy is like any other housewife in Rose Park –

organized, attentive, and sweet. Lois' attention to detail aids her in many aspects of life. Until she seems to notice slips in time, her family's personalities distorting, and her own past rearranging itself around her.

When you can't trust your eyes, your ears, and your own memories, what is there left?

Chapter *1*

Eyes flitted open in the dark. There was a quiet groan as a hand slowly moved to check if someone was still beside it— they were, and the hand patted the sleeping form. As always, Lois McCarthy woke up at 5:00 AM, no longer needing an alarm. Slowly rising out of bed, Lois turned and put her slippers on, got up, reached over for her robe, and silently padded into the master bedroom's attached bathroom. Without even needing to think, Lois followed her routine: shower, shave, get dressed, do hair, do makeup. She was done by 5:40, the ten minutes extra from this being a hair washing day.

Lois silently left the bathroom and glanced over at her husband, Paul. He didn't need to wake up until 7:30, so she left the room. Her kids needed to be up by 6:30 for school, so Lois headed downstairs and started on breakfast. As everything heated up, Lois gathered up any spare school supplies her two daughters had left scattered around the house, packing their bags up and putting them in the designated chairs.

Breakfast was scrambled eggs, toast, bacon, ham, fried apple rings, and pineapple juice. Lois knew she was right on schedule when she heard the pattering of feet just as she began putting food on plates. She'd been sure to leave enough to cook when it was time for Paul to wake up, smiling as Mary came down the stairs.

"Morning, mommy!" Mary called, smiling.

"Good morning, sweetheart," Lois said on instinct, bending over and kissing Mary on the cheek. Her older sister Linda followed down shortly, yawning and quiet.

"Good morning, sweetheart," She repeated, pulling Linda into a sleepy hug as Mary sat down for breakfast. The child waited patiently for Lois and Linda to sit down; she knew that they were on a schedule, though it wasn't conscious for her yet. She was only seven, and such things were less her concern. Linda, at nine, was much more aware of it, but she didn't feel the pressure the way Lois did. Lois ran on a clock, constantly chasing after the impossible prospect of somehow getting ahead of schedule.

Mary and Linda began eating as Lois slowly munched on some spare eggs. Paul liked to eat with her, but so did the kids, so she ate a little with them and had her full breakfast with her husband.

"What's school going to be like today?" she asked pleasantly. Mary, as always, answered first.

"Today we're going to be doing multiplication and division, and we're going to do something with newspapers. She said we get to cut them up and put them on a collage."

Lois smiled. Mary was good at math, and as much as the teacher encouraged Lois to push her daughter in a more 'female friendly' direction, Lois was determined to feed Mary's interest.

"Do I get to see your collage when you're done?"

Mary nodded, then paused. "I have to turn it in, but when we get it back I'll bring it to you," the child promised, and Lois nodded with a grin that made Mary smile. Much of Mary's—and Linda's—work hung on the walls and fridge.

"How about you, Linda?" Lois asked, turning to her older daughter. Linda looked at her with bleary eyes.

"We're reading through a few books and comparing them. And we're peer editing our short stories today."

Lois gave her daughter a grin and Linda smiled a little. She was still too tired to be up for much conversation, but Linda had always been good at writing.

"Oh, good, honey! I'm sure everyone will love it."

Linda nodded and turned her focus back to her food just as Mary finished eating. Lois got up and swept up her and Mary's dishes, putting them into the sink and pulling on rubber gloves to wash them without ruining her manicure.

"Mary, get your school clothes on, make your bed, and get ready for school, darling. Linda, just give me your plate when you're finished and do the same." The children replied with a unanimous 'yes, mama,' used to this.

Lois waited with Mary and Linda on their porch for the carpool that came to pick them up and bring them to the elementary school, over in the town next to the suburban development. While this wasn't one of Levitt's Levittowns, it had been built with the same idea in mind: every house looked almost identical, the only changes being colour and if they mirrored the one next to them or were exact structural copies. Lois's lawn was recognisable by her well-manicured garden with agreed-upon flowers, which she'd mapped out with the homeowner's association.

As they sat on the porch of the mint green house, Lois could see several of her neighbors doing the same. Lois waved at Nancy and Cynthia, who were out with their kids and used the same carpool that Patricia's husband Harold drove. Something else flashed in the corner of her eye, perhaps another person waving, but when Lois turned she didn't see anything.

It wasn't long before Harold's station wagon pulled up, right on time. Mary and Linda gave Lois last kisses and took the paper bags with their lunches from her before running over to climb in. Lois stood on the steps and waved as they drove away. She waited until they were out of sight before fetching the newspaper to put on the table and going back into the house at 7:25, heading up to the master bedroom.

Going through the dark, Lois bent down next to Paul's half of the bed where he was still sleeping.

"Honey," she whispered, before saying a bit louder with a hand on his shoulder, "Paul. It's time to wake up." In the dark room, she could see him open his eyes, looking at her with a soft smile.

"Morning," he mumbled. Lois smiled as he pulled her over into a sleepy hug. He kissed her on the cheek as she wrapped her arms around him, chuckling quietly.

Lois had always felt lucky that she and her husband got along so well; most of her friends didn't actually love their husbands. She didn't talk about it, as it was rude and bad show, but she knew it and they knew it. If she really thought about it, Patricia and Harold, along with Nancy and James, really seemed like the only ones who loved each other, and even they didn't seem to get along as well as Lois and Paul did. Cynthia and Winston were more like good friends, and the others were trapped in more or less loveless marriages. It hadn't escaped Lois's notice that they had all gotten together in high school, whereas she had met her husband later on like Patricia and Nancy.

Once it was 7:30, the alarm next to them went off and Paul's hand slapped onto the off button on instinct, groaning a little.

"We need to sleep in more," he murmured as Lois got up, heading into the open bathroom to fix her hair back up.

"I'd love to, but you know how it is."

Paul got out of bed, stretching before following her, his arms wrapping around her from behind as he bent over to put his head on her shoulder.

"Ah, yes. The schedule."

Lois nodded and he turned and kissed her cheek, eliciting a smile as she put her hands over his.

"This weekend?"

Lois paused.

"But the store."

Lois edited gossip and makeup columns for the local newspaper, but their primary source of income was Paul's general store in town.

"Just Sunday, love."

She paused before slowly nodding. Paul gave her a wide grin, turning her so he could kiss her proper this time. Lois smiled into it, and as he pulled back she reached forward and wiped the lipstick he'd rubbed off from his lips.

"It's your colour," she joked, and he laughed as he turned to get ready to shower. Lois turned to the mirror and reapplied her lipstick from the tube in the cabinet behind it before heading back downstairs to cook his breakfast.

Lois was putting the plates on the table as he came downstairs, wearing a pair of dark gray slacks and a tucked in plaid button up without a tie. It was very casual compared to what most of the husbands—aside from Harold, who was a mechanic—wore, but Paul insisted that it made people more at ease in the shop, finding him friendlier. He sat down next to her, grinning at breakfast and taking the newspaper as she put down a mug of coffee in front of him.

"I see it's Monday," he observed before beginning to eat. Lois nodded. With every day being more or less the same, her husband had some trouble remembering what day it was sometimes. His wife's rigid agenda—like the daily change in menu—helped clue him in before he opened the newspaper. Lois always knew, but it was because she made a point to know—if she didn't check the papers and keep mind of it, her days blended together too.

Paul scanned the paper quickly before folding it back up

and putting it to the side. He always left the paper for Lois, as he could read one at the store between customers.

"How were Linda and Mary?" He asked as Lois slowly ate.

"Mary is excited for a project at school. Linda's too tired in the mornings to tell, but they're checking their stories today, and hers is quite good. I think she'll be happy."

Paul nodded with a wistful smile, staring for a few moments as his wife looked down at her food. Paul didn't have the chance to spend a lot of time with his children during the week, though occasionally Linda would come visit him at the store after school.

"What are you up to today?"

Paul reached forwards and took one of her hands, intertwining his fingers with hers as she looked up at him.

"Oh, we have knitting club today," she said with a smile, and he nodded.

"That's good. Are you almost done with those next blankets?"

Lois was quick with her fingers, so they'd decided to sell some of her blankets at the general store to try and get some extra cash.

"I've gotten about fifteen of them done, darling."

He could tell she was a bit melancholy, which was another part of why he wanted to have her sleep in more. Paul and Lois had moved from the city to Rose Park five years ago, and since then their lives had taken up such an endless repetition that Paul felt stagnant. That was nothing compared to what had happened to Lois, however, who seemed to have become so controlled by their schedule that she had to be convinced to take a night out. She'd become more rigid and more withdrawn—scarcely resembling her spirited younger self.

Paul had talked with the other husbands, and while most of them seemed to like their wives being so sedated and dedicated to this monotony, Harold had understood. Harold's wife, Patricia, was a very artsy type who had felt stifled until she joined Cynthia's knitting club. Paul's brother, James, had a similar opinion, telling him that Nancy had been happier after joining the knitting club as well. Paul had immediately gone and convinced Lois to join, and while the company had seemed to cheer her, Paul still made an effort to try and give her variety.

"You said that Barbara joined?" He asked, trying to remember anything she'd told him about the club in the past. She never really talked about it.

"Yes. It's Cynthia, Nancy, Patricia, Eleanor, Barbara, and I." Somewhat small, but comfortable. The neighborhood wasn't even half full, so it was plentiful for the options available.

Paul nodded and watched as Lois got up and took his plate, which he looked down at just in time to realise he'd emptied it. She put all the dishes in the sink and pulled on her gloves to start washing them.

He glanced at his watch to see that it was 8:00, which meant that he had to leave in the next fifteen minutes in order to open the store at 8:30. Lois had an innate sense of the schedule that both impressed and unnerved Paul. Before he could say anything, Lois turned to him.

"You should get everything you need together, dear."

Paul finished his coffee before getting his coat, his keys, and his shoes. He didn't need anything else that wasn't already in his pockets, so Lois was practically dragging him to his car by 8:10.

"You don't want to be late," she insisted as they walked through the house to their garage, a paper bag with his lunch in her hands. The two car garage held their car, tools, and other supplies that didn't have a place in the house but needed to be easily accessible, including another refrigerator and a large freezer.

"I'll be there with more than enough time," he countered as he paused outside the car, put off by her antsiness at him possibly breaking schedule; her hands were fidgeting and she nervously gestured for him to get in.

"Lois. There's plenty of time," he assured her, but she wasn't convinced. Paul opened the door and put his lunch in before leaning over and kissing her, slightly reluctant as he got in their car and drove off for the store.

Now that everyone else was out of the house, the daily cleaning routine began. Lois cleaned the bathrooms before making her bed, putting in a load of laundry, going to the kitchen to clean out the coffeemaker, and mopping the linoleum floors. As it was a Monday, Lois went through the weekly tasks of scrubbing the oven clean, going through the refrigerator to throw out old food and clean it up, and finally doing the same with the cupboards. She then swept up the rest of the rooms, dusting and taking the rugs out to beat the dirt out of them.

Once she'd replaced the rugs, it was time to put the laundry in the dryer and load the washer with the second load. Lois gathered all the clothing that couldn't be run through a dryer and took it to the back porch, going past it into the yard to hang the clothing up on her clothing lines. She knew she was on time because she could see other lines being filled with clothing just over the fences that separated backyards.

Lois then proceeded to hunt the house for spare articles of clothing that needed to be washed, gathering them in a hamper to be put in the final laundry load. After that, she went back and opened the windows to air out the rooms, took out the garbage, and put anything out of place where it belonged. That was it for Mondays, and it took her a good few hours— Lois was done with everything by 11:30, at which point she began her daily exercise regimen. Lois made sure to dedicate at least half an hour to this every day, turning on the radio to listen as she did stretches and simple exercises. At 12, Lois changed into gardening clothes and headed outside.

In the backyard, Lois maintained several flowered plots and a small garden with herbs, spices, and simple foodstuff that they used often like potatoes, tomatoes, peas, lima beans, onions, and carrots. Lois, at 30 despite appearances of youth, had lived with parents who hammered home the concept of growing your own food out of necessity. Even now, when Paul's store offered them enough money and food to live very comfortably, she couldn't let it go.

Chapter 2

Lois spent the next two hours in one of her favourite places, picking weeds and tending to her plants. She only stopped when her internal clock warned her of the imminent arrival of her children—she got changed and cleaned up just in time for Mary and Linda to come walking up the sidewalk at 3:45. Her nieces, Maureen and Jane, were walking with them,

"Hello Linda, hello Mary," Lois greeted them with a grin and kisses as she met them at the sidewalk.

"Hello Maureen, hello Jane. Tell your mother hello for me."

She gave her nieces a hug and a kiss each, watching them walk to Nancy and James's house next door before taking both of her children by the hand. They slowly walked up the porch and into the house, Mary swinging her arms as Linda yawned.

"How was school today?"

"We started our collages! I found a picture of someone who looked just like you, mama!"

"I got an A on my story."

Lois congratulated both of them, turning with more attention to Linda.

"Oh, that's great, honey! Did everyone like it?"

Linda nodded with a summery smile, and Lois grinned.

"I'm so proud of you. You're such a great writer."

Linda turned to the ground, embarrassed but grinning.

Lois prepared them a snack as they—well, as Mary talked more about what they'd done. She deftly cut an apple into chunks, cutting the skins off of Linda's. She then smeared some peanut butter on them before serving them on two plates, sitting across from her children as they ate. There were oatmeal cookies cooking in the oven, but those were for the knitting club and the kids knew it.

"And we went through all these magazines, and there's a lot about fashion, but I just cut out everything purple 'cos we're supposed to do a theme, and I chose a colour theme, so

I chose purple, 'cos that's the best colour. The lady that looks like you is wearing a purple dress, mama! It's real pretty. And then we cut out letters from headlines to make our own false headlines, and they're supposed to catch your eye, so mine is about purple becoming the national colour of America!" Mary beamed. She'd babbled this all very excitedly, only pausing to take and swallow bites of food.

"Well, that sounds wonderful, Mary. Perhaps when you are a scientist, you can write about how purple makes people happier, or how it's the best wavelength." Lois herself had been quite keen on science as a child—which was a big part of why she was determined to let Mary follow this passion—but her knowledge was not very extensive.

"Yeah, mama!" Mary agreed. Lois turned to Linda, who had been perfectly happy to let Mary ramble on and on. Mary was much more outgoing than Linda had ever been. Linda was quiet and speculative, much more interested in being a writer and perhaps a journalist. Lois was even saving up to get her older daughter a fancy camera.

"So, tell me about your story, Linda."

Linda, voice sweet and quiet like her mother's, explained how her story had been about an alien coming to a neighborhood and trying to fit in, finding it easy due to the fact that everyone acted the same and worked on a schedule.

"Very creative, Linda. That's a great idea for a story," Lois said with a grin, surmising that this must have been a creative fiction prompt. Linda smiled and went back to focusing on her apple halves as Mary finished and jumped up.

"I'm going to go draw!" she announced before running out of the room, and Lois got up and began to wash the dishes.

"Linda, do you have any plans for today?" Lois asked, glancing back to see Linda shake her head.

"Would you mind going down to the store to see your father? He likes to spend time with you, and you can write while you're there. It'll be quieter there than here." As if on cue, a rock record began sounding through the house.

"Sure, mom."

Linda got up and brought her dish over to Lois before

leaving the kitchen to get ready to leave.

Lois wandered over to where Linda was pulling on her shoes and organising what she'd take to the store after the dishes were done.

"Linda," She started, pausing slightly, "Could you tell your father that I love him, and give him this?" She held out a little paper bag.

"Of course, mom."

Lois gave her a kiss on the cheek and a hug before walking out onto the porch with her and watching her bike off in the direction of the store, only sitting down when she was out of sight. While she was there Harold came walking up the street, waving before coming over up onto the porch. Lois jumped to her feet.

Harold and Paul had become very good friends after taking the car to his garage, and from that, Lois had become friends with him as well.

"Hello, Harry. Shouldn't you be at the shop?"

Harold was wearing his jumpsuit and a jean jacket; judging by how messy they were, it was apparent he'd been there sometime that day.

"I'm on break. I'll be going back soon. I just wanted to stop by to talk."

Lois nodded and they sat down on the porch, Harold tactfully choosing a chair without a cushion.

"I got the part, for the next time you bring the car in. I can show Paul how to keep it up, too. Just to let you know. But, uh, Patricia saw Cynthia today, and I overheard them talking about something that had to do with a case Winston has."

Lois was clearly interested, leaning in a bit.

"Oh?"

"Yeah, you not hear about it?"

"No, I haven't seen Cynthia since the last knitting club meeting."

Harold nodded, thoughtfully rubbing his short beard.

"Alright. Just wondering. Also, could you help me out in the garden real quick, before I go back to the shop?" Patricia wasn't a gardener by any means, so Lois wasn't at all surprised that he was coming to her.

"Sure. Let me just tell Mary."

With Mary in tow, they went with Harold down a few houses, just past where Lois's was visible. Harold and Patricia's house was light purple—something Mary quite enjoyed—and identical structurally to Lois and Paul's. Harold led them around the side of the house to the back where they kept a large flower garden. This was entirely Harold's garden, and Lois had learned quickly that he spent a lot of his time in it, similarly to her.

"I've been having trouble here with the azaleas."

He gestured to a few flowered bushes on the edge of the garden. They were drooping and had fewer flowers than more healthy bushes. The plant seemed dry but had obviously been watered recently.

"Oh, you need more mulch on those," she explained, and Harold snapped his fingers.

"Right. Yes."

At this point, Daniel had come out of the house. Very like Harold, the quiet eight year old was silently curious of the activities in the backyard. Seeing his dad, he ran over and gave him a hug.

"Daniel! Did you pass your test?" he asked, and Daniel nodded.

"I'm very proud of you."

"Hello, Danny!" Mary greeted him, and before Lois or Harold could say anything she was leading Daniel over to the back porch to colour with her.

Lois and Harold worked on his garden together for about a half hour, until the now rather muddy mechanic explained that he had to go back to the shop. Lois, Daniel, and Mary walked out to the front yard with him and waved as he drove off, at which point Patricia came out of the house.

"Oh, Lois! Did you help Harold with the azaleas?" she asked, and Lois nodded, walking over to the front porch.

"Yes, they just need some mulch," Lois explained, and Patricia nodded.

"Listen, I—" she began, but paused.

"—can't wait to see you at knitting club tonight!" She looked pointedly at Mary and Daniel, who were muttering something amongst themselves.

"Yes, I'll see you tonight. It's at Cynthia's tonight, right?" Lois asked in an almost overly polite voice; the rotating schedule of homes for the knitting club was common knowledge amoungst members.

"Yes." Patricia kept up the pleasantries with a smile for the sake of the kids.

"Well, I'll see you then, I should get back home to start dinner. Goodbye, Daniel." Lois departed with a smile, Mary waving as her mother led her away by the hand. They were quiet as they walked back home, and Mary ran into the house to keep drawing as Lois went to the kitchen. She'd prepared some ham aspic the day before, so she started working on side dishes of canned tomato soup and buttered pan—fried vegetables using carrots, onions, and lima beans from her garden. The tomato soup simply needed to be heated, so she set it to simmer on the stove before cooking the vegetables and turning the heat way down to keep them warm.

She'd just set them to stay heated when she heard the car drive in, right on time—5:15.

"Hello, mom!" Linda greeted before going into the living room where Mary was colouring.

"Hello, dear!" Lois called out, stirring the vegetable as she felt two arms wrap around her, careful not to disturb her cooking.

"Hello, my love," Lois greeted, turning to see Paul's grinning face. He kissed her before settling his head on her shoulder, watching her turn the heat up so the soup and vegetables would be at a better serving temperature.

"Hello, my darling. Thank you for sending Linda down. And thank you for the package." He kissed her cheek again before letting go and taking the plates and utensils out, setting the table. She turned to see he was wearing what she'd sent in his hair, tucked behind his ear—a particularly bright blue Morning Glory flower.

Dinner was served at 5:30, as it always was on the nights that Lois had knitting club. The kids were at their seats already as Lois put down the ham aspic, Paul pulling out her chair for her as she sat before settling down himself.

"It looks delicious, dear."

Paul grinned as he served her, the kids, and then himself. The rest of dinner was a drone of conversation, the girls repeating what they'd already told Lois to Paul as she pretended to really be paying attention. She was listening enough to respond, but her mind was clearly somewhere else. None of her family noticed.

"Lois?"

The voice brought her out of a deep thought, and she blinked as she realised that Paul was staring at her. Mary and Linda had excused themselves, leaving her alone with him. He looked concerned.

"Oh, yes?"

He reached over and put his hands over hers, intertwining their fingers. The look hadn't left his face.

"You looked a bit spaced out. Were you thinking about something?"

She nodded, shaking her head slightly before giving him a reassuring smile.

"Oh, sorry, honey. I was thinking about what I have to do tomorrow."

Paul gave a sigh. He pulled his chair closer until he was right next to her, one of his hands leaving hers as he raised it up to cup her cheek. She leaned into it slightly and he gave a weary smile.

"Darling. You worry too much. We're supposed to be living."

"I am!" She insisted, but her expression contradicted her tone. She bit her lip and didn't meet his eye as his thumb gently stroked her cheek.

"Lois," he murmured, and she sighed. A few moments of silence.

"You're right," she admitted in a whisper, and Paul drew her into a hug. She wrapped her arms around him tightly and closed her eyes.

"I know, I know."

He kissed her cheek as he readjusted, and she gave an 'Oh!' and a little chuckle as he pushed his chair back and pulled her onto his lap. With Lois's head cradled against his chest and shoulder, Paul moved to rest his chin atop of it.

"You have to live in the present."

She nodded in response.

"Remember right after our honeymoon? We visited my parents for dinner. The whole evening all they cared about was getting to the next thing—while we were greeting each other, they were worried about cocktails. While we were having cocktails, they were worried about dinner. While we were having dinner, they were worrying about desert…but we were having a great time, because we were just having a dinner."

"It's different now that we're a family and we're taking care of a house."

Paul looked down and gently put his thumb to her chin, tilting her head to face him.

"Lois. The house being taken care of is important, but it's not as important as having time to enjoy yourself."

She stared at him for a few moments, almost as if she didn't get it. He was about to say something else when she finally nodded, leaning up and kissing him.

"You're right," she admitted, pulling back a bit sooner than Paul would have liked; she gave a ghost of a giggle upon seeing him still leaned forwards, eyes closed.

"Glad you agree," he murmured before leaning forwards and kissing her again.

PREVIEWS
BEL NEMETON
JON BLACK

UNCOVERING MERLIN'S TOMB

A globe-trotting quest for the treasures of the historical Merlin.

From the Preditors and Editors Readers' Poll
Award-Winning Author Jon Black...

Carvings have been unearthed in the Middle East. They bear impossible names--Arthur and Merlin, albeit in a native transliteration. How did these names come so far? Do they imply the existence of a historical Arthur and Merlin? The scholars do what they always do. They arrange a press meeting.

But scholars aren't the only attendees. After heavily-armed mercenaries steal the stone, Dr. Vivian Cuinnsey is forced to work with Jake Booker, a self-professed treasure hunter. Can he be trusted? Or is he just one more force after Merlin's treasure for personal profit?

From the Middle East to the caves of Israel to German record rooms to Oxford's secret underworld, chase Vivian and Jake in their pursuit of Merlin's greatest treasure.

Prologue

The dream was over. Tears streaked down his wizened face as he surveyed the landscape. Bodies lie strewn throughout the Camlann Valley. Chill winds carried the stench of smoke and blood into his acute nostrils. He arrived too late, taking too long to escape the bewitching Nimue's imprisonment. His escape was a tale worthy of Arthur and his best knights, but it didn't matter. He had failed in his duty as his king's advisor, wizard, and friend.

In his mind, Myrddin saw how the battle unfolded, as

surely as if he had been there. Without the benefit of his counsel and his knowledge of tactics learned from the old Romans, Arthur and his men had simply charged, trusting that valor and strength of arms alone could carry the day against the traitorous Mordred and his Saxon allies.

He envisioned Camelot's finest as they charged the Saxon's fluttering banners along the broad, flat valley. Recent rains swelled the ancient River Cam, threatening to flood its banks. As the king and his company advanced, their formations grew ragtag and discipline frayed. Caring only about being first into the fray, the men ignored the high ground on either side of them. And so they remained ignorant of the surprise Morgana and Mordred concealed there. Myrddin would have done the same had he been in Mordred's place. He shuddered at the thought.

Still, Arthur and his knights had turned the tables, won the battle, and destroyed themselves in the process. Britain's king lingered for several hours afterward, so Myrddin was told. But the old man had not reached the Camlann in time to say goodbye.

He could not believe Arthur was gone. Arthur, whom, as a swaddled infant, Myrddin had cradled in his arms and sang to. Before Uther. Before even Ygrayne. Gone. Now, Brittan was without her king, the foe vanquished, and Mordred no more. Myrddin did not know if Morgana numbered among the living or the dead. He hoped it didn't matter. Without Mordred, Morgana amounted to nothing. Didn't she? But there would be another wave of Saxons. As far as Myrddin could tell, there would *always* be another wave of Saxons.

"Myrddin."

He looked up, it was Cei. The solemn and sober knight numbered among the handful of Arthur's host not only to survive the battle but remain, mostly, unscathed.

"Is it done?" Myrddin asked, wiping the tears from his face. Cei nodded gravely. Myrddin noticed the wound to the knight's face. His cheek would always have a scar. It would match the one on his heart.

How strange that, at the end, it should come down to the

two of them. There had been no love to lose between Myrddin and Cei. Neither made any secret of it. Myrddin found the old warrior tiresome, self-righteous, moralistic, and utterly mirthless. He could only imagine what Cei must think of him. Despite that, each man understood and trusted the other's unconditional love for Arthur. That had been enough to unite them.

Cei surveyed his surroundings, searching. "Bedwyr?"

Myrddin shook his head. "Not yet returned," he clarified, lest Cei should misunderstand him and fear another of their company had fallen. Cei had completed his task, as Myrddin knew he would. He hoped Bedwyr possessed the mettle for what he'd been assigned. The venerable cavalier reminded Myrddin more of a grandfatherly otter than a fearsome Knight of the Round Table. With his gentle voice and kind heart, Bedwyr deserved birth into a better time and place. And yet, they also gifted the knight a curious kind of power. Even dead-hearted Mordred had possessed a soft spot for Bedwyr.

Time moved in circles, Myrddin reflected. It had been the three of them, Cei, Bedwyr, and Myrddin, with Arthur at the beginning. And it was the three of them here, at the end. He had known it would be so. More years ago than Myrddin carried to count or admit, he had dreamed. The kind of dream that Bleys, his ancient mentor, taught him to always pay attention to. In his dream, Camelot burned. Stone. Mortar. The rock foundation itself. Everything consumed in flames. Camelot burned and it fell to the three of them to dispose of the ashes.

And so they had. His dream had come to pass.

Myrddin studied the knight, "What will you do now?"

Cei considered the question. "Stay here. Rally the others. Try to pick up the pieces. You?"

Myrddin, too, thought before answering. He plumbed the depths of logic and reason as well as his intuition for omens and portents. Though tempted by Cei's answer, he could not allow himself to go there. "Darkness descends upon this land," Myrddin pronounced, "and no man shall stop it. I shall walk the wide world searching for Arthur's spirit. And, if I do not find it, I shall simply go home."

"God be with you in your quest," Cei said.

"And the gods be with you in yours."

Chapter One

"Damn it," Vivian Cuinnsey swore at her computer. Once again the document she was preparing failed to format properly.

"Everything okay, Doc?" Grant, her graduate assistant, poked his head through the door.

"I'll get this. Eventually. It'll be fine."

That stretched the truth. Since becoming department chair last year, she had been immersed in a world of budgets, policies, and academic politics that bordered on vendettas. Keeping a department full of idiosyncratic Celtic Language scholars running was a full time job.

Then there was the graduate seminar she taught. Only one class, but an important one, complete with rubrics, lesson plans, and grading. Vivian thought the move from undergraduate to graduate studies was a bigger transition than going from high school to undergraduate. Both high school and undergraduate revolved around what you knew. Graduate school involved coming to terms with what you didn't know. A little acclimation went a long way in helping new graduate students adjust to that shift.

And, of course, Vivian functioned as her department's chief fundraiser and its public face—to the university's administration, alumni, and the world at large.

Now, she faced additional pressure from an impending meeting with an Irish-American CEO, who, having embraced his roots, was considering a sizable endowment to her department. The document which had frustrated Vivian all afternoon was part of her campaign to make the donation a reality.

Another half-hour resolved the formatting issue. Sending Grant home for the evening, Vivian also prepared to leave.

Checking email once more before closing her laptop, she was surprised to find a message from Dr. Weldon Grassley, a venerable professor emeritus with her university's department of archeology. Well past retirement age, Grassley remained on the university's payroll and perpetually in the field at excavations throughout Central Asia.

"Dear Vivian, I found this at an excavation in Uzbekistan. I would be very interested in your thoughts."

The attached photo showed a stele, an upright stone plinth, bearing inscriptions in three alphabets. She did not recognize the top two. The first was all thick shapes and dramatic lines. Thin loops and lines characterized the second. At the bottom, however, Vivian found the familiar Latin script she encountered a thousand times a day, the letters used by English and dozens of other languages.

Though uncertain why Grassley sent the photo to her, it piqued Vivian's interest. Greek inscriptions, courtesy of Alexander the Great, were sometimes found that far east. Latin was another matter entirely. A glance told her that, while the script was Latin, the language it recorded certainly wasn't. That came as no surprise. Many peoples had borrowed the script of the far-reaching Romans for recording languages not previously written. Excluding the cumbersome Ogham script, that included her beloved Celts.

Unraveling the Latin script's phonetics, Vivian saw familiar patterns. They were far better suited to the tongues of long ago Britain, Ireland, and Gaul than to the dusty caravan routes of Central Asia. The inscription seemed to be some form of Insular Celtic, the language family to which all living Celtic languages belonged. The words preserved on the stone stele manifested distinctly Insular Celtic traits like verb-subject-object word order and inflected prepositions. At the same time, they lacked traits associated with the other branch of Celtic, the now extinct Continental Celtic family, such as a third gender form.

Having determined the inscription to be Insular Celtic, Vivian's next task was deciding to which of that family's two sub-branches it belonged. The Brittonic language family, still

272

called "Brythonic" by some older linguists, included modern Breton, Cornish, and Welsh as well as their parent languages and a half-dozen extinct linguistic dead-ends. The Goidelic family of languages included modern Irish, Scottish, and Manx, all of which evolved from Middle Irish.

Dr. Grassley's inscription gave every indication of being Brittonic, specifically the tongue called "Common Brittonic." Between the fifth and seventh centuries, that language held sway from Scotland's River Clyde to France's Brittany Peninsula. After the Romans left Britain, distinct dialects of Common Brittonic began to emerge. Those dialects would one day become the separate languages of Breton, Cornish, and Welsh. Perhaps Cumbrian and Pictish, too. Opinions differed as to whether Cumbrian represented a distinct language or just a dialect of Welsh. And, while everybody had a theory, no one really knew what Pictish was.

Having, at least in broad strokes, placed the inscription's language in time and space, Vivian grabbed pen and notepad. Scanning the weathered letters again, she made a quick translation. Words she thought likely to be proper nouns were put into brackets while she offset confusing or unclear sections with parentheses.

The Great King [Tarkun] (causes to be raised?) this monument. (Unclear) house of the Great Counselor [Mirdin] in his honor. (Unclear) Great Counselor to King [Tarkun] for this (two-ten years?), formerly counselor to Great King [Arturus] of the sunset lands. With Great King [Tarkun's] blessings, [Mirdin] departs to the sunset lands to look upon (its?) green trees and endless water (one last time?).

The inscription was a potential bombshell. A career could be made, or broken, by those few lines in stone. But it might have implications far beyond that. A quick mental calculation told Vivian it was too early to call Uzbekistan. By the time she got home, made dinner, and settled in, it would be the perfect time to catch Dr. Grassley at camp before he left for the dig site.

Leftovers put away and coffee in hand, she sat at her

computer. Dart, Vivian's black cat, orbited her legs, occasionally staring up at her with his yellow eyes and big ears. She thought about the scrawny kitten he'd been when he first appeared on her doorstep, one ear inexplicably smudged with motor oil.

Initiating a video chat, Vivian was rewarded with the image of Dr. Grassley's birdlike features, mop of white hair, and thick black-rimmed spectacles. "Dr. Cuinnsey, I thought I might be hearing from you."

"Dr. Grassley, what have you dug up?"

"It is a puzzle, isn't it, my dear? We're excavating near a small structure the locals venerate as the tomb of a Sufi saint. But we've dated it to the sixth century, a couple centuries too old for a Sufi." Grassley paused and cleaned his glasses. "Were you able to translate the Roman script on the stele? Was it Celtic?"

"It was. Common Brittonic, to be exact. And I was, most of it, anyway. I'm emailing the translation now. How did you know it was Celtic?"

"An educated guess. After making a phonetic transcription, I consulted the standard references and did some online research. Celtic was one of the few language families I couldn't rule out. So, I thought I'd see if you could shed any light on this little mystery."

"What are the other languages on the stele?" Vivian asked. "I didn't recognize either script."

"They are both in the Sogdian language," Grassley answered. "The first is the classical Sogdian script. The other is the slightly easier Manichean script. With the caveat that we understand rather less about Sogdian than Celtic, they both give translations broadly matching yours."

That pleased Vivian. Of course, it didn't really answer any questions about the stele or its inscriptions.

"Sogdian is distantly related to modern Farsi," he continued. "The spelling of this word 'Mirdin' on the stele is equivalent to 'Lord of God' or 'Noble of God.' I imagine this would translate conceptually as 'pious leader' or something like that, which sounds like a title. But notice that the word already accompanies the title 'Grand Vizier,' or what you translated as 'Great Counselor.' So, I am inclined to believe 'Mirdin' is a name, not a title."

Grassley flashed a mischievous smile. "Of course, 'Mirdin' would also be phonetically identical to the Celtic name of the individual commonly called Merlin, wouldn't it?"

"Careful, Grassley," Vivian shot back with hard-earned caution, "You're about to open one of the biggest cans of worms in Celtic studies. The historicity of Merlin, or Myrddin in Celtic, is very controversial. Even the affirmative camp posits Myrddin is an amalgam of multiple figures stretching across centuries. Arguing for the existence of a single individual analogous to the character from mythology is a good way to end a career."

"An intriguing point, given the reference to the 'Great King Arturus' and the 'sunset lands.'"

Thrilled by those same implications just hours ago, Vivian was suddenly in no mood to discuss them with the elderly archeologist. Again, she cautioned Dr. Grassley about the rabbit hole he was circling.

"You can grasp the momentousness of uncovering Latin inscriptions in Uzbekistan," he told her. "To say nothing of ones used to transliterate Celtic. We're holding a press conference about the discovery next week. I'd really like you to be here in Samarkand for it."

Vivian thought it over carefully. "I'm going to follow this development very closely. But, at this point, I can't justify taking time off from my department based on one find, no matter how unusual."

"Regrettable. I always enjoy seeing you. But I understand. I will keep you informed of any developments."

"One more thing, Grassley."

"Yes?"

"Not a word about the whole Merlin thing. Not one word."